FLIGHT
FROM
ALEPPO

FLIGHT FROM ALEPPO

A NOVEL BY

BARRY R. SCHALLER

ROUND**ABOUT**
WEST HARTFORD, CT

Roundabout Press
P. O. Box 370310
West Hartford, Connecticut

ISBN: 978-1-948072-07-6

Cover illustrations by Donna H. Colburn
Cover and text design by James F. Brisson

Printed in the United States of America
10 9 8 7 6 5 4 3 2 1

CONTENTS

FOREWORD

by Carol V.C. Schaller

A FEW YEARS AGO, my late husband, Justice Barry R. Schaller, was contacted by the legal/philosophy department of the University of Nevada, Reno, to teach an all-day, two-week course to judges on "The Study of Law in the St. James Bible." The fall course was scheduled to take place during the last two weeks of October. The university provided a beautiful condominium apartment on Lake Tahoe, a rental car for Barry's daily one-hour drive to Reno, and an open voucher for groceries for the duration. Barry had not studied the Bible since his undergraduate days at Yale University, decades earlier, but he had recently published a textbook, *A Vision of American Law: Judging Law, Literature, and the Stories We Tell*, which had inspired the dean of the law school to contact him. Barry had just enough notice to brush up on the Bible before teaching his course.

The classroom was filled with about a dozen energetic and erudite judges, men and women from different parts of the country, who really cared about the topic and its application to "ethical decision making." I met the participants and learned about the course at the cocktail and dinner parties which took place most evenings after class. The conversation was electric, eclectic, and uproariously uplifting.

When Barry and I would take our early-morning or late-afternoon speed-walks to maintain our exercise regimen, he would invariably share his concern about a strange bit of dizziness and lack of energy. But he would shrug it off as a passing consequence of the thin mountain air. Our two weeks in Nevada were too soon finished, and we found ourselves back in our regular routine in Connecticut. Back home, Barry's notoriously high energy level suddenly vanished. We enjoyed the holidays in spite of his exhaustion and then one evening, soon after dinner, he felt "strange" and he took his blood pressure. It registered over 200, and we lost no time in getting to the Yale Emergency Clinic. His white blood count was found to be phenomenally high, and he was then immediately rushed by ambulance to the main hospital.

I will not go into detail about the illness, chronic neutrophilic leukemia with five genetic mutations, which eventually took his life. The head doctor at Yale School of Medicine, Division of Oncology, told us few people ever suffered the same malady, but that those who had been diagnosed— without the complicating negative mutations—had managed to survive, at best, five months from onset, which was probably about four months ago. He was sorry to have to tell us that it was "time to put your final wishes in order."

We reached for each other's hand as we sought to absorb the truth. And almost as quickly Barry asked a series of questions of the medical staff. He sought to determine the resources and locations for the latest research. Because of his determination, his life-long devotion to healthy physical activity, and most importantly, the spiritual devotion that permeated our lives, Barry managed to survive, not for one month, but a full three years from the onset of this rare disease. A miracle in and of itself.

The novel you are about to read, *Flight from Aleppo*, was written during those final years of Barry's life. He wrote it to help himself and others understand the shortcomings of human behavior and the exploitation of others to meet selfish goals. The city of Aleppo, for which the book is named, is among the oldest, continuously inhabited cities in the world. Syria suffered severely during the recent war. U.N. estimates cite at least 350,00 people killed in the conflict, 6.7 million people internally displaced, and more than 6.6 million refugees.

As he was writing the novel, Barry relied upon the military expertise of his revered law clerk, Dennis Carnelli, who helped him paint a historically accurate picture of the events depicted in the book. Dennis is a combat veteran of the Iraq War, who served in the United States Army as a forward observer with the 3d Brigade Combat Team, 3d Infantry Division.

I would also like to recognize our devoted friend of many decades, Fr. Jacques Bossiere, who passed away at an advanced age just one week after Barry was given the news of his fateful illness. Barry was saddened to learn that he could no longer receive the spiritual guidance of his wise French-speaking Anglican. The two had shared countless conversations over so many get-togethers and extensive regular correspondence.

An event described in this novel— where Conrad hears aloud a voice telling him, "Take courage; do not lose hope"—actually happened. I was in the master bath, getting ready for bed one evening, and Barry was in the hallway, heading toward our bedroom, when he heard "the voice of God, or Jacques, or somebody"— he couldn't believe I didn't hear it, but I had the water running— saying those words. They stayed with him.

Another dear religious leader and friend, Bishop Andrew Smith, came to our house regularly and kindly, to bring Communion. He said it was not the first time he had heard of that experience and that its specialness is recorded in the Bible many times.

On that note, Barry and I often discussed the nature of life after death with some of our elderly relatives when their time on earth was coming to an end. They wanted to assure us that they would try to give a sign that they were still with us, in a spiritual sense, after passing. One relative promised to "turn on a light in a room" when we were watching television. This later happened, but Barry and I both wondered at the time if there could have been some other explanation. So the next time we faced that scenario, we suggested that Grandmother Baldwin turn on the television. That came to pass as well— however, we wondered if the stormy late summer weather had played a role in the phenomenon.

So when Barry and I were standing in the kitchen, somewhat lightheartedly talking about what he might do to give me a sign of his spiritual presence, he said, "I know, I'll ring the doorbell!"

I said, "Honey, you can't. The doorbell has been broken for two years and we just haven't had the time to get it fixed." And he replied with a chuckle, "That won't matter!"

Two and a half weeks later, the disease progressed and Barry's discomfort proved unreasonable, so as medically advised, we checked in to Smilow Cancer Hospital, Hospice Unit. Family members came to visit. The farewells were full of love. Afterward, we were alone and we both needed a nap, so I climbed into bed beside him. The nurse came in to offer pain medication, and then we relaxed. Time, however, had come for eternal truth.

So I leave you with this truth: five days after Barry passed, I was in the kitchen cleaning the center island counter when the doorbell rang. I was not thinking about our conversation of several weeks earlier, just, "That's odd!" I went to the front door and opened it, but no one was there, not in any direction. The house is built on an L-shaped foundation with the front and back doors very near each other at the apex. I ran to the back door, opened it to a similar emptiness, then remembering Barry's promise, I returned to the front door, opened it again and saw a white butterfly hovering by the veranda column to my right and a beautiful dragonfly hovering at the same height to my left. I stepped down and the butterfly flew over to me and passing me flew directly to the dragonfly, and the dragonfly left its station and flew to me and landed on the column abandoned by the butterfly. I stepped down one more step onto the veranda; a sudden warm breeze caressed my feet and swept upward to my chin in a miraculous embrace.

⅏

PART ONE

ENCOUNTER

CONRAD FELT PARALYZED ALL DAY by a foreboding that some unspeakable harm was lying in wait for him. Given his peculiar circumstances, his sensitivity and extraordinary self-awareness, he might well have concluded that he was suffering severe depression. But he knew it was more than that. Something, some piece of information or some event, was waiting to pounce on him. Nothing yet had happened to suggest a cause for his unusual angst. But now, five o'clock in the afternoon, as the ordinary work day came to a close, he sat alone in his tiny cluttered office at the refugee center, thinking. Consciously delaying his departure for home, he reached for the still-folded morning newspaper. Casually flipping through the first few pages, an article on page five captured his full attention.

"This is it," he said aloud as he read the story of an eleven-year-old Syrian girl, a refugee named Samar, who revealed in an interview the details of her attempt to commit suicide with rat poison. "It was like the devil filled my head," the girl said to the interviewer. "I don't remember much about it when I tried to kill myself. All I could think about was that we have nothing. We will never have our lives back."

"They are all hopeless, these refugee children," Conrad said, "utterly hopeless."

The child vowed to try again to relieve her parents from their struggle to support seven children in the refugee camp in Syria, near the Lebanon border. The child had been found lying on the floor, foaming at the mouth and vomiting. She was in intensive care for eighteen days.

Reading on about the virtual epidemic of child suicides among the Syrian refugees, Conrad sat solemnly, transfixed by the horror of the apocalyptic situation.

His receptionist, Sylvia Reyes, called for his attention. "A group of Palestinians are in the waiting room," she said, poking her head into his office, which was divided from the crowded outer office by the flimsiest of partitions. "They've been here for quite a while."

"How many?" Conrad asked, without looking up from his desk.

"There's a young woman in her forties. She has a child with her. There's an older woman too."

"What's their problem," Conrad asked with irritation. "It could be important. The people come first, you know."

"I'm aware of that," Sylvia replied. "When I asked if she was a new refugee, she said no." Sylvia was one of those ambitious staffers who make themselves indispensable and then attempt to expand their control. "She says she's a former refugee. When I asked what her problem is, she says her son was kidnapped in Boston by ISIS, something about turning him into a child soldier or a suicide bomber. It sounds far-fetched to me. I asked whether she consulted authorities in Boston. I didn't get an answer I could understand. Oh, and, so you know, she calls ISIS '*DAESH*.' It's the new term that the Arabs and Europeans are using for all the different Islamic State groups."

"I was supposed to leave a half hour ago for a meeting at school and get home in time for a birthday party. My daughter's birthday," Conrad said, as much to himself as to Sylvia. "I'm in big trouble already. But this sounds serious. I'll talk to her but it would be good to let her know that I don't have much time."

"I tried to discourage her," Sylvia said. "I don't know why she's here instead of being in Boston. But she's persistent. She won't leave. I did everything I could but I'm only the receptionist." She had been the receptionist since the opening of the Global Refugee Organization office in New Haven. She was efficient but had her own set of rules and prejudices. It wasn't easy to find people to work long hours at low pay at a non-profit.

"We don't try to get rid of people who come here for help," Conrad said. "It sounds as though she could have a legitimate problem."

"Okay. Okay. It sounds like she has a serious problem," Sylvia said, sounding wounded by Conrad's rebuke, "but I'm not sure it's our problem. She's very upset, close to tears, even though she seemed stoic at first. She overheard someone saying that you're going to Jordan in a few weeks. She seems desperate to talk to you. I think we'd have to throw her out physically to get rid of her."

"We're certainly not doing that," Conrad said, jaw clenched. "I'll have to talk to her, meeting or no meeting, party or no party."

Conrad Paul Frisch had already logged off his computer in the shabby, run-down office of the Global Refugee Organization, known as the GRO or simply the "center." The organization was housed in an old factory building in an industrial area of the mid-size Connecticut city. Half of the building, which had sat dormant for years following the departure to North Carolina of a clothing manufacturer, had been lightly renovated to accommodate a collection of small offices, plus a waiting room, and a kitchen, thanks to a community funding project.

The GRO was not popular with some powerful elements of the city political establishment since it was perceived as likely to attract poor and homeless minority refugees into the area. Once here, they tended to stay, altering the demographic of the region. Nonetheless, there had been enough support so far to keep it going from year to year and the city became an important hub of refugee activity in New England. Challenges to the center became more aggressive, however, after terrorist incidents in Paris, Brussels, Nice, and other cities, reflecting the general American antipathy toward taking in refugees.

Conrad had been about to pull on his jacket when Sylvia entered with the information. He felt completely worn out tonight. In fact, he had been perpetually fatigued for weeks. He attributed that to his aversion to saying "no" to people in need. He was used to over-extending himself for refugees and students.

People had trouble describing Conrad because his features were so ordinary and common – a Caucasian man with mixed European background. In most groups, Conrad had a way of blending into the background. His personality did not command attention. He was often described as "unassuming" and "modest."

"My upcoming Jordan trip makes everybody envious," he exclaimed, mustering a tired smile. "You know what a soft spot I have for refugees. That's because," he added with an ironic laugh, "you're looking at a refugee from the human race. It's my fate. Anyway, I'll meet her. Just mention that I don't have a lot of time."

"I got that part," Sylvia said impatiently.

"But give me a couple of minutes. I'd better call home. I've already missed the university meeting, which is bad news. It looks as though I'll be late for the birthday party too."

"Okay. Remember I said she has a child with her, a girl maybe ten or eleven. Should she bring her in?"

"Sure, if the mother wishes."

"What about the older woman?"

"Oh," Conrad said, his mind on the telephone call he had to make. "Whatever they want. Either way."

"The daughter is very intense, like an adult," Sylvia mused. "I think she wants to come in with her mother. There's something about her that is compelling. I'd say let the child come in. She looks upset too although she's very composed for a child, almost more composed than the mother."

As Sylvia left the room, Conrad dialed his home number. His wife Helen answered.

"I was just about to leave for the meeting," Conrad said, self-consciously, in an apologetic tone, "but I have to talk to a Palestinian refugee first. I know. I know I'm late. But this woman has been waiting all afternoon and no one else is here who can talk to her…No, Sylvia can't handle it. She'd be too abrupt…I know I don't get paid. What difference does that make? Well, I'll make it as short as I can."

He put the phone down, rattled by her words and by the guilt he felt for being late. He took a deep breath.

Sylvia brought in a tall, stately woman in her mid to late thirties, with an olive complexion and classic features of a Palestinian. She had an erect posture and moved with classic old-world dignity. Her composure did not quite conceal her distress. Her dark eyes conveyed confidence and a plea for understanding and help.

Accompanying her was a slender, delicate girl of ten or eleven who strongly resembled her mother and was remarkably alert. Her bright, penetrating black eyes first scanned Conrad, then took in the room, as well as the receding figure of Sylvia. Mother and daughter studied Conrad closely, probably evaluating how sympathetic he would be and how much help he would be likely to offer.

The office, which served as the GRO's northeast headquarters, was not very impressive. Run down and furnished cheaply, it was unlikely to instill confidence. But it was the only active refugee center operating in New England. It was remarkably effective, considering that the receptionist and the director were the only paid employees, modestly so, among the eight to ten who worked in the office on a volunteer basis. Conrad had been involved as a volunteer since the inception of the center, which had been an inconspicuous event that drew a few generous supporters, but failed to attract a single political figure of any stature.

The mother introduced herself as Ghadir Younis and her daughter as Ayah. Conrad motioned for them to take a seat, then explained that he had been about to leave and could spend only a few minutes with them. Ghadir looked disappointed but maintained her composure. He added that he would make an appointment to see them early next week, since this was a Friday and the office was not open for appointments during the weekend, although it had emergency telephone service.

"But don't lose heart. We do have a little time to talk. I understand that you have a kidnapping to report. Of course, this may be a police matter and there may be little I can do. If this happened in Massachusetts, you should report it there. Connecticut authorities can do nothing about it. But tell me about your problem."

"Yes, I will tell you," Ghadir said. She spoke perfect English in a soft voice but with more formality than most native speakers. The child put her arm around her mother and leaned against her while she spoke.

"I didn't report this and I don't intend to report this to the police," Ghadir said. "It isn't that kind of problem. My husband, the father of my son Jamil, is the one who kidnapped him. Jamil is only nine years old. He has taken him to Syria, as far as I can tell. The police will do nothing for me. I am a Palestinian-American, a Palestinian in their eyes. I'm seeking help in finding out where my son is in Syria and then help to find a way to bring him back. I thought that with refugees coming and going here, you might have a way of finding out. One of your colleagues told me that you are going to Jordan soon. That is not far from where they might be. It made me feel hopeful that you might help. This happened while we were living in Boston but I have moved in with my aunt in Connecticut now. She lives in this area. The rest of my family is still in Palestine, except for one brother, who I believe is now in Syria."

Conrad asked, "How did this happen? When?" He forgot about the time and about how fatigued he had been during the afternoon. He was determined to hear her out and face the consequences at home later. During the past few months, life with Helen was becoming more contentious and their relationship increasingly strained. She showed less patience with his compassionate activism, and his most compelling interests were no longer of interest to her. He could feel her tolerance level grow thinner and thinner.

Ghadir began. "I came to this country a dozen years ago on a Fulbright fellowship and got admitted to the Harvard Kennedy School in public policy and political science for graduate work. There's a long story how that came about but I won't go into that. While I was at the Kennedy School, I met a Syrian man who was studying economics and politics. We eventually got married. His name is Yousef. We had Ayah," she said, smiling at the girl. "Her name means 'a sign from God.' Ayah was born while we were still in graduate school. Jamil was born after we had gotten our degrees."

Conrad was fascinated by the story and the opportunity to learn all he could about Arabic life within the U.S., since many refugees were likely to enter the U.S. if the barriers were lowered at all. He had made education in this subject a goal for himself, since so many of the refugees were from the Middle East.

"After we finished graduate school, we stayed in Cambridge. Both of us managed to get low level teaching jobs. I won't go into detail about the struggles we had with visas. It was a nightmare. But we finally secured the right to stay. Ultimately, I became a citizen but Yousef did not. After a while he became bored and dissatisfied with research and teaching. He continually complained about the poor pay and about the way he was ignored and mistreated by regular faculty members. He became filled with resentment and bitterness about the school and the U.S. in general.

He began looking for work outside the university community. Finally, he got a better-paying job with a Boston management firm that did consulting work and was operated by people from Iraq. He seemed more contented, even excited at times. That seemed fine to me, although I never knew whether his resentment and hostility were justified. I had no way to see what he was like outside the home."

"Adjusting can be hard for some people," said Conrad. "That's a typical scenario. The U.S. isn't the easiest place for Middle Easterners to adjust to, especially these days. It will get worse as more terrorist incidents happen. But it sounds as if he were a fuse waiting to be ignited. What happened next?"

"He began spending longer and longer hours in Boston. Eventually he admitted that, after work, he was meeting with young men from a Muslim jihadist group in Boston. I never learned the name of the particular group but later I found out they were an affiliate of the Islamic state group – DAESH. They held very militaristic views and eventually they recruited him. I could see that they were making him feel important. In retrospect, I could see how their influence overcame mine day by day. Yousef drifted away from me and spent more time with them and less with me and the children, eventually abandoning our life together as a happy family."

"I get the impression this is happening more often," Conrad said, "that is, for extremists here to recruit fighters to go to Iraq and Syria."

"It's far more common than most people think," Ghadir replied. "Since this happened, I've learned a great deal about it. Islamist extremists come to this country specifically to recruit fighters to go to the Middle East. Most people would be amazed at how many jihadists have already infiltrated American society. The concern about terrorists slipping into the country among Syrian refugees is overstated. They're already here and working to recruit vulnerable people, people who are isolated and disenchanted with their lives. Usually, recruits are Muslims who feel alienated by American society. But they're not all Muslims by any means."

"I've read case studies," Conrad said, "about how our prejudice against Muslims drives some of them to the other side. We become the enemy."

"I'm not saying that the recruits are necessarily justified in blaming their problems on this country," said Ghadir. "Some simply can't or don't want to assimilate and they begin blaming the non-Muslims around them. Some recruiting takes place remotely too – from abroad I mean, usually online. I've thought a lot about why Yousef became vulnerable to the promises the recruiters were making, whatever they were. I think he felt demeaned by his colleagues at the university. He separated himself from them and perhaps they became disillusioned about him as well. Meeting the extremists may have been partly coincidental but he may have been looking for a group where he could feel a sense of belonging."

"I'm glad to learn about the recruiting operations here. We read more about it happening in Europe," Conrad said.

"I remember," Ghadir said, "how Yousef took Jamil with him on weekends for what he said were retreats. Jamil was not interested in belonging to any organizations so it seemed strange to me. When I asked Yousef about this, he refused to give me any information. He'd just say this was a father and son thing. I should keep my nose out of it. Jamil became more and more distant from me. He'd also be rude too, something that had never happened before. Jamil and I had always been very close, as close as with Ayah. All these realizations have come to me since it all happened. I blame myself for not recognizing fully what it could lead to and bring Jamil to safety. I weep for what I allowed to happen," she said, her voice breaking.

"I don't think you should be so hard on yourself," Conrad said gently. "You couldn't expect to see where it would lead. You had no experience with that. You were still holding onto the marriage and assuming your husband's decency, his sanity. But they cracked it, didn't they?"

"Yes, Yousef became verbally abusive to me at first and then it progressed to episodes of violence whenever I protested what he was doing. He struck me across the face twice. He said my place was to obey him. He had never said that before. Of course, every time he came home, we argued. About this time, I learned about Ayah's sickness. She was abnormally fatigued and I took her to the Harvard Health Services. She was about ten and Jamil was eight by that time. I went with the children. My husband didn't even show up for the appointment. It wasn't long before he began talk-ing about leaving to join the fight against Assad in Syria. He was so preoccupied that he seemed to have no interest in dealing with Ayah's problem or anything else."

"What happened next?"

"After two months of tension, unbearable tension, the matter came to a head one evening," Ghadir said. "I can still see and hear the horrible scene when Yousef came home. I've replayed it in my mind over and over. He was two hours late for our regular din-ner hour. That alone wasn't unusual. The door to our apartment opened and closed so quietly I barely heard it. I asked, 'Yousef, is that you? Why are you being so quiet? Aren't you coming to the kitchen?' He said, 'I have things to attend to. I'll be in my office. Send Jamil in to see me.' I told him, 'He's finishing his dinner. We waited a long time for you.' He insisted, 'Send him in now. I need to talk to him. Now. Don't delay, woman.'

"After that," Ghadir said, "Jamil was with him for nearly two hours. I was afraid to interfere. Something about Yousef's tone frightened me. I wasn't able to organize my thoughts. Ayah asked me, 'Yamma, what is wrong? Why is Jamil with our father? Should I go in there with them?'

"'No, sweetheart,' I said. 'Your father wants to talk to Jamil alone. We'd better let him do that.' I tried to keep the fear out of my voice for Ayah's sake but she knew something was terribly wrong. I think she grasped it before I did."

"What happened next?" Conrad asked. "Did you talk to Yousef before the evening was out?"

"No, he spent the night – or part of it – in his office with Jami. I stayed away rather than confront him. I was afraid of what might happen.

"When I went to bed about ten o'clock, Ayah was already in bed. I couldn't sleep. I kept hearing noises, like voices whisper-ing. One time, I woke up thinking that someone had opened the bedroom door and spoke. Then the door closed and there was a scuffling of footsteps and voices. I wasn't sure if all that really hap-pened or if it was a dream. I must have dropped off finally because I awoke later with a start and looked at the clock. It was two a.m. The house was quiet. I got up and went to Jamil's room. The door was closed so I opened it carefully, not wanting to wake him. But I had to reassure myself that he was okay. It looked as though the bed was empty so I turned on the light. It was empty and his drawers were in disarray, as though someone had ransacked them. I could see that some clothes were missing.

"I felt a wave of panic wash over me. I couldn't breathe. I knew Jamil was gone. Yousef had stolen him, his body and his soul. It occurred to me afterward that the sounds I heard – the whispering – might have been Jamil coming to get me and Yousef pulling him away. I feel such heartache over this. Maybe I could have prevented it.

"I went to the office next and pulled open the door. I already knew it was empty. They were both gone. Yousef had kidnapped Jamil. I panicked. I cried. I screamed. Ayah came running in and she knew instantly what had happened. We dissolved in each other's arms before pulling ourselves together. The worst had happened. I felt that a limb had been wrenched off my body. I had no idea what to do so I called my aunt. I decided against calling the police. I felt it would lead nowhere. They were not going to help a Palestinian woman for something that her Syrian husband did even if I proved I was an American citizen."

"I suspect you were right on that," Conrad said.

"The next day, I called Yousef's work to see if he had shown up or if he had contacted them. The call got transferred from person to person. No one was forthcoming. It was as though everyone was protecting him. It was a conspiracy, I knew. I finally learned from one of Yousef's co-workers that he had not shown up at work. He had told one person at work that he and his son were taking a vacation to visit family.

"I knew the name of one of the men, one of the extremists, that he spent time with. I had met this man one time when I stopped by Yousef's office. He was quite rude. He's the one I called. His was the only name I had. He was really threatening. He told me that Yousef had gone to fulfill his destiny and that Jamil was with him to do the same. He told me to forget about it and not to pursue it. It would do no good and it would bring harm to me and to Ayah. Here's what he said exactly. I wrote it down. He said, `Yousef has important work to do and he has left to fulfill his mission. His son is his rightful heir and an important part of his work. You should be proud that your son will become a fighter for ISIS. It will be an honor for him to serve as he is needed, even to die for ISIS. I advise you – warn you – not to interfere or to make any inquiries or any reports. You will be safe if you follow that warning but you and your daughter will be in great danger of death if you ignore it. It is closed. Let it remain closed. Ask nothing. Say nothing. Do you understand?'

"I hung up the phone. I was shaking. I followed that warning," Ghadir said. "Based on what he said, I realized that Yousef's intention is to turn Jamil into one of those child soldiers. You know about that, of course. DAESH uses child soldiers. It also uses child suicide bombers too. I don't know which is worse. I had noticed that when Yousef was at home he paid more attention to Jamil, trying to create dependence, telling him about what was going on in Syria, getting him excited about military things. He talked to him about being a soldier, even took him to a shooting range a couple of times. At the time, I didn't realize the full significance. I was horrified that he did that. I remember saying 'Do you want your son to become a killer?' I didn't like what he was doing but I was pleased that at least he was paying attention to one of us. I didn't suspect the worst although, looking back, I can see the signs I should have picked up on it. I never imagined he would kidnap Jamil.

"I have relatives in Palestine and Syria. They've done all they could to find Jamil and Yousef." Ghadir paused, unable to go on, with tears streaming down her face. Ayah reached out to comfort her.

"Yamma, I can continue the story," she said. "The last information we have is that my father is fighting somewhere in Syria and that he arranged to leave Jamil with his brother and his wife in Aleppo, my aunt and uncle. We also learned that my aunt and uncle had to leave their home in Aleppo and go to a refugee camp because of the bombing but we don't know where they are."

Conrad was beginning to feel overwhelmed by the enormity of what he was hearing. He felt a little dizzy and attributed it to his time pressure and fatigue. All the while, his mind raced through possible courses of action.

"We suspect," Ayah went on, "they probably are not in the original camp but have moved on – maybe more than once. They may even be in the horrible camp that we hear about, Yarmouk. It's mainly a Palestinian camp, about five miles from Damascus center, not too far from the Lebanon border. That is a danger-ous place now, we have heard. We are afraid for my brother. My mother doesn't sleep at night because she is so worried about him. I am heartsick too," she said, distraught.

Conrad was spellbound by the story. He had read about the recruiting of militants in the U.S. but had never heard such a story first-hand. When Sylvia appeared at the doorway and announced that she would be leaving, he checked his watch. More than an hour had elapsed. He was hopelessly late for the birthday party. But the problem he had just heard about, however horrible, was exciting to him. In just two weeks, he would be going to Amman, Jordan – his trip of a lifetime – to attend the annual meeting of the worldwide GRO. The topic was the Syrian refugee crisis and how to deal with the refugees and internally displaced persons in the member organizations, which included Turkey, Lebanon, Jordan, and the European Union countries.

Although his position with the GRO office was unpaid, Con-rad's dedication to helping refugees settle in New England was the most important and meaningful activity of his life. He loved teaching and counseling his undergraduate students at the univer-sity. That paid something, although far short of what he should be earning at this stage of life. He had always felt alienated from other people, an outsider within every community in which he had lived. Working with refugees was a natural for him.

The opportunity to be involved in saving a child from a hor-rible fate, even an early death, was the opportunity of a lifetime. He couldn't help thinking about Samar, that little Syrian girl in the news story, as he talked with Ayah. And he didn't know what this woman, Ghadir, expected of him but, whatever it was, he wanted to be part of the effort. He dismissed the possibility that her story might be inaccurate, exaggerated, or might even be the result of a domestic conflict over where the boy should live.

Conrad got contact information from Ghadir, scheduled an appointment for the following Wednesday, and walked them to the waiting room. Ghadir had moved to her aunt's apartment in the city so the woman could help with Ayah. Despite his curiosity, Conrad decided to defer asking about Ayah's medical problem until the next visit. Ghadir and Ayah seemed satisfied that he had heard and understood their story. The aunt looked worried and somewhat cross, perhaps from fatigue and emotional strain. She nodded to Conrad as they left the waiting room.

Conrad arrived home past the midpoint of the birthday party, well after the meal and birthday cake. No one in the small family gathering composed mainly of Helen's relatives and friends acknowledged Conrad when he entered. Obviously, the well had been poisoned as far as his late arrival was concerned. Conrad had no close relatives and so all family gatherings centered on Helen's parents, her aunts and uncles and cousins, and her friends. The birthday girl, Conrad's daughter Esther, who had just turned twenty-two and was in her last year of college, glanced up at her father when he arrived but turned quickly away. Paul, her brother, four years older, did the same, although he gave Conrad a shrug meaning 'what do you expect', which at least was some acknowledgement. Helen shot him several sharp glances and said in a low voice, just loud enough for the assembled group to hear, "Don't expect dinner to be served to you. How could you be so thoughtless?"

When the gathering was nearing a close, Conrad slipped away to avoid the farewells, knowing that he would be rudely treated. He'd spare himself that further indignity. He slept in the den, since Helen had turned the bedroom lights off and locked the door while he was in the kitchen searching for something to eat.

✑

On Saturday of the same week, Conrad was sitting across from his friend and fellow teacher at the city university, Levi Weller. They met frequently for lunch here, at a small coffee shop in the center of the small Long Island Sound coastal town where they both lived. Conrad frequently joked that Levi was his only friend. There was more than a kernel of bitter truth in the humor. Conrad had neglected to encourage ordinary friendships over the years and was considered a loner by most of his peers at the university and even by acquaintances in his own tightly-knit waterfront community.

Throughout his life, Conrad felt the need to create distance between himself and anyone who threatened to become close. Levi was the exception. Trust was the issue and Levi had never failed to meet Conrad's high standard. Levi was dressed as usual in black clothes. With his long black beard, he could have passed as a Hasidic rabbi, minus the hat. His wry explanation was simply that he was not a hat person. Conrad questioned him on whether looking *old world* would impede his teaching career at the university. Levi shrugged it off, saying, "Nonsense, it doesn't matter."

Conrad was feeling morose this morning. Earlier in the day, when he and Helen were in the kitchen together, he had tried to tell her about the Palestinian refugees. She had rebuffed him, expressing a total lack of interest. Esther and Paul, who had stayed overnight in honor of the birthday celebration instead of returning to their residences, had come into the kitchen looking for breakfast. After finding cereal and donuts that Helen had left out for them, they left the kitchen, barely acknowledging Conrad. They each nodded slightly in his direction when they were leaving, Esther back to the small college in the next town over and Paul to his apartment at the university, where he was a religion instructor.

Conrad's frustration with the way he was treated at home was palpable. He was aware that his absence for almost the entire party the night before was indefensible. He should put family obligations first. But he was unable to resist the pleas and needs of desperate refugees. Aside from teaching, working with the refugees was his only rewarding experience, his calling. He was eager to tell Levi about Ghadir and Ayah, even though he knew about Levi's dislike for Arabs in general and Palestinians in particular. Any individual or group that threatened Israel's prosperity and security was anathema to Levi. Levi was a hardliner. Still, Conrad felt confident that Levi would hear him out.

"I had a fascinating experience at the refugee center on Friday afternoon," Conrad began. "I was about to leave to go home for Esther's birthday party, which I missed entirely, of course. I'm persona non grata again. What else is new? Some Palestinians with a problem showed up. The young woman had her daughter with her. There was an older woman, the woman's aunt, with them too. They had a classic Middle Eastern look and were very well-spoken, articulate and educated. Very attractive people."

Levi looked skeptical at the mention of Palestinians, but he kept his gaze trained on Conrad.

"The older woman was wearing a hajib. Not the mother, though. At first, I couldn't be sure whether they were Syrian or Palestinian but I guessed the latter. The mother's name is Ghadir and the girl's Ayah. Last name is Younis. They had a tragic story to tell."

"I wouldn't pretend to tell you who you should help," said Levi. "What's their story, and what do they want from you?"

"The father, a Syrian, apparently got recruited while he was in graduate school by extremists from some subsidiary of the Islamic State group, DAESH, in Cambridge. It's scary to think how widespread the network is right under our noses. Eventually, he left and took his son, who is about nine, with him. The mother is convinced from what she has put together that he intends to turn him into a child soldier or maybe even a suicide bomber. I've heard that ISIS has multiple training units for child soldiers. The mother is devastated. She doesn't know where they are now although my guess would be in the area of Raqqa, where ISIS headquarters is. I've heard rumors that there's a major training facility for women and children up there. Anyway, father and son have disappeared somewhere in Syria and the mother is desperate to find her son."

"How do you know this is true?" Levi asked. "Maybe the father just wants the boy to be raised in Syria. It could be a parenting dispute. If they were Jordanian or Lebanese, I'd feel differently. But not Palestinians or Syrians. The Syrian rebels demand U.S. help but once they're back on their feet, they'll be at the head of the line to form a coalition to wipe Israel off the face of the planet. Just like the Palestinians and the Iranians."

"For God's sake, Levi, how can you paint everyone with the same brush? You're smarter than that. Why don't you come along with me next week and meet these people? You said you'd come with me to the center any time I asked."

"I have reasons."

"What reasons? Tell me and maybe I'll agree it's not just prejudice on your part."

"I will someday but not now. Let's change the subject," Levi said.

They talked about the university and how many courses Conrad could manage.

"Look, Conrad," Levi said, "sign up for all your courses and, if you can't teach them all, I'll take over at least one and find somebody for another. But get yourself on board."

"That's a generous offer," Conrad said, breaking into a smile. "I accept. I'll let the Dean's office know, that is, the *good Dean's* office," Conrad said with an ironic smile, referring to his dispute with the other Dean, the *bad Dean*. "But think about coming to the refugee center, will you?"

"Okay, my friend. I'll think it over. Maybe I will. But I tell you my feelings and my conclusions are based on evidence, not prejudice. You don't know what I've seen."

"Then you should tell me about what you've seen. Okay? Instead of just mouthing off. I have to go now. I'm really beat. I've felt wiped out for the past three or four weeks. I don't know what it is. It's really hard to get myself going in the morning and get through the whole day."

"See a doctor," Levi urged. "Make an appointment. I'll see you during the week. Let me know when a good time is for a visit and I'll think about it."

❧

Conrad sat in the municipal parking lot, catching his breath before attempting to negotiate the short drive home. He felt a wave of indecision and indifference. Just sitting in the car seemed to take more energy than he had. "What a weight on my chest," he whispered aloud. "This must be the way people felt who were put to death by crushing during the Salem witchcraft times, like Giles Corey."

He wondered how he had arrived at this position in his life. As far back as he could remember, he had never fit in with any of the popular social groups. He felt thankful for Levi's friendship but at the same time it was sobering to recognize that Levi really was his only friend. From one perspective, life had been a self-defeating struggle, constantly tripping over the stumbling blocks he put in his own path.

Reflecting on his childhood saddened him. He jumped from one memory to another with peculiar clarity. His most pleasant times had been spent alone. He was the youngest child of four, with all his other siblings at least ten years his senior, and he spent little time with them. By the time he was born, his parents seemed weary of child-raising. That gave him ample freedom for whatever he chose to do but also a pervading sense of loneliness at times. After his parents died in an automobile accident when he was just ten, he spent the next eight years moving from one relative to another, all within Connecticut, with no one claiming him as their own with any degree of permanency.

Lulled by the streaming rays of sunshine warming the car and the hum of the idling motor, Conrad allowed his mind to drift over his early years growing up in Buckland, the town where he was born. Buckland was a small, lower middle class factory town rigidly ordered by sectarianism based on race, religion, nationality and ethnicity. Everybody belonged to some group or other and everybody was an outcast from the other groups. The large majority, Protestants, used the Walker Funeral Home, although they attended a spectrum of Protestant churches. The Catholics, who were a burgeoning minority, because of the large number of children they had, used the Connelly Funeral Home, which was Irish. There were no Italian funeral homes so Italians used the Irish parlor based on some sort of cost-benefit analysis. Conrad could recall the arid smell of the Walker funeral parlor after all these years, even though he'd only been there once, for his parents' funeral.

The Protestants were suspicious of the Roman-Catholics. They spoke in whispers about Catholics praying to Mary and other saints, going to confession and Wednesday afternoon catechism for schoolchildren led by strict nuns, and promoting what they, the Protestants, saw as the "false notion" of the Pope. They were particularly suspicious of the belief that the elements, bread and wine, were physically transformed into the body and blood of Christ. To Conrad, that seemed possible although he never saw any proof. The few times that Protestants entered a Roman Catholic Church for weddings or funerals, the Catholics tended to conceal any evidence of this magical transformation. Rumor was that, for a wide variety of reasons, the priests kept close watch over their supply of Communion wine. Communion consisted of worshippers lining up in front of the priest and allowing him to place a small wafer on their tongues. Since wine was not present, the attention of the wary Protestants focused on the wafer. No one reported that it underwent any noticeable change into flesh, which confirmed Conrad's childish notion.

Conrad's memories of his Irish Protestant grandfather ranting about the evils of Catholics, and his siblings making derogatory remarks about Jews, were still vivid. Even at a young age, Conrad had an innate distaste for the irrationality and unfairness of bigotry. He kept his thoughts to himself, however, until he was no longer dependent on family members.

The few Jews in town, a small minority, did not have a funeral home. No one knew where they went to bury their dead. They were secretive and mysterious, according to popular speculation. No one knew how they lived, but everyone knew that they owned a majority of the stores in town. The word was that they had a network, a secret organization that would lend money to any member who needed it. No Protestant or Catholic ever set foot inside the synagogue, which even looked strange and unnatural, not at all like a Christian church. For these reasons, the Jews were not trusted by the Catholics or Protestants, a feeling that united the Christians against a common enemy. Some whispered that the Jews conducted blood rituals of some sort in the basement of the temple as a sacrifice to their Old Testament God, a God of harsh justice. It was their way of atoning for their sins. Conrad dismissed this rumor as pure fiction.

The Jewish God of strict judgment, with highly partisan views of who was and was not chosen, along with a panoply of odd traditions, appeared to be a completely distinct deity from the Christian God of mercy and forgiveness. The few Jewish students in elementary school kept to themselves, often gathered in a small group on the playground. Conrad rejected the remarks about them made by his relatives, although it was difficult not to have his judgment affected by stories of strange behavior that he heard repeated.

As for Muslims, no one in town had ever seen or heard of one. They were mysterious people from Africa or the Middle East who had waged war against Christians in the Middle Ages or other ancient times. They were reputed to be dangerous. Pictures of fierce, scimitar-wielding infidels in children's books in the church library reinforced that reputation. Conrad particularly remembered one such sword with the name of the *Sword of Ali.* He was taught in his Sunday school class that Muslims were the original descendants of Cain. They were responsible for causing a clash of civilizations, resulting in the launching of the Crusades by Christians to wipe out the infidels. Conrad mused about how some ignorant people continued to be attracted to predictions about an ultimate clash of civilization between Christians and Muslims. Even today, rumors of a clash of civilizations persisted and Islamaphobia had a resurgence in American society.

Everyone in town, except Conrad, seemed to be content with living in a world in which everyone was divided from everyone else by a host of barriers, some beyond their control like race and ethnicity, and others by choice like religion, or by circumstance like poverty. There was little social interaction among the groups. Commercial interaction took place because, after all, supply and demand were immutable rules. The children who grew up in the town had only brief glimpses of what the world outside was like until they went off to college, assuming they were part of the lucky few who could qualify and afford to go. People in Buckland were wary and suspicious of new ideas. Most people didn't know enough to question the system. Some people remarked that the stratification that existed was good. It made it easy to know where everybody stood with respect to everybody else. Life was simple that way.

Conrad's childhood memories were punctuated by recollections of being a favorite prey of bullies. He often pointed with pride to having been able to withstand near daily torture at the hands of a few bullies. He recalled the exact spot on the way to school where two older and larger boys jumped him nearly every day and then chased him the remaining distance to school. He was a slow runner in those days and he was hopeless when it came to defending himself. Striking back would only bring greater torment and pain so he swallowed his medicine and vowed that someday he would retaliate.

That was Conrad's first experience with what he surmised was the criminal class, people who had no compunction about hurting others, something that was beyond his comprehension. The word 'empathy' was not yet in his vocabulary. One reason why he planned to be a lawyer was to prosecute and sue people like that. Although that plan collapsed, his experience led him to form a club based on blood oath with the victims of the bullies, those who lacked the strength or the will to defend themselves. He later thought that these experiences, plus his rejection of prejudice were the first stirrings of a powerful sense of justice that guided his life.

Conrad's father made a few efforts to instruct him on the art of self-defense but his efforts fell flat on the boy. His father stopped trying after Conrad seemed unable or unwilling to learn how to hold his hands up and strike an opponent. After that, his father mocked him with a hopeless expression whenever he complained of a beating, thus adding another layer of bullying to the mix. His father's death added another layer of rejection on Conrad's experience. It was years before Conrad accepted that his father's passing was not his fault.

About two years before his mother's death, because of his tendency to injure himself accidently and bleed profusely, Conrad convinced his mother that he must be a hemophiliac and that he would bleed to death during childhood. Conrad became fascinated by the prospect and one summer he took to regularly cutting himself for sport to induce bleeding. He'd then time how long it took for the bleeding to stop. He soon realized that he was not going to bleed to death, at least not from minor cuts. He would alarm his mother by pretending to be hysterical about the minor injuries. She gave up her obsessive fear when the family doctor finally convinced her that he had no such disease.

Conrad realized it was not a joking matter when he read newspaper reports describing cases in which people had actually infected themselves or bled to death. Later in life, he was astounded at the irony of the whole business. He supposed that, if his mother were still alive when the disease was discovered, she would judge him guilty of causing his own downfall. His mother once told another mother about Conrad's self-destructive play, causing a rumor to spread at school that added to his personal torment. The teacher even called him aside and offered to arrange psychological counseling, which was virtually unheard of in those days. That did not remain confidential and caused Conrad additional humiliation.

In those days Conrad felt like a refugee in his own life, unrecognized, invisible – a displaced person. That was it, the perfect term. He was a displaced person, like the DPs, as they called the people who had lost their homes in World War I and II. Although his mother probably felt responsible for his problems, she chose to make him feel responsible so he would take charge of protecting himself when she no longer controlled his life. Conrad wondered whether she anticipated an early death for herself. In any event, Conrad internalized a powerful feeling of guilt. It could be said that he believed in original sin – *his* original sin.

This concept of personal guilt was reinforced by the interpretation of Christianity that was taught in his Protestant Sunday school in those days. The Catholics spoke more of sin than guilt, even dividing sin up into categories of seriousness, like mortal and venal, and creating the practice of confession to cleanse the soul. Protestants talked about guilt too, along with mercy, but there was no easy way to get rid of guilt. Throughout his life Conrad kept adding to the stockpile of things that made him feel guilty. By the time he was fifty-nine, he was lugging around a truckload of baggage, guilt having been laden on guilt.

Conrad strained to make sense of the hazy memories of the time before his parents died. He looked forward to a time when he could forgive his parents for their indifference and then cut himself off, completely distance himself from them. They would never have imagined that he would interpret their tragically abbreviated parenthood as not so much tragedy as disappointment, and disappointment with *them*. Each time he retrieved and reexamined a childhood experience, he relived some measure of disenchantment that they had let things happen as they had, that his life with them had not been different.

By contrast, one category of experience stood apart as times of great happiness. Both his parents believed they should share with him the excitement and the wonder of the natural world. Perhaps, he thought, his siblings had long ago lost interest and so they had no one else to share with.

Conrad never understood why, in light of everything else, they went out of their way to be kind and generous with their own sense of wonder about nature. This applied to common experiences such as the beauty of a starry night, the fierce winds of a hurricane, a night-time snowfall, the music of a summer concert of insects and birds, or unusual experiences such as a lunar or solar eclipse. He could remember myriad times when he had been sent to bed early as punishment because of who knows what kind of trivial misstep. Then, suddenly, his mother or father would wake him and tell him to come to the kitchen or living room windows or to the screened porch to see some natural phenomenon visible in the back yard, which stretched for nearly a mile into dense woods. He would wake, drowsy, but surprised and excited, and relieved that whichever parent it was had relented and forgiven him for his latest misdeed.

Those moments of wonder were imprinted in his memory. He could see, hear, smell, and almost touch or taste those scenes. Several experiences stood out prominently. On one winter night, a blizzard and ice storm had swept over the Connecticut countryside where they lived, far from traffic or the lights of other homes. An especially beautiful stand of white birches bent over in the back yard, weighted with snow and glistening with a covering of ice crystals. He would never forget that scene.

Another was a solar eclipse in which the late afternoon sunlight was obliterated by the moon's dark shadow, blotting it out for what seemed like hours, but which actually took only minutes. To a small child, the solar eclipse was particularly frightening, as it must have been to primitive societies.

But both of those events were overwhelmed by one particular lunar eclipse in which the earth's shadow slowly but methodically blocked the shining moon's surface and the moon's color turned to a deep, startling red, a color which he had never seen or read about, much less imagined. He remembered the scene vividly. It was a terrible scene on one hand, but awe-inspiring on the other. The moon turned a deep blood red for the duration of the eclipse. In school the next day, the teacher explained that the lunar eclipse was called a blood moon and that the phenomenon had religious and spiritual significance to some people. It was a famous event, repeated only occasionally, that was forecast in some religions to signify the end of the world. The idea of the end of the world both fascinated and terrified him. Enhanced by the meaning ascribed to the eclipse, the sight of that spectacle was indelibly etched in his mind.

৩

Conrad woke abruptly without having any sense of how long he had been asleep sitting at the wheel of the car. Without giving himself time to get his bearings, he pulled hurriedly out of the municipal parking lot to travel the twenty or so minutes it would take to reach home. He was half day-dreaming and half paying attention as he made a familiar sharp turn and pulled into an intersection that was partially obstructed, just one block from his house. He passed through this intersection nearly every day. He knew that a driver had to look hard to the left to see any vehicles coming from that direction. Usually, a quick glance left, then right, then left again, was sufficient. But this time, Conrad pulled out without the second glance to the left, leaving it to chance as to whether any vehicles were approaching.

Chance was not on his side. A bright red pickup truck was speeding from the left, out of sight until Conrad found himself immediately in its path, totally unprepared to take evasive action. He jammed his foot on the brake pedal, grinding the car to a sudden stop. It was too late. He was helpless, sitting in the middle of the road. The truck was bearing down on him, split seconds from an inevitable collision. Time and motion stood starkly still, in what seemed like a single frame of a motion picture, repeated over and over. Despite the pickup truck's teenage driver's effort to jam on the brakes, causing the truck to squeal and skid to the right, the vehicles collided savagely with a deafening crash of metal on metal. Conrad felt his body jolted sideways, then back, and then forward, striking his head on the windshield with a loud crack. No air bag deployed, since the mechanism in his older car had long ago been dismantled. Pain seared his body, like a jagged bolt of lightning as he came close to losing consciousness. Again, time stood still and he remembered hearing a harsh male voice, probably the driver he thought, shouting at him. "Are you okay? What the hell were you doing, asshole? You didn't even look, did you? Jerk!"

Conrad was incapable of responding rationally, although in his traumatic daze, he felt the stirring of a tiny impulse to protest that the truck must have been speeding. He slumped back and managed to murmur, "Call the police. Help me. Call an ambulance," before his voice trailed away into a whisper of an outgoing breath carrying his words somewhere into space.

"Oh shit," the driver said. "My father will kill me...his truck. You goddam asshole."

Conrad heard other voices. He opened his eyes and could see people staring in the window at him. He felt like a caged animal on display. Voices were not audible except for one woman who asked him repeatedly, "Are you okay, mister? Are you okay? The police are coming and an ambulance. Hold on there."

Later, he would remember her kind voice, among the indistinguishable sounds. He allowed himself to drift off into unconsciousness until he was awakened by the sounds of an emergency vehicle and then a furious wrenching at the door of his car.

He remembered being roughly moved onto a stretcher and rolled to the back of an emergency vehicle, lifted and rolled in. Two people – one man, one woman – secured him in the ambulance and sat next to him all the way to the hospital. That was the last thing he remembered until he awoke again lying on a gurney in the corridor of the city hospital emergency room. He had no idea how much time had elapsed during his period of unconsciousness. It was as if the moment of the crash had been drawn out in slow motion and repeated over and over. The whole time, his mind streamed his life before him, his childhood merging into young adulthood, and then right up to the present, then back again to childhood as the sequence played out all over. It was as though the introspective moment before the crash, when he had sat consumed in memories of his early life, simply continued to pass before him. He did not feel near death, but he sensed that he was fading in and out of consciousness. He was vaguely aware that he might have a serious concussion. Or perhaps he was just weary of life and giving in to the impulse to let go.

He wondered whether anyone had notified Helen or whether she would even come to the hospital. He was overcome with deep sadness, taking him by surprise. He let go of concerns and allowed his mind to wander at will over the segments of his life, as people passed by, some stopping to speak and some merely commenting on their assessment of the situation. Some asked questions. Promises were made that he would be given a room but all this did not matter to him. He was lost, strangely, somewhere in the past, wandering through a dark wooded place, reflecting on his observations, his mind intent on figuring out how he got from there to here, wherever *here* was. What was reality and what was imagination?

Conrad lay still, fastened to his gurney. He was unable to move except by shifting his hips slightly or raising one knee a few inches. His mind, perhaps seeking escape from the predicament in which it found itself trapped, focused on the disappointments of his childhood. It seemed incongruous to be recounting his petty memories and recriminations while his very life might be in jeopardy. Yet, his mind insisted, as though it knew it had to tell his life story before the body expired and the mind, by itself or carried by the spirit, the soul, drifted away to some other existence outside of space and time.

The sound of a clear, kind voice seemed to materialize out of nowhere, just as the hazy figure of a man seemed to materialize in the empty space before him. He saw a tall, dark man with an open-necked shirt and loose sweater, standing by his gurney.

"Good afternoon, my friend," the person said. "I'm Gaspar. I work as a chaplain here at the hospital – when they need me, that is. Otherwise, I just check on things," he said with a quick chuckle. "I've been expecting you. I heard you were coming in today. Do you mind if I sit on the end of your cot for a bit? I wanted to meet you."

"No, I don't mind," Conrad replied. "That's fine. You wanted to meet me? You've been expecting me? How is that? I don't think I'm staying long. But I'm getting tired of talking to myself, in fact," Conrad said. "I've been lying here ruminating about my whole life, especially my failures. Can you get me a cup of water? I'm dying of thirst." Conrad choked on the word 'dying' and laughed. "Maybe I'm *really* dying. Do you have a last name?"

"I don't think so. That is, I don't think you're dying...not from this little accident anyway," the man said in his deep voice. "I'll see if they'll let me...bring you water, that is. You have a lot of questions. Usually, the nurses say no water unless approved by a doctor. Of course, they never get around to finding a doctor. I don't suppose they know what's wrong with you yet."

Gaspar returned in a few minutes with a small paper cup of water. "Don't tell anybody I gave you water. AMA. Against medical advice, you know. How do you feel?"

"Not great," Conrad said. "Do you know what happened to me?"

"Something of it, yes, but tell me what you remember."

"I was in my car. Next thing I know a truck was there. Hit me, I guess. I think I lost consciousness. But I don't feel any head pain now."

"In a few minutes, I'll try to get you some medical attention, when the team is finished with their rounds," Gaspar said. "But tell me. You said you were remembering your life, telling your life story to yourself. Do you want to tell me? Or you could wait for another time. Sometimes it helps to tell your story about life here on earth, if you know what I mean."

"Life on earth," Conrad said. "Not exactly. That's a strange thing to say. What else is there? Where am I? My mind has been floating around but I'll try to put it into words."

Conrad surprised himself by rambling – even he could tell it was incoherent – about his life back in school. It was odd, having the whole of his life confronting him in a jumble. He always heard that when people saw their whole lives run by in front of them, it was like a movie, running chronologically in sequence. He was experiencing his whole life but it was in a geometric pattern, more like an abstract painting. It made no sense. What did it mean? Was it some sort of sign? Was it a personal apocalypse?

He recounted how his promising performance in grammar school faltered into a disappointing performance in high school.

He confessed to a few desperate attempts at cheating in high school in order to raise his class standing and how they turned out badly. He was relieved when the semester ended without being confronted for his crimes. He was lucky not to have been found out.

"My poor college performance followed on the heels of high school. My chances of getting admitted to law school faded. Eventually, I got a Master's degree in education and something else. My head hurts. Awfully tired. Hard to think."

"It doesn't matter," Gaspar said. "Don't worry. Just go on as long as you feel like it. You can fall asleep whenever you want."

"Isn't Gaspar the name of…? I can't find the words…."

"Yes. It is the name of one of the magi. He was Indian but the name is mainly Hispanic now. But I'm not Hispanic, actually." He laughed again. "Confusing, isn't it? I feel like saying 'You're entering the twilight zone.'" He laughed again. "Just kidding."

It felt good to talk. "Social Justice is what I cared about," Conrad continued, "although education was practical. I volunteer to teach courses in human rights, social justice, and global development. Global development is another way of talking about poor people and poor societies. That appeals to me. I'm one of the invisible people on the planet. I can't complain but still I have always felt like a refugee from the human race. But I've never been poor or hungry or miserable."

"You're not invisible," Gaspar said. "You're flesh and blood. You wouldn't be here if you were invisible. You know, sometimes people say I'm invisible, like an angel. Beside the point. By the way, it's okay to feel disappointed with life. Most people are, in the end, at least when the measuring stick is their expectations. But there's always hope. It never ends. Go on, please. Are you married? Have children?"

"Yes. Her name is Helen. My wife, that is. We weren't ever in love, I think, although I'm not sure I know what that would feel like. I used to think we had mutual respect at least, but I don't think so any more. We have two grown children. It wasn't always that way. It all looks good from the outside but, inside, that's a different story. I never said those words out loud before. It sends chills, you know, just to hear them out loud."

He wondered again whether Helen had been notified of his accident. He felt a rising concern but realized that she would be critical of him when she found out how it had happened. There was time enough to let her know. He didn't know whether he'd be given tests in the emergency room or admitted as an in-patient. It all seemed far beyond his control. Having decided with some clarity that there was nothing he could do, he turned back to let his mind continue the storytelling. Too bad no one was writing all this down. But it was hardly interesting to anyone but himself.

Conrad was silent for a moment. "The children are named Esther and Paul. We liked the idea of giving them Biblical names, one from the Old and one from the New Testament. My middle name is Paul. I like that because Paul is my favorite disciple. I don't much like my first name. I can't imagine where my parents found it. But I wish I could lose it. It's a stupid name. It makes me sound like some backwoods simpleton."

Conrad dozed off thinking how Esther had developed along the lines of the Biblical Esther, the star of the family at least so far, in her senior year of college. Paul was a religion teacher at a local college, an admirer of certain features of Islam and Buddhism. He was stuck for now at the assistant professor level. But at least he had higher rank than Conrad did on contract at the university. Paul would tease Esther about the fact that the name of God was never mentioned in her book of the Bible and that although the authorship was attributed to her namesake, it wasn't proven to be so. He reminded her that Paul was the greatest scholar in early Christianity. How did they turn out to be so competitive with each other, he wondered. Time passed. Conrad opened his eyes, realizing that he had drifted away for some period of time. He saw with surprise that Gaspar was still seated on his bed. He was as patient as an angel, Conrad thought. Maybe that's what he is, an angel. "We don't have much in common," Conrad said out loud, referring to Helen. "Sometimes I feel like an outsider in my own home, like a boarder in a guest house."

After a few minutes, Gaspar said, "I'll be back to see you. But I hope the tests go well and you're able to go home. I'll send a doctor over here before I leave. Here's a card, if you need to reach me. I'm sure we'll see each other again."

Conrad was not sure whether to be comforted or disturbed at Gaspar's prediction. Shortly afterward, he was wheeled into diagnostic radiology for a full body CT scan, which proved to be negative for internal injuries or fractures. After examination and a waiting period that turned out to be six hours to be sure no severe concussion had occurred, he was told he would not be admitted to the hospital after all. A social worker told him that his wife said she would pick him up in a few hours.

That left Conrad with more time to ruminate. A glance in the mirror in the rest room, which he was now free to walk to, told him that he was average looking, a little overweight, losing some hair, and shorter than he wished to be (five-eleven and probably shrinking). As an outsider all his life, he felt irrelevant. He had been contented with his marriage to Helen, not what he would call happy, whatever that was, but not sad either. He knew that Helen had not been in love with him when they married. He had learned some years ago that she was having an affair with a married man, a relationship that had started well before their marriage and continued for at least the first five years into it, ending only when the man had died of a sudden heart attack. On a chance encounter some years after the man's death, his widow had told Conrad more about it than he wanted to know.

Conrad had never confronted Helen's infidelity and managed to block it from his mind most of the time. To do otherwise seemed pointless. When he did think about it, the episode caused him to experience sadness. He often wondered whether Helen would be as deeply affected by his death as she had been after her lover's death. Conrad trudged passively through life, disturbing as little as possible and confronting problems only when unavoidable.

The saving grace of Conrad's life, he thought, was his dedication to the refugees he helped at the Global Refugee Organization. They were a special class of outsiders – people without a home, without any resources, and virtually without a country. He took secret pride, more than he dared reveal, in watching them succeed. He followed students and former students, many of whom sought him out because he alone had paid attention to them. They had been ignored by the regular faculty. The regular faculty wanted to be worshipped by the best students; he was content to shepherd the ordinary or less than ordinary. The use of his time teaching and advising received little or no respect within the college community. Even here he was an outlier.

Conrad was content to fill in gaps in the university programs, teaching courses that no one else wanted to teach. That brought him to teach the ethics of war and military conflict and the social and economic status of displaced persons, refugees and migrants in the Middle East and Africa. He taught a course in public health problems of refugee populations, although he had no special qualifications to teach public health from a science standpoint. These were not popular courses among the faculty, who preferred pure disciplines such as English, the Sciences and Mathematics. No university department claimed him. He was a journeyman teacher, a utility infielder.

Conrad felt invisible in all social and professional gatherings at the university. The only place where he felt important was at the refugee center and, of course, in his own classroom. As soon as Conrad had begun to teach refugee studies, he volunteered to help refugees get settled in New England. The way he saw it, America was composed of refugees of one type or another from the founding. Virtually all immigrants had come to this country to get away from something.

Conrad was amazed that, since his childhood, every U.S. war had brought a tsunami of refugees from the country it had fought. After World War II, the Germans and Japanese. Then Koreans. Next Vietnamese. You could tell the history of the Cold War from the arrival of refugees – the Hungarians after the 1968 uprising, the Poles after martial law was imposed in the 1980s. After the Cold War ended, Russians and Eastern Europeans flooded the gates of the country. Now, in the midst of ongoing wars in the Middle East, it was Muslims from Iraq, Pakistan, and Afghanistan. Next it would be Syrians, Yemenis and Libyans, along with people from the African countries engaged in civil wars. That was not to overlook the Chinese and other East Asians and all the Central American refugees seeking to escape drug wars and gang violence. Conrad was comfortable with all the refugees, with whom he felt a sense of belonging. Building a country by stages of immigrants and refugees, many of whom were fleeing war or its consequences, was an absolute miracle, he thought.

Tears flowed and chills went through his body every time he heard Irving Berlin's hymn to refugees, *Give Me Your Tired, Your Poor*. He felt his soul come alive with that song and could not understand why it did not rank with the *National Anthem* and *America the Beautiful*. Berlin's song spoke to him, more because he had spent his life as an invisible person socially than because he was a second generation Swiss-American and a second generation Scottish-Irish.

He prayed every night but his prayers were more ritualistic, if not perfunctory, than deeply felt. If he ever had a personal relationship with God – or with Jesus Christ – it lay unfulfilled in his mind and heart. He had trouble visualizing the Trinity and so he addressed his prayers to God directly, without having any particular image of whom or what he was addressing. He would say often, "When I pray, I pray to God. I just can't pray to Christ like the Catholics do and, certainly, not to Mary or other saints."

From Conrad's perspective, Helen had managed to conceal her secret life. He could not know that she continued to grieve privately for her married lover long after his death. She and Conrad had now been married close to twenty-five years. At the outset, Conrad had simply provided a convenient way of continuing her relationship with her lover. She had engaged in a masquerade, a colossal trick, her first but not her last, he would discover.

In a short time, Conrad would be off on his trip to the Middle East for a conference on the burgeoning refugee overflow from the Middle East. Conrad knew that Helen did not approve of this plan. She saw it as a waste of time and money. But he was undeterred. He planned to attend a conference in Jordan with the director of the refugee center in order to find a way to facilitate the movement of refugees from Syria, mainly, to other countries in the region and to standardize refugee camps among the major centers, in Jordan, Turkey and Lebanon. This was a U.N. sponsored conference with the promise of funding if agreement could be reached, especially if other countries in the region would agree to increase the number of refugees that would be allowed to enter.

The continuing wars in the region, especially the long Syrian civil war, provoked in large part by radical groups like ISIS, constantly changed the dynamic. Syrian refugees were growing in number and Palestinian refugees, fairly stable populations for some years, were being forced out of Syria by the violence and forced out of Lebanon as well. Conrad was excited about the prospect of being involved at the policy level and, although the trip was expensive and was not subsidized, he had looked forward to it for months. His flight departure was only weeks away.

Conrad wondered whether the unforeseen consequence of the accident would derail his plans. Had he suffered injuries so far undetected that would prevent him from going? He lay in quiet contemplation, his life flowing backward and forward before his eyes or at least within his brain. He felt entirely passive, helpless, knowing that his fate lay in hands other than his own. There was nothing he could do. It was a relief in a way. He finally released the stream of images and thoughts. He would have to leave to fate what the future held for him. He wondered if he should pray. It seemed like a good idea. But to whom should he pray and for what? He drifted back to sleep while he waited for deliverance from the emergency room.

PART TWO

REUNION

AFTER BEING RELEASED from the emergency room, Conrad took a week off to recuperate from the injuries he had suffered in the accident. His life was further complicated by having to replace his car, which suffered total damage. As the days passed, he became confident that his injuries would not interfere with his Jordan trip. The countdown continued toward the departure day. A persistent fatigue plagued him, however, which he attributed to the aftershock of the trauma.

His second meeting with Ghadir took place two days after returning to his normal routine. He had one university class to teach as well as students to counsel. He wanted to be on hand at the refugee center to greet and orient a new group of refugees just arrived from North Africa. Syrian refugees were still being blocked at the federal level because of the fear of domestic terrorism generated by the continuing European terrorist incidents, which had now stunned five countries of the EU. Other ethnic and national groups trickled in at the normal pace. Conrad scheduled the appointment late in the afternoon following his three-hour afternoon class. Sylvia alerted him that Ayah was with Ghadir again but her aunt was absent.

"I appreciate your seeing us again," Ghadir said, her smile reflecting a medley of anxiety, pain, relief and gratitude. "I can't keep my mind off Jamil, wondering how he is, where he is. There are news programs on television about how DAESH, in its ugliness and evil, is increasing the recruiting of young boys. They have set up a system of camps to train young boys they call *cubs*. The full name I've heard is *Cubs of the Caliphate*."

"Absolutely disgusting," Conrad said. "Makes it sound so harmless, as if they were boy scouts."

"They have systematized the kidnapping of young boys," Ghadir added. "PBS had a special program showing how they target, then hijack, busloads of children on their way to school or camp. They separate the boys from the girls and train them to become warriors or suicide bombers, the girls they just turn into slaves. They force them to watch beheadings and torture of all kinds including electric shock."

"Desensitizing the boys, I suppose. Think of the damage it does," Conrad said without realizing how insensitive his remark was.

"It's unbearable," Ghadir said tearfully, "to think that Jamil might already be in a DAESH camp being forced to watch their barbaric demonstrations and rituals. I simply can't comprehend how a father could subject his son to this brutality. I never saw this in Yousef. Do you know they even script and rehearse the beheadings? They film them so they can show them again in training camps and post them on the internet. This is torture at its extreme."

"For me too, Yamma," Ayah added, hugging her mother.

To Conrad, Ayah added, "Our mother raised us to reject all violence. That's what the Qur'an teaches. DAESH changes the teachings of Islam whenever they please. My brother and I started studying the Qur'an when we were seven years old. My brother must be confused by what his father is doing. He is so young."

"I know how you must feel," Conrad said, looking directly at Ghadir, avoiding Ayah's intense gaze. Conrad was afraid her emotion would draw him in. "If you can get me some information – some leads – I'll see what I can find out when I'm in Jordan. I leave just over a month from today. I won't have time to go to Syria but I expect to meet people from all over the region. There'll be some Syrians there, I'm sure."

"I'll try to reach my brother," Ghadir said, "although that's not likely to happen quickly. He's affiliated with a rebel group in Syria that opposes Assad and DAESH. He told me the last time we spoke that he moves around often. I don't approve of using violence to solve political problems but at least he's on the right side, if there is a right side to war."

"I've read about the huge number of rebel groups," Conrad said, "but I don't know much about them. What about other contacts?"

"I'll be able to speak to a contact in Palestine – the sister of my sister-in-law, Mona. Do you remember me saying that Mona and her husband, Hamza, my husband's brother, were taking care of Jamil temporarily? I'll try to find out if they still have him and where they are now. I'm so afraid that there isn't much time. Once my husband decides to retrieve Jamil, we are lost. There will be no saving him. Maybe I should go there myself. I don't know what to do."

"I'll do my best to make contacts to try and locate Jamil. It sounds as though your brother is the best bet, though. If you could reach him, maybe he'd go and get Jamil himself. If you get any information soon, I'll try and make contacts with the conference organizers before I leave for Jordan."

Ghadir and Ayah left the office with a plan to return as soon as they had further information.

Conrad did not hear from Ghadir during the next two days. On the third day, he observed, as he got out of bed, that his left leg was noticeably swollen. His right leg looked normal. He assumed that he had injured the leg somehow, perhaps in the accident. He ignored it. When the condition persisted for several days, he went to his primary care doctor and friend, Larry Martino. Seeing no obvious cause for the condition, Larry referred him to a vascular surgeon to treat the condition just in case there was deep vein clotting that could jeopardize his vital organs – and his life.

"Don't worry," Martino said. "This isn't unusual for someone your age. You've been jogging for years. And you have varicose veins. I expect it's just that some of your veins aren't fully functional. The vascular surgeon will check it out and might decide that some of them can be safely removed. You're in good shape otherwise. You know I always say, Conrad. I expect you to die from an infection in your hammer toe, nothing more serious than that. And, since you cut holes in all your sneakers and shoes to accommodate the hammer toe, you'll probably be ninety-five by that time."

They had a good laugh. Conrad made the appointment, relieved and confident that nothing of consequence was involved.

After an ultrasound showed that he had two superficial blood clots in the left leg, he was started on an oral blood thinner. Two weeks later, when the pills appeared not to be working, because another clot, this one a DVT, a deep vein clot, had appeared, the medication was changed to an injectable blood thinner, requiring Conrad to inject himself in his belly fat twice a day. After he had conquered his distaste for this process and gotten used to the minor pain, he went to the doctor's office two days before the trip to Jordan for a final ultrasound.

The vascular surgeon greeted him with news that his condition was stable, although all three clots still existed. "Hey," he said carelessly, "you're stable. The DVT is pretty low down in the calf and not much of a risk. I think there's no reason why you shouldn't travel. Better you travel than the clot," he joked, surprised when Conrad did not flinch and stared at him with disapproval.

"The clots mean nothing?" Conrad asked. "Are you sure the clot won't move up toward my lungs or heart? What about the risks of flying? What should I do if I feel pain?"

"I can't guarantee anything," the surgeon said with annoyance. "It's your decision. I told you what I thought. Do you have any *important* questions? I have another patient waiting."

Despite his doctor's reassurances, Conrad had misgivings about travelling. He knew the risks inherent in a long flight. But he did not want to pull out of this trip no matter what the risk, especially after being cleared. He left the office feeling concerned but he put aside his misgivings.

Despite the blood clots and the swollen leg, Conrad had continued to teach his courses and to attend to refugees at the Center. He had met twice with Ghadir who was struggling to get accurate information from sources in Palestine or Syria. Nothing turned up. No one could reach Youssef's brother and sister-in-law and no information turned up about Jamil. The intervening weeks had elapsed without any progress and Ghadir became more desperate. The situation was precarious as long as there was doubt that

Conrad would be well enough to make the trip. When Conrad was cleared, Ghadir and Ayah, as well as Conrad, were overjoyed.

Within hours after leaving the surgeon's office two days before the Jordan trip, Conrad's world collapsed. As he was sitting in his office at the university preparing for his final class before the trip, he felt a slight pain in his left side. He dismissed it to himself as nothing more than a "runner's stitch," the kind that a runner gets by going a little too fast without warming up. Slowing down to a walk or jog usually solved the problem. Conrad attributed it to tension about the trip. Still, he called the vascular surgeon's office. The receptionist got the doctor on the phone and Conrad explained what had happened.

"This is not my problem," the surgeon said. "A pain like that can have any number of possible causes. It has nothing to do with my treatment."

"But I just came from your office. I want you to examine me. That's the least you can do."

"Not appropriate," the surgeon said. "This does not concern me. But you should get it treated before you leave."

"But where? By whom?" Conrad asked.

"I don't know. Just take care of it," the surgeon said. "Go to a GI specialist or the emergency room." The surgeon hung up without a further word.

Conrad felt frustration, even panic. And anger at being rebuffed. Not knowing where to turn, he called Larry Martino. Since it was now after office hours, he left a message. Larry called back within twenty minutes. "I can't see you until morning. I'm out of town."

Raising the suspicion that the pain might be diverticulitis, Larry sent him to the satellite emergency room in the next town over for a CT scan and a CBC, a complete blood count. "If it's diverticulitis, you shouldn't go on your trip. The Emergency Room doctor will call me to let me know what they turn up. I'll stay in touch. Don't worry. It's probably nothing."

Helen accompanied him to the satellite emergency room, where he was examined, scanned and had blood drawn for the CBC. As they sat in the examining room for an hour, Conrad said that he was praying the condition was not diverticulitis, because it would prevent his travelling, a remark that he later regretted. Helen was impatient to get back home. Minutes later, a young male physician's assistant appeared in the doorway.

"Well, we got the CBC result back," he said, obviously amused. "Big surprise to us, something we don't see very often," the PA chortled. The medical assistant with him, who was of lower rank than the PA, laughed too.

"What is it?" Conrad asked. "Good or bad? What's funny about this?"

"You've got a white blood count of 160. That's 160,000." He whistled loudly, causing the assistant to grin again. She added, "This is one for the books."

"160,000? 160,000 white blood cells," Conrad asked, exasperated with the pair.

"Yes, per microliter. This is amazing," the PA said. "Never saw this high a number before."

"What does that mean?" Conrad asked, irritated at their amusement. "I don't even know what a microliter is or what the count is supposed to be. What's going on? What does it mean?"

"The only time we see a count this high is in leukemia," the PA said. "Wow, man, this is something."

"Leukemia! You've got to be kidding," Conrad said, gasping, with a sickening feeling coursing through his body, threatening to submerge him. "That can't be. I felt fine. *I feel fine.* It was just a little stitch in my side. I ran yesterday. I run every day. I have to go to the Middle East in two days."

"Hey, I don't think so," the PA said with a pleasant smile, the assistant shaking her head as well. "Only place you're going is the hospital in the city. You can't walk around with a blood count like that. It's suicide. Call an ambulance, will you," he said to the assistant, who left the room.

"Ambulance? I won't do that. I have to go on this trip. Can't you just do something to make it normal? I feel fine. I feel perfect, actually. It can't be leukemia. I don't even know what that is? How can I have something suddenly when I don't even know what it is? This is ridiculous. You are ridiculous," he said angrily at the PA. You think it's funny."

"No, I don't think it's funny," the PA said, his own anger visibly rising. It's not my fault. It's yours. We can't let you go. You can't leave. You can't check out. We'll call your doctor. He'll tell you what you have to do."

"You can't force me to stay here or go to the hospital. I don't want a damn ambulance."

The PA got Conrad's doctor on the phone and Larry Martino spoke directly to Conrad on a speaker phone.

"Conrad. I'm awfully sorry to hear this," Larry said. "I had no idea. Back in September, your white count was 11,000. I'm looking at your chart on my computer now. I don't know what happened, what went wrong. But this is very serious. Go right to the hospital and I'll come in and see you on Monday. I'd meet you there tonight but Edna and I are leaving for a wedding in Ohio. I can't back out of that. But I'll be back Sunday night. They'll start you on chemo to lower your WBC right away. It could be dangerous. You could die from organ failure."

Conrad felt abandoned and alone, forgetting that Helen was still sitting there, looking stunned, and no doubt weighing how this would impact her life.

❧

Conrad left the satellite emergency room in an ambulance in an hour and a half. "You said my condition was serious, an emergency. Why did it take over an hour to get me in an ambulance," he asked, annoyed.

The attendants ignored his question as they strapped him to a gurney and wheeled him out, then locked him in place in the ambulance. He wondered if the siren would be turned on. It wasn't. The attendant who rode with him was absorbed looking at his cellphone the whole time. Conrad occupied himself by staring out the back window, staring at the receding scenes playing like a movie in rewind mode. He found moderate interest in trying to figure out where he was on the familiar highway trip to the city.

He ventured a remark to the attendant. "It was no more than a stitch in my side, but it lasted for two days. How is this possible? How could I have leukemia without knowing it?"

The attendant looked at him blankly, shrugged and shook his head. "I don't know. I don't know nothin' about leukemia except that it's bloody cancer."

Conrad cringed. "Thanks a lot," he muttered. Ordinarily, he would have dismissed any concern about the tiny pain, which seemed to get tinier every time he repeated the story. He could easily have ignored it in the course of preparing for the strenuous trip to Jordan. But with the annoying ache lasting overnight he had followed his impulse. There was the mistake. He should have ignored it and maybe it would have gone back to normal. He said, "I can't have leukemia. It sounds so repulsive, so terrifying. Maybe it was just a temporary rise in the white cell count."

The attendant just shrugged.

It was an anomaly. Here he was in his street clothes strapped to the gurney in the ambulance for the half hour trip to the hospital. He felt like a prisoner who could have escaped, just walked away, but instead who capitulated to imprisonment. He shook his head, trying to clear it of the painful memories of the ER visit a short time ago.

He realized with a start that he would not be going to Jordan. A boy's life was at stake. Many more lives actually. All those plans were shattered when the PA spoke the word "leukemia."

The terrible realization that his entire life had changed descended upon him like a shroud. He could barely breathe. He felt like a different person. Or perhaps he was not a person at all. He was rather a disease embodied, a carrier for a lethal something he didn't understand. He recalled the drug ads in magazines showing attractive men and women smiling and saying, "I am not my disease. I am more than that." What a lie. He was *not* more than his disease. He was defined by his newly-discovered disease. He was leukemia, he was cancer.

He felt even more that way as he lay for hours—so many hours, he lost count—in the emergency room, waiting for attention from somebody, anybody. He was now in a different world, the world of a city emergency room on a Friday night. He saw gunshot wound cases, berserk people shouting. Once when he had nearly dozed off, Conrad came to with the wildly grinning face of a wild man stuck right into Conrad's face, the man's spittle spraying Conrad as he made incomprehensible noises. Shocked and furious, Conrad pushed the mentally ill man away so abruptly that he fell backwards, hitting his head on the opposite wall.

"Stop," Conrad shouted. "Get away from me. Don't touch me."

The man laughed hysterically, lying on the floor, before spouting a stream of obscenities at Conrad. This brought two burly security guards, barely suppressing their laughter, to pick up the strange man and say to Conrad, "Watch it, asshole. You use violence again and we'll call the police. You can't do that, no matter what happens. This is a non-violent place. That nutcase can't help it."

Totally chastened by these outbursts and outraged at being blamed, Conrad was fearful enough of what could happen so that he turned on his side and faced the corridor wall. He was afraid to move. He longed to escape. He was miserable. He wanted to cry.

This was a crazy place, a scary place. Now he was in trouble. He'd be labeled a troublemaker. Somebody with a white coat was writing furiously on his clipboard. "Oh God," Conrad said aloud, "What's next?" Now he was truly guilty, not just of somehow getting leukemia, but of committing a crime. He expected to see the police arrive any minute. On top of it all the sickening developments, he'd be arrested. What if he'd injured the mentally ill guy, maybe with that reflexive shove, causing a concussion? "What if he died? What if he was a doctor," Conrad muttered to himself, nearly breaking into outright nervous laughter.

"Now I belong to this place," Conrad said aloud in a quiet voice to no one in particular. "I must have brought this on myself. Stress, that's probably what it was. Maybe it was my dispute with the Dean last fall. Could leukemia be caused by stress? If my count was normal in September, something happened between then and now. I know that was a toxic battle. It made me sick." He was too exhausted to weep, which is what he desperately longed to do.

Finally, after two hours Helen arrived. She hadn't given a thought to bringing clothes for him. She was clearly upset, on the verge of tears but dripping with suppressed anger and frustration as well. "What am I going to do? I don't know what to do. How long will you be here? I can't manage everything by myself.

Why did you have to do this? You must have done something to bring this on? When will you be home? When will you get over this condition? I don't do well with adversity. This had better not last long."

Conrad was shocked to see her visible reaction, especially her annoyance and demanding tone. He felt physically injured by her battery of questions and assertions. She was usually very controlled. He expected her to take this in stride. After all, he was the one who had been taken prisoner and brought here against his will. At least that's what it felt like. He wasn't given a choice. He was told he would be taken to the hospital. What right had they to strip him of his freedom? He hadn't even thought about just walking out of the emergency room, going home, resuming his life. But, at the same time, he knew that was not possible. The emergency room people were just doing their job, responding to an emergency. He could have walked out but then what would he do? His chest tightened at the thought. He was suddenly short of breath. Panic was setting in. Outrage was giving way to fear, to panic, to surrender. He told Helen to go home, since she was clearly uncomfortable for herself and unable to bring him any comfort.

Conrad felt hopeless, abandoned, alone in the hellish din and chaos of the emergency room, a place that was bursting its seams in a continuing explosion of insanity. This place was an organism created by human pathology.

After waiting ten hours in the emergency room, he had been admitted as an in-patient and then promised medical attention, which was never delivered. He had no choice but to change into the torture device they called a "johnny coat" or "johnny gown". The purpose of this flimsy, short, loose-fitting garment, with its deliberate rear exposure, is unmistakably to humiliate patients. Patients are easier to manage when they are passive and obedient. Another day in a johnny gown, a "johnny" as the nurses called it, would totally demoralize him. Helen had left but he would call her first thing in the morning. He forgot the time. He was disoriented in time and space. It was first thing in the morning.

He'd been awake all night. It was nearly 7 a.m. He'd ask her to remember to bring sweatshirts and sweatpants to wear. He'd read about new sweatsuit designs for hospital clothing. Where was it, he wondered.

His first conversation with a doctor in the oncology-hematology unit was uninspiring. He wasn't even sure she was a doctor although she kept referring to herself as a resident fellow. Conrad didn't quite get her name. All she said to introduce herself was that she was "Becky." Conrad's questions about why and how this had happened to him were brushed away with long sentences describing obscure sounding names for genetic mutations that had not yet been identified in his portfolio of evils.

"But why, after all these years and after exercising a lot and working hard to stay in good shape, why do I have this crazy disease?" Conrad insisted.

"It's not crazy," Becky said. She was a bubbly, cheerful person who tried to calm him by repeating at least three times, "You are not responsible for this. It's not your fault. You didn't do anything to cause it."

"But something must have brought it on," Conrad argued. "My mother would have said it is my fault. I know. I had a big fight last fall with the associate dean at my college. It was very stressful. He tried to change my contract to cut back my courses, which I need to teach because of the money. It was in the middle of my contract term too. I won the fight but it was so toxic, I felt literally poisoned after the battle. It went on for a whole month and he has badmouthed me ever since. It must have contributed. The stress, you know. That son-of-a-bitch did me in."

"Hold on," Becky said, looking annoyed at being contradicted. No," she asserted. "Not so. It's just bad luck. It's a disease of getting older. We all get mutations to our genes but almost all of them are harmless. We'll do genetic testing of all the cancer-causing genes, but we already know that you must have some harmful ones. It's not your fault, no matter what your mother would say. Believe me." The short resident fellow smiled sweetly and said, "Get some sleep now. I know you haven't slept all night. The nurse will be in to take your vitals shortly. Don't worry. We won't let you leave without a plan now, will we?"

"But when can I sleep?"

"Just try to sleep whenever you get a few minutes," Becky said in an offhand way. "There are a lot of things to check. It's Saturday morning, though, so you'll have more time to yourself during the weekend." She left, smiling and waving, cheerfully telling him he had nothing to worry about.

Conrad wondered if he'd wandered onto the wrong movie set. He thought it was a tragedy but perhaps it was just a comedy about hospital life.

She repeated, "We'll take care of your disease. Don't think we'll leave you without a plan. Be positive."

Conrad clung to her words of optimism and confidence, despite his skepticism. But he found out later on from a brief conversation with her in the hallway when he pressed her on *the plan* that she lacked any specifics about what they would do. In fact there was no plan. In fact, she did not give any sign that she even remembered talking with him. Conrad concluded that there never would be a plan for him…just seat of the pants improvisation. Every time he saw her, she continued to look cheerful and upbeat, a posture that Conrad became increasingly suspicious about. In fact, it depressed him more than the gloomy messages from some others on the staff. They shook their heads and stared at him as though he were a lab experiment, an already half-dead curiosity with a rare disease at that.

Conrad didn't persist in the argument about the cause of his disease but he remained convinced about his guilt, at least his responsibility for this disaster. There had to be a cause, a specific cause, for something as dreaded as leukemia. He'd find out.

Conrad managed to sleep for a few hours, followed by an unappetizing lunch from a menu that posed as a bistro selection. He decided to take a walk to the roof terrace, which was optimistically called the "healing garden." He'd been warned that he couldn't go anywhere without taking his *dance partner*, the common name for the spindly device that looked like an old-fashioned coat rack on wheels. It held bags of fluids for patients including Heparin and glucose. He unplugged the device and hurried down the hallway, with his Ginger Rodgers staggering along beside or behind him, tripping him at every opportunity. The two clear plastic bags swung wildly as he pulled the device down the hallway, and onto the elevator. He felt like an idiot dragging the contraption.

As Conrad circled the bluestone pathway of the healing garden on his tenth and final lap of the morning, the alarm on his dance partner began screeching like a fox in heat, with its ear-piercing low battery warning. Startled and self-conscious at the attention it brought from the half dozen or so patients, some in wheelchairs, some with walkers, and a dozen visitors on the cool, sunny spring day, Conrad, still cloaked in his ridiculous-looking, despised johnny coat, hurried back inside and up the elevator to the safety of his eleventh floor room. To hell with the rule that you do not venture out without your dance partner, he thought.

Every time he thought of the little pain that had brought him here, he was reminded of Tolstoy's story, *The Death of Ivan Ilych*. As he hurried down the long final corridor to his room, he paused at the computer station of one of his regular nurses. She always seemed a cut above the rest, and Conrad shared an urgency to share the Tolstoy story.

"The protagonist, a bureaucratic judge who treated members of the public dismissively, fell off a chair one day at home and later noticed a little pain in his side. His little pain turned out to be pancreatic cancer. There was an ominous undercurrent in the story, which Tolstoy does not make explicit." The nurse had asked whether the judge's dismissive treatment of people had led to the pain and consequently his cancer. "Precisely," said Conrad. "As I must be responsible for my pain and my cancer."

Once safely back in his room, Conrad closed the door, plugged the dance partner into a wall socket, and slumped down on his sofa. He didn't know when lunch would be delivered and he didn't car. He slept on the sofa each naptime and each night because the bed was uncomfortable and, anyway, he felt more normal not being in a hospital bed. Anything that took his mind off his predicament was a relief. Anything that lessened the impact of transitioning from a normal, functioning person to a diseased, helpless patient was a blessing. He felt overcome by sadness, frustration, and despair.

Conrad felt that he still looked normal. Whenever he looked in the mirror, he saw a gray-haired, pale, slightly overweight man of about sixty – the "about" being because he was just a few weeks away from his 60th birthday. He had looked fit and healthy, in his view. At just under six feet and 175 pounds, he had taken pride in his fitness. Now he could see how worn out he looked. Healthy to diseased in 24 hours. Unbelievable.

Conrad didn't venture back into the garden for two days, afraid that his dance partner's battery life was so limited that he'd run into the same problem. Finally, after a few days had passed, he took a chance after making sure the battery was fully charged. His white blood count—"WBC" in hospital jargon—had been lowered substantially thanks to the twice daily doses of hydroxyurea, known simply to its *intimates* as hydrea. The drug killed everything in sight – every cell that was capable of dividing. He had already had two double blood transfusions to bolster the red blood counts. Hydrea lowered white and red blood counts and platelets. The chemo was so powerful that one of the nurses said not to touch the pills or it would kill skin cells in his fingers. "Just place it on your tongue directly from the plastic pill container." That didn't make sense to Conrad but he complied. He couldn't understand why the pills didn't kill cells on his tongue or in his throat. His WBC had come down from the 160,000 that it had ascended to over the course of seven months or so, per some unit or other, to a remarkable reading of 30,000.

Hydrea served to control the disease but was not a permanent solution. The doctors continued to dodge his request to give his condition a name. That was, until the day when the attending doctor, Dimitri Ulianofsky, who was initially assigned to his case offered a diagnosis. Ulianofsky was a huge grim-visaged, arrogant man, apparently Austrian or Hungarian, who had trained in Romania. Some staff members, behind his back, nicknamed him "Count D," the "D" standing for Dracula. Conrad was never told that Ulianofsky would be assigned to him until one day when he marched in followed by a parade in lockstep of seven assistants – a resident fellow, two interns, two medical students, a nurse practitioner, and two oncology nurses. With the entourage standing in a row at attention, occupying nearly all the empty space in the room, Ulianofsky – solemn faced, hovering over Conrad – announced in a booming voice that the first genetic test result had come back.

Conrad brightened, hopeful for good news. "I'm here to tell you that you do not have the Philadelphia gene," he announced proudly in his thick accent, clearing his throat repeatedly.

"Oh great, that's a relief, isn't it?"

Ulianofsky started shaking his head no, and smiling maliciously.

"What's the Philadelphia gene," Conrad continued on innocently, subjecting himself to another lightning bolt like the first news of leukemia.

"Oh, you don't know," Ulianofsky asked rhetorically, trying to control a smile from curling unpleasantly on his lips, and a guttural snicker emerging from his throat, before he delivered the lethal blow. "That's the gene that causes CML, when it's mutated."

"What the hell is CML?" Conrad asked, beginning to anger at what seemed like a reprise of the stand-up comedy – tragedy show at the ER, and raising his voice out of frustration. "For God's sake, what are you telling me? Is that good or bad, although I should know better than to ask that question, shouldn't I? Why can't you people just be plain-speaking – and perhaps a little kind – with patients?"

"Ha, it's bad," the doctor said, ignoring Conrad's admonition. "CML, chronic myeloid leukemia, is easy to treat. People live a long time by just taking Gleevac every day. Their leukemia goes into remission. They used to have the same poor prognosis that CNL patients have now."

"Oh, great." Conrad said angrily." This is bad news you're getting at, right? Pardon me for thinking that you announced that little bit of information happily. At least this is a little more humane than when I was told by some giggling PA standing in the Emergency Room that I had leukemia. At least I'm sitting down, lying down actually. But, dammit, I don't like it when you fill up the room and crowd me out, standing there hovering over me. I feel like a caged monkey out for public view. Do you have to bring your whole cheering section with you every time you have bad news?" Conrad asked, surprising himself at his anger.

Ulianofsky looked mildly offended at the criticism. "Ha. Of course not," he said resentfully with a shrug. "How many should I bring then?"

"Whatever, use your common sense. Just not the whole death squad. When do I get some good news?"

Ulianofsky shrugged, backing up a few steps. His entourage, which one by one had shuffled a few feet toward the doorway, stared blankly at Conrad, emotionless, speechless. Conrad later observed that the cheerleaders never said a word. They were afraid of saying the wrong thing, that is, anything that would contradict the captain of the team.

Conrad, exhausted and demoralized as he was, was not through attacking, although his better judgment warned not to offend the medical people on whom his survival would depend. It could come back to bite him. "Can any of you speak," Conrad said, staring first at one then the others in the lineup. "Are you afraid of being human? Do you see me as a human being or a disease? I guess I should ask – are you human?" No, Conrad thought. Being human was not part medical education or practice. More blank stares.

"Right," he shouted, adding to his diatribe as the parade marched out of the room in lockstep. "Medicine – cancer medicine, that is – is all science now, isn't it? It's all deterministic, isn't it? You're treating my disease, whatever that is, not me, not my body, right? I'm nothing but a disease to you," he said, his voice intensifying. As if what Ulianofsky said was the right thing, Conrad thought. Clinical. Deterministic. This gene, that gene. That's all there is to it. Fuck it, he thought to himself. Fuck them. Later, he wasn't sure whether he said the "F" word out loud or not. But he recalled seeing shock on their faces.

As days passed, Conrad felt increasingly demoralized and out of touch with the reality he had once belonged to. It seemed as though the world that he had been part of had spun off in some other orbit or perhaps had simply been sucked into a black hole. He had been totally absorbed in himself, in his disease and the hospital routine since getting the news and being institutionalized. The trip to Jordan, which he had looked forward to for months, had faded into obscurity. It seemed as unreal as the likelihood that he would ever regain his life. He had asked Helen to let the refugee center know that he wouldn't be going and to cancel the flight for him – unless someone else was available to take his place.

His spirit was initially crushed with disappointment about the loss of the trip but gradually his awareness dulled and slipped away. He hoped that the refugee center would let Ghadir know. He felt unable to cope with anything but the daily hospital routine. He let go of everything else, helplessly and hopelessly. He wondered if this was the way new prisoners felt when they entered correctional institutions. Being in a hospital was like being in a prison. He began to give up on life, to surrender to his fate. No other priorities seemed to matter.

He could tell that the shocking turn of events caused Helen to experience an awakening of sorts, not unlike Conrad's, although at lower decibels. He imagined how her routine was disrupted. But there was no comparison. She was not a prisoner. She could come and go at will. She could wear normal clothes, eat normal food, and she was not attached to the infernal dance partner, which clung to him, with the lines and cords tripping him wherever he went, including the bathroom or the so-called healing garden.

The news of his illness appeared to cause Helen to question the meaning of her own life. Whenever she was in the room during a visit, usually once a day, she seemed self-absorbed, as though she was concentrating mainly on the impact of the disease on her life, not on his.

At the very least, his hospitalization was inconvenient and burdensome for her. She had to do the chores that Conrad managed, paying the bills, taking out the trash, locking up the house at night, servicing the cars. Not that he did them happily or without reminders, but at least he did them. Now her life was cluttered with dozens of extra tasks, extra concerns, and uncertainty, all of a lower grade than his, which put life and death on the line. Conrad had viewed those tasks as tedious and undesirable. Now they took on the luster of life, of living. He longed to return to that hum-drum existence that he had called living – living on the ground level.

Conrad thought to himself that catastrophic illness has an insidious way of bringing out truth. It cuts inwardly into the raw flesh of human existence and makes even the most stable and confident people feel anxious and vulnerable. It breaks down the flimsy defenses that humans create to protect themselves against the inevitability of death. Death, when indefinite and remote, can easily be ignored if not entirely forgotten. Death, when specified in time, cause and means, becomes omnipresent and oppressive. Death becomes the owner – or at least the proprietor – of every minute of a person's life.

Not the least of the impacts on Helen was the fact that she might soon be a single person, a widow, rather than part of a couple. Her access to the social world, the world of couples, would be severely curtailed. Friends would offer gestures of welcome to her for a while but the gestures would fade quickly and she would be alone. Couples do not extend more than occasional symbolic gestures to single women. Now, with extra time to ruminate – and recriminate – about her situation, she began complaining about the sting of the rejection she would encounter. Conrad surmised that she also felt that, if her secrets and her selfishness were to be known, she would be disgraced and even more quickly rejected by her social community. She had nearly always had some other male relationship to count on for comfort or entertainment but that was not nearly as convenient as having a marriage and a spouse to provide cover.

Conrad could understand that reality and even to feel some sympathy for her. She was as much a victim as he was. But any thoughts about her future plight and any passing thoughts about her guilt for old transgressions quickly evaporated in seeking to blame Conrad for the situation. Why did he get himself in that faculty fight at the college? It was toxic and did no good. She had warned him that it would make things worse. He must have brought this illness on himself. The battle at the college had lasted all fall and that was when his illness was getting out of control. Why had he gotten so upset? What was so important about it that it caused this catastrophe? Conrad's sympathy quickly wore thin in the face of her blistering condemnation.

Conrad also found it difficult to deal with the medical staff. He felt helpless and abandoned, not to mention treated without respect. Conrad concluded that the familiar cancer slogan posted

on his wall that read, "I am not my disease," was nothing but superficial gloss, a flimsy pass at a humanistic approach to medical
art. It was, in short, a lie. In fact, patients were treated as though
they *were* their disease. There was no one to cheer him up except
Helen and she was usually so irritable and upset that he found
himself struggling to comfort her at times, that is, when he didn't
shut her off entirely. He even got so frustrated one day that he
barked at her, "For God's sake, I'm the one who's dying. Do you
want to trade places so you can get the sympathy? Do you want
me to just curl up and die to be rid of your problem?"

She recoiled visibly, and then wept bitterly, complaining that
he had wounded her and then unleashed her own inner rage at
the circumstances. "You're just a wretched numbskull! A vicious
one at that!"

His first reaction of dismay and guilt at attacking her gave
way to his own angry response. Exhausted at their outbursts, they
sat in silence. She finally found the energy for one more attack.

"For God's sake, Conrad, you're selfish and feeling sorry for
yourself all the time. Stop saying things like, 'If I'm still around
next week' or 'Do you want me to plan my funeral service or do
you want to do it?' How do you think that makes me feel? You
forget that I'm going through this too. If you die, it changes my
whole life, my whole world. I'm in this too. Don't forget it."

He mustered enough empathy to remember that admonition.
It was true. He felt shame, deeply penetrating shame.

Conrad felt properly chastised and had no remaining strength
to continue the battle with Helen. He was careful after that to try
and remember that he was not the center of the universe. But neither was she. Who had the most right to be narcissistic now? Conrad lay down on his sofa, turning his face from the room. Spent
and exhausted, he drifted off to sleep, his only refuge. Conrad
avoided the other patients. He wanted nothing to do with them.
They were aliens from another world, a world he wanted no part
of. Some of them appeared normal but others were bald and weak
looking. Some had complexions so dark and green-tinted that
he shuddered to see them. Nausea and fever were their constant
companions. They soon became his but without the discoloring.
He stayed in his room more and more except to get coffee in

the small kitchenette on the other side of the floor. Despite his lifelong self-identification as a refugee, he did not identify with the other aliens. He even harbored the irrational fear that their cancer germs would give him another form of cancer or otherwise complicate his condition. He did not want to breathe the air they breathed. He did not want to touch what they touched. He became addicted to hand sanitizers. Even in his current dark state of mind, he glimpsed the humor in his irrational reaction. He remembered when he didn't like being near friends with cancer for fear it was contagious. Ah, the irony of it all. "Ah Bartleby! Ah humanity!" The closing lines from Melville's story had long been favorites of his. Now they had new meaning.

Most of the other patients seemed to have a steady stream of visitors and the staff seemed to interact with them, even enjoy them. They had no need for him. And he had no wish to enjoy interacting with the staff. He wanted to leave as quickly as possible and to forget about what had happened. He could not imagine having to accept living with this disease for a long period of time. He began to feel that the disease that had conscripted his body in its deadly assault had kidnapped his body for some nefarious purpose, perhaps to torture it or dissect it or consume it. He sometimes wondered if he would awaken and find that this awful state of affairs was only a nightmare, a grim zombie movie.

The doctors were getting more specific about additional genetic testing results. The results trickled in one at a time. They had done a full test of some four hundred cancer-related genes. That was becoming customary with cancer patients, that is, with those who could afford it or had insurance. Thank goodness the university provided health insurance for contract employees. Other people were out of luck all the way around. They would send out the biopsy slides for testing all genes that commonly became mutated as life wore on. The first piece of the results, of course, had been that CML was ruled out because he didn't have a mutation of the Philadelphia gene. That was strike one.

The next report came in three days later. He did have a mutation of a gene called CSF3R. It was involved somehow with a receptor in his bone marrow. That was what was causing the deluge of neutrophils, the most dominant white blood cell, in his bloodstream. That was a good finding. He learned that a targeted drug existed that seemed to stop the excessive neutrophil production. Ball one.

Strike two came two days later. Yes, he had a CSF3R mutation but, "Sorry," the resident fellow, who had just introduced himself, said mechanically, "you also have two other mutations that are *negative prognosticators* for success of the targeted drug."

"Too bad," Ulianofsky remarked later in the day.

Now the count is one ball, two strikes, thought Conrad.

"But," the Ulianofsky went on, "we're starting you on the drug anyway. It might work for a while, but don't count on it for long. You better consider having a marrow transplant, you know, get an injection of stem cells, rejuvenate your immune system. That's your only hope. Otherwise, you have far less than two years to live and it won't be pretty after a year or so. One by one, bad things will be happening to keep you on a merry-go-round in and out of the hospital."

"Thanks for the encouragement," Conrad spat at him. "What's the prognosis for me surviving a transplant of stem cells?"

"Well, don't get your hopes up," Ulianofsky said, grinning." I'd say about a one-third chance of it being successful and two thirds of your dying at some stage of the process. Of course, you might get lucky and survive it and end up in a nursing home for the rest of your life." Again, the familiar twisted smile curled his upper lip.

"Oh, great," Conrad said, anger rising again. "One-third? And I'm supposed to consider that my salvation? That's what I should look forward to? What the fuck do you even talk to me about that for?"

Ulianofsky's head jerked backward at Conrad's use of the "F" word. "I don't have to put up with that," he said. "I won't."

Conrad apologized through gritted teeth.

The doctor went on, "It's probably the only chance you have, at least, a chance for a cure, if you can survive it. We'll see that you get to talk to the transplant surgeon, whether you want to or not."

Conrad wallowed in depression the rest of that day, his sixth or seventh in the hospital. The days were bleeding together until it was nearly impossible to distinguish one from another. He could understand how difficult it was for institutionalized people to keep track of time and space. He refused to speak to anyone, even Helen, who sat as far away from him as she could and made no serious effort to coax him out of his dark mood. "At least your white count is going down and you feel good physically, don't you," she asked in a bored tone.

Conrad lay still on the sofa, his back to the room. He didn't answer. Helen finally left. He felt badly about that but did not bring himself to speak. When the nurses and aides came in to perform blood draws and vital signs, he sat up in grudging compliance, and lay down as soon as they left. He felt abandoned, alone, hopeless, near tears. He had a sense that he was driving everyone away and that was exactly what he wished to do.

Conrad remained in the hospital for three more days during which his emotions rose and fell like changes in the tide. They would shift from joy, as a title surge of freshly aerated water when he got a good blood count, and back to despair floundering in the muddy stinking water of low tide. But his emotional swings were far less regular than the ocean tides. He never experienced outright denial of his plight but the reality that he had the disease faded in and out of his consciousness. He had glimmers of feeling the "Why me?" syndrome that cancer patients experienced. He quieted them down by remembering that he'd had nearly sixty years of life and lots of people got cancer when they were much younger. The sight of babies and children with the tell-tale wrist band and the dance partners trailing behind filled him with true sorrow.

"How could I feel sorry for myself," he announced aloud. "I don't like it but I can't say it's unfair. What do I have to complain about?"

He felt hopeful when, on her next visit, Helen handed him a letter from his longtime friend, Jacques-Paul Bouton. Jacques-Paul hardly missed a week in his communication, by letter, email or phone call. Conrad leaned on Jacques-Paul's words as though they were scripture itself. But Jacques-Paul never overstated his own insights, which were considerable and all the more so because of his deep sense of humility. "He's so old," Conrad told Paul, Esther and Helen one day, when they were visiting. "I want so badly to visit him in the Arizona desert, where he lives with one of his sons. I'm afraid, if I don't do that soon, I'll never see him again. I know he's ready to die and go to Heaven at God's will." He barely suppressed his happiness at seeing the letter. He tucked it behind him on the sofa bed.

As Helen was leaving, she asked, "Aren't you going to read his letter?"

"No, I'll wait until I'm alone so I can concentrate on what he says. Anyway, you wouldn't be interested. I'm sure it's spiritual advice on how to deal with illness and death. He tries to encourage me. He started when I went through that torture at the university and he's kept in touch every week since I got my diagnosis. He's a very loyal friend, the best I have."

"You're lucky," Helen said quietly. "I mean that. I have no friends like that."

Conrad shrugged. "He's all I have."

Conrad occupied himself during the day with reading, as well as writing all his thoughts down in a notebook. He dreaded the nights. He'd sleep for two or three hours and wake up abruptly with the stark realization of his plight. He'd feel himself plunging downward into despair and could stop the fall only with the strongest of will. Most of the time, he surprised himself by finding more reserve of mental strength than he thought he possessed. Sometimes, it took an hour of wrestling with the devil, as he termed it, but he usually managed to pull himself out of the deep well of despair and return to sleep for another two hours.

All his life, Conrad had awakened frequently during the night and when he did, his mind automatically focused on the gravest problem of the moment. He was familiar with the sinking, desperate feeling that now overtook him during his wakefulness. There was no escaping the despair. But that experience gradually eased with time and months later, he'd look back and realize that he was nearly free of the despair. He was free, liberated from what was at the bottom, the fear of death. Once the fear of death was conquered, fear was immobilized, rendered powerless. Fear of death lay coiled, ready to strike with one lethal move, at the heart of every other fear.

On this particular evening, after Helen had long since left and the nurses and aides had finished all their routines, Conrad fell asleep on the sofa with one light remaining on. Waking suddenly with surprise and sensing a trace of the despair that usually enshrouded him during the night, he sat up abruptly. His hand touched the letter beneath him. As he scanned the three handwritten pages, his mind centered on one paragraph that Jacques-Paul had no doubt composed with great care.

"My dear Conrad. You are facing quite unexpectedly two enemies, cancerous bone marrow and depression. In my mind, depression is far more destructive. As I know you, you are ready for a battle. One way or another, it has been a constant in your life since I met you, how many, some forty years ago. It is what made you strong and successful, although I know you don't see yourself that way. It is much harder to fight depression than cancerous bone marrow. You will be a loser if you fight it alone. It is time, Conrad, to re-examine your faith, not the horizontal way (through your church with which you have differences, I know) but the vertical one, deep inside the human face of God, which is Jesus. Try to close a few doors a few minutes every day to wake your soul enough to throw yourself at the feet (and mercy) of God-Jesus. Read again the Acts of the Apostles and the Gospel of John. A great supporting thought is the notion that anything which happens to us in our own life is known of God and permitted by Him. Amities, Jacques."

Conrad felt a soothing peace pass into his mind and throughout his body. A renewed confidence and trust bathed his soul in refreshing freedom. He relaxed and slept well for the first time in the hospital stay. He did not wake until the morning nurse's rounds for vital signs and medications. He was aware of feeling spiritually renewed.

※

One afternoon, as Conrad was lying on the sofa, about to surrender to sleep, he was startled by a light tap on the door. He considered ignoring it and lying motionless with his eyes closed. That was one way of dealing with the constant interruptions by the hospital staff, each signaled by a light tap prior to opening the door. Something tugged at him to reply. "Yes," he said concentrating on making his voice sound weary as though he had been awakened by the noise. The door opened slowly, revealing a remotely familiar face peering into the room, followed by the body of a tall slender man dressed in casual clothes, khakis and a light blue shirt garnished by a white clerical collar. The African-American man who seemed to float into the room appeared to be middle-aged in a way that defied further precision. He had dark, partially graying hair, and a pleasant face with a moustache and trimmed beard.

"Hello, Conrad, May I come in? Did I disturb you?" Without waiting for an answer, the man nodded in the direction of the only chair in the room, the uncomfortable padded recliner that Conrad sat in for vital sign checks and blood draws by the nurses who drew his blood every four hours, night and day. "May I sit," he asked politely.

"Yeah, sure," Conrad said. "That's my vampire chair. I can't guarantee that you won't be attacked. They probably won't even notice that it's not me. They see only a human arm to suck on. I was sleeping," he lied.

The man looked slightly crestfallen, leading Conrad to add, "But it's okay. No problem. Who are you?"

"We met before," the man said. "I'm one of the chaplains, from downstairs. Someone told me that you wanted to see a chaplain today and, since we met before, I took it on myself. I'm a Catholic priest, if you remember. If you're not comfortable with that, I can get someone else. Do you remember that my name is Father Gaspar, or just plain Gaspar, whatever you like."

"I'm not Catholic but I have no problem with that, Father," Conrad said, "but I didn't ask for a chaplain. I don't know who told you that."

"Oh," Gaspar said, "I don't know. I got the word on very good authority, you know, the *Word*." A glimmer of a smile crept over his face, illuminating it in a way that defied description, as Conrad thought back on the moment.

Conrad liked the man. He must have encountered him when he was in the emergency room, which was all a blur. Gaspar, was the first person who was respectful, who seemed to see him as a human being, not just a pathogen on a slide, or a lump of flesh to be stuck, or to be choked while forcing down a dozen pills four times a day, or a patient to be awakened at the pleasure of the staff and then left alone, until the least expected moment.

"No, no, you can stay, I mean, if you want to. Sure, that's fine. Maybe it would be good to talk. The staff ignores me; the doctors bludgeon me with bad news, and my wife doesn't like me. I am nobody." Conrad burst out laughing, with tears welling in his eyes.

"What did I say that was funny…and sad," Gaspar asked.

"Nothing," Conrad said. "I just thought of the song, *Mr. Cellophane.* Ever hear that? 'Mr. Cellophane shoulda been my name.' That's me. Mr. Nobody, the invisible man."

"Oh, I get it. I looked at your chart," Gaspar said. "I saw your diagnosis. This must have been a terrible shock to you. The first few months are the worst. People adjust to news like this but it takes time. And it's different with every person. I think the more you talk about the way you feel, the quicker you get on an even keel. That doesn't make your disease go away but you'll handle the changes better. It's best taking things day by day. Don't get too far ahead of yourself. But do you want to tell me what you are feeling now, today? Only if you want to. Otherwise, we can just talk about anything you want."

"I would like to talk," Conrad said. "I feel sad. Deeply sad – I mean right down to the core of my being. Is that clinical depression? Never mind. I've never felt so sad. I feel lost in the wilderness. My life is over. My prognosis is bad, really bad. There's no treatment for me that will last and the prospect of a marrow transplant is a parade of horrors. The worst of it is that no one really cares. Well, I do have a friend, a priest in fact, who does care. What he says to me does matter. It does bring peace but I need that feeling renewed frequently. I can't hold onto the peaceful, trusting feeling of faith."

"There must be something that's good in your life," Gaspar said. "Is there anybody else who would care, once they know?"

"Well, yes, I suppose," Conrad said. "Some of my students would care. But the semester is just about over and they'll move on. I work with refugees at the center in town. Yes, some of them would care. This will affect them to some extent. I was going on a trip to a conference in Jordan about the refugee problems in the Middle East. I was really looking forward to it but now it's beyond hope. It breaks my heart."

"I'm sorry to hear that. That's a loss. But maybe you can go in the future. These days there are amazing advances in cancer, especially leukemia. Cancer is becoming more and more a chronic disease. Don't give up hope."

They talked for another half hour, with Conrad unloading his burden of distress and Gaspar responding quietly. At that point, Gaspar asked, "Would you like to know why I want to work mainly with cancer patients, especially leukemia patients?"

"Sure. I can't imagine why anyone would want to be here," Conrad said. "Judging by the appearance of some leukemia patients – the ones whose skin turns dark and greenish or grayish – it's a pretty horrible place to be. Hell."

"Not exactly, Conrad, and, incidentally, they don't all turn green. You might just be thinking of cyanosis although there are other reasons. Anyway, before I became a hospital chaplain, which was more than twenty years ago, I served as a priest in missions around the world as well as parishes in this country. My religious order was – still is – the Missionaries of the Precious Blood. Would you believe my order was located in Kansas City? Doesn't sound like a Kansas City thing, does it? We do missionary work abroad and in urban areas. We promote justice and peace. But as you can tell, we focus our attention on the life-giving force, the power, the uplifting spirit of Christ's blood to revitalize the world. You can see there is something special to me about people who have cancer of the blood. I believe in the healing power of the blood of Christ, through Holy Communion. Maybe it sounds mystical to you. Well, it is mystical. I truly believe in the healing power of blood, especially for leukemia."

Conrad said, fascinated, "It sounds good to me. Why did you pick that order?"

"I didn't always want to be a priest," Gaspar said. "It wasn't until after college and law school, when I was starting work for a Kansas City law firm. I was engaged to a wonderful woman. She happened to be a lawyer too. We planned to get married. Then she found out that she had leukemia. No warning. No symptoms or signs. It was a routine blood test. She had a type that is treated successfully now. She had CML, chronic myeloid leukemia. Now there's remission. Then it was a death sentence. There was no treatment. She died within a year. I wanted to get married anyway but she refused. She said she couldn't stand to make me a widower. It was too gloomy and she felt it would just be baggage for me to carry around. We lived together the whole time. I left the firm to take care of her. When she died, the light went out in my life. I had no interest in returning to law practice. It took a long time to get over my grief but, eventually, I went to a seminary in Kansas City. I chose the Precious Blood ministry because she had blood cancer. I had thought of becoming a priest as I grew up so it didn't come out of the blue. I've never regretted it… with one exception. I found Buddhism very appealing too. That would have been too big a leap, though. Still, my order practiced a similar kind of peaceful self-discipline."

Conrad felt the first blush of hope that he had felt since being hospitalized. It was irrational, he knew, but still, he felt it. "That's quite a story," he said, "very inspiring. I'd like to have some of that healing blood. Can you get me some?"

"We'll do that," Gaspar said. "I have to go now but I'll come back and give you communion if you want."

"Yes. Please. By the way, who told you that I wanted to see a chaplain?"

"I'm not sure," Gaspar said, as if trying to remember. "I'm not sure. Someone important. I have interesting connections, you know. But I had a reminder on my calendar to see you today. It was very much in my mind. No question about that." He smiled warmly as if sharing a secret.

With that, he slipped out the door as quietly as he had come in. Conrad watched him walk toward the door. He could have sworn that when he reached the midpoint of the room, he disappeared from sight. Conrad was mystified but left off trying to figure it out. He attributed it to his fatigue. The conversation stayed with Conrad the rest of the day and during the night but he had trouble visualizing Gaspar. He felt eager for his next visit.

⁂

After more than a week in the hospital, Conrad had his first visitor from the outside world, his friend Levi. Helen and the children had come on several occasions. Esther and Paul seemed awkward about talking with him about his illness. Conrad wondered if the tension between him and Helen was responsible or whether it was his new vulnerability. He did not like the feeling of vulnerability either. Somehow, he felt he should examine his body in a mirror to see whether the genetic mutations were visible. Perhaps they had turned him into a strange and frightening creature. All he could think of was Kafka's story, "The Metamorphosis." Did Conrad look like a giant insect? Once, when Helen left the room to get coffee, he asked them if his condition made them think of Gregor Samsa. That seemed to break the tension and they shared a good laugh. He assured them, without much confidence, that he would walk out of the hospital one day soon with his disease under control. The incident made him feel closer to Paul and Esther than he had felt in some time. "Nothing is all bad," he said aloud to them, hugging them goodbye after Helen returned.

When Levi visited, he was full of apologies for not coming sooner. He explained that he had been in Israel teaching and visiting friends. Levi looked forward to teaching special courses in Israel during his periodic trips. As an adjunct, even lower on the faculty scale at the university than Conrad, he got little respect despite his academic credentials. He was a former rabbi who had a Ph.D. in literature. He was several years younger than Conrad, in his early fifties. Unlike Conrad, he was content to view teaching as his second career rather than feeling that he had failed because he could not achieve tenure.

Levi had powerful feelings about the Middle East situation. He had been raised in Conservative Judaism, which continued through his years as an active rabbi. Fifteen years into his career, he was established with a congregation in a small town in Massachusetts. His marriage was an unhappy one which had led to a divorce. A faction of his congregation disapproved of his situation and he ultimately resigned. A turn to teaching was a logical move.

He eventually married a woman who practiced Orthodox Judaism. Their union produced two children. He moved to Connecticut and found an adjunct position at the university, thanks to a mutual friend of the president of the college. He became observant and, as an orthodox Jew, he joined his wife in a very strict congregation. Conrad knew that, by virtue of some tragedy, his wife and children had died but Levi had never revealed the details.

Conrad was well aware that Levi became influenced religiously and politically by the right-leaning rabbi of his new congregation and developed strong antipathy for Arabs, especially Palestinians. The subject of Palestinian claims of injustice and suffering sent the usually calm and peaceful Levi into ranting that was distressing to Conrad. Conrad generally tried to avoid the subject. Conrad had difficulty listening to fundamentalism of any kind, especially in religion. It seemed, in his view, to be the antithesis of the tolerance that every religion should exhibit. Levi's inflexible hostility towards Palestinians in particular troubled him acutely because Conrad felt that there was fault on the part of all participants in Middle East conflicts and wars.

As outsiders within the university community, he and Conrad struck up a friendship. Since Conrad was opposed to any form of fundamentalism, he and Conrad argued constantly and vigorously about religion and all other forms of fundamentalism.

Levi was the only friend who took time to visit him and to offer help to Helen. Levi was a loyal friend with whom Conrad could talk freely and openly with on every subject except the Arab world. During the previous fall, when Conrad was engaged in a bitter feud with the Dean who was trying to eliminate contract employees entirely, Levi was his only vocal supporter. Levi himself was fairly sanguine about the policy move and not inclined to get into a personal battle with the Dean. He tended to accept whatever came his way. He was confident that he would find a position elsewhere if necessary. Conrad, on the other hand, was geared for battle partly because he was desperate for the income his contract provided.

The matter came to a head when Conrad spoke out at a faculty meeting in opposition to the Dean's proposal to eliminate adjuncts and contract faculty. The Dean had anticipated that and had arranged for various faculty members to attack Conrad. The meeting went badly for Conrad. He was shouted down, criticized and condemned by the regular faculty members. Only Levi spoke in support of Conrad despite not being as deeply invested in the controversy.

Conrad finally walked out of the meeting, sickened by the sting of defeat and humiliation. Levi provided moral support by joining Conrad in his painful exit.

Conrad was unable to think of the conflict without feeling ill. The months of contentiousness had a toxic effect on him. He had never felt so badly treated, and so totally defeated as a person. In the end, the university president deferred the measure and the Dean backed off for the time being. But Conrad suffered from the months-long battle. Levi had supported him all the way, however, and their friendship was strengthened.

During his visit to the hospital, Levi offered to help Conrad after his return home. He promised to stop by and see him and to drive him to the clinic for his frequent visits.

Conrad searched assiduously on the laptop that Helen brought him for any information about his tentative diagnosis, which was either chronic neutrophilic leukemia (CNL) or atypical chronic myeloid leukemia (aCML). There were very few articles and those were so technically dense, so full of genetic code, meaningless numbers and letters, and medical jargon that he absorbed only a fraction of the meaning. But the more he read, the more familiar the terms became, and the more he understood. He began pressing the doctors with questions to the point at which they would begin retreating toward the door. Their patience could tolerate only a certain limited number of questions. Questions that contained an implicit challenge to the superficiality of prior answers were considered out of bounds. Their scientific determinism about what was impossible continued to disturb him. Doctors were used to giving answers to patients' questions but not necessarily the correct and complete answers. Answers were given to halt the questioning, not to bring about understanding. They wanted to give answers that could not prove them wrong at some later date but they had to be aware that most answers were not necessarily correct; they were just temporarily safe answers. The writers of medical journal articles, usually long lists of collaborators from multiple medical schools, were shackled by specific research findings. Their conclusions were repeated over and over without reasoning and without knowledge gained from other related disciplines. Multiple authorship or an article was hazardous to patients' health because the article often tended to settle for the lowest common denominator or a compromised conclusion.

Conrad, simply applying his common sense, decided there was nothing wrong with sticking to scientific findings. They served as boundaries to sheer speculation. The problem was the lack of imagination and thinking about what was or might just be on the other side – just beyond – the boundary. Conrad made some discoveries of his own, however. That was the fact that the articles that limited the current scientific thinking, the new discoveries, the brilliant insights that were possible, were old. For example, the leading article on his possible diagnoses was based on research studies from two and three years ago.

After the studies had been completed, it took months, even years, to write and rewrite the articles. By the time they were published, they might well be ancient history. Exciting discoveries were being made even then, but it would be many months, sometimes years, before they were published. The reality was that much more was known about the diseases but the process of exposing that knowledge to the light of day was vastly delayed. In the meantime, the old information, old discoveries and knowledge prevailed and impeded the thinking of the bright people who should have been exposing their ideas to the world of patients and treating physicians.

Samuel Beckett's astute description of Murphy's brain as being *hermetically sealed against the exterior universe* came to mind as a perfect description of the scientific approach to disease by the medical profession. The professionals struggled to adopt viewpoints that were not confined to prior limitations. In other words, outside-the-box thinking about treatment solutions was a mental stretch that only a few could manage. It seems that medical school did not teach how to think about problems innovatively or to consider individual responses based on the whole person.

Most medical people in the oncology field practiced the *science* of medicine, not the *art*. Seeing him as a whole person was beyond their comprehension. He was, to them, no more than an accumulation of genetic mutations with highly predictable results as evidenced by studies and clinical trials. The fact that the genetic mutations kept changing confounded the problem, creating obstacles as well as opportunities. "What about the rest of me," Conrad asked more than once of Ulianofsky. "This bone marrow is mine but so is my brain, my heart, my lungs, my soul. Why do you say that I cannot affect the progress of a stupid mistake or two or three? Do I have to sit idly by while a few genetic mistakes destroy the rest of me?"

"That's bullshit," he shouted one day at Ulianofsky, who abruptly stalked out of the room, shaking his head. It seemed to Conrad that some Europeans were the worst thinkers – rigid, closed-minded, with brains that labored heavily to assimilate new facts and slammed shut at the mention of anything outside the realm of genetics and hematology. While he knew that was an overstatement, he felt as justified in being as stubborn as they were in making up his mind about the matter.

Conrad shouted after him, "Are you telling me that there's no room for individual response? I'm a human being. I'm unique, and I'm in good physical shape – or at least I was until you all put me into this hellhole of a prison and threw away the key. I feel like a lost soul in a living version of Solzhenitzyn's *Cancer Ward*. I'm a healthy person. I just happen to have a disease." He was surprised how angry he was and how out-of-control his anger was. His anger stop switch must be mutated. Now he began second-guessing the doctors all the time. Every statement, every move, was subject to his relentless scrutiny, interrogation and disputation.

His body was subjected to a bone marrow biopsy, the first of many. He was told that it would be painful, but it amounted to nothing – that is, until he received a second one which somehow resulted in an injured nerve and caused him to hobble around for two days. Then he was wheeled to the operating room, the OR, for insertion of a port in his chest. Why on earth couldn't he be allowed to walk? The port would be connected to the jugular, they said. "The jugular? Won't blood gush out?"

"No, you're thinking of the carotid artery," the surgeon said, laughing. "The jugular is a vein. When you want to kill someone, you cut their carotid, not their jugular. It's a popular misunderstanding."

Conrad pondered that one, reflecting on the dozens of times the phrase "going for the jugular" was misused.

He stayed awake for the whole procedure, listening to the conversation, some of it disrespectful and trivial, but shielded from the surgery by a plastic tent over the operating table. He was amazed at how quickly and unquestioningly he had agreed to have this small plastic box placed under his skin, with its connecting tube to his jugular vein. The spot was painful that evening and became black and blue, or "developed a hematoma," in medical jargon.

Weeks later, when the area of the surgery took so long to heal and the hematoma so long to fade away, the nurses joked about it. "Where did you have that done?" a new nurse asked. She seemed embarrassed when he said, "Right here, downstairs." It took months before it began to heal and look as normal as a raised square box under the skin could look.

Apparently, his port surgery was grotesque by any standards. When he was back home, a visiting nurse said with a laugh, "That surgery looks like it was done with a sledgehammer." Conrad wondered if he would have this installation for the rest of his life, which he then caught himself short by remembering that the rest of his life might not be all that long. He laughed at the thought. How his perspective had changed. That realization was followed, as it usually was, day or night, by several hours of depression that he had trouble pushing away. Conrad became skilled at classic black humor, the medical equivalent of gallows humor, which never failed to generate a laugh at his own expense, even if it caused temporary discomfort for others.

⁂

Finally, the day came when Conrad was discharged to return home, after a false start the day before they were to release him. Levi appeared midmorning on Saturday, as scheduled, ready to liberate him from his confinement. Alas, Conrad had to tell him that Ulianofsky decided he needed two units of blood because his hemoglobin was down to 7.0. While Levi stayed to chat, the infusion began, all six hours of it. Two hours per unit was the standard rate. Add in the delays, taking of vital signs, and an hour at the end to watch for reactions, and the day was swallowed whole. Levi left about noon, promising to be back on Sunday morning. He explained that Helen had asked him to do the pickup because she had too much to do. "I got the feeling," Levi said, "that Helen feels burdened by this herself. I'm not sure what she has to do that makes her so busy. Maybe it's just the emotional burden of facing the unknown. She doesn't know what to expect."

"To be fair," Conrad said, "I can appreciate that what has happened to me affects her. Her life is changed, too, but it's the second-hand effect. She doesn't have the actual physical burden and she isn't about to die either. But I will try hard to understand."

"You're a good man, Conrad," Levi said, patting his arm firmly. "I'll see you tomorrow. Let me know of any change of plan, okay?"

Sunday morning came at last. For Conrad, it was a strange feeling to contemplate leaving the institution. "I feel as though I've been away in a foreign country for years, maybe decades. I feel like a refugee, a discard onto the garbage dump of society. I hate to admit it but I also feel scared, scared that no one will be checking my vital signs and my blood."

"You'll be fine. And you look great," Levi said. "You don't look like a refugee or a patient, for that matter. You don't look any worse than you always did," he said, punctuating the remark with a grin.

"Thanks, old friend. But I feel as though I no longer belong to the world of the living. I'm here on a visa from the land of the dead and the visa can be cancelled at any moment – like my life."

Riding home in the passenger seat, it appeared to him that a whole season had passed by. It was early April when he entered the hospital. Now, just eight or was it nine or ten days later, it seemed that spring was over and summer was beginning. He felt so out of touch that he didn't want to talk to anyone or see anyone. He must look strange. He was a different person. He wondered what the effect of his double blood transfusion would be. It was his first blood ever. It felt strange to have someone else's blood flowing through his body. Too bad the solution wasn't as easy as substituting fresh blood for contaminated blood. It was, in a way, by substituting stem cells, but that wasn't so simple.

It took several weeks before he felt like emerging from the house even though he felt that Helen resented his being there, intruding on her newfound freedom. She demanded that he take over his old chores and would get impatient when he pleaded that he was too tired. "Too tired to take out the trash? Too weak to empty the wastebaskets? You've gotten used to a soft life. What good are you," she said under her breath, not expecting to be heard.

Going back to the hematology clinic every other day for blood draws kept him occupied – more than he wanted. The clinic felt more familiar than the world outside. He'd have his blood taken, with a slight pinch in the arm or, after healing had faded some of the bruising, they'd use his port. That hurt more than the arm but they said they had to use it or the port could get clogged and they'd have to remove it, and then do the procedure all over again. He wanted no part of that so he agreed to use the port half the time. Then he'd wait for an hour or so that it took to get the CBC and blood chemistry result.

His life revolved around his blood tests and treatments. His mind frequently resumed thinking about the Middle East and his disappointment at not going to Jordan. But he was still obsessed with his disease to the near exclusion of everything else. He believed, based on what the doctors had said, that his remaining life was short – less than two years and probably more like one year. That view controlled his thinking, and his imagining. It was difficult to visualize that his life amounted to anything more than controlling the disease until he breathed his last breaths a matter of months from now.

After blood tests, he was eager to look at the printout and see whether his white count had increased or decreased. If it went up, he'd be depressed the rest of the day. But if it went down, even a point, he'd be elated. Most of the time, he fluctuated between denial and hope, depression and optimism. Only if he got engrossed in a book did he forget who he was, what he was and what his bleak prospects were. Once a week, he'd see Ulianofsky, whose pitch was, "Remember, we're working toward a transplant. That's the only cure. Otherwise, you've got less than two years and the second year won't be pretty. I want you to see Julia Reinhard, the stem cell transplant doctor. We have to start working you up. Your white count could shoot up any day now. This disease is devious and insidious. It can turn acute at any time without warning."

No one ever explained why he always saw Ulianofsky. Of all the doctors he'd see in the clinic area, he was the least pleasant, least interested in him. One day he told the charge nurse that he'd like to see the young cheerful doctor from the Middle East – Syria, he thought – instead of Ulianofsky. "I saw him one day in the hospital when he was willing to answer my questions and lay out some treatment possibilities. I think his name is Husni."

"You mean Husni Bitar. When you come in on clinic service, you have to take whichever doctor is assigned. For you, it happened to be Count D. That's what the nursing staff calls him, you know," she said, softening her voice, "but don't tell anyone! We could all lose our jobs! And I'm really sorry, you can't see anyone else. Everybody wants to see Husni, Dr. Bitar. He's nice to everyone, listens to everyone. He's smart too. All the nurses love him. Your only chance is if the mad Russian goes on leave at some point. I'll keep that in mind."

As she was gathering all the protective medical trash for disposal, the irrepressible doctor himself strutted into the room and boomed an inane greeting. "Well, what's our patient deciding today?"

Conrad felt most depressed when he contemplated a transplant. It was a parade of horrors, one nightmare scenario after another for a whole year, until he had either survived it or was on his way to a horrible death. He resisted the idea despite the pressure Ulianofsky put on him.

"No way would I agree to a transplant," Conrad said, "unless I'm convinced there's no backup therapy to the Jaktinib. Why can't you come up with something? There has to be a backup drug. Think of something."

"There's nothing that would work for longer than a couple of months," Ulianofsky said. "You'd better think transplant before you lose the window. After that, it will be out of the question. Once it turns acute, you're a dead man. It'll be too late," he said in his thick, Romanian accent, making sure that he bore down on Conrad so he understood he had no choice.

Conrad found Ulianofsky's dismissive behavior crude and intolerable. He postponed visits with him and would walk the clinic halls looking for Bitar, whom he had found out was Syrian but trained in Jordan. Several times, he was lucky and engaged Husni in conversation about his case. Husni seemed willing to talk and seemed to be familiar with his case, probably from the team's weekly meetings. Although no permanent option came to pass, Husni Bitar had a sympathetic attitude and was more encouraging about his success with treatment. "Don't let them push you into a transplant if you don't want it. It's no bed of roses and the success rate is still low."

Conrad nodded.

"But if you do want a stem cell transplant," Bitar added, "go somewhere else. Go to one of the major cancer hospitals where they do tons of transplants. That's a good rule for treatment in general, actually."

Conrad thanked him and they went their separate ways. He saw the charge nurse watching from her hallway station. She smiled, acknowledging that he had managed to have a good conversation with Bitar after all.

Conrad made the rounds of other cancer clinics, searching for someone with better options. He travelled to three different places, the farthest away being the Maynard clinic in Minneapolis. In the end, he found no one with better alternatives so they settled for what they already had, resigned to a limited universe of ideas, hopefully inspired by a consultant from a New York City hospital. If bad luck had brought him to this discouraging and nearly hopeless situation, perhaps some stroke of unexpected good luck would enable him to deal with it successfully and gain remission. The consensus was that *that* was very unlikely.

Levi visited Conrad faithfully at least three times a week. He had made contacts with people who had attended the conference in Jordan. It turned out that the conference had ended with little agreement as to how the burgeoning numbers of refugees should be handled. Few countries that had not already increased their in-take of refugees changed their policies. Three countries – Jordan, Lebanon and Turkey - continued to bear the heaviest burden by far.

European countries were varied in their response but most were experiencing growing resistance to the overflow of refugees. There would be another conference later in the year if the refugee situation continued to worsen. Conrad was heartsick, wondering whether he would be able to continue his work with the refugee organization. He even wondered if he would be well enough – or even alive - to resume teaching in the fall. It seemed too uncertain to make plans and he feared that he would fall by the wayside in both endeavors. He sent out inquiries about Ghadir's situation but so far she had not responded. He had let Ghadir know by email that he had cancelled his trip but had not yet had a chance to explain the details. He worried whether she and Ayah might feel abandoned.

The two friends had long talks about what Conrad's life would be like after he returned home. Levi was optimistic; Conrad less so. Although he argued with the doctors about their fatalism and genetic determinism when he was face to face with them, their forceful opinions carried weight with him. When they weren't around, he found himself taking up their arguments to counter more optimistic views. He firmly believed that individual varia-tion played a role in response to drugs.

"But," Conrad asserted, "the only evidence is that people with my mutation – CSF3R – plus the others – ASXL1 and SETBP1 – do poorly in the long run. If I had only the CSF3R mutation, I'd probably be fine for a long time with Jakafi. But with the others, I'm doomed. The treatment team is unanimous that I'll be dead in less than two years."

"That's not the whole story," argued Levi. "That conclusion is based on very few cases, a mere handful. That conclusion isn't, well, conclusive. You may do just fine. So far, you are fine."

"But the doctors can't say that," Conrad said. "They have no basis to say I'll do fine. They're pushing me to a transplant. And that sounds more like a death sentence than the disease itself."

Levi, in his regular visits, managed to drag Conrad out of his daily despondency for a while at least. It was like pulling someone out of quicksand onto solid ground and watching the person slip back. The transplant issue was a major bone of contention in Conrad's life and one on which he and Levi did not see eye to eye. Levi felt that he should not rule it out absolutely. It could possibly be worthwhile. Advance would undoubtedly be made in the procedure.

Conrad was adamant that he didn't want to go through that, only to have only a thirty percent chance of success, at best. The specter of giving up a year of his life, battling infections, graft versus host disease, rejection, and relapse overwhelmed him. Even with success, it might so affect his organs that he could end up surviving in a nursing home, with a chronic, disabling condition, stemming from the transplant. That terrified him. To be fair, it was the strong opinion of one doctor – a consultant at another institution – that had firmed up Conrad's opposition to transplants. He had read and then heard first hand horror stories about the year of confinement after a transplant. That doctor had been influenced by one bad experience and made it her cause to dissuade potential recipients. Conrad would never know whether he had mistakenly ruled the procedure out for himself without reasonable consideration.

"What kind of choice is that?" Conrad asked on one of his periodic visits with the transplant surgeon, Julia Reinhard. "Why should I give up a year of my life now while I'm at least able to function, all for what is probably a futile transplant?"

Julia repeated the standard explanation – the "only chance at cure" line - but refused to look him in the eye. Conrad had overheard several doctors discussing why the hospital was eager to *build* its transplant practice. Conrad speculated that accounted for Reinhard's willingness to continue to meet with him to discuss stem cell transplants despite his challenges and insults. Conrad was glad to know a vital piece of information that Reinhard and Ulianofsky did not realize he knew. There was no way he would get bullied into an unwanted transplant.

He continued to seek out Dr. Bitar whenever possible. Conversations with him raised his spirits, even if there was no new information. Bitar was the only one willing to communicate by email outside the secure server. Apparently, the hospital policy forbade that practice, ostensibly to protect patient privacy, but it went on anyway. Why was it that every HIPPA privacy rule was interpreted and applied to work in favor of the hospital and against the interest of the patient? Didn't hospitals realize that privacy was not necessarily the prime value to be served?

A week after Conrad returned home, he called a neighbor who was a dentist. Bernard Leviton had often boasted of knowing genetics. He claimed to have attended medical school for two years before dropping out in favor of dental school. During his two years, he asserted that he excelled at pathology. Although Conrad sensed that Bernie, as he called himself, overstated his medical knowledge in a typical way, Conrad was impressed. He had learned from past experience that having a pathologist for a friend was an advantage. Pathologists seemed to know everything, every illness, every treatment.

After pathologists, general practitioners were the next best category of doctors to have on your side. That did not include internists because, considering themselves as a specialty, they tended to refer patients to other specialties rather than assessing illnesses themselves. Surgeons were the most worthless as consultants but, oddly, the most convinced about their superior standing in the medical community. They knew little substantive medicine and were interested in less. They were mechanics, in the view of other doctors. In their own eyes, they were the gladiators of the medical arena, the fierce, bold warriors who would face every foe without fear. In this era of fractured medical practices, it was difficult to find doctors willing to bridge the gaps among medical specialties.

Bernie seemed oddly guarded at first, questioning Conrad as to why he was calling him. But eventually he acquiesced in Conrad's request. He appeared at the front door within an hour and listened carefully to Conrad's rendition of the story of his illness, how it was discovered and where it stood now that he was on Jakafi, as an outpatient. He had never heard of CNL, since it was so rare, or about the studies involving Jaktinib, but he promised to find out. Conrad thought it was odd that Helen insisted on sitting in on the conversation. She laughed heartily at Bernard's feeble attempts at humor, especially off-color remarks.

The next time they met, Bernie said he had talked with his retired pathology professor. His conclusion was that it was too early to give up hope although no researcher or physician was going to give a favorable prognosis based on the results so far. They simply couldn't, given the negative experience to date, even though the patient base was tiny because the disease was so rare. But that did not mean that the results with a greater number of patients would be so skewed toward failure. He said he'd even get his professor to visit with Conrad sometime. Bernie brought along a few articles that his professor had found. Conrad spent the next two days poring over the articles, which were dense and full of undecipherable jargon. Acronyms prevailed as they did throughout medical practice. When he could penetrate the fog, he was sent reeling into despair. No studies had positive results for his disease. The news was all bad but, of course, most articles were about studies more than two years old, some much older.

He left that enterprise alone after that for the most part. Only when he felt strong and confident, early in the morning on some days, did he dare search the Internet or read medical articles about his illness. If he read any articles dated before 2013, he immediately clicked off. Until Jaktinib came into the picture in 2013, CNL was a death sentence. In 2013 approximately, CNL had been distinguished from other leukemias. Only then did research studies get focused on CNL and the literature began to grow in due course over the following years. The only thing worse than failed treatment was a marrow transplant, which was a death sentence from the cure, not the disease itself – and transpired much sooner.

Hope was not to be found in medical journals. They contained no section entitled the *Gospel – good news*. In fact, hope and a positive attitude, along with nutrition or exercise or, *God forbid*, spiritual belief, were given little more than lip service by any practitioner in this field. They were irrelevant to the deterministic approach. Nonetheless, Conrad determined to keep Bernie informed and to ask him questions.

❧

Conrad had been home three weeks when at eight am on the third Sunday morning after his discharge, he received a telephone call from John, the son of his oldest friend, Jacques-Paul. Bouton was an Episcopal priest who had left the Roman Catholic priesthood in his mid-thirties. Born and raised in Paris, Jacques had then travelled to Canada and from there to the U.S. where he join a major university, teaching French literature and serving as a chaplain.

The two had met by chance when Jacques was giving a talk at Conrad's college and they had become life-long friends. Jacques, after retiring, had relocated in Arizona, where one of his three children lived. For a while, he spent half the year in Paris, and the other half in Tucson. Conrad and he had continued to visit back and forth and kept in touch by phone and email when they were apart. Conrad was fond of saying that Jacques was his spiritual advisor. The strength of Jacques-Paul's faith far exceeded Conrad's but, perhaps because of that, it inspired Conrad to pray daily and to aspire to have faith. Their spiritual relationship seemed remarkably unrestricted to normal means of communication.

Jacques-Paul was the first person outside the immediate family whom Conrad had informed of his diagnosis. He had responded with daily calls and emails with counseling as to how to deal with life and death, both of which were gifts from God, according to Jacques-Paul. Conrad felt buoyed every time he spoke to him.

John was typically abrupt and to the point.

"Conrad. I have bad news. Dad died last night. He had a fall at his trailer and they operated on his fractured femur. He seemed to be recovering and was in good spirits when we left him last night at eight o'clock. I want you to know that the last words he said as we were leaving were, 'I'll see you in the morning. Tell Conrad what happened. He'll be expecting to hear from me. I'll call him as soon as I can. Tell him that I am praying for him.'

"We got a call at three a.m. saying that he was failing and that we should hurry to the hospital. We were there in a half hour. He was peaceful, just barely awake. He seemed to know we were there but he couldn't speak. In an hour or so, he just slipped away very peacefully. I'm still in a state of shock. I wanted you to know right away. I'm so sorry for what this loss means for you. I hope everything will be okay."

Conrad was thoroughly stunned. A wave of grief enveloped him and he let himself be washed away, drowning in grief. Tears streamed down his face and he was unable to hold back his sobs. "This is unbelievable," Conrad said to John. "What a loss, for you and for me. But I'm mostly grieving for the loss to the world. He was a great man, the source of spirituality for so many people. John," he said choking with sobs, "I don't know what I'll do without him and his guidance."

Conrad was in grief for the next three days. The loss was unbearable. His consolation was to reread all the email exchanges. He found that Jacques had provided him, in more than 50 emails starting last fall when he was embroiled in the dispute with the dean, up to two days ago.

The emails amounted to a course in Christian spirituality. They were positive and optimistic, full of hope for future life and for life after death. He read and reread them. Then he turned to the passages in the New Testament that Jacques-Paul had recommended – the Gospel of John and the Acts, basically the story of Paul's conversion, plus psalms, and passages from the Gospel of Matthew.

Jacques-Paul had urged that he not bother seeking out a church if he didn't feel like it. Conrad had been separated from his church for six months as a result of a dispute with the minister. Jacques had enjoyed a deep relationship with Christ, going back to his boyhood, when he experienced what he never doubted was a personal contact with Christ. Jacques-Paul had been cruel to one of his sisters in refusing to speak with her for an entire year over an incident in which he was convinced that she had violated his privacy by reading his diary. He begged forgiveness and felt Christ's presence forgiving him and redeeming him. In his words, "Christ virtually *forced* his way into my life."

Conrad felt himself, in his time of need, opening himself up to communication with Christ, in a way that he had never before experienced. Perhaps cancer at last had driven him back to the church – to Christ anyway – through his great need despite his skepticism about religious faith. He had never doubted the existence of the soul and a spiritual presence but the details of organized religions fell flat for him. Perhaps this was at last a rebirth of faith inspired by Jacques-Paul's life and teaching.

⅗

"ADMONITION: HAVE COURAGE. DO NOT LOSE HOPE."

Two nights after learning of Jacques-Paul's death, Conrad awoke after three or four hours of restless sleep. He lay still for several minutes, composing himself. Finally, he rose and began to walk carefully across the pitch-black hallway to the bathroom, concentrating on keeping his footing. Suddenly, without warning, he was startled – *seized* might be more accurate – by a flash of bright lights spelling six words: *Have courage. Do not lose hope.*

The words seemed to come out of nowhere, Conrad said later as he explained the vision to Levi and others. He saw the words but they also seemed to be accompanied by sound, according to his brain. He could not actually recall hearing them when he tried later to reconstruct the event. They were palpable but beyond any of his senses, multi-sensory. They transcended any attempts to explain the event in ordinary language. He was certain beyond doubt that the words did not come from within himself. That was not the way he spoke. The experience was unlike any he had ever had or heard of. He had read of all types of visions, of course, in the Bible, but he did not pursue this fleeting thought until later when he read about Paul's experience in the Acts of Apostles.

Conrad had not been thinking those thoughts, nor would he use such language but the words were directed to him. He was certain they were meant for him for some purpose, the first occurring to him being his terminal illness. The source was supernatural and beyond ordinary explanation. But still, there was no doubt as to the authenticity of the words and their message. His immediate reaction was that the words were conveyed by God or Christ or perhaps a soul lingering after death. Jacques-Pierre? The vision was powerful, with the voice of God within, outside, surrounding, enveloping him, dominating his mind or was it his soul? Fatigued as he was, the message seized him as vividly as if it were flashing in neon lights at Times Square and announced by a loudspeaker.

Earlier in the day, Conrad had been lying on his sofa for hours, in grief over the news he had received from his doctor. He now knew what would cause his death. He knew approximately when it would happen, years before he had anticipated. Death as an abstract concept was meaningless. It had no sting, no bite. It could easily be denied or simply ignored. But death as a concrete prediction was entirely different. It had teeth to it.

Conrad was overcome, speechless – with joy and exhilaration – and total confidence. He remained motionless, standing in the hallway, until he recovered his bearings. After returning to his room, he sat stunned for a long time. He said aloud, "The words are inscribed in my heart, my soul – directly – by God. That has to be it."

They were not his words. He had not spoken or thought them. The words did not come from his conscious mind but rather from deep within – or perhaps from outside, however contradictory that was. The words were not accompanied by sounds but still they were vividly displayed in a way that he had never experienced and could not find words to describe. Were they God's words? Or were they Christ's or the Holy Spirit's? Were they from the Holy Spirit, speaking for God or Christ? Perhaps these words appeared within him – in his spirit – or perhaps they came from far away. Could they be Jacques-Paul's words? He had never heard him say those particular words. He had not heard anyone speak or write those words. No matter from whom or what the cause, they were truly miraculous.

The words – the message – brought him immediate comfort, strength, and confidence. They meant *something*. They were a sign, a message, that he had asked for, begged for, to help him cope with his condition. Had God ever spoken to him before? Certainly not. Maybe it was the fact that he had opened up the channel of his soul and his heart, not just his thinking mind, to Jesus in the past few days thanks to Jacques' urging and teaching. It was as though Jesus or whoever spoke them had taken over his mind to convey them – just as Jesus took over – *forced himself on* – Jacques-Paul when he was sixteen and in agonizing humiliation at asking forgiveness for his cruelty.

Regardless of the source, he felt that God, Christ – *Someone* – knew he existed. And that he suffered. He thought, yes, this was a thought of his own, there is no god but God. The source of the words strengthened his resolve. He vowed that he would never forget these words. Of course, he didn't know what they meant. Did they mean Hope for life or Hope in death? Did it matter? How could he know? These were words etched in his heart directly from God. They meant, above all else, that he was not alone in the universe. God had acknowledged his existence. God knew he was there in the darkness.

Conrad returned to bed, and lay awake until dawn. He was amazed and humbled at the experience.

There was no promise of a magic solution for his body's tragic mistake in permitting a tragic mutation that caused it to destroy itself. There was no promise of continued life, or an easy death. Although he did not know what the words meant, they were a sign that he had been heard and that his existence was known to God. He knew that was true even though the experience was beyond his capacity to grasp.

He thought about it all the next day. In the late morning, while ascending the stairs to his office, he was moved to tears and fell to his knees, like Saul, overcome with joy, sadness, grief, wonderment, amazement. He wept. Later he did the same sitting by the water at the jetty, alone, tears streaming, not caring who saw or heard him. He wept uncontrollably that he had been heard. He existed in the universe. And God existed. Conrad felt a sense of purpose, of meaning, in the universe. He wondered if this would ever happen again. Was this the way God spoke to humans in the New Testament? In the Old Testament, God roared. He spoke in words or wrote in words. He was a God of Drama, theatrics, a God of fireworks.

Why had God spoken to him? He was not worthy. At the mere thought of equating himself with prophets, Conrad felt frightened. The audacity of it, he thought. I must not become enchanted with myself. I must be humble. He wept aloud once again, heedless of where he was and who might hear him.

He felt deeply that Jacques-Paul was now happily joined with Jesus. He would think of this often and he believed that he should tell others that, yes, God existed. "I believe. I believe," he repeated over and over, in exultation. That was the only word for it. Exultation as he had never before experienced it. "I believe in God and Christ!" His children and someday his grandchildren must know.

"Someday, great-grandchildren. Why count them out? I have to tell everyone. That's my moral obligation. I have a purpose. He had begun to think about whether every soul had a purpose in human life. Why not, too, a purpose in leaving life, that is, to join the multitudes in death?"

He knew already, however, that the certainty of his spiritual experience would face a challenge as time and the seasons wore on and doubt put down roots and sprouted seedlings. The feeling of the moment would be difficult to recapture. There was no physical evidence of the experience. No one else could attest that it had really happened. No one could help him interpret its meaning or its source. The affirmation that he felt was amazing but also so unlikely.

Suppose that God or Christ attempted to communicate all the time but found mostly unavailable recipients, recipients so immersed in worldly affairs, so walled off from spiritual matters that communication fell, so to speak, on deaf ears, and blind eyes. Perhaps in his despair, he, Conrad, had been open for an instant to what was already there, always there, always inscribed in his heart. Perhaps this was always the way humans received Divine communications and inspiration. By being open in heart and soul, by opening a channel or by discovering what was already there.

He would have to recreate it. Was it ambiguous? Not at all, he said to himself. The words were not his and the voice, or whatever the means of communication, voice, sight, deep feeling, was not his. He continued to call up the memory of the timeless moment, and immerse himself in it. That left no doubt but he could understand how the disciples who encountered Christ after his death could be momentarily overwhelmed but experience a fading of the experience followed by creeping doubt about its authenticity. He would not let that happen.

Ah, he worried again, a human failing – doubt, anxiety, worry, over-thinking. But what did the words mean? Were they addressed to the present, to his life which was under assault by a virulent disease that could take off at any moment and consume him with pain and disability? Or were they addressed to the afterlife? To Resurrection? Did courage refer to facing life or facing death? Was hope channeled toward longer life or Resurrection after death? He had no way of knowing.

Was it possible that Jacques-Paul's soul was permitted to linger in order to deliver a message? Or was it God himself? As these questions spun around in his head, he could not dismiss the thought that this was the kind of mystical, other-worldly thinking that he had always rejected. But how could it not be other-worldly and mystical when the experience indicated it was authentic? "For now," he said aloud, "I will savor the experience and not let doubt dispel the exultation at being heard and seen, acknowledged by the Divine." How could this be anything but wonderful, inspiring, hopeful, whatever its meaning? This was just the beginning. That much he knew. He would never forget and he would not hesitate to tell the *good news*.

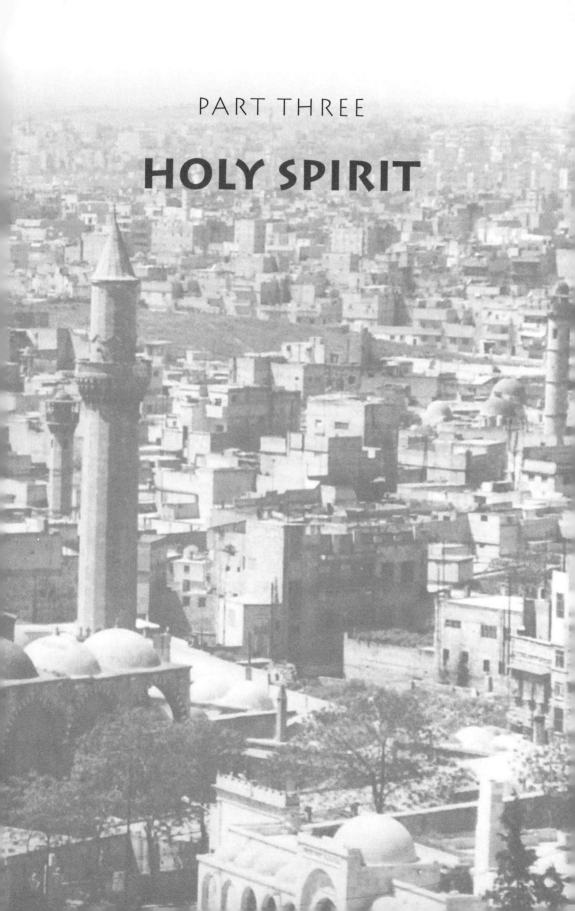

PART THREE

HOLY SPIRIT

As DAYS BECAME WEEKS and weeks became months, Conrad adapted to the changes in his life. Although he occasionally enjoyed the relief that forgetting could bring, he was hardly ever free of a spiritual ache that reminded him that everything he had ever known, past and present, were immutably changed. They no longer belonged to him. His visions and dreams for the future – however indefinite they had been – seeing his children mature, delighting in grandchildren, experiencing the seasons of life – no longer seemed within his grasp.

Oddly, much of the time he felt fairly normal in a physical sense and found it hard to imagine the sinister and destructive forces at work inside his body. He shuttled between various planes of acceptance and denial. Helen kept her distance from him but Levi worked tirelessly to convince him to remain positive.

"Don't surrender to depression," he'd say. "Be realistic but don't resign yourself to an early death. Resist, fight, defend yourself. You have to be ready to die – we all do – but until you do you must be determined to continue living. Don't waste the good time wallowing in misery."

Levi continued, "I can imagine what it feels like to you. When I was in graduate school, I did my thesis on works of literature that dealt with disease. The central piece was Thomas Mann's *The Magic Mountain*. It's still my favorite."

"I read it in college," Conrad said. "Pretty gloomy, I'd say. Not my favorite."

"I also wrote about *Cancer Ward*, by Solzhenitsyn," Levi added. "You read that, right?"

"Yes, but not seriously," Conrad said. "I didn't enjoy particularly reading about sick people, even though I knew these stories were really metaphors for the sick societies the authors perceived. I thought they were creative and clever, although depressing. Tolstoy is a good example. There are lots of jokes about Tolstoy. Everything he wrote presented a gloomy view of life. Look at *Ivan Ilyich*, *Anna Karenina*, and *War and Peace*."

"Okay, I can't dispute that," Levi responded. "*The Magic Mountain* consists of hundreds of pages about life in a TB sanitarium. It isn't exactly fun to read, except that it takes place in what is now one of the fanciest resorts in the world, Davos. But what I'm referring to is that the protagonist, Hans Castorp, a healthy young man, arrives for a one week visit with his cousin, gets diagnosed with TB and stays for thirteen years! I figure that's the way it looks to you. You show up at the emergency room for a routine CBC and, bingo, you get a life sentence."

"I see what you're getting at," Conrad said. "Yeah, that's about the way I feel. Let me out of here!" He laughed heartily, though it was the laugh of dark comedy, humor tinged with pathos. "So how am I supposed to stay positive?"

"Maintain equilibrium, find your internal balance between reality and hope," Levi said.

"That's difficult," Conrad said. "I have to accept my fate without surrendering to it. The paradoxical nature of the situation baffles me."

"Exactly," Levi said, brightening. "Life brings pain, no doubt about it. But if you accept the pain as opposed to resisting it, you'll minimize your suffering."

"Count me as still baffled," Conrad said. "But I want to tell you about a new insight that has occurred to me. It's a vision, a hallucination some might say. It flashes through my brain and then disappears until the next time. During this moment of insight, like a glittering shard of glass, I feel as though I know life and I may be ready for death. For a moment, I feel excited about venturing into death, the realm of death. Then it's gone, and I revert to my fear and anxiety about death. I like that moment of relief from fear and anxiety."

"Whoa," Levi said. "Don't start getting excited about dying, my young friend. You have years to go, miles to go before the darkness descends, if that's what happens. But I can relate to your insight and I am certain that it does provide some relief."

Conrad struggled to shield himself against the doctors' predictions. They seemed to be helpless in the face of scientific facts that left little room for individual variation or hope. But Conrad told himself he was not helpless. He was a whole person, whose reality encompassed not only the physical, but emotional and spiritual dimensions as well. Those dimensions were as real as his physical being.

Why must he accept the absurd proposition that it was impossible to prevent part of his physical being to wage war against his whole being, thereby threatening his life? The ironic aspect of this was that these virulent cancer cells were so determined to proliferate that they would kill their host – Conrad – and themselves in the process. In a moment of inspiration, so he thought, he drew an analogy from his study of global conflict. It was like the civil wars in Syria and Yemen, and so many other places. One part of society was pitted against the other, seeking to destroy all order, and inflict as much pain as possible in the process. In his case, a battalion of suicide bombers was stalking his healthy cells.

Sometimes he felt like screaming at his body to stop the plundering, stop the self-destructive behavior that would kill every cell in his body including the culprit itself – the gene mutations in the pathway system in his bone marrow.

Prayer helped because it made him feel as though he were sharing his own burden. He realized that the strength of his faith was not consistent. He had been a doubter most of his life. But now he had received the insight that hope was essential and that to hope meant to have faith. Hope cannot exist without faith. And faith cannot exist without trust – trust in God, trust in a greater power than his weak, flawed self. After he spent time praying, he always felt that he understood the situation better than before, even if he couldn't put it into words. In fact, putting it into words diminished it somehow. Whenever he felt doubt, he thought of Jacques-Paul's death and the six *miraculous* words that had caused him to weep with joy.

In good weather, he'd wait outside in the so-called healing garden, the place, or so it seemed, where no one ever got healed. Its function seemed to be to allow patients to breathe outside air, albeit city air, and to give work to the maintenance workers who were lucky enough to draw gardening duty. No garden of its limited size ever received more attention and painstaking care per square inch.

Since it was spring and the weather had yet to turn hot and humid as it no doubt would by late May, Conrad always went outside to wait anxiously for the lab results he received two or three times a week. He'd find a spot in the sun, if possible. There were usually very few people outside. He saw patients dragging their dance partners or lumbering along in wheel chairs or with walkers. He saw small children in strollers, being wheeled by nurse assistants or family members. The sight continued to touch him deeply. That comforted him somewhat, although the feeling didn't stay with him. If his CBC (complete blood count) was bad, he was discouraged for the rest of the day. If the report showed improvement (more red blood cells) he was elated.

Despite being deeply self-absorbed, Conrad began to recognize the regulars, the patients who were on his time schedule, the Monday, Wednesday, and Friday routine, that usually put them in the same proximity at around 2 p.m. One day, three weeks after he had begun the outpatient visits, he noticed a young girl who appeared to be eleven or twelve years old. She was at the far end of the garden, examining with obvious delight small figurines of children and animals that some volunteers had placed in the garden. They were stationed along the stream that meandered through the garden. The stream had no beginning or end, with the water circulating underground and emerging only to flow downstream again.

The garden was otherwise empty of visitors. The girl was accompanied by an older woman, perhaps in her sixties, about Conrad's age. The girl was wearing the telltale wristband and a headscarf that only partially concealed her baldness. Despite being pale and very thin, the girl, who looked familiar to Conrad, was energetically bouncing around the garden paths. The pathway was decorated by a rich variety of plantings, alongside the artificially created stream. Some plants were just beginning to bloom but most were patiently awaiting warmer weather. The temperature was cool enough to make a light jacket feel comfortable.

The garden itself received good sun in the early part of the day, Conrad observed this from his infrequent, yet lengthier hospital stays. Thus he knew the would-be-welcoming benches sprinkled around the outside of the pathways, were mostly in shade by early afternoon. The garden area was surrounded by high buildings on two sides and the lack of afternoon sun disappointed most visitors.

Conrad was fascinated by the inner happiness and peacefulness reflected in the girl's expression and her rhythmic movements around the garden. Her companion, an aunt or grandmother, Conrad guessed, had a sad expression on her face.

Conrad couldn't figure out exactly the nationality of the two, but assumed they were Middle Easterners because the woman was wearing a scarf, a *hijab*. He knew the names of the various types of coverings worn by Muslim women from his experience with many of *his refugees*, as he called them at the refugee center. He mainly saw Middle East refugees from Palestine, Syria, Yemen, and Lebanon, along with others from North Africa.

The girl glanced briefly in his direction and smiled as she rounded the far corner and Conrad couldn't help but smile, despite his anxiety or perhaps because of it, at her inner happiness. She continued smiling as she danced on to join the older woman. The woman whispered something in her ear, perhaps warning her against being friendly to strangers. They departed before Conrad's results came in, leaving his curiosity unfulfilled. His attention quickly returned to his own concerns.

Conrad thought afterwards, though, that the girl's demeanor and energy, despite her paleness, reminded him of his own daughter when she was the same age. He and Esther were close then and he took pleasure in her cheerfulness and high spirits. Now she was very much immersed in her own college life. Career decision time was on her. He was hopeful that, once she settled into her life after graduation, they would see more of each other. They might regain the close relationship they once had.

Conrad was struck by something compelling about this child in the garden. He could see that she had no fear of strangers. In fact, he felt that she had welcomed his presence despite the older woman's reserve. He wondered what kind of cancer the girl had. He felt sadness, his only unselfish feelings these days, at any child having to deal with cancer. It was bad enough at an older age.

The girl and her grandmother, or whoever she was, did not reappear that week on Wednesday or Friday when Conrad was in the garden or in the solarium. But the week after, as he was sitting drowsily in the sunshine on a bench tucked along the edge of the garden stream, the woman and child reappeared and sat at the opposite end of the garden. More flowers were in bloom in celebration of early warm summer-like weather. Once again, Conrad and the child exchanged smiles, this time in close proximity as she passed by on one of her frolics around the garden.

Conrad nodded and greeted her simply with, "Hi. How are you?"

The girl responded happily with, "Well, and you, sir?"

"As well as I can be under the circumstances," he told her.

She laughed and danced away. This time it was Conrad who left first without exchanging any greetings with the pair. But he did emerge from his own despair long enough to realize that the child looked familiar. But he still could not place where he had seen her before. But he speculated that he might have seen her at the refugee center. Then again, he had seen dozens of children there over the years. How far-off the Refugee Center seemed to him now! He had been so absorbed in his own medical problems that he felt a distance between himself and the entire world surrounding him. It was as though he saw "life outside himself" through a thick layer of fog.

༚

On Wednesday of the following week, the child reappeared, this time in the company of a younger woman who wore a *shayla*, leaving her face and neck exposed. She looked more pleasant than the older woman and the child seemed to be even more free spirited. When the child spotted Conrad, she smiled from across the courtyard and whispered something to the woman, who Conrad speculated was probably her mother. The mother, like the child, had a complexion and clothing that Conrad knew was Middle Eastern. The mother looked fit and thoroughly healthy, unlike the child.

When the child was doing her usual rounds of examining the garden, she stopped in front of Conrad and greeted him with a simple, "Hello, sir. You are here again. We are glad to see you." Her manner of speaking was clear and articulate, with a quality that would suit a well-educated adult. Conrad emerged from the days of self-absorption that obscured his perception and immediately recognized that she was Ayah, the daughter of Ghadir, who had visited him what seemed to be ages ago at the refugee center – in his prior life before the diagnosis.

"I remember you from the refugee center. Are you a doctor too," the child asked.

"I remember you too and no," Conrad said with a laugh, despite himself. "I'm just a patient, like you."

"Do you have cancer?" she asked innocently.

"I do," Conrad said. "I have CNL, chronic neutrophilic leukemia. Do you know what that is?"

"No, I don't. I have childhood AML. Do you know what that is?"

"No, I don't really," Conrad said. "Would you explain that?"

"It's acute myelogenous leukemia," she said without stumbling over the term. "It's the second most common type of leukemia that children have. Is yours similar to that?"

"No," Conrad said. "Chronic neutrophilic leukemia is very rare, so rare that fewer than two hundred people have ever been diagnosed with it. That's because no one identified and classified it until a few years ago. But my leukemia might change into AML at some point, when it enters the acute phase."

"That's amazing," she said. "I was diagnosed two years ago," she said, "so the doctors say I have a good chance to recover. Children have a very good recovery rate from leukemia. It's not as good for AML but better than adults. The doctors are very encouraging to me. I've been getting treatment all that time. We used to live in Massachusetts but my mother moved here so now I come to a doctor here. I get treatments here. I like this hospital better."

"I didn't realize that you had leukemia. Your mother mentioned your illness when the two of you came to talk with me at the refugee center. Your mother is over there on the bench, right? Let's go talk with her. I want to explain what happened to me and why you haven't heard from me."

They walked to the long arched bench that was now half in sunlight and half in shade. Ghadir was sitting in the shade. She pulled aside her hijab and looked up with an expression that reflected surprise and curiosity.

"Yamma, you remember Mr. Frisch, don't you?" Ayah said with a lilting voice that belied the circumstances. "He's a leukemia patient too. I didn't recognize him when I was here with my *khala*. That's my aunt, really my mother's aunt," she said looking at Conrad before turning back to her mother. "Mr. Frisch has CNL. I though he was a doctor before. We were talking about our illnesses."

"Ghadir," Conrad said. "I'm so sorry that we lost contact. I don't know if anyone at the center told you what happened to me a couple of months ago. I tried to reach you by email but I didn't get an answer."

"No, I didn't hear anything," Ghadir said stonily. "I went to the center twice after our second meeting. Both times the receptionist, Sylvia, said you weren't in and she wasn't sure when you'd be back. I gave up after that. No one offered any other information and no one seemed interested in my case."

"That's terrible. I'm sorry. I got diagnosed with leukemia. There was no advance warning. I was hospitalized for eight days. My life totally changed. My white cell count was at a dangerous level. They were afraid my liver and spleen could shut down. I thought of you and your dilemma often but I lost track of everything but my illness. I'm an outpatient here. I come three times a week for blood tests and go to another hospital in New York also. The doctor there is an expert consultant on treating this disease."

"I'm so sorry to hear of your troubles," Ghadir said, her mood shifting. "I imagine you were surprised to see Ayah here. We never got around to telling you about her leukemia. She's had the disease for a few years and we transferred her here from a hospital in Boston. We're hoping her disease will go into remission. There are some good treatments and a good outlook for what she has but we have to take good care of her."

"Ayah was telling me about her type of leukemia," Conrad said. "I think she knows as much about hers as I do about mine. She's extraordinary."

"She is that. You see, this is the reason why it's difficult for me to think of leaving her if I decide I must in order to rescue Jamil."

"Is there anything new about Jamil," Conrad asked. "Do you know where he is?"

"Yes," Ghadir said. "We believe he is still with Yousef's brother and his wife in the eastern part of Aleppo, the part controlled by various rebel groups. I'm sure you've read that. We are uncertain about the future. Yousef could come to take him away anytime. Yousef's brother Hamza and his wife Mona left their home and moved to a small town outside Aleppo for the sake of safety. The eastern part is under constant attack by Assad's forces and his allies. They moved into a vacant apartment that belongs to Mona's family. They want me to come there and bring Jamil to the U.S. I am considering that right now."

"I want to help you," Conrad said. "I'm sorry I didn't keep in touch with you. I wasn't able to go to Jordan for the conference. When I told the medical staff I had to go on the trip, the doctor said, 'You'll be going to the hospital by ambulance instead.' That was a terrible blow to me. I have no leads to report, I'm afraid. It's been difficult to think of anything beyond controlling my disease. There is no cure or even remission for me. Control only. But I am getting stronger. We should talk about a trip, if you can leave Ayah."

"I would have to do just that. Ayah is not strong enough to undertake a trip like that," Ghadir said. "I will have to go to Syria eventually."

Seeing Ghadir outside in the sun and wind, Conrad was struck by her appearance. She looked younger and more vibrant than in his office. Conrad supposed that her stress level had been lessened somewhat because she knew that Jamil was safe at the moment. She was seated in the sun-drenched portion of the stone bench. As Conrad sat down in the shade, she offered to move so he could be in the sun.

"I've been here enjoying it here for an hour," she said. "You take a turn in the sun."

"Thanks," he said. "I appreciate it. I feel self-conscious with my wristband and my mask. They told me to wear the mask whenever I'm inside the hospital. They're worried about my immune system."

"It's okay," she laughed. "I tell Ayah that she has to do the same to stay healthy. Do you live near the hospital?"

"No, I live in a small town just outside of the city. I come in three times a week for a blood draw. I haven't started working again at the refugee center and I'm not teaching any courses."

"Ayah has to have blood tests and she comes here for medical treatment too."

"How often?" Conrad asked.

"Once a week, on Wednesday. Ayah is in school in New Haven. I pick her up and then bring her back after the treatment. I'm trying to give her a normal life. But sometimes she needs hospital stays to get intensive chemo." She looked down at Ayah and put her arm around her. Ayah responded with a similar gesture, making it difficult to tell who was comforting whom.

At that moment, the solarium door opened and the hematology nurse emerged, holding a print-out of Conrad's CBC results.

"Good news, the white count is down today," she said cheerfully. "Hello, Ayah. How are you today? I didn't see you. No lab today?"

Ayah got up quickly and approached her, giving her a hug. "Not today. Just a treatment. I'll be going back to school as soon as they clear me. We're waiting for the doctor."

"Okay, sweetheart. I'll see you next time maybe. Come in and see me." The nurse glanced at Ghadir. "I love to see her. She makes me feel better. Isn't that something? If I'm having a bad day, all I need is to see Ayah's face."

Ghadir laughed. "I know what you mean. Everyone says that. I wish I had her inner happiness. She takes everything in stride. She never complains about the restrictions she has because of leukemia. She's a gift every day, a treasure."

Conrad left soon thereafter, since he was meeting Levi for coffee, but not before finding out the details of Ayah's next appointment. He felt more uplifted and confident than he had since the night of the miraculous message. He wasn't elated, just hopeful. The nagging fear that had plagued him since the devastating diagnosis had lifted like early morning fog in the mid-morning sun. He felt at peace for the rest of the day.

When he awoke the next morning, the feeling was still there. With it was a new sense of excitement that he could do something worthwhile in what was left of his life. He'd go to Syria and help bring back Jamil. That would fulfill his destiny.

ᘒ

Since Conrad had no teaching to occupy him, having declined to teach a summer semester course due to his compromised immunity and his energy level, he had a struggle maintaining his emotional equilibrium. Reading and writing provided some relief from obsessing about his condition.

He continued on the schedule of three blood draws each week. The process consumed a good three hours, including the travel. After starting Jaktinib, his targeted drug, ten days after getting out of the hospital, his white count, which had been reduced to below 20,000, thereby nearing the normal figure of 10,000, soared to 80,000.

But when the doctors raised the twice a day dose of Jaktinib, the count crept back down to 40,000. On blood draw days, he awoke with anxiety that plagued him until he saw the printout. One day he mentioned his suffering over anxiety to a psychologist at the hospital.

"Don't put yourself through that," the psychologist said. "If you allow yourself to react to every change, you'll drive yourself crazy. You have to realize that the counts will vary up and down. Accept that and find a steadying factor – like the way you feel. If you permit those mood swings, you're letting the disease run your life. Cancer will run your life – and ruin your life if you let it. You need to take charge."

"You make it sound like cancer is some evil creature inside me," muttered Conrad, "and that it's trying to make me miserable – as well as kill me."

"It isn't that at all," the psychologist said. "Cancer is just cells, a mass of cells but it does act like it has a will of its own –

consuming glucose, growing in size or proliferating in number. It is in a desperate fight for survival as your other cells are."

Conrad realized he had made an illuminating point. From then on, he controlled his mind to expect variation in white count numbers and to realize the world did not end with a bad result. It was easier than he imagined adjusting to that approach.

After reaching 40,000, the four tiny Jaktinib pills, each 5 mg, taken twice a day, stopped reducing the count. The consulting doctor trumped Ulianofsky's insistence on raising the dose to the maximum allowable of 25 mg twice a day. The count lingered at 41,000 for two long weeks. Conrad resisted going to the maximum for fear that losing the cushion would be depressing. In any event, Ulianofsky had been the strongest advocate for a transplant aside from Reinhard. The two of them just wanted to get the Jaktinib treatment over with and get on with the transplant. Conrad resisted this plan in view of the ridiculously poor prospects for a successful transplant.

Suddenly, without warning the Jaktinib took off and demonstrated a second life, a second kick. Day by day the count went down until after three weeks, the white count had reached 13,000, honing in on normal. Conrad would not forget the day when the count hit that lowest ever after diagnosis. He went to New York city to the consulting hospital. Helen, in a moment of cooperation, went along. There, meeting with the supervising doctor, he saw the printout with 13,000 for the WBC and a little over 10,800 for the neutrophil count. He was elated. Both of them were elated and began dreaming that with this strong a reaction, surely the Jaktinib would not fail Conrad. The most recent MRI was equally encouraging, showing a significant spleen reduction.

꒰꒱

A few days later, Conrad was sitting on the long stone bench in the healing garden with Levi, who had been driving him to nearly all appointments recently. Conrad was delighted to have the company and also wanted Levi to spend serious time talking with Gaspar as well as Ghadir. So far, although Levi and Gaspar had met briefly in the solarium, Gaspar's schedule had not allowed a real conversation. Inquiry at the desk when they arrived revealed that Gaspar was expected in the clinic within the hour.

While waiting for his lab results and for Gaspar's arrival, Conrad was recounting an incident that happened on the last trip back from New York, after visiting with a consulting physician.

"Everything that was said during the visit was so encouraging that Helen and I began thinking, gosh, the drug is working so well, maybe it will actually keep working. It even got us talking about our future together. Maybe the dire prediction that I have less than two years will fall by the wayside. I began to speculate out loud about future plans. Should I take on my full course load next semester? Should I accept the offer from Florida International to teach the American Studies course again? Should we spend two months in Florida this winter? If I don't work, our income could be down twenty-five thousand dollars. How can we manage that? Should we this or should we that?"

"I can see why Helen got so excited," Levi said. "She had mentioned to me that she felt life was closing in on her. She was just a bystander, with no control. That has to be frustrating, no matter what else you might think about her."

"But then," Conrad said, "I was overcome with fatigue and discouragement for the rest of the train ride. I couldn't even find the strength to talk. I pretended I was asleep. I wanted to be asleep. I felt that I was getting ahead of myself, dangerously so. I'm not cured. There is no cure. I have no chance of remission. A few weeks of good results doesn't mean that the Jaktinib will work over a period of months or years. It's working now, which is good, but that's all we can say. I was exhausted when I got home. It was close to 10 p.m. I was so tired this morning and so discouraged that I didn't feel like getting out of bed. Some of my discouragement has been shed by sleeping but I'm left with decisions to be made that are beyond me. Morning has brought a little clarity. Do you know what I'm discouraged about? It's not bad medical news. Not at all. It's the *good* medical news. Strange, right? You're probably thinking, 'How can this be?'"

"I'm not sure I understand," Levi said. "But go on."

"When I was in the hospital and the first genetic testing results started coming back to my doctors, I got one item of bad news after another. One major blow was finding out that I don't have the Philadelphia gene – the one that is involved in CML. That's the disease that Gleevac puts in remission or cure. That was a serious blow to me because it would have given me a chance to resume a perfectly normal life. I also realized that, had it been CML, the threat of illness would have faded away and my life would hardly have been changed. There went my dream recovery. Instead, I faced increasingly difficult odds. I learned that my situation is one of the worst nightmares – absolute and indefinite uncertainty.

"The good news that Jaktinib is working so well has restored that dream of recovery, maybe even remission. Maybe all the dire predictions will fail, that is, the ones based on the extra mutations I have. Then it started to be clear, as I was sitting there on the train. My dream is no longer just to go back to the life I had. It isn't enough to pick up where I left off and carry on as though nothing has happened. This experience – living and walking with death, staring it in the face - has changed me forever, not that forever is all that long," Conrad added with a burst of laughter.

"I'm not trying to be melodramatic," Conrad said. "But I have confronted my death. I've looked in the mirror day after day, when I can stand staring at the specter of myself. I've seen that I'm a different person. My body has changed. My values are changed. My priorities have changed. And of course, I'm far from being out of the woods. The dire predictions that every doctor has solemnly pronounced have not changed. I can't go back to my former life under any circumstances. The problem is that the moment I appear to be recovering, people, especially my family and friends, will start believing that I should fulfill their expectations of the way I should live my life. Helen has so much as said that. I'm not up to that."

"That's a natural reaction," Levi said. "A person who has had a catastrophic disease knows he can't go back to the way things were. Everybody else expects him to do that. The way people see things diverges completely."

At that moment, the solarium door opened into the garden and Gaspar emerged, waving in Conrad's direction. A few minutes later, the three of them were seated on the bench engaged in animated conversation.

Conrad continued, "Gaspar, I was just explaining that part of me wants to go back to a normal life, whatever that is. Practical necessities like making money dictate that I can't go off and do nothing but write or teach to my heart's content or run off to help the refugees who need my help. I don't want to run away from my life and my family. Not really. But my priorities are very different than they were before. I have been changed by the experience but others have not, at least not to the same extent. Time is now even more precious than it was. Every hour I have to spend is a treasure to me. Each one must be spent doing God's will. After all, if good comes to me, it's not my doing. It's God's mercy and grace."

"So cancer has made you think you have faith that you didn't have before," Levi asked in a skeptical tone.

"Yes, it has. I am tuned into higher frequencies than before. I truly believe I've heard the voice of God, not because I'm special but because I happened to be tuned in to the perfect channel, because I was so vulnerable and open spiritually. The word of God is everywhere. We just can't hear it most of the time. We tune it out deliberately or we simply aren't listening."

"True," Gaspar said. "I know that to be true."

"You *know* it to be true? I don't believe that," Levi said. "I think that's nonsense. Everybody gets religion when they get cancer or when they get caught and sent to prison. We all know about *cancer Christians* and *death row Christians*. You're desperate and so you reach out to anything and everything in a way that would have seemed foolish before. Now it doesn't seem foolish. That's the difference."

"Bull," said Conrad. "Don't you believe in the soul? What do you think the soul is if not a glimpse of the Divine, a very small glimpse, like a receptor, that is just turned off most of the time? Maybe it's just blocked from hearing by all the noise of everyday lives."

"Go on," Gaspar said to Conrad. "I think you're inspired."

"I can't be far away from my doctors. I am still hanging by my fingertips on the edge of a cliff. Isn't that hysterical? We – the cancer victims, those who are engaged in a death struggle with cancer – are the *extreme athletes* of our culture. It's not the mountain climbers, the race car drivers, or the ski jumpers. We are the risk takers. Every day of our lives, we hang on the balance between life and death. We live on the edge every day of our lives, out of desperation, not by free choice. And we are not thrill-seekers. We have no vacations from this task. It's a 24 hour a day job and there are no sabbaticals."

"Fascinating perspective," Gaspar said, while Levi sat shaking his head in disbelief.

"I may suffer a devastating setback next month, or the one after that," Conrad said. "The doctor I trust the most has said the time will never come – *never*, did you get that? – when he can say that I'm free of the cancer. To use military metaphors, there will never be a cease-fire when the cancerous cells pause in their mission to destroy me. There is no DMZ or no-fly zone. That's the nature of my disease. Sure, maybe other drugs will come along and work for a while. I might get more than two years – maybe even five if I'm really lucky."

"I get that," Gaspar said, nodding. Levi shook his head slowly from side to side.

"That night on the train," Conrad said, "I felt like retreating, escaping into my illness to avoid grappling with all the expectations and needs that I don't feel able to cope with. I don't want to lean on my illness as a crutch. But this will be very difficult to explain and justify to Helen, to my children, even my friends. They won't understand how a person is changed by coming face to face with death.

"This is a dilemma and totally unexpected. In some way, down deep, I'm glad the disease changed me, changed my life, my expectations because I now have a much greater appreciation of the gift of life that I now have and of the preciousness of each hour. I now see everything differently. To be frivolous about it, I could say I'm like Yossarian in *Catch-22*. He said, if you recall, 'I see everything twice.' Yossarian was making it up in order to stay in the hospital. I'm perfectly serious. It's as though I see through a clear lens now and no longer darkly through a clouded glass. Corinthians, right?"

"That's why the New Testament doesn't do anything for me," Levi said emphatically. "When God speaks to me, or I should say, if God ever speaks to me, I'll hear it loud and clear like Moses, from a mountaintop." He laughed heartily. "None of this whispering in your ear - or whatever - in the dark. I remember your telling me about the six little words. That's not the way my God speaks. My God is a shouter, not a whisperer."

Gaspar laughed but did not argue with Levi's words, which he took to be partly in jest and partly in seriousness. "I understand," Gaspar said, "but I've never been there. I've experienced the word of God, though. I believe. And I've heard lots of people tell me about similar experiences. It's not communication the way we normally think of it. I see that you want a different life, a new life, for the time remaining. You understand how little time may be left and don't want to waste it. But you have to be tolerant and understanding of other people who do not understand this. There's good reason to take each day at a time, not to get ahead of yourself, or too far ahead of other people."

"It will be difficult," Conrad said, "because Helen will feel that it's lack of love on my part or selfishness, maybe even self-indulgence. On some strange level, I like my newfound state of being. I like struggling with death and what it means and reconciling with my mortality, with death that lies waiting to lead me through that closed door. There is a different plane of existence. I glimpsed it and I don't want to lose it in the mindless occupations of life, unfulfilling work and deadening vacations. I know this will be difficult to maintain. It sounds humorous but my best hope is to die *with* the disease; the likelihood is that I will die *of* it.

"What I didn't say," Conrad added excitedly, "is that I also pray every day and commit myself to trying to understand God's will. I feel that writing and teaching how I feel about facing illness and death may be part of my mission. Writing about the consequences of war and combat and the importance of truth may be my mission. Writing about the horrendous plight of Middle East refugees, the importance of finding common ground in human life, and reducing conflict among the three Abrahamic religions may be part of my mission. I have to find out what my mission is, which is to say what God's will is. I'm not so presumptuous as to think I can really figure it out but I have to try.

"This is my story this morning, friends," Conrad said. "I am feeling less fatigued and stronger every day. I know that holding onto whatever insights I've gained and explaining and negotiating all this with the people I love will take unselfishness, diplomacy, caring, and love. With whatever meager resources I have, I will try to carry out my mission, whatever it turns out to be. "

"I understand," Gaspar said.

"I applaud you, my friend," Levi said as he nodded slowly, accepting Conrad's passionate response, "even if I don't understand everything you feel."

"The doctor, Ulianofsky, has switched me to once a week labs," Conrad said. "He did it because he thinks my time is limited and my quality of life is more important than ever. He thinks I'll be dead in less than two years. I'd rather have Dr. Bitar. He's a Middle Easterner who has everything going for him. We're on the same wave length, but I'm stuck with the mad Russian for now. I'm still working on that one, though. I don't agree with Ulianofsky's reasoning, values or priorities. Everything is different now for me. I can't help but think of St. Paul. He knew he couldn't ever go back to being Saul again. Everything was different. In a way, trauma has changed me. In another way, I've been converted too. You might laugh," he said, looking straight at Levi, "but I've heard the voice of God and been brought to my knees. I can't go back. I don't want to go back. This is a wild thing to say but sometimes I feel curious, even eager, to see what lies beyond. I feel that way when I'm the most confident," he said, laughing. "Most of the time, I'm a full-fledged coward."

Conrad scheduled his next lab appointment for 2:30 Wednesday afternoon, the day of Ayah's next appointment. Now that communication was restored, he was intrigued to know more about Jamil's plight. He was concerned about Levi's reservation about getting involved. He was afraid that Levi's feelings arose more from prejudice than from rational thinking. He hoped that when

Levi accompanied him to this appointment, he could meet Ghadir and Ayah and hear their story firsthand. Conrad saw no reason to be skeptical about Ghadir's story merely because she was Palestinian. Besides, there was something unusually compelling about the child, Ayah, that lent credence to the story.

Conrad couldn't stop wondering about the coincidence of meeting up with Ghadir and Ayah again – here in the cancer hospital – after meeting them at the refugee center. The coincidence that Ayah was being treated for leukemia right here was amazing. He didn't believe that God arranged coincidences in some mystical way. But coincidences that brought people together were marvelous, if not miraculous. Blood had brought them together again. Blood, the source of life, medically and theologically, was like a river flowing among people, carrying the vital elements of life. He couldn't get out of his mind that Ayah and Ghadir had been carried on that river into his life for some purpose.

When Conrad went out to the garden after his blood draw, he was pleased that Ghadir and Ayah were already seated on the long, curved bench, huddled together at the sunny end. Conrad waved and, when they waved back, he approached them and asked if he and Levi could join them. Conrad briefly introduced Levi and they sat down, welcomed by Ayah, who turned toward Conrad.

"How are you feeling today, sir? You look healthy."

"I am feeling well, Ayah," Conrad said, amused at her adult composure. "I'm hoping for a good blood count today. It's the white cells that are my problem – the neutrophils. Do you know anything about white blood cells?"

"Yes," she said. "I looked them up on my computer. I read about your disease but I didn't find much about treatment."

"That's because there isn't much written about it. It's rare, much rarer than yours. You have a much better chance than I do at being cured or at least going into remission. Do you know what that is?"

"I do," she said quickly. "Remission is when the disease doesn't advance. It's not the same as a cure but it can last for a long time if you're lucky. Will you tell us how you found out about your disease?"

As Conrad was about to begin his story, Gaspar appeared at the doorway to the solarium, looking expectantly in their direction. Ghadir waved for him to come over.

"I'm glad you're spending time together," said Gaspar. "I've known Ayah and her mother for many months. I knew you all would have a lot in common."

"We met a few months ago at the refugee center," Conrad said. "I know what has happened to Jamil."

Moving to the end of the bench so he could see all three of his listeners, Conrad began. "To answer Ayah's question, right after Christmas, I had unexplained swelling in my left leg. That led to my seeing a vascular surgeon. He treated the blood clots but did nothing to ascertain the cause. My story actually begins before that. In the preceding fall, I had a battle that lasted for months with one of the deans at the university where I teach. I'm a contract teacher. I teach whatever odds and ends no one else wants to teach. This dean has a lot of power over me and my future opportunities, including my earning capacity.

"It's a long story how I ended up with such a low position, that is, a non-tenured one. I won't go into that. I love teaching my students, especially those who need support and don't get it from the regular faculty. Last year I taught global problems in public health, war ethics, bioethics and American cultural ideas. My friend Levi here teaches there as an adjunct.

"This particular dean wants to do away with contract professors, including me, maybe especially me. We've had skirmishes before. He can't stand anyone challenging him or criticizing him. That's a story in itself. He proposed to phase all of us out. I criticized this plan at a faculty meeting. He was furious. He attacked me in front of everyone. No one on the regular faculty spoke in my support. I finally walked out, badly beaten up. Levi, here, stood by me, spoke out, and walked out with me.

"The dean hasn't been successful in terminating contracts yet but he's my sworn enemy. He wants to get rid of me. I believe he will attack based on my illness. I'll have to fight to stay there and it's my only livelihood. I can't help but think that this toxic situation wore me down and accelerated my leukemia but I can't be sure, of course. I think emotional trauma can affect the immune system."

Ayah's face expressed her compassion, as though she were experiencing his pain and his humiliation. She placed her hand on his as though she could not withhold it. Conrad was moved and felt near tears. He went on.

"All spring I was treated for the clots. They got worse, then seemed to get better with the blood thinner that I had to inject twice a day. In April, I had a small pain in my left side. It was like a stitch that you get when you run too fast."

Ayah and Gaspar nodded.

"My doctor ordered a blood test and sent me to the Emergency Room in my town for a CT scan to check for possible diverticulitis. I had a trip to Jordan planned a short time after that. Ghadir knows about that. I was going to make some contacts to help find Jamil. Anyway, the staff there looked at the blood count, the CBC, and told me I had a sky-high white cell count and that it was probably leukemia. My wife and I were stunned, absolutely shocked. I was taken to the hospital; the trip was cancelled, and I got a diagnosis of chronic neutrophilic leukemia, which is rare. They told me it was caused by a genetic mutation in the bone marrow – which itself was just bad luck. It was nothing I did or didn't do.

"There's a drug that targets this mutation but, because of two other genetic mutations, my chances are not good. I might well not live more than two years maximum, probably closer to a year. That is, unless I get a bone marrow transplant. But that's such a parade of horrors with a poor survival rate, about thirty percent, it's hardly worth considering.

"Having a transplant is like playing Russian Roulette with four or five chambers of the gun filled with bullets. It takes nearly a year out of your life trying to survive all the horrors of each stage. So here I am, almost sixty years old, a failure in life, facing a terrible disease and painful death, with my career in jeopardy. There's more to tell another time."

Conrad stopped, looking as though he could burst into tears but, instead, emitted a small ironic laugh. No one else dared laugh. Gaspar, who was used to hearing desperate stories, broke the heavy silence.

"Conrad," Gaspar said, after a pause, "I know this is a terrible blow and you've had only a short time to adjust to it. I see patients day in and day out who are on emotional roller coasters. It's important to put doctors' opinions in proper perspective. You have to consider they are primarily scientists, especially in technical fields like hematology and oncology. They have to warn patients based on science and statistics, as documented in studies. They're afraid to create false hopes so they present the worst case scenarios.

"Hope and optimism are not part of the recipe. I can't think of a scientific study that takes into account a patient's emotional or spiritual state of mind. I'm not saying that's right but that's what happens. We know there is more to getting well than medicine alone. You're a whole person, an individual with body, mind and spirit, and you may well react in a unique way to a disease or to medication. You're not limited by the way other people respond. You should not lose hope. Focus on the positive side and be strong. Have courage and *determination* - not *determinism* - as you face your illness."

Conrad stared at him, struck by his words and how they resembled the words he had *experienced* a short time ago. "I've heard those words before," he said to Gaspar. "They remind me of my spiritual experience. I have no idea where the words came from. And I don't know what they mean except that I feel that I am not alone. The words were otherworldly."

"You will eventually come to understand those words," Gaspar said confidently.

"That would be a miracle," Conrad said. "Hearing or seeing them at all was a miracle. I know they are powerful. I call this the *first miracle*. I guess that means I'm hoping for more miracles."

"I will pray to Allah for you," Ghadir said firmly, "and in fact I already did after meeting you at the center. I had no idea of your background. Stay strong and positive, believe and have faith in Allah - in God - and he will be with you."

Ayah was silent but kept her hand on his shoulder as if to recognize his need to be healed.

"I believe that I am meant to carry on my work, humble as it is," Conrad said. "One of those missions is to bring Jamil back home." He laughed, looking down at his body in a sweeping gesture. "In my condition, that will take a lot more than courage and hope. I'm far from stable and certainly not strong. Recovery is out of the question. I will have to work with what I have."

After a pause, Gaspar turned toward Ghadir. "Would you go next" he asked. "Levi and I can tell our stories, that is, if Levi wants to, another time." Levi shook his head in the negative. Conrad was not surprised that he was not ready to reveal himself, but appreciated that he seemed willing to listen.

Ghadir smiled, nodding in agreement. With a glance at Conrad and Levi, she said, "Yes, I hope I can fulfill that, but there is sadness in my story. Do you want to hear it?"

"Absolutely," Conrad said.

As Ghadir began, Ayah stood and put her arm around her mother's shoulder. Sensing her eagerness, Ghadir said, "Sit down please, Ayah. You may join me in telling the story. But we can't both talk at the same time. I'll tell the short version." Scanning the group, she continued, "If you're not familiar with the history of Palestine, it's complicated. Of course, it plays a role in my personal story and in some sad things that happened to members of my family. I'll save that for another time.

"I was born in Palestine in a small town outside the city of Ramallah, in the occupied Palestine Territories, the West Bank region. Before I was born, my family lived in one of the suburbs of Jerusalem. They were forced out by Israeli authorities who just decided to take over the area. They moved to the Ramallah area because they had some family members there. That's another story. I'm the fifth of six children. I have two sisters and two brothers still living. Two of my brothers were killed, one while we were still living on the West Bank. I will not go into those events. My family had a modest house with a small yard and a vegetable garden. It had been owned by relatives of mine for a long time. Most people in that area now live in apartment buildings. Although we were a little crowded, we managed. We were fairly well off, much better than many other families. We loved having our own house. I was doing very well in high school, getting good grades.

"Eventually, we were forced to move again, abandoning our home, because of the arrival of Israeli settlers. We had very little time, only a few days' notice. We had to leave behind almost all our belongings, including furniture and anything else we couldn't carry with us. Basically, we took what we could manage in one trip. It was heartbreaking. We moved in with relatives in the city of Ramallah for a while but eventually it got to be too much for everyone. So we moved out and went to a refugee camp in Ramallah. That was Al-Am'ari Refugee Camp.

"The conditions were terrible. It was crowded, dirty, and unsafe. There was very little supervision or protection. While we were there, my father died of a heart attack. He died on the way to the hospital. He should not have died. But we had to go through a check point and were forced to wait so long that he died before we reached the hospital. It was the only hospital that we felt comfortable going to, one that was under the supervision of a Palestinian medical staff. Hadassah Hospital was closer but we didn't think he would be admitted there. That's an Israeli hospital."

"I'm sorry to hear that," Conrad said. "It must have been a painful loss. Life must seem very arbitrary and unfair."

Levi shifted uncomfortably, but held his tongue.

"My brothers were teenagers by this time," Ghadir continued. "They took over the family leadership to an extent and tried to protect us. I should add that my parents were not involved in politics at all. They were barely able to feed us and send us to school. That took all their energy. They raised us to avoid conflict even when we suffered indignities or abuse. They wanted us all to survive and be part of a solution to the conflict, not part of the conflict itself.

"My family decided to make a move to Syria for reasons that I don't understand. I believe that some Palestinians were forced to migrate to Syria after 1948. The situation there was not promising for Palestinians. We knew that it would not be a home in the full sense and that we would be treated forever as refugees. At least, though, Syria was peaceful at that time, unlike the horrible turmoil now.

"We were directed to a camp for Palestinians near Damascus, called Yarmouk. It was the closest one so we went there. It wasn't bad at that point but you know what it's like now. It's a horrible place now, with conflict, and without supplies. After Al-Nakba, Palestinians suffered from very bad treatment. It's a sort of battlefield too, a microcosm of the war, in some respects. But at the time we were there, it was decent enough. We got settled there, expecting it would be temporary, although we didn't have anything definite for the future.

"We clung to the tenuous hope – or dream – that we might someday return to our home in the West Bank. My brothers had trades and they expected to get work. That didn't happen and we just scraped by day by day. We were very poor. I continued to do well in school, despite everything. My parents had always wanted me to get a college education.

"My mother was able to borrow money from relatives back in Palestine so I could go to college. I got a degree from Birzeit University. The years I spent at the university were tumultuous. I won't go into detail on that. I wanted to get a graduate degree so I could become a teacher in Palestine. I came to the States on a Fulbright fellowship and got admitted to the Harvard Kennedy School to study public policy and political science. I was incredibly lucky to get in. That's a long story too. While I was there, I met a Syrian man, Yousef, who was studying economics and politics. We eventually got married and the children followed.

"I should fast forward, as the expression goes, over a few years. After we finished graduate school, we stayed in the Cambridge area and both of us managed to get low paying teaching jobs. I won't go into detail about the struggles we had with visas. It was a nightmare. But we kept finding ways to stay. I thought my husband's interest in being in the U.S. was the same as mine. But he got disillusioned with teaching and found a job with a Boston management firm. He began associating with young men from a Muslim extremist group in Boston. You'd be amazed at how many extremists there are in the States, people who came here perfectly legally, usually with European passports."

"I hear the same thing," Gaspar said. "I don't think people realize that when they put all the blame on refugees."

"At first," Ghadir said, "I knew nothing about this group. But my husband began to stay away longer and longer. He told me some startling things from time to time. For example, he would boast that they held extreme views and plans for violence. I was alarmed when I discovered that he had brought weapons into our home. I begged him to stop seeing those men.

"At first he just argued with me but eventually he'd get furious if I raised the issue. I could tell that he was won over. People call it becoming radicalized now. They must have worked hard to recruit him. I could see their influence overcoming mine week by week. He drifted away from me and spent more and more time with them and less with me and our family. Islamist extremists, you know, frequently come to this country specifically to recruit soldiers to go to the Middle East and fight. I'm certain these people were connected to DAESH directly or indirectly.

"My husband became verbally abusive at first and then more and more violent as I protested what he was doing. Every time he came home, which was not every night, we argued. He struck me more than once but, of course, as a Muslim woman, I wasn't about to go to the police. I became more and more frightened of him. I had very few friends, no one to talk to. My husband had discouraged my having friends. He also tried to force me to stop communicating with my family. About this time, I learned about Ayah's illness. She was abnormally fatigued and I took her to the Harvard Health Services. She was about ten and our son was eight. I went alone with the children. My husband didn't even show up for the appointment. He would go into diatribes about Assad. He finally said outright that he was becoming interested in fighting against Assad in Syria. He was an entirely different person.

"Then one night he disappeared and Jamil with him. I discovered it during the night. We had an argument that evening when he got home and his behavior was strange. But I did not imagine the worst. I had noticed that when he was at home he was paying more attention to Jamil, trying to create dependence, telling him about what was going on in Syria, getting him excited. I discovered that he was telling Jamil about war and military things that were beyond my knowledge. I didn't suspect the worst. But looking back, I can see the signs I should have picked up much sooner. If I had, I'm not sure what I could have done anyway. I had only my aunt and a cousin living nearby and there was nothing either of them could have done. I told Conrad that I also had a frightening conversation with an acquaintance of his who was part of the extremist cell."

"You were in a bind. It's an old story about this," Gaspar said. "This was probably a typical brainwashing as part of the radicalization."

Ghadir continued. "I have relatives in Palestine and Syria. They have tried to find out where Jamil is and where Yousef is." Ghadir paused, unable to go on, with tears streaming down her face. "We did find out that Yousef left Jamil with his brother, Hamza, and his wife, Mona, in Eastern Aleppo, but that he is planning to return to get him. But Aleppo is under siege more and more. It is an extremely dangerous place. We don't know how they are or even where they are exactly. I live in fear that any day now, Yousef will show up and take Jamil away to some camp. Raqqa, DAESH headquarters, is not far away, for example, and there are all types of training camps there."

Ayah reached out to comfort her. "Yamma, may I continue with the story?"

Ghadir nodded.

"The last information we have is that my father is fighting somewhere in Syria. My uncle is a doctor. My uncle and aunt are not extremists. They are good people, I believe, from what my mother says. We haven't seen them in a long time.

"They have lived in Syria as long as I know. They may want to protect Jamil. But I don't think they could resist my father when he comes to take him. He may already have taken him away. My mother didn't want to say it aloud but we fear that my father may intend to turn Jamil over to be trained as a soldier or suicide bomber. It's bad enough to become a child soldier, to learn to kill, and to be exposed to an early death. We think that my uncle and aunt may have left Aleppo because of the fighting and destruction there. If they do move, we don't know whether they will stay in Syria or go to Lebanon, Jordan, or Turkey. We try to make contacts every day."

"Horrible situation," Gaspar said. Conrad was silent, emotionally choked and unable to speak.

"We've had no contact with Jamil since he was taken," Ayah went on. "He is just ten years old now and is the age at which the Islamic State likes to train and brainwash boys to become suicide bombers, snipers, and soldiers. We are desperate about this, as you can imagine. My mother cries every night. We left the Boston area to stay with our aunt in New Haven. You saw her here on several occasions. We are hoping for someone who can help us. Will you please help us?"

Ayah sat down next to her mother, gently taking hold of her hands.

"Thank you, Ayah," Ghadir said. "I'm sorry for breaking down but this is a desperate situation for us. We don't know what to do."

After a pause, Conrad said firmly, "I'm going back to the refugee center. My medication is working and I feel well enough. It's time to get on with my life. I'll make some inquiries at the center, as I was going to do weeks ago. If we can get current information, it would help."

After Ghadir and Ayah left, Conrad said, "Being in the hospital is demoralizing. It sucks the vitality out of me. Since I got out, I can't seem to get going."

"I hear that a lot," Gaspar said. "Patients become dependent. It weakens them. They lose their will to survive. They begin to see themselves as less than whole people. They become diseases walking. They lose their interest in being autonomous."

They agreed to meet on the following Wednesday.

As he drove Conrad home, Levi seemed to be absorbed in his own thoughts. Conrad felt strength flow through his body as he considered the problem of Ayah's missing brother. His interest in life and living was refueled and he was excited at the prospect of helping to locate Jamil. He caught himself up short when he realized that Jamil was in grave danger. "This is tragic," he thought. "This is not some adventure for my amusement. This is serious. It isn't about me."

❧

Conrad was eager to tell Helen about the meeting. She greeted his enthusiasm with skepticism bordering on hostility.

"What do you want to do? Rush off to the Middle East? Don't you have enough problems of your own to worry about? Don't I have enough to worry about because of your problem? I don't know what is going to become of us. We're in no position to take on someone else's problem."

"I know. I know," Conrad said. "But these people face a desperate situation. It takes my mind off my own problems to think about theirs and to try and help. Maybe there are some Syrians at the center who can help with contacts. We're talking about a child who is about to be forced into being a soldier or a suicide bomber. Doesn't that matter to you?"

"No, frankly, it doesn't," Helen said emphatically. "We have enough to worry about. You should be taking care of yourself. That's your priority. If you have extra energy for a diversion like this, you should use it to work more to pay our bills. The only health insurance we have is mine. Maybe you haven't noticed that our medical bills are mounting. Are you going to work in the fall? Have you been in touch with the university?"

"Yes. I'm going to teach," Conrad said. "I've signed up for two courses. I hope I can follow through. Why don't you come to the hospital with me next week? Meet these people. It would be an eye-opener. You might change your mind."

"I'm not interested and neither should you be. If you're not going to take care of your health so you can keep earning your meager salary, I'll change my own priorities and you won't be one of them," Helen said, revealing a strain of hostility that he had not noticed before. "All you think about is yourself."

Conrad didn't say what was on his mind which was, *All you can think about is yourself.* Instead, he said, "I've come to accept my illness and accept that I face an earlier death than I ever thought would happen. The chaplain told me that both life and death are gifts. There's nothing wrong with resisting an illness and trying to live longer. But I won't go running around in desperation trying to avoid death."

"Oh, that's great. Accept it all you want. You may have one foot in this life and one on the other side. I'll take care of myself."

"Why do you have to treat me like the enemy?" Conrad asked. "I'm the one who has a terminal illness. I'm the victim, the one facing death. Why do you beat me down? You act like you're the only one who counts."

"I don't want to listen to any more of this," Helen said. "I suppose you remember that our children are coming over tonight for dinner, right?"

"Sure," Conrad said, realizing that he hadn't the slightest recollection of that plan. "I intend to tell them about it. We have a family tradition of helping refugees and immigrants, giving them a helping hand. I want our children to know that. I might even enlist the children to help. They're adults. They can take some responsibility."

"Good luck with that," Helen said, walking back into the kitchen.

An hour later, Paul and Esther arrived in separate cars, Paul from work, Ester from the college. The evening progressed on a superficial plane until, at the dinner table, Conrad told them about his conversation with the refugee family. Both expressed polite interest.

"Do you feel up to this, Dad?" Esther asked.

"Sounds like a lot to take on to me," Paul added.

"Your father told me he was going to tell you about this," Helen said, barely suppressing her anger and frustration. "He's all excited about getting involved. This is plain foolishness. We have priorities and they don't include a couple of Arabs who have been victimized by another Arab."

"Helen," Conrad exclaimed. "There's no call for such harshness. These people can't be written off by simply calling them 'Arabs,' as though that was some sort of curse."

"They deserve what happens," Helen went on, ignoring Conrad. "They made their lives and they have to live with them." Turning to Esther and Paul, she added, "Your father should be concentrating on getting well so he can work full-time. If he can't, we're in trouble. Esther won't be able to finish college. We might have to borrow money from you, Paul."

Alarm registered on their faces. Helen went on without breaking stride. "If he isn't able to work again, it means he probably won't last that long anyway. He shouldn't be wasting his precious time on some Arabs. It's one thing to fool around at the center, as you do," she said, staring at Conrad. "It's another to take on their problems personally."

Conrad gasped at Helen's harshness. "Do you realize what you just said?"

"Yes, I do. Someone has to speak the truth."

Esther and Paul seemed to take their mother's remarks in stride, and glanced nervously at each other, looking for clues as to what to say next. Helen left them in no doubt.

Staring first at one, then the other, she said, "Tell your father that he's crazy to get involved in that mess."

"Yeah," Esther finally said, "Mom's right, I think. I know how much it means to you but you have to focus on your health now. You always say that your students and the refugees are important. Sometimes I think they're more important to you than we are. We need you to get your health back. You might not survive a trip like that," she said with some compassion, despite the pressure on her to agree with her mother.

Paul, squirming in discomfort, nodded but said nothing. Conrad knew that he shared his own interest in the global refugee problem but was afraid to challenge his mother.

Helen shook her head, endorsing what Esther had said at her prompting. "See," she said. "I told you the children wouldn't think much of your misdirected energy. She's right. If you have attention to spare, give it to your children. Not to mention to your wife."

Conrad lost his temper and railed. "How can I give them more attention when we hardly ever see them? Any time I've ever asked anything of the two of them, they're too busy. Maybe you all should pay me a little more attention. I'm the one who's suffering here. Do you all face suffering and death? No. Why don't you all understand?" Conrad got up from the table, his dinner untouched. "I'm going to lie down."

Conrad went to the den, slumped onto the sofa, and fell asleep in his misery. He felt attacked, abandoned, and unloved. He was vaguely aware of hearing the front door close, but he drifted back to sleep. When he awoke two hours later, the house was still. He went to the kitchen. There was no sign of Paul, Esther or Helen. Checking the garage, he discovered that Helen's car was gone. There was no note.

Two days later, Conrad received from Ghadir a forward of an email that Mona had sent to her sister. Ghadir explained the background.

"You know that Mona and I grew up together in the West Bank. She and Hamza met when he was in medical school in Jordan. They went to Syria, where Hamza had a residency. They lived in Idlib, a town just south of Aleppo. They have one son, Karam. They are traditional Sunni, like most of my family.

"Hamza's father is Syrian and his mother, Lebanese. After medical school, his residency and post-doc were in the U.S. Unlike so many others who remain in the U.S., he returned to take care of his own people. I haven't seen them since I came to the U.S."

The short email text followed.

"When fighting broke out in the Aleppo region, including Idlib, and two larger cities, Horns and Hamah, our home was severely damaged by bombs. We were lucky to be away at the time but it was dangerous to stay there. We had to find another place to live. The four of us went temporarily to a refugee camp in that vicinity.

"That camp is no longer safe and we will head south to a safer camp, eventually going to Jordan. We might have to stop along the way at other places, such as Yarmouk camp. It was known to have both Syrian and Palestinian refugees, mainly Palestinian. The northern part of Syria, in the region of Aleppo and Raqqa, where DAESH has its headquarters, is definitely unsafe. We must leave Eastern Aleppo. The bombing is reducing the city to rubble. The Russians are bombing everything, including hospitals and schools. There are no humanitarian limits."

Ghadir said, "That was the last communication that Mona's family received. They are hoping Mona will communicate again. They have a decent car and, I would imagine, enough money to make the trip. My hope is that they will do what they can to prevent Yousef from taking Jamil. Their sympathies do not lie with the Islamic State. They hate the idea of exposing children to violence. They may purposely be avoiding Yousef by not telling anyone where they are. I fear that Yousef, with all his contacts through DAESH, will find them before I do. It has been a long time now since Yousef took Jamil. I worry that they might go to Yarmouk. It has been attacked by both DAESH and the Syrian army.

"My brother Hussein is also engaged in the war in Syria. He fights for a rebel group that opposes DAESH as well as the Assad regime. He might be able to help us find Jamil if I can locate him. His group opposes recruiting child soldiers."

❧

The next morning Conrad headed to the refugee center, accompanied by Levi, who offered to drive him. The center was located in an unused warehouse that had been vacated when a new VA social center was built near the VA hospital. It was funded by a variety of public and private sources, the private sources being mainly church-related organizations. Business had been booming for some time with people coming in from Central America, the Middle East and Africa.

Although most Middle Eastern refugees had previously come from Iraq and Afghanistan, Syrians, Yemenis, and Libyans were now joining the flow of homeless people finding their way to the center. This was taking place despite opposition from an array of American politicians who feared that radical fighters would slip unnoticed into the country, posing a lethal threat to security. Conrad was hopeful he would be able to make some contacts. He knew that Syrian refugees had a special network using social media that connected them to refugees in the Middle East, Europe and other destinations abroad and also was accessible to people who wanted to help refugees. Just as travel conditions were difficult and unpredictable, so electronic communication such as cellphone service and the Internet, was primitive and often unpredictable but it did exist, thanks to the ingenuity of aid agencies and individuals.

Despite Levi's cynicism about Muslim refugees in general and his concern about exposing Americans to terrorists, he listened patiently while Conrad circulated through the building as well as going through the indexes of Syrians who had already been relocated in New England. Conrad tried to pick up shreds of information about the likely journey and stopping points of Ghadir's brother-in-law once he decided to make his way to safe territory to the south. He also learned names of journalists who were on their way to or back from Lebanon, Jordan, and Turkey, to interview

Syrian refugees. Conrad persisted beyond his fatigue level. On the way home, Levi berated him for wearing himself out.

"What are you doing? This is crazy," Levi said, exasperated. "No one will find them. Anyway, why do you have to jump in the middle of this situation? You don't even know she's telling the truth about what happened. You should take care of your health, for God's sake. What does Helen think?"

"She's fed up with me," Conrad said. "She wants me to save my strength and teach more courses to make money. She has no use for refugees, never did. Would you believe, she's a second generation American? What do you think of that? She doesn't realize that I don't want to go back to what my life was. I want to do something worthwhile with the rest of my life, no matter how short it is. Anyway, I haven't told you yet that we're not getting along at all. There's history you don't know."

"I'm sorry to hear that," Levi said. "But back to what I was saying. What if this woman and her precocious kid are giving you a line? You can't get people to grab some kid just because she gives you a story. I mentioned your idea to my brother, who practices immigration law in New York. He thinks you're crazy. You'll wind up dead or in a prison cell in Syria or Jordan or maybe even federal prison. You'll be violating God knows how many laws besides risking your neck – not to mention your life."

"Why don't you come to the hospital clinic with me again on Wednesday?" asked Conrad. "Hear more of what she has to say. Ask questions. Challenge her. Make your own decision. That would be a help to me."

"If I can, I will. For your sake. But I'm not staying to listen to any contrived story. She probably wants to get money out of you. How do you know she went to graduate school at Harvard? Seems unlikely to me."

"Fine," Conrad said. "I believe what she says. The child is special, perhaps even in a religious or spiritual way. For all I know, she could be a descendant of Muhammad. She's like a wise adult in a child's body, very composed and confident. She has a remarkable sense of justice. Gaspar believes them. He's impressed with Ayah, too. I can tell."

"Yeah but what kind of gullible fool is he? What do you know about him? I mean, he seems nice enough. But I'm skeptical about a Roman Catholic priest who can't make his mind up what he is, a Christian, a Muslim or maybe even a Buddhist?" Levi said. "These types fall for a good line. They have no critical judgment."

As they pulled up in front of Conrad's house, he asked Levi to come in for a drink. "It'll take the heat off me with Helen. She's going to be upset that I went to the center."

The two of them walked up the driveway. Opening the door, Conrad heard voices, Helen's and a male voice, both laughing. The male voice was familiar. He motioned to Levi to close the door quietly and they made their way down the narrow hallway, which was in desperate need of repainting, to the kitchen and sitting area. As they entered the kitchen silently, Conrad stopped before appearing in Helen's view. He could see her sitting on the loveseat close to a man. She was facing him, with her arm on his shoulder, stroking the back of his neck. When she turned toward him, she had a warm and adoring smile on her face. He knew attraction when he saw it. Conrad recognized instantly this was an intimate scene – and an intimate relationship. The back of the man's head was toward Conrad. Helen spotted Conrad and was so startled that she jumped away from the man.

"Conrad," she said sharply, the word tinged in anger. "What are you doing here? Why did you sneak up on us?"

The man was startled as well and turned abruptly to look at Conrad. It was his neighbor, Bernie, the dentist. Bernie? Conrad was incredulous at first. Then it began to make sense.

"What do you mean, sneak up? We just walked in," Conrad said, his own shock turning to annoyance, ascending quickly to anger. "Is there a problem with that? Is this my house? Do I live here? Am I dead yet? Sorry to disturb you. I don't mean to break up your little conversation."

Levi took it all in. He looked uncomfortable but slightly amused. "Hi Helen," he said, with a smile curling on his lips.

She glared at him. "Think what you want," Helen said. "Where were you, Conrad? I can imagine. At the refugee place, right? Are you encouraging him, Levi? Are you crazy too? You should know better. For all I've been through the past few months, you'd think I'd deserve better treatment."

"I'd better go," Bernie stammered. "Conrad, this is nothing, nothing. We were just talking, mostly about your medical situation. Come and see me anytime. I want to be helpful. You know Helen and I are good friends too. You're both my friends. That's it. That's all there is to it. Conrad, we're still friends, right," he said, slapping Conrad on the back lightly as he moved past him toward the door, causing Conrad to wince with repulsion. "Hey, man, come and see me, anytime, okay?"

"Yeah, right," Conrad said. "Anything else to say, Bernie? This is your chance. Do you have any medical advice for me? Maybe you'd like to advise me on assisted suicide?"

"Yeah," Bernie laughed nervously, mistaking Conrad's sarcasm for humor. "Yeah, physician-assisted suicide," Bernie said, feigning a laugh. "Hey. Come on. Don't be like that. This was nothing. I came by looking for you."

"You came by?" Conrad said, bearing down on the word 'came.' "Yeah, right. See you later, Bernie. You know your way out. I should say, you know your way in, right?"

Bernie hurried down the hallway, closing the door quietly.

Levi pulled Conrad back into the hallway in the wake of Bernie's departure.

"I should go, Conrad," he whispered. "But I'll stay if you need me. Are you all right? This must be a shock."

"Let's go outside," Conrad said.

They stepped outside. "Am I overreacting? What did you make of this?"

"You need to take this seriously. Do you think this has been going on a long time?"

"I don't know," Conrad said. "We're not getting along. We're on different wavelengths. She doesn't have a clue what I'm going through. I wouldn't want my old life back even if I could have it on a silver platter. Death is around the corner. She's written me off. She's preparing for her new life. Time is precious and I need to do things that mean something."

"Oh shit," Levi said. "This is terrible. You need support. She's throwing you overboard – and for that jerk, that asshole. I know him. I used to go to him. He's so full of himself. I never told any-body this but he's been accused, privately so far, of coming on to female patients. He's a total creep."

"I never cared much for him but I thought he was some sort of friend."

"What do you want to do? Stay? Or come with me. You can use my spare bedroom any time you want, Conrad. My door is always open. You don't have to call even, just come over."

"Okay, thanks Levi. That's good to know. I'd better stay and have it out with her."

"I'll stay if you want. Just say the word," Levi said.

"No. Thanks. It's okay. I'll be okay. I'll call you later."

Conrad went back inside. Helen was still sitting on the love-seat, staring ahead. She didn't look up when Conrad entered and stood by the fireplace across from her.

"What's going on, Helen? What's this shit? Out with it."

"I don't know what you're talking about," she said. "He came over to see how you are. We were just talking. Is that a crime?"

"I saw something that I'm sure about. You and he have a rela-tionship, don't you?"

"Yeah, right. A relationship. We're neighbors, same as you. You're overreacting. You're a sick man. Now I know you have a sick mind."

"Thanks for the support. Obviously, l can't count on you. The hell with you. You can leave any time you want to. I'm sure Bernie needs the company. He doesn't have many friends. He's a creep. You need companionship? Bernie? That asshole. You amaze me."

"Leave? Me leave? Not likely. You're free to leave any time you want to," she said, with her face contorted into what Conrad recognized as disgust. "You're calling him a creep? Take a look at yourself. You're selfish. Just because you're dying, you think you can treat me like a piece of crap."

Conrad was aghast. "I'm treating you like a piece of crap? You're a selfish bitch. I want no part of you or your life."

He left the room, heading upstairs to the spare room. He heard the sound of glass smashing against the floor or the wall. It was probably her wine glass or the wine bottle. That reminded him how disgusting her drinking was to him. He moved some of his clothing from the master bedroom to the guest room. He lay down, feeling exhausted, unmoored, and depressed. He felt totally alone, as though life had caved in on him. He felt like the outcast that he had much of his life. He should be the one smashing things. If only he had the energy. He felt washed out, worn out, ready for the garbage dump.

Suddenly, as though lifted out of his despair by an unseen force, he determined not to wallow in despair. He knew what he would do. He would go to the Middle East – to Jordan, to Lebanon, even to Syria, wherever it was necessary to go – in order to rescue the boy. He'd find out soon if the mission was feasible. First, he'd have to see Ulianofsky, although he dreaded that encounter. He'd need some reassurance. He'd make an appointment to see him. And he'd pursue getting Levi involved. Levi would be good support. He could trust him, if no one else, in this uncertain and painful world.

On Monday morning, Conrad went to the local hospital cancer clinic. Monday was physicians' day at the clinic. The waiting room was full. He'd been lucky the scheduler made the effort to squeeze him in. He hadn't been switched officially to Dr. Bitar yet and Ulianofsky was filling in for another physician. He was stuck with him at least one more time. Of course, he'd be in for a long wait. Half the people in the waiting room were wearing masks. He hated to wear a mask. He hated this place. It reminded him how sick he was, how much he belonged here with all the other dying people. Well, dammit, maybe he wouldn't die as fast as they thought he would. At least, he'd die doing something worthwhile.

Two hours elapsed before he was ushered into the tiny cubicle of an examining room. Then more waiting. Finally, a resident came in to interrogate him so the *physician* wouldn't have to waste his precious time finding out what was going on with the patient. The resident was a thin, unattractive young woman who tried hard to appear confident. She was better than some of the others who acted as though they were above talking with patients. At least she listened to his answers, while she was scribbling down notes. Conrad explained all that had happened.

"What brings you in today, sir?" she asked.

"I'll get to that with the doctor," Conrad retorted. "No point in our discussing my question. That's why I made the appointment with him."

The resident looked chastised. She flushed and responded with, "How are you feeling, then? How's your energy level? Your bowel movements?"

"They have to ask every damn time," Conrad muttered to himself.

"Your blood counts are quite good, actually, better than we expected," she added.

"I feel pretty well," he replied. "My energy is good. I do stuff all day, go out sometimes. I started going back to the refugee center where I volunteer. I'm preparing three courses for the fall semester, adjunct courses. I get really tired by the end of the afternoon though. I usually need a nap before dinner."

"How about emotionally?" she asked carefully. "Is everything all right, I mean, at home? I mean, with you?" The resident paused.

Conrad looked at her, a blank expression on his face. "Wonderful," he said finally.

"Does it depress you that the medication does not have durability, I mean, is not likely to keep working because of your combination of mutations?"

"That's a lot of questions," Conrad said. "Of course it depresses me." He wanted to say, "Of course, you idiot. What do you think? Why wouldn't I be depressed? Anyone who would not be is crazy." He thought immediately of *Catch-22*. He'd figure out a new *catch-22* from this one. But he held back. No need to offend everyone. It was impossible to keep from insulting Ulianofsky. He was so condescending, so insensitive. But with the resident, he simply said, "That remains to be seen. Every person is different, if you haven't noticed. As far as home is concerned, what business is that of yours?"

The resident ignored the rudeness. "I'm supposed to find out why you made the appointment. Why the urgency? Would you please just tell me the subject?"

"Okay, I will. I want to take a trip, basically the same place I was supposed to go in April when I got kidnapped and institutionalized. It's been three months, actually, more than three months."

"You were kidnapped?" the resident asked.

"Another word for it is *hospitalized*. My question is, what do I need to do, to take, what precautions, for going to Jordan and possibly Syria? It's something I need to do. But it isn't definite yet. I just want to find out."

"Oh, I see. I don't know what Dr. Ulianofsky will think of that. Not much, I suspect. It sounds as though you couldn't pick a worse place to go than the Middle East – you know, with all the violence, turmoil, and disease. There's a lot of disease you know. Think of the crowds of desperate people. Why do you need to go?"

"Trying to find someone, help someone, a child, actually."

"I'll fill the doctor in," she said, visibly relieved to depart the room.

He could hear murmured speech on the other side of the door, the one that led to the doctors' area, the portal that separated the providers from the needy, desperate, dying patients.

After another half-hour wait, Conrad left the cubicle to go to the rest room. When he returned, the resident was there. She announced in a hushed tone that the doctor was upset because Conrad was not there when he came in. There would be a delay while he saw another patient. This is going to be a really pleasant meeting, Conrad thought. Finally, after another twenty minutes, Ulianofsky breezed in and took a seat, looking irritable. "My time is valuable," he said in his heavy, oppressive accent, obviously seething. "I expect patients to be ready when I am. Next time, don't leave or I won't see you at all."

"Oh, pardon me. I thought after waiting for three hours, I could be allowed to go to the rest room," Conrad said testily. "Your time is all that counts, right? Next time I'll go ahead and pee right here."

Ulianofsky looked disgusted but declined to escalate the quarrel. "What brings you here," he asked. "What is so urgent?"

"Didn't your assistant tell you? I told her the whole story."

"Tell me the story, the short version, that is."

Conrad repeated most of what he had told the resident, who had now joined them and was standing uncomfortably against the wall. The underlings were always expected to stand. There were never more than two chairs in any of the cubicles. If a patient brought a companion along, someone would get an extra chair but never for one of the medical assistants. Conrad observed to himself that it must be part of disciplining of the staff to wait, by standing at attention.

"In my view," Ulianofsky said in his thickest, leaden accent, glaring at Conrad, "that would be the most stupid thing you could do. You propose to leave the country and go to one of the worst, most dangerous – perhaps the most dangerous - disease-infected parts of the world? Are you crazy? You're a dead man if you do that. I guarantee it."

"Finally a guarantee," Conrad exclaimed loudly with sarcasm. "My life here isn't worth crap," Conrad said aloud, surprising himself with his harshness. "I want to do something worthwhile. It doesn't matter if it's the last thing I do. What do you think of that?"

"I'm speechless," Ulianofsky said, feigning shock at Conrad's bluntness. "What's so bad that makes you feel that way?"

Perhaps the man had some feelings after all, Conrad thought to himself. "I'm dying. My wife is having an affair – with a dentist, of all people. Imagine that. A *dentist*. I have no support system, other than one friend. My kids don't give a damn about me. I'm losing my job." He spoke with vehemence.

"Do you want to talk to a psychiatrist? Or maybe the social worker?" Ulianofsky asked with amused indifference.

Conrad laughed harshly. "Are you kidding? That's the last thing I want to do. I'm not imagining this. I'm in touch with reality. What on earth would a shrink say? What I want is for you to prepare me with what I need to go over there for two or three weeks. Everything, including names of doctors and hospitals. I'll prepare an itinerary and then I need to pack everything I'll need, meds, needles, everything."

"All right. I can get my staff to do that. When is this?"

"Not sure. It isn't definite. I'll know within the next two weeks," Conrad said, feeling suddenly anxious at being so definite, so committed about doing the trip.

"I have to go," Ulianofsky said. "Let me know." He was gone as quickly as he had appeared, trailed by his assistant, closing the door heavily behind him.

Conrad was alone, feeling hopeless, not buoyed up or encouraged. He went to the coffee machine, a concession to patient comfort, without speaking to anyone. All the staff were occupied at computers or busy chatting with each other. He felt invisible. No other patients were in sight.

⅜

That night, after heading directly upstairs, bypassing any of the areas where Helen might be, he sat in the guest room, eating a sandwich that he had bought on the way home. He watched the small TV set on the corner table for an hour. He caught the last half of a movie about a four-year-old boy who had a near death experience. When he recovered and returned to his family, he began telling stories about being in heaven and spending time with Jesus. He offered detailed descriptions of Jesus, and met for the first time a sister who had died in the womb.

The movie purported to be based on a book written about the boy's experience by his preacher father. Conrad was fascinated by the story. The premise was that the boy had information that could only have been acquired by being in heaven, right down to his description of Jesus, which matched a portrait painted by a teenage girl who claimed a similar experience. Conrad thought he might get the book. He wondered again whether he was nothing more than a Cancer Christian, one of those late-comers to the faith.

Cancer Christians, Conrad reminded himself, were the civilian counterpart of Trench Christians, soldiers in World War I who discovered religion when they faced death on the front lines.

Conrad thought sadly how Jacques-Paul, with his deep and abiding faith, had advised Conrad to develop a vertical relationship with God. He believed that the thin places, those places and times celebrated in Celtic belief systems among others, when spiritual communication was most likely to be heard and received by humans, included times of fear, grief, and suffering. He had assured Conrad, both during his dispute with the dean and after his diagnosis, that he should not hold back on expressing his faith just because someone might argue it was contrived as part of a bargain to survive.

Conrad took Jacques at his word then without expecting miracles. Having positive faith in something or someone greater than himself was a vital part of healing. Conrad clung to the belief that the appearance of the six words was a miracle, an acknowledgement that he existed, even if he couldn't be certain about the source or exactly what the words meant. There was no other way to view it.

Conrad was exhausted but at least he had regained a sense of equilibrium, close to peace. He lay down on the guest room bed. He felt like a ghost, invisible to the world of the living. As he lay still, drowsily approaching sleep, he thought about the miracle of the *word* as he drifted off to sleep.

Conrad woke frequently during the night. Each time, he could feel his attention being drawn powerfully, like sinking in quicksand, to his fear and grief about the disease that was struggling to prevail in the competition for his body. But each time, he repeated the six words along with a simple prayer, counteracting the force that was trying to destroy his will along with his body. Each time he managed to return to sleep, the unconsciousness that brought temporary relief from the demon that sought to defeat him.

He was glad to see sunlight streaming in the window when he awoke. Sunshine, especially accompanied by a breeze no matter how strong, always buoyed his spirits. He could see a patch of blue sky through the window and hear a chorus of birds that sang every morning just an instant before daybreak and continued to midmorning.

He felt – then pushed out of his mind – the threat of another gut-wrenching conflict with Helen this morning. The house would be full of palpable tension this morning, unless she had already gone out. When he went downstairs quietly, hoping to get a preview of the atmosphere before disclosing himself, he discovered that the house was empty. He was relieved to be alone.

PART FOUR

ROMANCE

THE SOUND OF THE TELEPHONE stirred Conrad from a morning nap on the living room sofa. At the second ring, he debated whether to rouse himself and rush to take the call in the kitchen. He was glad he did when he saw the name of his college roommate and friend, Henry Robinson, on the caller i.d. He answered on the fourth ring.

Although they lived only a few towns away from each other, they had seen little of each other in recent years, especially since Henry was homebound waging his personal struggle against bladder cancer. They did exchange emails from time to time, usually initiated by Henry, who loved to circulate the absurd humor that floods the internet. Conrad had little interest in that humor but was glad for the contact. He thought of Henry often and had meant to let him know that he too had joined the ranks of cancer victims, the not-so-elite club.

Conrad had procrastinated visiting Henry even after he heard from Helen that Henry had experienced a setback in his condition. Two months ago, it appeared that the cancer had spread to his liver and other vital organs. Helen had maintained over the years a tenuous but cordial relationship with Henry's wife, Virginia, whom Conrad had known since college. Conrad had dated Virginia for nearly a year before they broke up. At that time, he had sensed that Virginia was not as devoted to him as he was to her, leading him to stage a painful confrontation, which ended badly for Conrad. Conrad remembered being acutely jealous when Virginia and Henry started dating, even more when their relationship became serious.

Conrad had many moments of regret in later years about his impetuous behavior but he never blamed Henry or Virginia, for that matter. At the time, he had made clear to Henry that he was no longer interested in Virginia, true or not. Over the years, whether at church or neighborhood parties, Conrad liked to imagine that a strong attraction existed between them. But if that did exist, they had always kept that firmly in check within the bounds of friendship and loyalty to their spouses.

"Henry, how are you? I'm so glad to hear from you," he answered the phone enthusiastically, expecting to hear Henry's voice.

He was startled to hear Virginia's mellifluous voice, tempered with sadness. "Conrad. I'm so glad to reach you. I have bad news about Henry."

Conrad's heart sank, fearing what was coming next. "Oh, No. Not that."

"I'm sorry to have to tell you. Henry was taken to the hospital three days ago. It seemed as though every organ was shutting down. I couldn't manage him at home any longer. He died very early this morning, about 5 a.m. I got a call from the hospital, thank goodness, and was able to be with him for the last few hours."

"Oh God," Conrad said. "I'm so sorry to hear that news. I've been meaning to call him for weeks but I've been putting it off."

"He understood. Helen told me that you've been diagnosed with cancer. I let Henry know that. He wanted to call you but, somehow, he didn't get around to it either. I meant to call you myself, but the last few months have been a blur. Henry stayed occupied the whole time, writing and more writing about his disease progression and how he felt. He said it kept his mind off the worst part of it. I wasn't so sure. I felt that it caused him to be obsessed with the disease but it's what he wanted to do. He said it seemed as though he was writing about someone else. I'll show you his journal sometime, if you want, but it's not exactly cheerful. It's too bad that you two couldn't have gotten together to comfort each other. But that's often the way."

"I thought about him a lot," Conrad said, "and you too. It must have been difficult for you."

"It wasn't easy. Henry didn't have a lot of physical suffering. I'm glad for that. But he was devastated at leaving life behind.

He wasn't ready to go. He was a happy person, you know, and he hated to give up that happiness."

"I can understand why he was a happy man. You gave him a wonderful life. I'm sure he was a great husband too."

"Yes, he was. He was a fine person and we were happy. Thank you for saying that."

"Will you let me know the arrangements?" Conrad asked. "Is there anything I can do? I'm glad you called me. I'd like to drop by and see you sometime too. Perhaps I can help in some way that would make up for my failure to stay in touch with Henry."

"We'll have a memorial service in a month or so. Will you say a few words about him? If you feel well enough, of course. Henry made very clear that he wanted me to get in touch with you."

"I'd be honored," Conrad said. "I should mention that I might be going away for a couple of weeks. That's not certain. I don't know when exactly – if it does happen, that is. Please keep it to yourself. What I mean is, please don't mention it to Helen. Actually, we're having a bad time right now. I want you to know in case you talk to her."

"Of course I will. I'm so sorry. If you ever want to talk, please call me. I'm Helen's friend but my loyalty is to you, just as Henry's was. We both knew you, for goodness sake, when we were in college. Such a long time ago. Henry cared deeply about you. I do too, Conrad. I want you to know that. I'm fine and you can just call anytime. I'd love to see you."

"Great," Conrad said, surprised at awakening to the intensity of his feelings for her. He forgot about his grief – for Henry and for himself – for a moment. Virginia could give him moral support during this crisis, that is, not only the disease but the breakdown of his marriage. It could be more than that as well.

He added, "I'll call you."

"I'd like that," Virginia said.

They signed off warmly. Conrad felt his spirits buoyed. As he walked around the house that morning, he felt a distinct bounce in his steps, the first time in a long time. He had resorted to a shuffle these days, as much from discouragement as physical fatigue. Although he hadn't seen Virginia in at least a year, he remembered that she had aged well, preserving her natural beauty, far more than most people approaching sixty. He found visions of her entering his thoughts as the day wore on into evening.

⁂

Conrad's goal on the following Wednesday morning was to visit the refugee center to see if anyone had contacts with Syrian refugees. After that, he wanted to get to the hospital early for his blood draw and talk with Ghadir.

Conrad felt his mental state on an even keel today despite the continuing conflict with Helen. It was a relief to be spared the usual wild swings of emotion. He had not foreseen the deterioration of their marriage. He must have been oblivious to warning signs. He had kept at bay intrusive thoughts about his plight so far today. He worked at convincing himself that human lives exist, in reality, on a continuum, without distinct segments, flowing in a seamless river of time. Clinging to a theory that life was a process without measurable segments of months and years made it less painful for him to contemplate the likely ending of his life in middle age.

He argued to himself that all humans emerge as conscious beings into the continuum. They move through life, changing physically in the process, until they exit. He thought of the simplistic analogy of an airport people-mover. Conrad mused that we know neither where we came from nor where we are going. It is best if we don't know when that final exit will occur. If we happen to find out with some degree of certainty, as he had found out, we lose the capacity to ignore the certainty from that point on. Today he felt normal whether he was or not. He determined not to think about what happened *after life*.

At the refugee center, Conrad searched out Alec Fernandez, the director of the Center. Alec had been a volunteer and now was the only paid employee besides Sylvia. He had once worked for the State Department in Syria and had closely followed the Syrian civil war since the beginning, even making a few trips there. Born in Lebanon of Latino parents, he had travelled widely throughout NOME, the favored acronym for North Africa – Middle East. He knew enough to have an overview of the entire refugee camp network, if one could call it that, for IDPs, that is, internally displaced persons, the term used for Syrian citizens as well as Palestinian refugees in Syria, those who were homeless in Syria.

"There are close to two million IDPs at all times in Syria," Alec said. "These are people who have lost their homes, in addition to refugees who fled to Syria from Palestine. Some of them have moved to other countries, especially Jordan, Lebanon and Turkey. Of those, more than half a million are Palestinians who were in Syria as refugees prior to the civil war. There are lots of refugee camps mainly down the Western part of Syria. Some are populated mainly by Palestinian refugees, called PRS, Palestinian Refugees from Syria, when they try to leave Syria. Others are mainly for Syrian citizens. Some have both Syrians and Palestinians living in them."

"I suppose," Conrad said, "that would make locating any particular individuals very difficult. Is there any central record of who all these people are or where they came from?"

"Not really," Alec said. "Some camps are more organized than others. Some have registries of sorts. Others are completely unorganized. A lot of them have been attacked, especially the Palestinian camps. There has been a lot of destruction. People move frequently, especially from the ones that have suffered attacks during the war. They don't leave forwarding addresses."

"Suppose I wanted to find a family who originally lived in Aleppo. Assume they lost their home because of bombing or invasion of the area by DAESH or the government and its allies. Assume they were trying to get their children to the safest possible place by heading south rather than to Turkey. Where would they go?"

"There are quite a few camps as you move south from Aleppo," Alec said. "One that's well known is Atimah in Idlib. That area was attacked at some point after 2013, though, so many people moved south toward Horns and Hamah. There are some Palestinian camps, some Syrian, and some mixed in those regions. But there have been attacks throughout the region."

"Is it likely that they would keep moving south toward Lebanon and Jordan," asked Conrad, "until they could find a safe place? Assume that one parent is Syrian and the other, Palestinian. Would they be welcome in the camps?"

"Probably so," Alec said. "They'd be on the move south, most likely toward Jordan, which is far safer than Lebanon and typically more welcoming, especially for Syrian citizens and for Palestinians. But even Jordan has imposed serious restrictions on both recently. Jordan is not a wealthy country and it's overwhelmed with refugees now."

"I hear bad things about camps in the Damascus area, especially Yarmouk," Conrad said. "It used to house a large number of both Palestinians and Syrians, right?"

"Yes, it was well settled, mostly by Palestinians," Alec replied. "But then both sides – I should say *all sides* because it isn't bilateral – in the war started attacking it for different reasons. ISIS attacked it and took over most of it. The Assad forces attacked ISIS there. It became a living hell. Everyone who could leave did. It isn't far from safe passage to Jordan though. Does this family have Syrian passports or Palestinian? Jordanian?"

"The husband has a Syrian passport. The wife is Palestinian. She's not likely to have one. That could be a problem, I suppose," Conrad said.

"Yes, I think so," Alec said. "Most of the refugees don't have proper papers. The ones who do have the best chance. Maybe Lebanon would be a better goal for them. I'm not sure."

"Anywhere is better than Aleppo," Sylvia interjected. Conrad had not realized she was in a position to overhear the conversation. "It's horrible there, just horrible," she went on. "We had some people come through last week from Aleppo by means of a northern route. They didn't stay here in Connecticut though. They have relatives in New York City."

"That's right," Alec said. "We could probably locate them if you need to talk to them."

"Thanks," Conrad said. "We hope to intercept these four people before they reach either the Jordan or Lebanon border. We can figure out how to escape Syria then. First things first. Do you have any idea where someone might start to try and find them?" Conrad asked. "By the way, in moving south toward Jordan, let's say, how do people usually travel?"

"Most people start off with cars or trucks if they're reasonably well off. A lot of bad things happen – breakdowns, thefts, damage. The roads are terrible in some places because of the bombing and the IEDs. I just thought of the name of a camp near Aleppo, where they might have gone, at least in the beginning. It's a logical place for them to have gone, anyway," Alec said. "It's called EinAl-Tal camp. It's only twelve kilometers from Aleppo. Quite a few Palestinian refugees were housed there. I would look for camps that have both Palestinians and Syrians, since the couple has mixed nationalities. They might feel most welcome there. Maybe you could start there asking about them and then work your way south. You should know, though, that while twenty percent of Syrians in Jordan live in camps, eighty percent live in urban areas. Some Syrians are lucky. They have relatives in Jordan so they're not even considered refugees. They just move in with their relatives. Those Syrians would cross at Daraa and perhaps stay at a camp before locating and joining their relatives. But let's not get ahead of ourselves. Is it possible that this family has Jordanian relatives?"

"I have no idea," Conrad said. "It seems like trying to find a needle in a haystack in whatever country, without any central record system."

"Afraid so," Alec said. "But there are usually informal networks in camps where people from the same towns seem to find each other. The grapevine is alive with information. Some people stand out and others don't. Some try to make contacts within the camp but others try not to call attention to themselves."

"I think these people might have tried to network," Conrad said, "and certainly would have started with a car or truck. They were fairly well off, comparatively speaking, that is, before the civil war. The father is a physician. People from Aleppo might know of him."

"My guess," Alec said, "is that they'd head for Jordan and they'd be looking for safe places along the way. They might stop and stay a while if they find one. If he's a physician, he might stay in order to take care of people. How about his wife? Is she a doctor too?"

"I think she's a nurse," Conrad replied. "Do you know of any contacts in any of the camps? I suppose most people have cell-phones, right? "

"Yes, but as you can imagine, service is not dependable, with all the destruction," Alec said. "The whole country is a war zone. Tons of damage. I'll do some checking and keep in touch with you. Let me know what you find out."

As Conrad drove home, he realized that Virginia had been on his mind most of the day.

※

At the thirteen-week stage of Conrad's treatment, his response to the targeted drug was so strong that Dr. Ulianofsky wanted to publish an article proclaiming success. Ulianofsky had an assistant summon Conrad in to discuss it.

"You're a pharmaceutical phenomenon," Ulianofsky said. "With all the extra mutations you have – negative mutations – by rights, this drug shouldn't work at all. I want to get a case report out there telling doctors to use Jaktinib for your disease."

"No, no," Conrad replied with urgency. "It's too soon. That would make me really nervous. Please, give it more time. You said yourself that duration of response is the key factor. It feels like a recipe for disaster, a set-up where I end up taking a fall. It's bound to stop being effective at some point. Let's see what happens in six or eight months. I might feel more comfortable if the response lasts that long. It isn't going to do a thing for me. Incidentally, why wasn't I prescribed this drug in the first place?"

Ulianofsky ignored the question and bullied him for a full hour on the issue. "You'd be doing a service to other patients and other doctors. They should know to try Jaktinib even with the other mutations. How can you refuse? How can you be so selfish? Don't you care about other patients?"

The insinuation offended Conrad. "No! Not now. And don't lecture me about being selfish. You're the selfish one. You just care about yourself. It's all about your career. I'm not going to sacrifice myself for your ego."

"If you want my cooperation, you'd better think about this," Ulianofsky said threateningly. "Why should I go out on a limb for you? Why should I take a risk with treatments if you won't coop-erate? Look, I actually don't need your consent to publish this. I wouldn't identify you by name. I just thought it would be decent of me to alert you."

"Decent? You want me to be grateful to you for asking me? No. And despite what you say about not identifying me, I bet you will be saying enough about me that others would know ex-actly who I was."

"Yes, to some extent. I recommend that you think about this before you…."

Before Ulianofsky could finish his sentence, Conrad stood and walked briskly out of the small consultation room and down the narrow hallway lined with windows overlooking the mental health center. Then, suddenly, he thought better of it and went back to the room. The doctor was gone. The door from the in-ner office area opened and a resident whom Conrad had not seen before entered with a scowl on his face.

"I heard you walked out on the chief," the resident lectured him. "Big mistake. If you want his cooperation, you'd better be willing to cooperate. You're doing a disservice to the medical pro-fession and to all patients too. You can leave now. I was told to come back and tell you to make your next appointment." As he opened the door, he added with a sly grin, reflecting amusement at what had happened, "You sure ticked off the big man."

"I'm not being selfish here," Conrad called after him. "It's just premature, too soon to be touting success. It's not going to keep working like this. There's nothing funny about it, by the way. You're not fit to be a doctor."

The resident shrugged, mouthing a profanity, and left without another word, closing the door abruptly behind him.

Conrad sat down for a few minutes, upset at the conflict. He wondered when he could switch doctors or at least see Dr. Bi-tar some of the time. Bitar was smart, personable, and far more reasonable than Ulianofsky. Everybody wanted to have his medi-cal care. He was modest and slow to take offense when a patient challenged him. Why had he been so unlucky as to draw the Count, Ulianofsky, with his supreme arrogance? He was the chief of the hematology group but that didn't entitle him to be a bully.

Conrad determined to look into that. He was not optimistic he'd be allowed to switch. It would be a blow to the ego of the department head but it certainly made sense.

Conrad's skepticism about the continued effectiveness of the drug was well-taken. In three weeks, the white blood count began rising until it had reached 30,000, roughly triple the high normal count. The drug had lost some control, just as he had feared. The platelets and hemoglobin counts remained strong so the doctors made no change. With that slippage happening, waiting for the blood test result each week was a heart-thumping exercise in exquisite anxiety.

The CBC during the following week was even more disappointing. As Conrad waited in the solarium for the printed result, he wondered whether the count would show a drop toward the normal range. The nurse came into the solarium, revealing nothing in her expression about the result despite Conrad's careful searching of her face for the slightest hint.

"It went up a little," she said, in an even tone. "Not too much. Just five points, five thousand, that is."

Conrad's heart sank and his disappointment must have been written over his face. "Oh, damn. It went up. I didn't expect that. I hoped it would settle where it was, not go up again."

"Not to worry. That's not much. We knew it wouldn't keep dropping."

Conrad shrugged, choked up and unable to answer, and took the paper. He stood and gathered up his things, walking past the nurse toward the door. She called after him. "I think it might drop next week. See you next week. The doctor said no change in treatment plan." He nodded that he had heard.

❧

Conrad regressed to the poor sleeping that had plagued him for weeks leading up to the run of favorable test results. After waking up in the middle of the night, he was unable to return to sleep. He'd lie awake for hours worrying about the white count rebounding. Once awake, the windmills of his mind were spinning endlessly as they circled in on whatever problem was troubling him most.

He and Helen coexisted in the house, barely tolerating each other and rarely communicating. They were two people living separate lives, passing through the same space and time without connecting. Conrad asked himself time and again, How had she turned out to be so deceitful, so treacherous? Had all their years of marriage meant nothing? How had he misjudged her so badly? He had been no great bargain all these years but she had seemed to care for him. He would have it out with her but he was too tired most of the time, too preoccupied with his illness, and too resigned to an early death, which made the relationship matter less.

Helen's mother came by one day while Conrad was home alone. She was surprised that Helen was not home and seemed concerned about his appearance. When Conrad told her about the estrangement, she was shocked. "What happened? Did you have a fight? George and I always fought but we always made up too. That was the fun part," she added with a silly grin and a knowing look, which Conrad found inappropriate.

"No. There are no fights," Conrad said, angered by her silly references to her own happy marriage. "It's like she isn't here anymore. Her head – and heart – are somewhere else. I think she wishes I'd die quickly. But you know, she is disloyal to me again. It isn't the first time."

"I can't believe that," she said, recoiling in disbelief. "I won't hear it. That's not true, Conrad. She isn't like that. Don't say that again." She walked away quickly into another room and shortly made excuses why she had to leave sooner than expected. She paid no more social visits to Conrad.

On the following Friday, the first one after his appointments were changed to Fridays, Conrad drove to the hospital clinic and took the elevator to the seventh floor of the leukemia wing. He was anxious and depressed, two conflicting emotions. At the beginning of doctors' visits, the nurse doing the vitals and screening asked in the litany of questions, "Do you have anxiety or depression?"

Conrad thought that was a strange question to ask a terminal cancer patient. Sometimes he said simply, "No," but at other times he'd say flippantly, "Of course I do. Are you crazy? I'm dying of cancer. Do you think I'm a robot or something?" That usually stunned the questioner into momentary silence. It was followed by a question in a measured monotone, dripping with fake concern. "Do you want to talk to a social worker?" Conrad's answer was always, "Absolutely not." The next question on this occasion was: "Do you have a safe place to live?" Conrad spit out, "Safe but miserable."

The nurse left the room and returned with a social worker, a somber, patronizing woman, who launched into a half hour of deadly serious, but inappropriate, questions despite Conrad's repeated protest, "It was just a joke." He avoided playful answers in the future regardless of the ironic nature of the interrogation and his impulse to unsettle some staff members.

"You're quiet today," the nurse observed. "How are you feeling, Conrad? You seem to have less energy today."

"I'm worried," he said. He spoke so quietly that she had to ask him to repeat it. "I get so depressed when my white count goes up. I'm afraid of the worst, the predictions that every doctor has made. I feel like I'm halfway into the grave."

"Don't talk that way. You have to stay positive. Keep your immune system strong."

"But this is all about my *immune system*!" he retorted. That's where the cancer is. How do I strengthen an immune system that is trying to kill me? Besides, I read that these strengthened immune systems are turning on their hosts, something the researchers didn't count on." Conrad failed to suppress a distinct laugh at his own black humor.

When the result came in, the nurse delivered another discouraging result. "It's up just a little more, ten thousand points, but that isn't so much. Just a little more than the margin of error. Anyway, the blood counts vary from hour to hour. It's nothing. But don't worry. The doctor says we need to see more results before we can see what's happening. Keep your spirits up."

That was more than Conrad could manage to do. To add to his gloom, Ghadir and Ayah did not appear at the solarium on the next day Conrad went for a lab test. He had expected them to be there. No explanation. He was worried. Was something wrong? Had they left for some unexplained reason? Were they not coming back? He emailed Ghadir when he got home but, by bedtime, no response had come in. That night was the worst in months. It took all his will power to hold himself from slipping into despair. He recalled one of Jacques' prayers, the one he used when flight turbulence unnerved him. Conrad repeated the prayer over and over. "Oh Jesus Christ, son of God. Have mercy on me, a miserable sinner."

He dropped off to a deep, satisfying sleep.

❧

The next two blood draws produced more increases in the white cell count. The count was now up to 50,000, nearly five times the high-normal reading. Most of the gains made by his targeted medication were wiped out. Had the drug run its course, as Conrad had feared?

Conrad was still haunted by the ominous prediction of a scientist who was the principal researcher for a study of his originally-diagnosed disease. In a no-holds-barred conversation, Dr. Carla Rothman had said in brutally frank language that the drug would probably give him a good response for a few months, allowing him to look healthy and feel well. At some point, without warning, the successful response would disintegrate like a meteor burning up in the earth's atmosphere. His white cell count would skyrocket, his organs would swell to massive size, and he would experience a rapid descent, ending in a crash. At that point, any possibility of a bone marrow transplant would be out of the question.

The disease would then be in its acute form. He would experience a parade of secondary consequences marching through his body, "one after another." Sooner or later, he would be blindsided. His death would finally result from an out-of-control infection or an organ failure or, beauty of beauties, a brain hemorrhage. He would be unlikely to survive for longer than the median survival period for the disease, twenty-three months from diagnosis. In fact, Rothman assured him he would die far sooner than the median.

Although he had sought her opinion and assured her that he could handle a candid assessment, her words had devastated

Conrad. Even thinking about Rothman's apocalyptic predictions now sent him spiraling into depression. He was acutely aware that cancer specialists readily make predictions of how long patients will live. In doing so, they attribute base line status to certain numbers acquired from clinical trials and case studies. Dr. Rothman's prediction of survival became his negative base line. Along the treatment path, other case studies of particular drugs had become positive base lines. Although patients inevitably engage in these personal predictions, they hardly ever prove to be true.

For the next two days he stopped whatever he was doing when he felt the panicky, hopeless feeling welling up inside him, threatening to drown him in grief – grief for his own inevitable demise. At those moments he prayed in desperation that the medication would start working again.

"Oh, God," he prayed, "Oh Jesus and the Holy Spirit," he added, covering all his bases, "please give me more time on this sweet earth. Please, in your mercy, give me a few more years - my life expectancy if you will - in your mercy. But if you can let me live to my nineties, that would be best, in your mercy of course."

Conrad admitted to himself, with amusement, that he feared that if God were a literalist, he might get only what he asked for. A few more months or years weren't enough. His life expectancy, nearly fifteen years, would be ideal. So he prayed carefully, crossing each T and dotting each I, in case God delivered not an hour more than what was asked. He recognized the absurdity of this chicanery. Who was kidding whom? Could God really be a literalist? Wouldn't God understand what he meant without the detail? But then why take chances, he thought. He couldn't picture God with a sense of humor. His thought process made him laugh out loud.

His local doctors weren't ready to give up but all the hope they could promise consisted of cycling in well-known drugs that might have short bursts of effectiveness before they too burned up in the combustible atmosphere of his body.

Early in the disease process Conrad had consulted a nationwide expert in myeloproliferative disorders. The recommendation of Dr. Leopold Podolsky came from a friend who ran the Middle East refugee center in New York City, in the upper East side.

Conrad made an appointment to see Podolsky at the Stone-Kimberly Cancer Center, where he was based. The trip was uneventful but mildly encouraging. Leopold Podolsky was from Czechoslovakia, a big man, friendly, cheerful, and exuding confidence. He made Conrad feel as though he had nothing to fear but his own doubt and pessimism.

Podolsky was less concerned about the course of the disease than Conrad's local doctors. He had prescribed the targeted drug, Jaktinib, many times in various types of myelofibrosis and was not afraid to mix and cycle in other drugs, in hopes not only of boosting its performance but sometimes giving it restored potency in a second round. Conrad determined it could be useful to get Podolsky's views on critical decisions in the future. He'd let his local doctors carry on but Podolsky would be a good resource and eventually a last resort when the future looked its bleakest.

After all, he was chief of proliferative leukemias at the top cancer center in the country, if not the entire world. "Relax," Podolsky said as Conrad was leaving. "Leave the worrying to us. I know your doctors. I see them at medical conferences. We get along. Call me anytime. Email? Sure. Anytime."

As Conrad was leaving, the doctor gave him a hearty clap on the back, gentle but powerful enough to propel him out the door and halfway down the hall. Podolsky's optimism remained with Conrad throughout his travel back to where he was staying. His mood remained cheerful throughout the grueling trip back in the noisy, crowded Metro-North train, complete with a leaky window that let in a spray of rain during two hours of drenching rain.

It was fine, Conrad thought, that Podolsky was upbeat and chose to phrase his observations in euphemistic language. But another four weeks of rising white cells propelled Conrad into a tailspin. Even reaching for Podolsky's lifeline did not reassure him. He made an appointment with Podolsky and explained what was happening. "Let's not jump to conclusions," the doctor's voice boomed. "It's true that the drug is not working well enough on its own to keep the white count down but it's too soon to say it has failed. Jaktinib is not known to keep white counts down in myelofibrosis, the disease that we use it for. The real test is whether the spleen and liver enlarge, whether you get night sweats and extreme fatigue. A rising white count is not alarming on its own. It doesn't signify disease progression. With fibrosis, we mix in Hydroxyurea to bring the white count down."

"You say it hasn't failed," Conrad said, imitating the doctor's calm, even tone, "but it isn't succeeding either. You're trying to pacify me. That's a trick. It is the beginning of the end. All this bullshit is what cancer patients go through. Promise this, promise that. But you think you're doing great if you screw around with the meds and keep me alive for six months. Tell me the truth. Don't bullshit me. The hope is gone that Jaktinib will keep me alive for years. Sorry, I don't mean to be rude but let's be honest."

"I can't say that," Podolsky said. "It's too early. Not to worry. There are too few cases with your disease, CNL. Don't give up. I'm not making any promises I can't keep. There's no reason why Hydrea won't go on with the Jaktinib for a year or more. Let's see what it looks like in two months, okay? Keep your spirits up."

"What good is that," Conrad said abruptly. He excused himself to go into the staff area. A conversation took place in the background while Conrad waited. Eventually, a resident came into the room, stammering something about having the secretary get in touch about the next appointment in the city. Conrad felt chagrined at his own lack of control. It seemed that nearly every conversation ended with his rudeness and anger. He had lost his grip. One noticeable change that he detected was loss of resilience. He was so brittle that he could lose his temper in an instant of frustration or irritation. His temper went over the top without a moment to rein it in. He had been like that as a child but he had learned to control it. Now it seemed that the veneer of civility and reason had worn thin. He had no reserve left. He felt like smashing anything within his reach. Sometimes he carried it out.

"Doctor," he said politely to the resident, catching her by surprise, "would you please arrange with my local doctors for me to have a complete set of my medications – enough for two weeks – with instructions? I'll be going away in September for two weeks to the Middle East. It will be remote and I won't be able to obtain these meds or replace them. So I need a two-week supply plus a backup. Can you work with the local doctors to arrange this?"

"Yes, of course," she said, relieved at the change in Conrad's tone of voice. "I'm sure the doctor will order that supply for you. We'll give you instructions too in case something goes wrong. I'll get contact information there if you tell me where you'll be. We're in touch often with Dr. Ulianofsky."

"I'll do that as soon as I know," Conrad said as calmly as he could manage.

❧

After leaving the hospital, Conrad decided to walk to Grand Central rather than taking a cab. He was in no hurry to get back to Connecticut. He walked down First Avenue for a while before crossing over to Lexington, then to Madison Avenue. It was good to be outside in the fresh air and in the midst of crowds. He belonged to humanity after all. He enjoyed making his way on the busy New York sidewalk with the flow of pedestrian traffic and against it, cutting this way and that, as though he were negotiating white water rapids. The ebb and flow of human beings of all ages, sizes and races was energizing and equalizing in some satisfying way.

Some professional men and women, well-dressed, carrying briefcases, in a hurry, carried themselves with an air of importance. Tourists strolled along, chatting happily and lingering at store windows that caught their fancy. Others stood chatting with people they knew. The vast majority of the people looked ordinary, revealing no particular identity or claim to being special. Many were poor, some panhandling along the sidewalk, in myriad sizes, shades and disabilities. Rich and poor walked side by side in unrelated missions and with occasional smiles, stares, nods or greetings. The movement – the flow of the crowd – seemed to offer a sense of purpose and meaning to every participant, aware or not. The dynamic of the activity and the common humanity temporarily suspended life's problems, if only for a few minutes. Conrad felt a keen sense of belonging to the throng, this endless stream of common humanity, struggling to live, to work, to enjoy the simple pleasures of life, and some like himself, simply trying to survive. He enjoyed the brief respite from his problems. He felt a kind of intimacy with the crowd. His problems were mysteriously shared by his fellow humans.

Conrad often felt uneasy in a crowd but today he appreciated the energy that surrounded him. He soaked it up. It absorbed him, buoyed him, made him feel alive, a state of mind that he no longer took for granted. He was in a happier frame of mind by the time he reached Grand Central. He ended up boarding with minutes to spare, as usual. He even enjoyed dodging and weaving through the crowd and the last-minute sprint down the platform to join the dozens of people hurtling toward their cars of choice. The train was crowded on this Friday afternoon before a long weekend. He wanted to read the novel he had brought along but the clutter of conversations made it difficult to concentrate. Again, he was glad for the company and did not recoil from the crowd or the noise. He listened in on several conversations, feeling amused instead of annoyed with the casual exchanges.

A young couple, apparently just friends but trying too hard to be appealing to each other, sat across the aisle and chattered constantly in their strange version of contemporary campus jargon. It was incessant, repetitive and without substance, words and phrases strung together in a disjointed way – or so it seemed to Conrad, although the meaning of the *code* was clear to them. Each sentence celebrated the buzzwords of the college and high school generation. "Awesome" and "chill" punctuated many sentence fragments. They spent the whole two hours saying nothing, it seemed to Conrad. He could barely stand to hear that noise because it was one level too loud for comfort. How could they stand each other? How could they stand themselves? Finally, they seemed to wear each other out and fell into silence for the second half of the trip. Then he realized that he had been fascinated by their interaction. He so rarely paid attention to the detail of everyday living – his own and that of others. It was a joyful luxury to take the time and appreciate it. He felt badly for being so critical of them now that they were silent – as though he was responsible for muzzling them.

When Conrad reached home, the house was empty. There was no trace of Helen and no messages from her. He went to bed and locked up at 10 p.m., assuming that she had found someone else's bed, probably that idiot, Bernard. That was fine with him. The next morning, he awoke so fatigued that he felt like staying in bed. It was hard to tell where emotional fatigue – depression – ended and physical fatigue began. No question, his emotional state of mind trumped his physical. What did it matter? He felt like crying from time to time after he got up. He didn't give in but did not struggle against the temptation to indulge briefly in his grief and an oppressive hopelessness that made it difficult to breathe. Oh yes, he had to remember to breathe, as a tiny gasp emitted from his lungs reminded him.

That night Conrad had one of his frightening nightmares. He was leaving a hospital in the winter dressed only in a flimsy johnny gown. On the way out of the hospital, he had to traverse the first-floor corridor past the urgent care area. It was populated by dying patients with green complexions, moaning loudly, calling out to him. It looked like a scene from a refugee camp infirmary or perhaps from hell itself. He took in dozens of people slumped on hospital beds, half-naked and not caring who saw them or what kind of a picture they presented to the world. He shuddered and hurried toward the exit as quickly as possible. When he reached the main hospital door, he found it locked. No one was there to help, as the army of sick and dying patients came after him, shrieking and moaning. He woke shuddering, weeping and gasping for breath from what seemed to be a scene from a zombie movie, an oddly popular genre of television and cinema.

Several times that night and the next day, Conrad thought of calling Virginia. He finally picked up the phone two days later. It was a hot August Sunday morning. He felt a wave of relief akin to happiness to hear her voice.

"Hey, Virginia, it's Conrad."

"Conrad," she said with enthusiasm, "I'm so glad to hear from you. How are you? I've been thinking about you all the time. I started to get anxious when I didn't hear from you but I know it hasn't been that long."

"Not great. My white cell count is going up and frankly I'm scared. The doctors try to put a positive spin on it but I don't buy that. They're trying anything that might work for a while. It's the same old cancer story – promises and more promises."

"Why don't you come over? It would be good for you to talk about it or, if you don't want to, to just let go of it for a while."

"You mean right now?"

"Sure, why not? It's a short drive. I'll put something together for lunch. Something simple."

"Okay, I will. It'll take me a little time to get ready."

Conrad was excited. He was ready to leave in a half-hour. For the first time in months, he paid attention to the clothes he selected. He felt more alive than he had since receiving his diagnosis. He was barely aware of driving to her house.

As he approached her front door, he felt nervous. He could hear his heart pounding. He was self-conscious about his own appearance, suddenly fearing that his illness had transformed him into a hollowed-out skeleton with a pale green complexion. He felt like a high school student on his first date, a teenager with a face full of acne who had misplaced his tube of Clearasil before an important date. He doubted that Virginia had similar doubts and fears. She'd never lacked self-confidence.

When Virginia opened the door, Conrad was relieved to see that she was as attractive as he remembered. She had aged gracefully and had retained her figure. She was thinner than Conrad remembered. He attributed that to the toll on her physical strength while she took care of Henry during the final months. Her face revealed not only that she was not horrified by his appearance, but that she was pleased by it. He allowed a smile to brighten his face. It was the first time he had smiled in how long? Weeks, months? He'd had no reason to smile since the devastating news last April. It had been months of persistently somber news, punctuated by one siege of discouraging news after another. He had nearly forgotten what it was like to experience a normal day with steady emotions.

"Conrad, come in," Virginia said enthusiastically. She threw her arms around him hugging his body close to hers with a spontaneity that took him by surprise. He felt a cascade of warmth, comfort and love, not to mention excitement – another surprise – fill him and wash over him. This was life, he thought. Life was not over. He responded with slightly more reserve, and they finally stepped away from each other like a well-rehearsed dance. Conrad avoided stumbling despite his overwhelming emotions.

"Virginia," he said, savoring the sound of her name. "It's so good to see you. It's been a long time."

"Too long," she said. "I shouldn't say this but I've longed to see you during the difficult weeks and months that I've had. I had a good life with Henry. I loved him and I miss him. But I've missed what we had – our friendship and more. Those feelings were never in conflict for me. Henry knew that and accepted it. The last two years of the illness took a heavy toll on us but I think we did well. Come on into the kitchen. I haven't been out shopping in a week so I made do with what I had in the house."

They spent the next hour sitting at the kitchen table catching up. Conrad talked about how he felt and what had happened with Helen. Virginia told him about Henry's last year. They felt as though the intervening years had slipped by seamlessly.

"What will you do," she asked, "about Helen? Are you going to get a divorce or just separate or keep living together?"

"I haven't thought much about it," Conrad said. "Until now. It didn't seem to matter. I felt as though, with such limited time left for me, it wasn't worth the trouble. But seeing you, I feel alive, as though I've recaptured something worthwhile. It does matter." He felt a warm flush pulsate through his body, reaching a climax when it reached his face.

Conrad became aware later on that his usual midafternoon fatigue was overtaking him. He knew it was time to leave, difficult as it was. They talked about plans for the next visit and parted with reluctance. It was too soon to think about the future. But he knew he had a future.

※

The week passed by without incident. Conrad went to his university office every day despite moderate fatigue. Virginia was on his mind nearly all the time. They exchanged emails and confirmed plans to go out to dinner on the weekend. He had a distinct sense that the new happiness and hopefulness made his physical symptoms and his anxiety easier to bear. He had a renewed interest in his mental and physical health – exercise, diet, positive outlook, dreaming about the future.

By Wednesday, Conrad was already preoccupied, wondering whether Ghadir and Ayah would be at the clinic on Friday. At lunch on campus with Levi on Wednesday, he urged Levi to accompany him again. Levi resisted until Conrad told him how fatigued he'd been feeling all week. At that, Levi relented.

Conrad called Gaspar to explain, "I've persuaded my friend, Levi, to come with me again. I'm hoping he'll hear more of Ghadir's story. If we go to Jordan or Syria, I'll need Levi's support on the trip because of my disease. He needs to be persuaded that her story is legitimate. Levi's a tough sell. This is what I've been waiting for – a way to spend the rest of my short life doing what I've dreamed of. Do you think we can pull this off?"

"I'm amazed at your determination," Gaspar said with admiration in his voice. After a long pause, he added, "I don't know. This is difficult and dangerous. Are you up for that physically? Is Levi physically able? Ghadir would have to be part of the mission. I'd go myself but I'm not sure I'm up to it. Let's see what happens tomorrow. I'll contact Ghadir. Where shall we meet? Is the garden okay or shall I find a room?"

"I like being outdoors," Conrad said.

On Friday morning Conrad was apprehensive about how Levi would handle this meeting with Ghadir, given his outspoken political views. Levi picked up Conrad and they set out for the hospital early. After the blood draw, they settled outside in the garden. He and Levi sat in the bright sunlight on the long semicircular bench in the far corner. Ghadir and Ayah emerged from the solarium doorway with Gaspar.

"Ghadir," Conrad began, "As you know, Levi is a very good friend. He's been a loyal supporter. He's my main support system now," he said, smiling at Levi, hoping to soften him. "Levi is a former rabbi. He teaches religion and philosophy courses at the university. Levi was raised conservative but he became orthodox. He has strong feelings about issues in the Middle East." Conrad paused to catch his breath and glanced apprehensively at Levi.

"But he promised to be open-minded." Another glance at Levi. "I wanted him to hear your full story."

"I'm very glad to have you with us, Levi," Ghadir said. "I appreciate that we probably have different views about events and issues that have happened in Palestine and Israel over the years." She paused to study Levi's reaction for a moment. "If you have visited Israel or have friends or relatives there, I'm sure our experiences have been worlds apart. Perhaps we have observed the same things from different perspectives."

Levi nodded and managed a slight smile.

"I think you have heard me describe my early life and what brought me to this country. My family was originally from Jerusalem," Ghadir said softly, "but they lived in Ramallah at the time I was born. Conrad has probably told you that we lost our home there and lived in one after the other refugee camps. I came to Massachusetts for graduate study and have been in the U.S. ever since."

"I remember that from the last occasion," Levi said. "I'm anxious to hear more of your story, especially the current problem that you face. I didn't grow up in Israel but I have family members there and, yes, I've visited Israel many times. I admit that I have always viewed the clashes there from the Israeli point of view. What else can I do? That's all I know. I don't think I'm wrong in my perceptions."

"I'm sure we'd both say that the overall situation and the specific events have a very complicated – and controversial – historical background," Ghadir said.

"I hope," Levi said sharply, "that you won't start in about the *occupied territories* business. I object to that characterization. That's just an argument, to call them the occupied territories. I won't listen to the usual political arguments stated as though they were facts."

"Levi," Conrad said, "You'll get a chance to tell your story if you want to. The Palestinian view that Israel occupies portions of its land is as legitimate as the contrary view. You don't have to agree with it."

Levi nodded silently and sat back in his chair. "Okay, I'll hold my peace but I don't agree."

Ghadir remained calm and Conrad was relieved she did not feel the need to respond to Levi's provocation.

"I've had some pretty terrible things happen to my family," Levi said, with a slight flush, almost imperceptible. "There's been a great deal of suffering, mainly at the hands of your people. Look at the violent attacks that go on every week. But, of course, some of the claims made by both sides are hotly disputed, such as the right of the Palestinian people to claim land as their own." He paused. "No more of that now. I'm here to listen and to support Conrad."

"I've had very painful things happen in my family too," said Ghadir. "We share much suffering. I too am open-minded and I believe that most people in both our nations are not responsible for causing suffering to others. Most of us are those who suffer, not those who cause suffering."

"That's true," Levi said, nodding.

"Great," Conrad said, relieved that the meeting had remained peaceful and that no harsh words had marred the chance of what he envisioned as a kind of reconciliation of different beliefs.

"Where shall we start today?" Conrad asked. "You know Ghadir's basic story from our last meeting. We should ask Ghadir if she has any more information about where her brother-in-law is and whether there is new information about Jamil. That's Ayah's brother. Do you know any more?"

"I do," she said with a slight smile. "It isn't all good news but there is some. Since we saw you last, I talked to every person who might know where they are. Mona's sister, who still lives in Ramallah, was the most helpful."

Looking at Levi, she added, "My sister-in-law Mona has always been very close to her wife of my husband's brother, Hamza. Mona and her sister stay in touch on a weekly basis, sometimes more often. Mona has been giving her sister updates frequently, either by email, texting or phone calls, whatever she could manage, as often as possible.

"There was internet service in Aleppo before the bombing intensified. It still works intermittently. Mobile phone service is the same. When all fails, she writes letters and mails them when she can. As you can imagine, postal service has been disrupted too so communication is uncertain from day to day. Mona is trying to keep an account of their lives since the situation became dangerous in Aleppo and her sister is doing her best to create a journal. She had training as a journalist and wrote for a newspaper."

"This is great news," Conrad said. "So her sister is making a record of all the communications?"

"Right. Mona's sister passes it along to her family and tries to write and edit the oral messages so there will be a complete journal account to read someday. It's just luck that I thought of contacting her. I didn't realize they were keeping so current with what is going on. I call, text or email her sister every day. Actually, I originally tried to reach Mona's mother but didn't know she had died a year ago. Fortunately, I found someone at her home who knew what her sister had been doing. We have information up to a few days ago. She'll keep forwarding as she hears more."

"I'm sure we all want to hear the details," Gaspar said, "but what's the bottom line? Are they safe and well?"

"Yes, so far as we know. I received Mona's account of what happened in her own words since departing from Aleppo."

Ghadir sat, holding her tablet, with Ayah looking on. "It's about three or four days out of date now. It takes Mona time to communicate with her sister and then it comes to me after that. Then I translate it."

Dearest Family. Today is Monday, the first of June. I am waiting for Hamza to finish loading our van. We bought the vehicle used about six months ago. Doctors' salaries are low and, with the government under siege, he hasn't gotten paid regularly during the past year.

We spent the last three days packing and loading everything we possibly could from the house — or what remains of it. It has been more than a month now since that horrible day when we returned home and found our house severely damaged by bombing. The whole neighborhood that we live in was a scene of destruction. We learned that a great many civilians had been killed.

There were at least three or four separate bombing attacks that had struck our neighborhood. First, the rebels bombed us because the government had taken control of the eastern portion of Aleppo and had built a large base in a central area. Then, the government forces bombed extensively throughout our part of the city, trying to drive the rebel forces out. In addition, rumor has it that both the Russians and the Americans did bombing runs over selected areas. Our neighborhood is centrally located. It took a severe beating. The news reports speak of collateral damage, which makes it sound insignificant and even justifiable. Nearly half of our house was destroyed but we managed to salvage a sizable portion of our household goods, bedding, food supplies, cooking utensils, and clothes. The worst damage was to the living and dining rooms plus one of the bedrooms. It was a small house but large enough for the four of us.

Jamil has been with us for nearly four months now. His father left him and ordered us to guard him until he returned. Yousef is fighting with DAESH somewhere in Syria. He would not tell us where. He said he would come to get Jamil and that he would make him a soldier for Islam. He said Jamil was excited about that. We know that isn't true. Jamil is terrified at the prospect. We see the effect on him firsthand. Hamza and I were very distressed at the time about Yousef's plans. Yousef has changed so much that we barely recognized him. He seems obsessed with violence. We not did object, of course. We are glad to have Jamil with us and hopeful that Yousef will not return to carry out his plan. Jamil and Karam are like brothers.

We continued living in the house for a while after the damage but, finally, when the weather turned colder, we had to go to a refugee camp. We secured our belongings and began making plans to travel to a safe place to the south, in the Damascus area and then to Lebanon or Jordan, whichever seems best. We expect it will be Jordan because Hamza has contacts in the medical field there.

Hamza was sad to leave his medical practice and I am heartbroken about leaving my nursing position at the hospital. Hamza intends to resume practice when we reach our destination, wherever that may be. Many refugees on the road are sick or injured and need help. Our first priority is to bring the boys to safety outside Syria. Syria is still our country but we do not recognize it now.

It seems likely that the war will go on for years and years unless Assad leaves or is killed. Then some other group will fill the void. We have virtually nothing, not even safety, not even a guarantee of enough food or water or shelter. As a Palestinian refugee before being what I am now, a Syrian refugee, I have lived with danger, violence, and hopelessness all my life. We found new lives together only to see them shattered before our eyes. But we have not surrendered our hope for the future. We will face what we must for the sake of the two boys.

The time we spent in Bab-al-Salameh camp, which is at a very important crossing between Syria and Turkey, was frightening. We lived in a small tent among 17,000 other refugees. Nearly a third were children. Conditions were terrible. There was no security or safety for anyone. The communal toilets were horrible and water was scarce. We were better off than most people because occasionally we could bring supplies from the remains of our house.

We considered going to Turkey but decided it is too dangerous. Rebel forces have been in control of the region near Turkey, at the Bab-al-Salam border crossing, but we don't know what they stand for. We imagine that the government has done the bombing but that is just a guess. That is an area that has seen brutal violence over the years, particularly during conflicts between Syria and Turkey. Life is very bad for the children, who suffer the most and whose futures are in doubt.

While we were at Bab-al-Salameh, we were bombed a number of times and militias drove through the campsite looking for enemy forces. When bombing raids happened, there was no place to go. We just had to pray. We knew we had to get out of the Aleppo area and travel toward safe territory. Hamza was very busy helping injured people and sick people.

Hamza just told me that the car is ready. We hope that we can complete our journey before it breaks down, or runs out of fuel, which is scarce. We are taking extra cans of fuel *but they won't be enough to make it all the way to Damascus. We know there is a danger that the car may be damaged by bombs or explosions or that it may be stolen by rebel groups or government troops. We are vulnerable and there is no way to prevent that.*

It is time for us to leave. We hope to travel through until we can reach Hamah. We will stop to sleep briefly along the way. We expect that there will be military checkpoints along the highway so we will have to travel much of the time on back roads. They have their own dangers but we are afraid to be stopped by DAESH since we have Jamil with us. We know that Yousef will be on the lookout for his son, once he finds out we have left our home.

The distance from Aleppo to Damascus is about 310 kilometers. We estimate that the driving time ordinarily would be five or six hours. If we don't run into unusual problems, we hope to be in Hamah within two or three days. But if we lose our vehicle, it could take us weeks to reach Damascus. We hear from others in the camp that there are some taxis or buses or trains but that many people are simply walking, which we are prepared to do if we must.

We leave now. I will write again as soon as I can. We have mobile phones but no idea of whether they will be of any use. We will call if we can find service. We ask your blessings on us as we begin our journey. May the peace, mercy and blessings of Allah be with you.

When Ghadir stopped reading, no one spoke. Only Levi appeared unmoved by the story.

"I'll break the silence," Levi said. "It's all well and good to go weeping over the plight of these people. But Muslims brought this on themselves. Now you want sympathy. Palestinians caused their own troubles with late-discovered territorial claims, hatred of Jews, and intolerance. I do not weep for these people. All these battles are among Muslims. It's Turks against Syrians against Libyans against Jordanians and everybody against Palestinians. This violence is the scourge of the Middle East. The Middle East will never be stable except through Israeli strength."

Ghadir gasped and Ayah appeared stunned at Levi's stinging words. Tears welled in Ayah's eyes and began to stream down her face.

Conrad was first to address Levi. "Where did that rage come from? Why do you condemn all Arabs? All Palestinians? What did Ghadir and Ayah and their families do to warrant that? What harm have they done? Your remarks are violent. Do you think this is an Arab thing? A Muslim thing? How can you say that? Is this what your Israeli God of war demands of you? I have never heard you speak like this before."

"I suppose that comes across as harsh," Levi said unapologetically. "I don't mean this personally to your friends, Conrad. But you know, I suffered at the hands of these violent people. It was a long time ago now but I relive that moment every day of my life."

"I understand," Conrad said, "but you're not the only one who has suffered losses and it is not just your people who have suffered. Everyone suffers. Your people were once refugees. You should know what that feels like. Do you want to tell the story of what you suffered? It might help if everyone understands the meaning of what you have just said."

"No, not now," Levi said. "It's too long and painful a story. Sometime I will. I was probably too harsh. I can appreciate whatever heartache Ghadir is going through. We share a common humanity after all."

The distress in Ghadir's face faded slightly at hearing this concession. "I understand," she said quietly, "why you feel hatred toward Palestinians if you suffered a personal loss because of some violence. I would like to know what happened but I respect your wish to be silent. I too suffered a deep loss to my family at the hands of the other side in the conflict between Israel and Palestine. I feel every day the pain of that loss. We may have suffered similar losses. I am willing to share mine but this is not the right time. I hope you do not hold your loss against Ayah and me. I do not hold you responsible for what I have suffered."

"I think," Gaspar interjected, "we're reaching toward an understanding. I know what Ghadir went through but I don't know what Levi has experienced. If you ever wish to talk about it, I'll listen. Do we not have a common goal? A child has been taken, kidnapped, by his father, not by anyone else. No one blames this on anyone except the man who has turned against his own people and his own God – and his own flesh and blood. I know Conrad wants to help. But I do worry that you," he said, turning to face Conrad, "are not in good enough health to undertake a mission to do this. If you can manage it and your doctors can prepare you, you will need help. A young woman and a man with a serious disease cannot cope with the conditions that exist in Syria, or even in Lebanon or Jordan. These are dangerous places. How can you manage this?"

"It is my child who is in jeopardy," Ghadir said with determination. "I must do what I can to save Jamil. Ayah has reassured me that she is prepared to manage for a time without me. She will stay with my aunt. Ayah has a vision that we will save her brother. I have finally reached my brother. Although he is with a rebel group that opposes both Assad and DAESH, I do not support his resorting to violence. But it is the way he has chosen. At least, his group opposes the use of any children as soldiers or as suicide bombers. He understands this will pit him against my husband. I believe he would kill Yousef if it came to that, in order to save Jamil. I have no doubt that Yousef would kill Hussein as well. This is a terrible prospect but Jamil's life is at stake."

"I'm prepared and ready," Conrad said with confidence. "I've discussed this with my doctors. They advise me against it but they will supply me with medications to get me through the trip. This is what I want to do with the rest of my life. We do need help. Levi, will you join us?"

"I need to think about that," Levi said, with a troubled look, shaking his head in a way that signaled his ambivalence. "This is not my cause. I've been to the Middle East many times, mostly to Israel. I've also been to Jordan and Lebanon and to what you call the Palestinian territories. On one trip I went to Damascus. I still have relatives in Israel and friends in Jordan. There's quite a bit of commuting between Israel, Aqaba and the Dead Sea. As a Jew and an Israeli citizen, I would be at risk in Syria. But that would not necessarily deter me. I know all of you are taking risks. Give me a few days. I will make contact with a friend in Jordan. He lives not far from Zaatari, one of the large refugee camps."

"My brother may be in the Damascus area," Ghadir said. "I am counting on him to find out where Jamil is now. I'm hopeful I can make contact soon. I have no idea how far Mona and Hamza have gotten or whether they are still travelling by car. We don't even know their destination except Hamah, presumably a camp there, and a camp in the Damascus area after that – before they attempt a border crossing into Jordan. My guess is their ultimate destination will be Jordan, not Lebanon."

"Even though she's married to a Syrian," Conrad said, "my understanding is that Mona does not acquire Syrian citizenship. Her child would but she would not. Once a refugee, always a refugee. Without that citizenship, does she have a chance of entering Lebanon or Jordan?"

"Neither country will be easy for my sister-in-law to enter because she is Palestinian. We are considered undesirable immigrants in some places. Actually, she is a Palestinian refugee in Syria, a PRS. The best I can hope for is that they will find a way to enter Jordan together."

"It is so unfair," Gaspar said, "that Palestinians should be so discriminated against when they are the victims of so many decades of abuse – from occupation, disenfranchisement, then expulsion or confinement. Where's the justice?"

"I can't stay silent when I hear that argument," Levi said, with bitterness again distorting his face in a way that disturbed Conrad. "You talk about occupation and disenfranchisement. But you forget that the Palestinians were nomadic. They made no territorial claims until the Jews, who truly had been persecuted and treated as underclass refugees for centuries, finally got their rightful place in a homeland. They had a claim to that homeland. Then Palestinians woke up to what was happening and decided to make a claim to the land. They have no rightful claim. They are lucky to be treated so well given the destruction they have brought to Israel. They deserve whatever they have and no more."

Ayah moved to her mother's side and hugged her closely, comforting her with her gentle touch and calm voice.

"If those are your true feelings," Conrad said to Levi, "then you are not fit...."

"Wait, please, Conrad, before you continue. Let me speak," Ayah interrupted gently. "I think," she said, looking directly at Levi, "that you do not know what my mother and my family have suffered. We do not know what you have suffered. We must forgive you and you must forgive us. It is not my mother's way to respond with anger as some people do. She believes in peace. Our people and your people want peace but our leaders do not carry out our wishes. They bargain for themselves. We must not fall into hatred or anger. And we must not resort to violence, as some people on both sides do."

Levi was visibly moved by Ayah's words. He began in a conciliatory tone, with direct eye contact. "Child, forgive me. I do not mean to hurt you or your mother with my angry words. I have suffered great losses at the hands of Palestinians, which I will tell you about some time. But I'm sure that your mother and her family have suffered equally. We will hear each other out someday. Perhaps we will understand each other better."

Ayah moved to his side and hugged him, saying, "Thank you." Levi did not resist the gesture.

"Can we plan to exchange information and then meet next week – a week from today?" Gaspar asked. "I will consider going with you."

Conrad felt encouraged but filled with anxiety at the same time. He knew he lacked the physical capacity to deal with conflict, much less survival in conditions of wartime in which a healthy person would struggle to survive. He kept his misgivings to himself. But as he drifted off to sleep later, he thought to himself that, in addition to fighting their main adversaries, diseases, secondary effects, and side effects of medications, patients are engaged in a relentless struggle with their doctors and hospitals, all of whom have their own personal or institutional agendas. Patients are essentially alone with no one to trust completely, no one to rely on.

After resolving to join the expedition to Syria and Jordan, Conrad was pushed beyond the limit of his endurance one night. After a day in New York meeting with Dr. Julia Gerhard, the consulting transplant doctor, he felt encouraged. Gerhard said she recommended postponing any decision on a BMT, the acronym for a transplant, for six months.

"Conrad, I'm amazed at how healthy you look," Gerhard said. "I know you've put up your defenses against further consideration of a stem cell transplant. Given your mindset and your quality of life now, I couldn't justify putting you in suspended animation for a year. Then there's the risk of infection or relapse, not to mention the poor prognosis. Let's defer this for six months. That brings us to March of next year. Schedule an appointment in March. Let's see what things look like."

"That sounds good to me," Conrad said. "You think I can hold my own until then?"

"We can't tell," Gerhard said. "We don't know. But if anything goes wrong, we can be in touch. I see no reason why you can't control the white count with Jaktinib and Hydrea. You haven't shown any blasts yet, which is a good sign. You know what they are?"

"Not sure," Conrad said. "Explain, please."

"I thought you knew everything," Gerhard said, a smile of condescension crossing her face. "When the lab does a manual differential," the doctor said, "that means they look at the slide under a microscope. They're looking for highly immature cells, which we call blasts. They actually look at the size and shape of the white cells. When the marrow is clogging up the blood with blasts, it's a bad sign. You will always find some blasts in the marrow but there should not be many in the bloodstream."

"Good to know," Conrad said.

"Your white count is going up and the hemoglobin is going down a little, but it's not critical yet."

Conrad left feeling hopeful because of Gerhard's optimism. That would bring him to a year from diagnosis and an additional six months from the likely onset of the disease.

That evening Conrad was watching television. Helen was not home. He had no idea where she was or how she spent her days or nights. Although neither of them had said the word "divorce" since their confrontation over her relationship with Bernard, each of them proceeded as if the other didn't exist.

Then, just as Conrad was eating a cookie with chocolate and nuts, he tasted something acrid. Rushing to the bathroom, he stared with horror into the mirror to see fresh red blood gushing out of a tiny incision in his tongue an inch from the tip.

"Oh God," he said aloud. He was frightened. It took him fifteen minutes to find the doctor's on-call service number, all the while trying to stem the gusher that was filling his mouth. Excitedly, he explained the problem to the receptionist, hung up, and waited a half hour for the call-back of the on-duty resident. When the phone rang, the caller was a doctor whose name he had never heard before. She listened and then explained the protocol for stopping a bleeding tongue – pressure, ice, astringents, more pressure. "If that doesn't work," she said in a confident tone, "just go to the ER, that is, the city ER because they'll have more to work with."

"No way," Conrad spat out. "Are you kidding me? Go to the city ER at night?" I'll never be seen again."

"Suit yourself. That's your choice," she said, suddenly bored with the conversation. "Call your doctor or his nurse in the morning if there's still a problem."

Conrad hung up abruptly, muttering a sarcastic, "Thanks a lot."

With pressure, he stemmed the flow, but a few hours later, bleeding resumed. That scenario repeated itself three times during the night. He was exhausted in the morning and felt traumatized, as though he'd been hit by a truck. He staggered through the day, worried about the future. That was silly, he told himself. "This is not the disease problem; it's probably the blood thinner." Later the next day, he went to the satellite ER. He spent nearly the whole day while a young doctor bravely tried one procedure after another with hours of waiting in between. When Conrad left at 5 p.m., the bleeding seemed under partial control, at least enough to get some sleep.

Conrad woke early Saturday morning to discover the bleeding had resumed. His heart sank. After pulling himself together, he made another trip to the emergency room. Finally, after stopping the blood thinner for a whole day, the bleeding tapered off.

At that point, an older, experienced doctor volunteered to tie off the offending vein and suture it. If it worked, he said, it would probably solve the problem. He performed the exquisite surgery on Conrad's tongue in a busy corridor of the main room with Conrad sitting on a cot. It worked.

Despite the ultimate outcome, Conrad left discouraged and anxious about his future wellness and the feasibility of a trip of any kind, much less to a war zone in the Middle East. His determination prevailed. "If it's the last thing I do, that will be fine," he said aloud. "At least I'll die doing what I believe in." He called Levi to tell him what had happened as well as his resolve to overcome the problem. He followed up by calling Virginia.

Virginia urged him to come and spend the following long weekend, Labor Day weekend, with her at the beach cottage that she and Henry had bought and fixed up years earlier, situated in a small village on the Rhode Island coast. "It's a wonderful spot, pure delight," she promised. "We'll have daily swims. The water is still warm enough. I believe salt water will heal you. Come and try it. We - I mean, I - have, a very private spot on the beach and half the cottages are deserted now that school has started. We can stay as long as we want."

"That's so tempting, Virginia," Conrad said. "I've reached my limit of frustration these past few days. I need a break. I'll throw some clothes into a suitcase and come over, say, on Thursday night or Friday morning. What's best for you?"

"Come on Thursday," Virginia said. "We'll make it a five-day weekend at least, longer if you want. Actually, why don't you come on Wednesday and we can get an early start on Thursday morning."

"I'd love to do that," Conrad said. "It will have to be late Wednesday. I'll reschedule my usual Friday labs on Wednesday. I should try and organize a meeting of the group that's going to Jordan and Syria, hopefully. We can't afford to lose momentum."

"I'd like to hear more about that," Virginia said. "I'm not really a worrier but I am concerned that you'd take that on when you're not in good health."

"I'll tell you about it when we're together. Maybe I can get you interested in the trip," Conrad said, laughing.

"Tell me more," Virginia said. "Just come here as soon as you're free on Wednesday. We can relax and leave when we feel like it in the morning."

Conrad was excited about the prospect. He hoped he could reschedule his Friday lab. That was a better day for him but it was not a sure thing. Come to think about it, he wasn't sure why it got changed to Friday from Wednesday. It was probably for Ulianofsky's convenience. He'd see if Ghadir, Levi and Gaspar could meet on Wednesday for an update and, hopefully, make some progress in planning.

A phone call to the scheduler's desk at the cancer hospital bore fruit even on Saturday. He was all set. The scheduler added, "You have an appointment on Friday with Dr. Ulianofsky. Do you want to reschedule that too? He has no more time available until the week after next. He sees patients only on Fridays now. He cut out the Wednesday appointments."

"Aha, that's it then," Conrad said under his breath.

"What did you say?" the scheduler asked.

"Oh nothing," Conrad said, brightening. "I guess I have to. How about switching that to Wednesday," he asked, ignoring the information he just received about Ulianofsky's schedule.

"Oh, I can't do that," she said. "What I just said was that he doesn't see patients on Wednesday any more. He does clinic only on Fridays now. I see that you used to come in on Wednesdays. That's why you got switched to Fridays."

Conrad was excited. Maybe this was his opportunity to get rid of Ulianofsky. If he came up with a story that made Fridays impossible, they'd have to switch him. He'd find out if Dr. Bitar saw patients on Wednesdays. If he did, he should be able to make the switch.

Three more phone calls and he was two-thirds on the way to setting up a meeting on Wednesday afternoon at the clinic. Ghadir and Levi were available. He left a voicemail for Gaspar, whose message said he would be away for the weekend. He remembered now that Gaspar was going off to a retreat center run by a group of Zen Buddhists for a weekend of meditation. Conrad was curious about Gaspar's interest in Zen, given his Roman Catholic background with the Missionaries. Gaspar did believe in nonviolence although he was not strictly a pacifist. The Missionaries, Gaspar had said, spend time ministering to people who have been victimized by family violence as well as to people in hospitals, veteran centers and other institutions. Conrad could see that Buddhism would be appealing to a priest who had taken vows in the Missionaries.

Conrad spent the next three days anticipating, first, the meeting and second, spending Labor Day weekend with Virginia. When Wednesday came around, Levi picked him up and brought him to the hospital. As they waited in the healing garden for Ghadir and Gaspar, who had not returned his call, one of the hematology nurses came out with a message from Ghadir.

"Conrad, I know you're waiting for Ghadir. I have a message. She's with Ayah in her room. Ayah had to be admitted. She came in for her IV chemo and had a bad reaction – a high fever, inability to keep food and liquids down. She's on an IV for that before they proceed with the chemo. Usually she tolerates the chemo amazingly well."

"Oh, I'm so sorry to hear that," Conrad said. "Is she going to be okay? Has this happened before?"

"Yes, it has happened before. It's not that uncommon. Children usually tolerate chemo much better than adults but sometimes they react badly. Our concern is that we need to keep controlling her cancer but we have to curtail the chemo for a short while to let her regain her strength. Ghadir will be down shortly."

Conrad and Levi sat in silence on the long bench, trying to capture the warmth of the sun's rays as they were disappearing behind the tall buildings surrounding the garden.

"Poor kid," said Conrad. "She has an aggressive form of cancer, but she does remarkably well, considering. When I think about having to deal with that as a child, I can't complain about my own condition. It's just so sad when children can't live a normal life and do normal things. It seems so unfair. I wish Gaspar were here so I could ask him why God – why any of his Gods – allow that to happen."

"I know what you mean," Levi said quietly. "I don't understand it either. Maybe we could visit the child briefly. What do you think? Do you want to ask the nurse?"

Conrad looked at Levi quizzically, stunned at his suggestion but all in favor. He went to find the nurse. She called Ghadir in Ayah's room in the Children's Hospital. The answer was positive and, armed with directions, Levi and Conrad set out for the cancer floor of the Children's Hospital, room 510. When they stepped out of the elevator, they were surprised that visitors were allowed to walk around in the midst of the bustling activity of medical providers. "I'm surprised that we can just walk around on this floor. There seems to be a high level of activity. But of course the hospital would want families to have free access to their children all the time. No barriers here. It's great, really."

They found the room without trouble and knocked on the door, which was three quarters open as it was.

"Come in," Ghadir said. "I'm so glad you asked. Ayah is very excited to see you both, despite feeling quite sick. She's having a hard time with this chemo. It's a new drug. The doctors started her on it just two days ago. They thought it could be done as an outpatient but she reacted badly to it so they're keeping her here for a few days. This drug is layered on top of her previous one. The doctors believe in using multiple drugs, after testing, of course. I know she's very uncomfortable but Ayah doesn't complain. Come in and say hello to her."

Conrad and Levi both walked to the bed. Conrad bent over to give her a hug. Levi was more restrained but clearly was moved by the sight of the young girl looking pale and drawn. Ayah brightened at the sight of both men and broke into a warm smile.

"How are you? You look very well," she said to Conrad with more energy than Conrad felt he could muster, himself.

"I'm doing well, Ayah. This must be difficult for you. I'm sorry you have to go through this. But you look as though you're handling it well."

"I know I'll get used to this chemo," Ayah said. "The next cycle will be easier. I know this is good for me so I can bear it. That's what we have to do, right? You know what that means."

Directing her attention to Levi, she said, "I'm so glad you're here too." She smiled with warmth at him. "Did you come for a meeting with my mother?"

"Yes, we are hoping to do that," Levi said. "I am glad to see you. I hope you can go home soon. I think you are a very brave young lady."

"Thank you," she said shyly. "I cannot see anything good come from being gloomy or pessimistic. I try to see the happy side of whatever happens. Everything that happens creates opportunities for good or bad. Everything that happens has been allowed by Allah. How we react is up to us."

"Shall we go to the garden to talk, Conrad? I think we can leave Ayah to sleep for a little while."

"Yamma, please just talk here. I'd like to hear what your plan is."

Ghadir looked over at Conrad, as if to ask what he would like. Conrad said quickly, "Whatever you wish, Ghadir. Either way is fine. Do what's best for yourself and for Ayah."

"I think you should sleep, my dear. We'll just go downstairs for a half-hour. I'll come right back."

Ayah looked disappointed. The three left, with Conrad and Levi saying goodbye.

As they traversed the hallway to the elevator bank, Ghadir said, "We don't have to go all the way to the garden. That involves crossing over into another area of the hospital. Let's just sit and have tea or coffee. I have to talk with Ayah's doctor and then return to the room."

"Are there any new developments?" Conrad asked. "I see that horrible things are happening in Aleppo. The bombing goes on and on. There is very little left to destroy. The Russian and government planes seem to have nothing left to bomb but rubble left from previous raids. It's painful to watch the destruction on television news. Nothing is off limits, not schools or hospitals."

"I'm so glad they got out of Aleppo before the total destruction was underway," Ghadir said. "There will be nothing to return to. I am worried, though, about where they are and what is happening. I'm hoping for news very soon. I think we should continue our plan. Ayah will be able to leave the hospital as soon as her treatment is finished in about two or three days. Her system will settle down during the period when she is not getting the drug, that is, before the next cycle of IV infusion. We should be back by then. It's a week of treatment, then four weeks off."

"If you email me the date of departure and return that you prefer, Ghadir, I'll get your ticket and mine before I go away for a long weekend. I'm assuming that Gaspar will go but he can take care of that himself. Levi, I'm hoping you will decide to go by the next time we get together, after Labor Day weekend. We'll be in touch, right? I'm going to the Rhode Island beach with Virginia tomorrow through Monday or Tuesday. I'll contact you as soon as I return."

Levi nodded approval. "I'm leaning toward going to make sure you come back in one piece, Conrad. I'll let you know by Labor Day."

Conrad smiled approvingly. After saying goodbye, Conrad and Levi headed for the parking lot. Levi inquired, "Do you still need me? I understand Virginia is a nurse. I suppose she'll take care of your medical needs while you're away. Is there anything for me to do?"

"Of course," Conrad said. "This will be a dangerous mission. We will have to deal with militia, possibly including Yousef himself. These are serious soldiers and ruthless ones at that. Anyway, I haven't asked Virginia to commit yet. I'm not sure whether she will choose to go."

"Okay, just wanted to be sure," Levi said. "I don't want to be a fifth wheel."

Conrad was excited but slightly on edge about the prospect of spending so much time with Virginia. The prospect of intimacy and rediscovery of the mutual physical attraction, so long shared but so long dormant, was stimulating and challenging. If this relationship worked out, it could mean some happy months or even years if he survived, instead of a lonely, loveless existence. They would need time to get to know each other again and dispel the cloud of Henry's death after so many years of marriage. The timing had to be right. He wondered whether Virginia would consider coming along on the rescue mission. He was still married to Helen, which posed a complicating factor. No closure there, he thought.

He had to line up next week's meeting with Ghadir and Levi. Medical doubts notwithstanding, Conrad felt compelled to make the trip to Syria. It became his life line, the goal that kept him going, rather than giving up and resigning himself to mere survival. He emailed Ghadir that he was counting on meeting again the following Wednesday. He'd bring Levi to the hospital again if he could and hopefully they could persuade him to join them if she felt comfortable with that, in view of his outspoken views on Palestinians.

That task done, he hurried to pull together what he'd need to stay with Virginia for a long weekend. He had no idea where this would end but he felt more physically alive than he had in months, perhaps years.

When he arrived at her house, he recognized that she was glowing with anticipation as much as he was. After loading their clothes and supplies into her van, they departed for the beach. It was still daylight when they pulled into the driveway of the beach cottage.

Few of the cottages showed signs of life. The row of well-spaced and landscaped cottages had a deserted look despite the fact that it was Labor Day weekend. Virginia's cottage was set back several hundred feet from the wide sandy beach and was situated on the curve of the cove, lending it privacy and spectacular views of the coastline. The natural combination of sea, sky and sand in that harmonious configuration was awe-inspiring. The sight was not only a visual sensation but an audible one, with the waves breaking in a rhythmic musical pattern. Conrad was spellbound by the beauty of the setting.

Only a few people were walking on the beach. No one was in the water. Midway on a rising tide, the waves were beginning to roll in, bubbling with aerated foam, reaching farther and farther up the wide sandy beach and sparkling in the light of the descending sun. The sky was streaked with clouds and the reddish orange glow of sunset illuminated the sky. After bringing their belongings into the cottage, they changed quickly into bathing suits and hurried out to the beach, walking barefoot for a mile or so down the beach. They ventured out knee-deep into the surf, feeling the cool water on their legs. They reveled in the sensation of being jostled and rocked by the surf, which was gaining power as the tide continued to rise.

He took Virginia's hand to help steady her when they ventured waist-deep into the water. They continued to hold hands as they walked in the rising surf back to the cottage. It seemed as natural and magical as when they were college students dating. Conrad was amazed at the buoyancy of his mood, a vast change from his anxiety and gloom just twelve hours ago. Suddenly, he felt a lightness of being that he had rarely experienced in life. The grim realities that stalked him disappeared carelessly in the joy of the fresh sea air, the openness of the sky, the life-giving force of the salt water, and the thrilling newly-discovered intimacy.

Delighting in being soaked to their skin by the waves by the time they approached the cottage, they dashed into the oncoming surf again, holding hands, and falling into the waves, then let their bodies be washed to shore, tumbling on the sand as they reached shallow water. They regained their footing, laughing and eager for another breathless dash into the rolling and cresting surf. Finally, when they had enough, they collapsed on the sand together, thrilling in the abundance of sensation body to body, before walking up to the cottage in the magical twilight.

Conrad felt carefree for the first time in many months. Virginia was radiant.

❧

While Conrad explored the cottage and then sat on the front porch, overlooking the ocean, Virginia prepared light food and drinks. They talked for more than an hour before going inside for the night. Conrad felt uncertain how to raise the subject of the sleeping arrangement. He decided to leave it to her. He had purposely left his overnight bag downstairs.

"Conrad," she had without evident discomfort, "this is a little delicate but we have to decide where to sleep. I'm open to anything but I don't know what you would be comfortable with. It feels so good to be together again after so long. I can hardly believe we're here. I've had a little time to adjust to Henry's death and I'm not hung up on it. I don't mean to be pushy about it because I respect you if you're not ready to be ... well ... to share a bedroom which is pretty intimate by itself, regardless of … other implications." She laughed outright, causing Conrad to join her in releasing his nervous tension through laughter. The two of them were aware that they were a unique couple – two adults, lovers in their youth, coming together again after a long hiatus. Language was not adequate to express their complex emotions.

"I'm very comfortable with this," Conrad began. "I like the idea of sharing a bedroom with you. I'd say I'd be honored if it didn't sound so darn awkward. I feel as though you've lifted a load of anxiety and gloom off my back. I haven't been so happy in a long time."

They were standing close to each other; their bodies were in full contact. Virginia looked straight into his eyes and reached out her hand to grasp his. He took it and reached forward to give her a hug. They fell into an embrace and kiss that went far beyond a polite, warm gesture. They kissed again.

"This is not at all like old times," Conrad said. "This is brand new. I feel as though I have a life, a new life. I keep saying that I live for the moment now, with my illness, and now I want this moment to go on indefinitely."

She nodded and kissed him again deeply. "I feel the same way. Let's go upstairs. It's been a long day and we have many ahead of us here and, well, let's take it a day at a time."

"Sounds good to me," Conrad said softly.

They went upstairs and settled in the master bedroom, leaving their suitcases in the other bedrooms. They changed into nightclothes. No need to rush matters. In bed, they embraced again and fell asleep holding each other. Conrad could taste the sweetness of the moment. He was confident that Virginia shared that feeling. The cares of the world seemed as distant as the stars twinkling in the dark night sky.

※

Conrad was accustomed to waking before dawn to a feeling of mental and spiritual depression. For the first few months after learning his diagnosis, he would wake frequently during the night as well, to a sinking feeling of imminent doom. It was as though dense fog hovered over his being, preventing any light or fresh air to penetrate, draining him of energy and hope. He taught himself over time to regain control over his mind, training it to resist surrendering to pessimism.

During the past few months, after learning to keep a firm hold on his mind during the night, he would still wake in the morning with a sense of futility. On some days, it took effort to rise and go about routine chores, even making coffee, checking his email, making conversation, getting the newspaper. Three or four cups of coffee would ease him out of the mood. Occasionally, he would feel a wave of determination and hope. He would go about his day, immersing himself in one task after another, forgetting about the fate that lay in store for him.

On this morning, with Virginia by his side, it took only a short time for Conrad to orient himself to where he was. The elation, the peace, and the joy that he had felt the night before was not present at the precise moment he awoke. Within moments, gloom had dissipated like morning mist rising over the gentle surf. He heard Virginia's peaceful, musical breathing. He raised himself on an elbow so he could enjoy the sight of her face. He lay back on the pillow to enjoy the sensation, content to relax the need for mental control. He could feel his body reveling in the lightness of being that he had dreamt of enjoying. If he wasn't careful, he thought he might float away in ecstasy. He felt connected, not only to the earthly life, but to the ineffable.

He lay still for another twenty minutes, drifting off to sleep again briefly, before slipping out of bed quietly, to avoid disturbing Virginia. He managed to fold the covers back without waking her. Before he rose, he saw her hand outstretched toward his. He smiled and squeezed it gently before rising. She stirred and returned the smile, her eyes still closed. He held the grip and her gaze for a few minutes. He walked out through the cottage to the porch. He took a seat on the wicker loveseat and gazed at the softly rolling ocean at low tide, glistening in the sunlight. He glanced at his watch, noting that it was a quarter to seven. He felt happiness well up inside him, recognizing at once newfound hope for the future tempered by the realization that he could not predict anything, even a few weeks from now.

As he sat there, he contemplated his decision to assemble the group to travel to Jordan and Syria. The determination that had led to that resolve had arisen from his need to accomplish something meaningful before his life ended. His decision had been reinforced by the message of courage and hope received after Jacques' death. He had returned time and again to examine that message, the vision that he called the first miracle.

He now felt a higher level of spiritual understanding and sensed a second miracle. He felt confident as he bathed in the intensifying light that brightened the sky and illuminated the gentle ocean waves.

Conrad pondered again the specific meaning of the first message. *Have courage. Do not lose hope.* Did it refer to courage to fight his illness, hope that he could subdue or conquer it? Or did it refer to courage to face death and hope of life thereafter? They were powerful words. He had not been able to ascribe any single meaning but it did not detract from the significance of the message.

He sensed the meaning more clearly now. Perhaps it was the courage to face *whatever had to be faced,* and hope instilled by trust. He now believed that anything was possible. He now heard himself *summoned* to carry out the mission to find Jamil, regardless of what it entailed and what it would mean for his health and longevity.

If the first message he had received was the *Word,* the second must be spiritual understanding, that is, the *Word embodied* in the context of meaning. Now he understood that there was a deep, rich context to the words. What they meant for him personally, for his life and for his death, was not so much the question. The question was what was he to do? He understood, although on a level that he found difficult to express in ordinary language.

A new element was now part of the equation. He was confident that what he felt was more than optimism, more than hope. A year ago, he would have dismissed his present state of mind as merely wishful thinking or perhaps as mysticism or delusional thinking. Things were different now. Coming face to face with death and the unknown and unknowable had brought him to a spiritual and emotional level that he had not experienced before.

A person under those circumstances connected with God or Yahweh or Allah. The name attached by humans to the Deity wasn't the point. He had broken through another of many barriers to human understanding.

As Conrad sat lost in thought, gazing inward as well as outward at the magical scene before him, he felt a hand on one shoulder and then on his other shoulder. Virginia, who was standing by the side of the loveseat came around, arms still wrapped around him, and slid into his lap. He felt the warmth of her body, the scent of her just-awakened face and neck. He responded by enfolding her in his arms, rocking slowly back and forth on the glider until both of them were stimulated to the point of near unbearable sweetness and desire.

They let themselves fall sideways until they were stretched out on the loveseat, laughing at the awkwardness of the positions they found themselves in. In a moment, Conrad lay on top of her, entering her as they spoke sweetly to each other. Laughter evolved seamlessly into passionate urgency as they gave themselves to each other freely. When they were finished, they lay still, basking in the sun, salt air, and sights, and savoring the tenderness of the moment. And so it had happened – their coming together – without thought or planning, without hesitation, without condition. There were miracles to understand but this miracle was complete. He had found, amidst the debris of his aging and infirm body, the love of his life, and the passion for which he had waited a lifetime.

After savoring the exquisite luxury of complete surrender to each other, body, heart, and mind, they sat looking out over the sea and sky, still streaked with the gentle hues of sunrise, which colored clouds passing by in the mild onshore breeze. They were in a state of sheer joyous exaltation at their discovery of the redeeming power of new love and rediscovered passion. Over breakfast and coffee, they talked about the future.

"Have you decided definitely to go on the rescue mission to the Middle East?" she asked.

"Yes. I'm sure it's the right thing to do. It seems like the culmination of everything I've done. Everything I've failed to do, actually. The doctors aren't in favor of it of course. They see it as too risky even if I didn't have this cursed disease. I don't expect anyone else to understand."

"I understand," she said. "I can see why it means so much to you. It's a chance to do a wonderful thing. But are you convinced that you'll be able to take care of yourself medically while you're there. What about testing and keeping up with treatments? It is dangerous, isn't it? What if the boy's father shows up? He's a dangerous person, a ruthless killer, isn't he?"

"I would say he is. Ghadir's brother should be able to help. He may be just as dangerous but, at least, he's on the right side in this fight. Both of them are used to killing, I'm sure. They're on opposite sides, although they both oppose Assad."

"Conrad, it seems so dangerous even if you were young and healthy. I understand but I'm not sure you should go. I couldn't bear to lose you now that we've found each other."

"I was going to ask if you would consider coming along on the trip," Conrad said, glancing at her for a reaction. "I'd love to be with you and to have you share this experience. I know you trained as a nurse, too." He laughed. "You could take care of us and drum some sense in me when I need it."

She laughed while a serious expression clouded her face. "I worked as a nurse for quite a while. I haven't practiced for more than ten years. I was actually thinking of taking a refresher course at the nursing school and looking for work again. I could help you stay healthy if I were to go. But it's a frightening prospect. I'm not as courageous as you are."

Conrad hovered between understanding and hope. "Now that makes me want even more to have you come with me. I'd love to have you there. I hate to leave you now. I want us to be together for all the time I have left, whatever it is. It bothers me to expose you to danger but maybe we could protect each other. Sometimes I feel optimistic, sometimes pessimistic. I get so easily frustrated and impatient."

"You seem to handle it well, as far as I can see," she said.

"You don't see the worst," Conrad said. "I can't control my temper when things go wrong, like the bleeding, or the constant interruptions, or scheduling mistakes. I just flip out completely.

I lose control. Sometimes I feel self-destructive too, not suicidal, but reckless, impulsive, like when I'm driving. I visualize letting go and smashing into another car or a tree. It scares me when I feel as though I could lose my grip that way."

"I hate to hear you say that," Virginia said, reaching over to hug him. "Please promise me that you won't let go, that if you feel desperate or frustrated, you'll tell me. Call me, whenever you need to. I'll reach for you and tell you, 'I've got you now,' and you'll be safe. You have so much to live for, like me, for instance," she said laughing and climbing into his lap. "I've decided. I can't bear to have you go without me. I can handle it. I'll go."

"Wonderful," he said, jubilant. "Let's see if we can pull this trip together this week. Will you come along on Wednesday to join us when we talk about it with Ghadir? I'm hoping Levi will agree as well and maybe Ghadir knows more about where her brother is. We need him in the picture."

"Yes, I will." With that resolved, they changed for a swim while the beach was empty. Not a soul was in sight. The two of them were alone in the universe.

⁂

It was still only a few hours after dawn. The light sea air was fresh and pure. Gulls and sandpipers had the beach to themselves, scurrying away when their space was invaded. Conrad and Virginia crossed the beach toward the water, wading in without hesitating, then splashing their way through the surf.

Virginia was wearing a two-piece suit that was easily removable and Conrad, a pair of shorts. No one was in sight in either direction as they crossed to the water, which was deliciously clean and vibrant, and cooler than yesterday. The air had a faint touch of autumn and they predicted that the ocean would start cooling off in a week or two. They walked hand in hand into the water, finally diving headlong into the fast-moving surf now at mid-high tide. As they swam out some fifty yards, they realized they could still touch their feet easily on the silky bottom. No shells scratched their feet. The water was as clear as crystal.

Virginia ducked under the waves and removed her top, exposing her firm shapely breasts to the morning light – and to Conrad's sensitive hands. As he gently stroked her breasts, she reached down and pulled his shorts down, exposing his aroused private parts. He removed her bikini bottom. They hugged and fell into the waves, with peels of silly laughter, in case a passerby should happen along and glance out at them. To Conrad, the sensation of feeling the salt water was a healing experience. He felt like a baby floating in amniotic fluid or a sea creature swimming at ease in the sea. If ever there was a healing experience, it was being naked in the life-giving, buoyant salt water of the vast oceans of the earth. This was where life began, was nurtured, and where healing could take place.

His wholesome feeling gave way to excitement as he and Virginia explored each other's bodies. Both of them rose to a pitch of excitement and they longed for each other. They continued swimming, diving and embracing intermittently for the better part of an hour, until they could stand it no longer. Putting on their shorts, but with Virginia leaving off her top, they raced through the surging waves and up the beach to the cottage. They wasted no time hurrying to the screened porch where they again released not only hours of longing but days and weeks of frustration and suffering, all in joyful celebration of life.

❧

As he was dressing, after their latest passionate embrace, Conrad heard the vibration of his phone signal the arrival of an email. When he checked, he found an email from Ghadir translating the most recent communication from Mona.

> *We were forced to change plans as we headed south toward Damascus. Jamil began showing symptoms of illness about a day into our journey on foot after losing our vehicle to a band of rebel soldiers, who took it at gunpoint. They came upon us at once when we slowed down briefly to cross a bombed-out section of the roadway. That was a terrifying experience. There were eight or ten of them, all heavily armed. They didn't harm us but their harsh words left no doubt that resistance was impossible. We begged them not to leave us stranded but they ignored us. It all happened in the course of a half-hour.*

We were sure Jamil was running a fever with his respiratory symptoms. We aren't sure where he got the illness, although we did give a ride to a family with three children about a day's drive from Aleppo. The children were all in the back area of our vehicle for about an hour. Of course, the weather conditions are not ideal. We had rain and one very cool night. We are all exhausted from the strain of the trip and the stress of trying to avoid capture.

Jamil was having trouble walking. He was out of breath and coughing. Hamza carried him for a while and then realized that he could not continue. We would have no choice but to backtrack a half day's walk to a small (15,000 people) refugee camp just south of Homs. We would have to stay there until he was ready to continue. We found a vacant tent. Hamza had antibiotics with him and started Jamil on a course of treatment. The camp was very crowded and dirty. It was not safe. We heard that an intestinal virus causing diarrhea was spreading through the camp as well. We were very worried that, in his weakened condition, Jamil would pick up another illness. Fortunately, that did not happen, but Karam did get the intestinal bug.

Many health risks exist for all of us who are on the road and a large percentage of people we meet or pass each day are suffering. Most camps and even temporary refuges are vastly overcrowded and lack ordinary sanitation and clean water. Conditions of some are filthy with unclean community toilets and garbage dumps everywhere. Insects and rodents control the territory. Illnesses can be as serious as tuberculosis, hepatitis, MERS, malaria, leishmaniasis, dysentery, even cholera. We have seen or heard of all of these and many more in our short time on the road. All kinds of injuries are very common. The deprivations are bound to cause long-term health problems for many children. We are doing everything we can to avoid more sickness.

Jamil and Karam have recovered. We are about to set out on foot again. Unfortunately, the first half day we will spend retracing our steps but we have learned a good deal while in the camp about conditions of travel, warfare, and the dan-

gerous people to avoid between here and Damascus. We understand that as we get closer to Damascus, the chances of getting a ride increase. There are some taxis and some buses. But the danger of running into military units of all kinds also increases. We are vigilant all the time and Hamza and I stay awake in shifts during the night.

We are on the lookout constantly as we walk, often with many other people on the road or through fields or down railroad tracks, for soldiers – any soldiers. We also try to spot bodies or parts of bodies lying alongside the roadway before the children can see them. Many people of all ages, children as well as adults, and old people, have died along the way. The causes probably are injuries sustained from bombs or mortar fire as well as diseases, or simply hunger, thirst or fatigue. The saddest sight is to see people carrying babies and small children who are so thin, so emaciated, you wonder how they are still alive. It is pitiful.

There's very little food available. Some areas look like desperate war zones, with extensive damage to houses and public buildings. Some towns are like Aleppo – nothing but piles of rubble. People search for garbage to eat. They will eat anything. We can hardly bear to think of it but we have heard stories of people who eat human flesh. I know it is happening when starvation is near. It is too horrible to think about or speak. But it is the truth. If the truth isn't spoken, how will people ever understand what it is to have millions of homeless, starving, desperate refugees walking to safety – walking to have a chance at surviving this ordeal.

We still carry some supplies but we have to keep them secret. It breaks our heart not to share what we have but if we did, we would have nothing and the boys would die. We would all die. We must continue for their sake, if not our own. I will write again before we reach Damascus, which is about ninety miles from where we are. We could cover that distance in two days if we are lucky enough to get a ride. If not, it will be another two weeks. We hope for the best and leave our fate in the hands of Allah.

That was the end of her message, wrote Ghadir.

I'm relieved that the siege of illness has ended. I'm hopeful about Internet communication with them as they get closer to Damascus. I've heard there are new apps that allow clear messages when there is a basic Internet connection. It may not be consistent but, hopefully, she will be able to get some messages through.

I've given Mona's sister my email address, which Ayah uses too, so she can copy me directly. That will be useful once we leave here, avoiding the need for three-way communication. How can they manage the rest of the trip? This reminds me of my childhood and one journey on foot to a refugee camp. I had hoped that neither of my children would have to suffer what I suffered as a child. I suppose it made me stronger and I can only hope that it does for them. I pray for the cycle of suffering to end with this.

I feel desperate to get to Syria. I would like to leave within a week or ten days. Ayah keeps begging me to go with us but that is out of the question. She will guide our mission from here.

❧

By the time Wednesday came, Levi told Conrad on the phone that he was close to a final decision. Virginia had not changed her mind and, in fact, had arranged to attend informational sessions on public health conditions in the Middle East. On Wednesday, Levi picked Conrad up and then headed for Virginia's house. Levi expressed surprise to hear that Conrad and Virginia had become so deeply engaged in a romantic relationship in the short time since he and Conrad had talked. He listened quietly but did not show any special signs of happiness for Conrad.

Virginia gave Levi a warm greeting when she entered the car.

"What's your final word on the trip?" Conrad asked Levi. "As I said on the phone, Virginia has given in to my persuasion to join us."

"I expect to go with you," Levi said with slight hesitation. "I know the region and I could probably be helpful. Besides, who will protect you from DAESH? I don't know, though, how I can bear easily being in such close contact with a Palestinian terrorist for that long."

At the last remark, Conrad detected a half-concealed smile on Levi's face. Conrad took it seriously.

"You must be joking. She's hardly a terrorist," Conrad said, feeling agitated. "I thought we had worked through that accusation the other day. She was born a Palestinian. She's suffered as much as you have, if not more. She is a human being with a serious problem. Can you imagine how you'd feel if you had a child kidnapped and in grave danger of a horrible fate?"

Levi paused for several seconds. Conrad thought he wasn't going to answer. Finally, he said, "Yes, I do know how she feels. I was really only half-serious," Levi said, making direct eye contact with Conrad. "A poor attempt at humor. Sorry. I don't see Ghadir that way anymore but I still maintain my views about Palestinians in general."

"I thought you were serious," Conrad said. "That's a relief. I know what you went through, maybe not the whole story. The two of you have a lot in common. The difference is that you can do something about her problem."

"Okay, I'll commit to going. She seems decent enough. I don't know about the rest of her family though – her brother, her husband and his brother. They all sound like bad news to me. I don't have any more use for Syrians than I do for Palestinians."

"She probably feels the same way about you," Virginia said. "I don't know exactly what she experienced in the past but what she's going through now with her child kidnapped is more than anyone should have to bear."

Levi listened silently, as though he realized he had one more voice to pressure him into accepting the Palestinians and other Arabs.

When they reached the healing garden, they sat on the large corner bench waiting for the others. Ghadir and Ayah came out from the solarium, Ayah was virtually bouncing along, accelerating her pace to greet Conrad.

"Ayah," he called out. "You are amazing. All recovered." Her eyes sparkled as she approached to give him a hug.

Conrad noticed that Ghadir's aunt was walking behind them. Conrad couldn't tell if her grim look was directed at Levi or at him, or was merely her natural visage. Ghadir looked subdued, in contrast to her usual happy disposition. She genuinely welcomed Virginia to the pilgrimage they would undertake in Syria.

"I have more information from my sister-in-law," Ghadir said, looking from one to another. "The news is not good. But it could be much worse. Mona was able to place a phone call to her sister because the family was picked up and taken to a government military base with phone service. What happened could have been a terrible tragedy. As they were walking south on the road along with hundreds of other people, they were caught in the middle of furious air strikes. No one expected strikes in that area but there are many different encampments in the region – government, ISIS and several rebel groups. There have been skirmishes in recent weeks. Here's what she said in her words," Ghadir related, looking at her notes.

PART FIVE

TERRITORIALISM

N O ONE KNOWS FOR SURE *which party is responsible for the air strikes. It could have been any of the participants including the U.S. or European countries, maybe France, maybe Russia. They dropped bombs and were strafing the roadway and railroad tracks in the area. It may have been a mistake. Of course, no one ever admits they made a mistake. The result is lethal whether a strike is inadvertent or intentional. We all know that strafing and bombing civilians is often a deliberate act.*

It was the worst thing I ever experienced. Bombs were dropping very close by and many shots were fired. We thought everyone would be killed. Some people were injured and quite a few people, including some children, were killed. It was pandemonium for a half hour, as long as it lasted. Hamza got hit by something; we're not sure what. We hear the government is using cluster bombs. He was bleeding from his head and face. The boys were terrified. I was too. Luckily, some soldiers came along in a Humvee and took pity on the wounded. They took all four to their base and gave Hamza medical treatment. I'm not even sure what group those soldiers belonged to. It didn't matter as long as they helped.

The soldiers said we'd have to leave in the morning. One group, the ones who picked us up, said they would give us a ride in the morning as far south as they could before they had to change direction. I said our immediate destination was Yarmouk, the camp near Damascus. They warned that fighting has been taking place inside as well as outside the camp. Apparently, both government forces and ISIS warriors are in the area, maybe in the camp itself. Still, we need a destination, even briefly, and it's the closest to where we are. We will hope to leave there for Jordan or Lebanon as soon as possible, whichever is safest at that time, according to what we can learn. We hope to meet up with you. We are aware of your plans.

"Oh my God," Conrad said. "I hoped they would avoid getting caught up in the middle of the war, on top of all the other problems with such a strenuous journey. We have to get there as soon as possible. At least we know their destination."

"This may be the last word we'll get before we're on the ground," Ghadir said. "They could be in Damascus within a week, if they're on foot the whole way. We can't be sure how long they'll stay at Yarmouk. The latest reports from that camp are disturbing. It's like a battleground. Reports say the conditions are inhumane. There is not enough food or water. Sanitation conditions are terrible. It is starting to get colder too. Nights get cooler at this time of the year and they probably have very little in the way of clothing or supplies. If they can stay safe and well, we should be able to find them in time. Thank goodness we're not running into winter conditions as they are farther north. That's an added danger that makes it difficult to survive when health is already jeopardized."

"I know," Conrad said. "They're going to run into border-crossing problems too. Jordan and Lebanon are getting stricter with refugees. They are barring, as well as expelling Palestinians, most of whom are PRS. Mona should be okay but you never know."

"I've talked with an expert," Levi said. "He studied at the University of Michigan which has one of the top refugee studies programs. We may run into serious travel problems ourselves."

"On the light side, if there is one," Conrad said, "I can't help laugh when I think of the image we'll present as we go on our journey to Damascus and wherever else destiny takes us. We have a bearded Orthodox Jew, a former rabbi with a fierce countenance, a tall, thin African-American priest, who is a reformed lawyer committed to nonviolence, a young Muslim woman wearing a hijab, a sickly white scarecrow of a man beaten up by life and shuffling along on his last legs. You'll recognize the last one," he said, raising his arm in the air. "Finally, we have Virginia, our beautiful companion, a battlefield nurse dressed in full medical regalia and ready to save everyone." Conrad's remark brought a pause, followed by an enthusiastic laugh from everyone.

"We are quite a spectacle," Conrad went on. "We could be straight out of Don Quixote, a band of medieval knights off on a quest riding our exhausted horse Rocinante, and by our side, our own Sancho Panza."

Levi laughed. "I think we're more like the cast in a production of *The Wizard of Oz*. We have five characters on a mission – Dorothy, the Tin Man, the scarecrow, the cowardly lion, accompanied by Glinda. Ghadir is Dorothy, the young lady leading an urgent mission. Virginia would make a good Glinda, the powerful force for good in the world. I nominate myself for the cowardly lion. Gaspar can be the scarecrow and, Conrad, the Tin Man. Is there any question but that Yousef is the wicked witch of the West? We are going to solve the great mystery of Oz and return home with our reward. The trouble is we need miracles – not just magic."

"I'll try to provide the final miracle, God, or Allah or Jehovah, willing, of course," Conrad said. "I've already been blessed with two miracles. The first was the Word presented to me. *Have courage. Do not lose hope.* The second was meeting all of you and understanding deeply what those words mean. I believe a third miracle is yet to come. That is the wisdom and strength on our part and mercy and grace from God, to carry out our task of bringing Jamil home safely. That's my Christian version but you all can translate what is happening into Judaism and Islam.

"I may break out laughing at any time when I get a vision of what we'll look like to other people we meet," Conrad said, with tears in his eyes. "We're a remarkable troupe of, shall I say, un-superheroes, so formidable that we may frighten our enemies away – or more likely cause them to die laughing. One thing is for sure. We're bound to attract attention when we try to cross into Syria and when we have to return to Jordan."

"I don't know the story of Don Quixote," Ayah said, "but I've seen the *Wiz* on Broadway. I like this but I think I should be Dorothy. Can't I please go along? I'm as well as Conrad."

Ghadir hugged her. "No, my love. I need you to stay here. You will be our mission center and our spiritual power. I wish you could come with us but we need you to take care of your health and pray for our success. You are a child, a wise child, but a child still, and you have a much greater task ahead of you. You are the inspiration for our journey."

⁂

Energized by the lighthearted depiction of their heroic quest, the travelers discussed a feasible departure time within the month. Conrad faced the most problems in getting ready, since he had to deal with Helen, whom he had not seen in over two weeks, and finalize his medical treatment. Before he left the cancer center, he met with Dr. Bitar's nurse to discuss whether he would need a blood transfusion before departing. The switch of doctors had been accomplished. Based on the last three CBC reports, which showed a pattern of rapidly decreasing hemoglobin and platelets, the answer was a definitive yes. The nurse speculated that he should have platelets and two units of blood on Friday.

The prospect of the transfusion troubled Conrad because of horror stories about infections and bad reactions, reinforced by the litany of warnings on the waiver form given to patients prior to being connected. There were warnings about reactions with a long list of symptoms, including fever, chills, breathing problems, excessive iron, and allergic reactions. No beneficial treatment was without its downside. Conrad was taking seven medications, enough to cause a cascade of side effects. He counted his blessings that he had not suffered serious side effects so far. In the end, he could not refuse because the risk of having an infusion in Jordan or Syria was unacceptable.

Once he set aside the fears of side effects, he felt glad for the promise of vitality and new life that came with fresh, wholesome, blood. Perhaps if he replaced all his blood with new, pure blood cells, he would recover. That procedure would virtually be a stem cell transplant. The litany of evils combined with the anemic prognosis for success made that seem like a death sentence. He would never agree to a bone marrow transplant, even if his life depended on it – which it very well might. Even if he survived it, what good was life that required constant medicating to prevent infection, rejection, graft versus host disease, and relapse? Besides, the BMT surgeon, a misnomer if he ever heard one – it was not typical surgery at all – practically guaranteed that he would lead a miserable life for a few years if he survived the six to twelve-month isolation. Better to die quickly than drag out a horrible death over a period of years. He would be alone in some dreary nursing home with no one to care for him. Although the renewed relationship with Virginia was exciting and promising, how could he expect her to be willing to care for an invalid, after nursing Henry for years?

Conrad came to grips with his next task, tracking down Helen and taking steps to close up the house while he was away. Where on earth was she? Had she and Bernie moved somewhere together? He decided to call Bernie's wife, Janet, damn the consequences. Janet answered and was silent when he identified himself.

"Janet. We haven't talked in a long time. I'm trying to track down Helen. It's been two weeks since I've heard from her."

She interrupted. "She and Bernie moved to an apartment. He left here, good riddance, two weeks ago. I found out what was going on and kicked him out. Why didn't you tell me what was going on," she asked with barely masked anger.

"I didn't feel it was my job to do that. I wondered why you didn't tell me. I just found out. I'm dealing with a lot of stuff, Janet."

"Okay. I get it. Here's the phone number. Good luck. We're both better off without those losers," she said with bitterness in her voice.

"Thanks," he said. "I'm taking a trip, not a pleasure trip, but a serious one. I'll be gone two weeks, just in case you want to know. I may not survive the trip either. But that's neither here nor there. No one cares."

"I'm sorry to hear that but I've got my own problems. I can't afford to keep the house and I have my own medical issues. I'm sorry for yours."

"Good luck to you then," Conrad said halfheartedly.

Conrad dialed the number. Helen answered. He was surprised at the wave of mixed emotions that flooded his mind as he heard her voice.

"Helen. I'm closing up the house within two weeks. The trip, you know. If you need anything from the house, now's the time to arrange it. I will be securing it and having it checked by the police while I'm away. Sorry but you won't have access until I get back."

"You have no right to lock the house," Helen said angrily. "It's mine as much as yours. I'll come by to pick up a key. I'll access it whenever I want to."

"I'm not arguing the point, Helen. You heard what I said. There's no extra key for you. I'll tell you what I'll do. To the extent I have time and energy, I'll put your stuff in plastic bags and leave them in the garage. I'll leave the garage accessible. Have it your way. Pick up what you need this weekend or access the garage. The house will be locked and my new alarm system will be on. It rings in police headquarters. They will be notified that you do not have legal access."

The connection ended as she hung up. He felt dizzy, his heart racing, as he put the phone down. Conflict always disturbed him deeply. Open warfare with Helen was new and very upsetting. He knew she might find a way in and that disturbed him more. He had bluffed about a new alarm system but he would stop by police headquarters and ask them to check periodically. The title was in his name so he had the right to say who entered and who did not.

For the next hour, he had trouble settling down and concentrating on planning what he needed to do. The cost of the trip would be split evenly among them. It was expensive but everyone was capable of coming up with the necessary resources. Conrad insisted on paying Virginia's way, however, since Henry's unreimbursed medical expenses had left her in financial straits. His real estate business had diminished to nothing over the course of his illness so there was no reserve. Ghadir's aunt insisted on covering her financial needs.

Ghadir was in charge of the itinerary, after consulting with her brother. Levi would make reservations once Conrad had researched them. Gaspar would make contacts with priests he knew in the region. Levi would do the same with relatives in Israel and Jordan. He was hopeful that one of his cousins might agree to meet them at some crucial point but that was indefinite. He was a very resourceful lawyer, although he shared Levi's general antipathy toward Palestinians. He lived in Jerusalem where tensions were usually high. He would not sympathize with the mission, seeing it as an Arab thing – Arab against Arab – but he cared about Levi.

※

Three days later, Conrad and Virginia returned to his house in late afternoon. They had spent the previous day together, concluding it with a quiet dinner. They spent the night together at her house, making love twice, once in the evening and again in the morning. He was amazed at how he felt revitalized despite his medical situation – and his fluctuating hemoglobin. He felt renewed confidence that once he returned – if he returned – from their mutual quest, they would begin their future life together. She accompanied Conrad to his house to help him organize and pack.

When they approached the house, Conrad was shocked to see a black pickup truck backed up to the open garage door. As he pulled into the driveway, blocking the truck in the process, he saw Bernie walk through the garage carrying a large box. Helen appeared carrying two smaller boxes. Alarm registered on their faces as Conrad got out of his car and approached, waving his fist in the air.

"What the hell are you doing? You have no right," Conrad shouted. "You broke into the house, you bastards," Conrad shouted, approaching Bernie, who put the large box into the truck bed. Conrad reached out for the box, which was perched on the edge of the truck. Bernie grabbed him and wrestled him away from the truck. The box went down, making a large crash. Conrad went down at the same time, falling on top of the box, twisting his left arm. He crumpled on the ground, crying out in pain. His left leg was bent underneath him in an awkward position.

Bernie stepped back, surprised at what had happened. Virginia rushed forward and pushed Bernie backwards into Helen, who was nearly at the scene of the crime. Helen kept her footing but dropped the boxes she was carrying, screaming at Virginia. "You bitch. Who do you think you are? This is my house."

Virginia helped Conrad up. He shook loose and started to charge at Bernie but stumbled and landed on top of him. Virginia lunged forward and tried to pull them apart. Conrad got to his feet. He realized that he was bleeding from his left arm and the left side of his face.

"Get out of here now and leave what you just took. You just committed a crime. I'll have you arrested if you ever come back."

Bernie, now on his feet and furious at being attacked, yelled, "You son of a bitch. Move your goddam car. We're out of here but we'll be back."

After they had left, Virginia drove Conrad to the emergency room in the next town. They spent the next four hours there while Conrad was examined, cleaned, and had his injuries treated. The medical team sent home instructions to watch for internal bleeding signaled by swelling and pain in his extremities, both arms and legs. A CT scan showed no signs of internal injuries to his head or body.

The white-coated nurse practitioner and the blue-suited PA seemed to be in charge of the ER, aside from an MD who came in briefly to chat with Conrad before disappearing. Conrad was surprised that the nurse practitioner was robed in the traditional white coat but the only MD in the large facility was dressed informally in an open-collar shirt with no tie or jacket or white coat. It seemed that white coats, once reserved as the special mark of MDs upon becoming licensed, were handed out so freely that the only way MDs could distinguish themselves was by declining to wear one.

Everybody in the food chain of medical practice wanted to be called doctor except for the nurses, of course, who seemed to be the hardest workers and most attentive staff members. The white coats were seated at their computers most of the time. The nurses, who wore dark blue scrubs, and the nursing assistants, or PCAs (patient care assistants) who donned light blue scrubs, had the most patient contact. Conrad made a tally of the number of medical staffers who saw him during this visit. He counted eight, virtually all for repetitive questioning and mostly empty promises about the timing of his care.

"What happened to white uniforms," Conrad asked. "You should be wearing white."

Everyone was polite this time, which was Conrad's eighth ER visit since his diagnosis. When he was in-patient, many of the nursing assistants and nurses tended to be bossy and condescending. Thankful for small favors, Conrad waited and waited patiently, sometimes lying back on the bed and sometimes sitting upright.

The grim-faced and obtuse PA told Conrad they were worried about compartment syndrome. When Conrad asked what that was, he looked astonished and laboriously explained that it was the natural reflex of the body to react to a severe injury to a limb, especially a leg, by cutting off circulation. It was the body protecting itself – its organs – from death. So Conrad should check during the night to be sure the leg wasn't turning white or getting cold or swelling a great deal more. "If you awake to numbness or tingling, be sure to come back right away or, better still, go to the ER in the city hospital. They can operate right away," he said, "and save the limb."

"Oh God, help me please," Conrad exclaimed. "How can I sleep at all if I have to worry about that? That doesn't seem likely to me. It's just a muscle tear, right? All that other stuff. That's bull," he added.

The PA and the nurse who was standing by the door looked shocked. "Have it your way," the PA said and stalked out, leaving the nurse to pick up the pieces of the situation.

"It isn't too likely," the nurse said, "but you have to be aware, and you shouldn't talk to the doctor like that."

"He's not a doctor," Conrad said. "Why the job inflation around here. I don't call myself a professor. I teach but I'm just an adjunct. I don't pretend."

"Good for you," the nurse said, turning on her heels, leaving them alone.

"Conrad, sweetie," Virginia said. "You shouldn't talk to them that way. I know you're distressed and angry but it isn't their fault. You need their full cooperation." She massaged his back until he began to relax and let go of his bitter rage.

❧

Virginia slept over and checked Conrad during the night. No swelling was evident but, in the morning, he was in pain and they returned to the ER for further examination. Swelling had begun in his left leg and a purple patch had appeared on his left arm. An ultrasound was performed to be sure no blood clots had formed. The technician left Conrad in the cubicle where he was scanned, saying that she'd be back as soon as the doctor in charge had examined her findings. Conrad said, "Wait a minute. Did you find any clots or not?"

The technician smiled apologetically. "I'm so sorry. They get angry at me if I tell the patient what I found. You'll have to wait for the doctor. It won't be that long."

Conrad resigned himself to waiting. He lay there uncomfortably on the examining table with only a sheet over him and without any pillow to support his head and neck. He was cold but there was nothing to do about it. He felt helpless. He was discouraged.

He said aloud, "I'll never be ready to go on the trip. It's over. With my swollen leg and internal bleeding, clot or not, I'm sunk." He felt like crying but, instead, allowed himself to descend into depression. He lay there lifeless, uncomfortable, miserable, but resigned to his fate.

He was startled by the door opening and realized that he had dropped into sleep. The doctor entered. He was a tall, young-looking man of perhaps thirty-five. He had a sour look on his face, as though this visit was an annoyance. "No clots," he said. "But one ultrasound isn't enough. It's not definitive. You will need a follow-up within four to seven days. Schedule it before you leave."

"What do you mean it isn't enough? Who says? I've had four ultrasounds in the past six months and no one ever said one wasn't definitive. Anyway, I can't. I'm leaving on a trip out of the country. I don't have the time."

"You'll be risking your life if you don't get one. I'm telling you to do it," the doctor said. "It's for your own good. Anyway, there's no chance you can take a trip. You can't get on an airplane. Are you taking a flight?"

"Yes, of course. A long flight."

"No way," the doctor said. "That would be foolish, a big mistake. Does Dr. Ulianofsky know?"

"Basically, but he's not my doctor anymore," Conrad said quietly. "Dr. Bitar is my doctor."

"I'll talk to Dr. Ulianofsky," the doctor said. "He's very respected, you know. You're lucky to have him. His name is still on your medical record so he's the one I have to contact."

"That's idiotic. I'm telling you he's not my doctor any longer. But you go right ahead and do what you want," Conrad shouted, fearing that the chances of going on the trip were slipping away. He was so disheartened that he felt like giving up but he couldn't resist protesting the young doctor's arrogance.

⁂

The day wore on and Conrad wore out with the passing hours. Conrad and Virginia left for his house after a total of six hours in the ER. He was exhausted but relieved to learn that the swelling was due to the trauma, not to blood clots. A CBC, however, revealed that blood counts were going in the wrong direction – white cells upward again and red cells downward. His doctor ordered him to increase his dose of hydroxyurea, the champion serial killer of all cells. His hemoglobin and platelets would need monitoring even more closely until he left. He definitely would need at least one more double blood infusion before the trip. Now that he was off his blood thinner, because of the excessive internal bleeding, he would have to be concerned about clots on top of everything else.

"Talk about a cascade of problems," Conrad moaned to Virginia. He added quickly, "Forgive me. I don't mean to feel sorry for myself. I'm lucky to get the care I do. And I am so grateful for you."

That remark brought a warm smile to her face and a "thank you, sweetheart."

Once he was home, he got a phone call from Ulianofsky, who accused him of being crazy to think about a trip anywhere after all this, much less a war zone in the Middle East. "I won't be responsible for you any longer if you do that. I'm through. It's crazy. I advise against it. No, I order you not to go if you want me to continue. I'm not going to be …. Never mind. Don't be a fool."

Conrad was steamed. "Listen. I'm going. You're not stopping me and I'm not your patient. You can't dump me. I already dumped you. I'm going if it's the last thing I do."

"It will be that, all right. Good riddance, I say," Ulianofsky said. "You'd better come in to see me tomorrow. You need a blood infusion, a double, actually. I want to make clear that I oppose this trip and I'm having you sign a release of me and the hospital. You have to acknowledge that you are doing this contrary to medical advice. We'll plant a big 'AMA' on your chart. Maybe I'll plant 'AMA' on your forehead too. I presume you've read Hawthorne."

"Fine, frankly, I don't give a damn. Of course I have," Conrad blurted out.

"If you insist, I'll give you the name of a hospital in Amman and one in Syria, if I can. You have to check in Amman for a lab and have an exam before you leave the city. My associate trained in Jordan. He was from Syria. He has contacts, but I'm telling you, you have to follow through with that or we're not responsible for what happens to you. This will be your last trip and you'll be coming home from Syria in a box."

Conrad hung up but he did call back to set up an appointment for Monday, which was a week before the flight. He was not intimidated by the prediction that he would come home in a box. "What good is life the way I'm living it," he said aloud. All the same, as he was lying in bed that night, Virginia curled up beside him with her arm across his chest, he offered his usual prayer for forgiveness and for help in doing God's will and for mercy and grace to live through the trip and beyond it. As always, he asked for longer life and as he often did, fearing that God was a literalist, he prayed, "And, God, please let me live longer, my life expectancy if you will. But I'd be happy with fifteen years. If you would do that, please, I ask for that grace even though I don't deserve it." He had to make sure that God didn't misunderstand.

Conrad wondered again whether God could really be a literalist or if God listened at all to prayers. Did God have a sense of humor? There was no evidence of humor that he had ever heard about. He – or she – certainly hadn't done anything to help so far. Well, he was still alive, which was something. Here he was, about to go off to hell on earth to save a child from being a victim – and a coerced perpetrator – of violence. God was supposed to oppose violence, at least the God of the New Testament. But Levi's God did his own brand of violence and ISIS – DAESH – and the other jihadists happily dispensed violence in the name of their God. Who was God anyway? Did we humans even have a clue? Sometimes it seems fruitless, he thought, this praying and begging for mercy and grace.

Maybe Don McLean was right, the way he put it in his song, *American Pie*. The father, son and Holy Ghost had caught the last train for the coast. God was gone. He or she created matter and energy and left it to explode or implode. God was in absentia from the universe. What was the use in praying? He caught himself up with the sudden realization that saving Jamil was an important thing, perhaps *the* most important thing. Perhaps this was God's will and a symbolic action that could help redeem the human race – and Conrad, himself. The insight or revelation remained with him during the night. He awoke with it foremost in his mind and with new confidence – courage and hope.

Inspired by this awareness, Conrad followed his own ritual prayers many times a day, fearing to deviate. Maybe another miracle would happen after all. Then he had another insight that caught him by surprise. God created humans and nothing would make God turn humans into gods. He was destined to die and whether he was 59, 79 or 99 made little difference. It was a flash in time, a fraction of a second in ultimate ongoing time. And how could he say that wasn't fair. No one ever promised he'd live out his life expectancy. That was just fiction. Well, anyway, he'd keep praying because it brought him some peace and enabled him to return to sleep when he woke, chilled by fear and apprehension during the night.

It helped to have Virginia here. He loved it when she held him and said, "I've got you now." There was something safe and permanent about that, as though it had to work, of course. This new relationship helped to sweeten the bitter taste in his mouth from Helen's final betrayal, the last of a long betrayal that had begun years ago with her treachery. He drifted off to sleep, satisfied for the moment that he had done all he could. Something about talking with God gave him temporary peace, as though he had put the matter in someone else's hands – Someone Else's Hands, that is. But he had a keen perception of what happens when one part of the body fails. What intricate organisms we are, he thought.

When something goes wrong, it's like a cascade of problems. Disease and treatment join in an evil conspiracy to bring down the whole organism. It's so critical to keep the body healthy – to avoid secondary consequences to the cancer. Oncology was one thing; good health was another. He remembered the advice that most deaths occur because of organ failure, infections, bleeding, or other secondary consequences. Stay healthy, Conrad thought. He said aloud, "I'm a healthy person with a disease; that's all."

The rest of the week was a blur – organizing, anxiety, packing, fear, and medical appointments, all without knowing for certain that he would be healthy enough to go. He had his infusion just in case the swelling diminished enough so that he could manage the trip as well as the long flight. He also made peace of sorts with Ulianofsky.

Conrad felt the worse for wear but he was excited about the prospect of dedicating his life and his health to a cause that he had long supported. He had before him the possibility of the greatest adventure of his life. How it would turn out, he couldn't predict. It was his destiny. He was determined not to give up on the trip at this point. With a mix of emotions ranging from hope and optimism to resignation and pessimism, from excitement to despondency, he would push ahead to the day of departure.

By early evening, the five travelers, Ghadir, Conrad, Virginia, Levi, and Gaspar, were checked in and seated in the passenger area of Royal Jordanian Air at JFK International Airport, waiting for their flight to Amman. They had been originally scheduled to depart at 10:30 p.m. and fly nonstop, arriving at Queen Alia Airport approximately eleven hours later. They took in stride a departure delay of two hours, which had just been announced. They found a quiet corner in a vacant area across from their crowded departure gate area.

"We've got at least three hours to wait before takeoff," Conrad said. "We could use this time to our advantage. It'll be impossible to talk with everyone once we're on the plane. We'll all want to get some sleep anyway. Since we're going to be together for a week under intense conditions, we'll have to depend on each other for survival. The more we can count on mutual trust, the better. We've all shared our personal stories to some extent. But we've held back some of the most painful details. I have two suggestions. One is that we could share the details in the interest of getting to know each other better. The other is that we can review the details of the plan that we have to implement as soon as we land. What do you think?"

"I'd be glad to share more about what happened to me," Ghadir said tentatively, "if you think it would be helpful."

"The part I haven't talked about," Levi said, "is the most painful part. I'm not sure I want to get into that. It's what causes me to feel hostility toward Palestinians. I don't see how that serves any useful purpose."

"Up to you, Levi," Conrad said as casually as he could manage. "Maybe it's time that you did unburden yourself and let us know the origins of your opinions. Why don't we start with Ghadir and take it from there."

"Okay," she said. "I'll keep to the facts. You know that I grew up in Ramallah. I was born there but some of my brothers and sisters were born in a village near Jerusalem. That's where my grandparents on both sides lived, too. We go all the way back to 1948. When the family property was confiscated by the Israeli government, we moved to the Palestinian sector. They were displaced out of Jerusalem. Eventually, that area changed when the Israeli government built the wall. Our home was on what became the Israeli side of the wall. It was eventually destroyed. My family lived in refugee camps such as Qalandia, and Al-Amari. Life was difficult; there were no basic services. They depended on food supplies provided by UNRWA for years until they had a chance to move into a small apartment offered by an old man who was living alone in Ramallah. They became his neighbors and, when he died, he left the apartment to my family.

"They were able to acquire a larger house after a while. Then Israeli settlers began to take over that area. That's a fact." Ghadir looked at Levi. "That practice led to what Palestinians call 'the occupation.' Some historians have described it in terms similar to what Irish Republicans call 'the implantation.' That's when Scottish Protestants settled in Ireland in the seventeenth century, displacing many of the Catholic residents. It's a fact that what some Palestinians call 'the Israeli occupation of Palestine' began in 1948 when the British mandate ended. That also marked the end of the Palestine War. That's all I'll say about this but, in my view, it is necessary historical background for what came later and, in particular, what happened to my family. I know Levi might disagree," Ghadir said. She avoided Levi's gaze and turned instead toward Conrad.

Levi had become agitated and looked as though he was having trouble remaining silent. Conrad glared at him and whispered, "Be still. Let her speak."

Ghadir went on. "We didn't have a large enough house, of course, so we stayed in the old man's small apartment in Ramallah until that became too burdensome, much too crowded. We moved to a camp called 'Dheisheh camp,' which was not far away. It was actually in Bethlehem, the famous city on the West Bank, known as 'the City of David' and the place where Jesus of Nazareth was born, according to the Bible. The population of Bethlehem consists of Jews, Christians, and Muslims.

"Very early in our stay in Dheisheh, a terrible thing happened. I don't remember all the details because I was so young. I do remember how much the whole family grieved and, of course, I heard the story many times as I was growing up. One of my brothers, who was then about seven or eight, used to go out with other boys and throw stones into one of the conflict zones near Bethlehem. I'm not saying that I justify that. Not at all. I'm sure they injured people on occasion. But they were children, after all. One day Israeli soldiers came out while they were throwing stones and yelled at them to stop.

"My brother wasn't a bad child, and he was younger than the rest of the group. He stopped what he was doing. But he didn't leave. He stayed there to see what would happen, I guess. A few older boys continued to throw stones, this time, at the soldiers. In fairness, I imagine some stones hit the soldiers. Without any specific warning, as I understand it, the soldiers opened fire on the boys. Three of them were killed. Tragically, my brother was one of those killed. Other boys were injured.

"I still remember vividly that one of the other boys' fathers came to our house and told my parents what had happened. He was carrying my brother, who was lying limp in his arms, and bleeding. I remember all the blood. A trail of blood across the floor. So much blood." Ghadir looked as though she might faint. "It was gushing onto the doorstep and then onto the floor as he entered the house. I had never seen bleeding like that before. I had the horrible realization that he was dead. I remember my mother and my grandmother wailing. It was terrible. And I remember the crying. It went on all night. Then there were services and a funeral and the burial. That was my first death, up close, in my own family. I have seen many more deaths since then."

"Unfortunately—yes, tragically—this sort of thing happens, often, both ways," Levi said, bowing his head slightly.

"The second tragic incident happened when we were still in Dheisheh," Ghadir continued. "Another of my brothers, who was no more than sixteen at the time, was involved in what you would now call insurgent activity. He was meeting with other young men, some teenagers like himself, to plan retaliation against the Israeli police and military for constantly invading our homes without warning and without specific reasons. One night the police came to take him away for questioning. He was frightened, although at this point he had not done anything except go to meetings. He tried to get away through the back door and one of the officers shot him from behind. We were stunned. He had no weapon. He was just frightened. I think he died quickly but they took him to the Palestinian hospital and we followed in our car. They pronounced him dead without giving any treatment.

"I remember most clearly the grieving we did over my second brother who was killed. The grief and anger is even more vivid. He had not committed any acts of violence or threatened anyone. He was unarmed and simply frightened. There was no need to shoot him. It took a long time for the anger and bitterness that we all felt to die down. I felt it myself but I could not hold onto it the way others could. I sensed deeply that nothing good would come of hatred and anger. We never would have peace. I heard all the talk about revenge and retaliation but I knew from my childhood that it would lead nowhere but to more and more bloodshed. I still feel that way.

"Our leaders in the community talked then, as some do now, about war and killing as the only way. I have taught my children that we must find peaceful solutions. War has been the medium of change in the Middle East for centuries, for millennia, and it has brought nothing but more war. War breeds war. Violence breeds violence. War accomplishes nothing in the long run. I vowed to become a leader someday and work toward a peaceful solution. I was on the way to doing that until my husband—and my marriage—turned violent. My husband was persuaded eventually that war was his answer. And now you see what has happened. He has brought his own son into great jeopardy. This is not the way. I know it in my heart. Bloodshed will bring nothing but bloodshed. This is what I have learned from these terrible events."

The group was silent, even Levi, who simply looked away and then down at the floor. Finally, Conrad asked, "Did anyone in your family ever retaliate? Was there more bloodshed?"

"No. There were many threats of retaliation but my parents begged our family members not to join any insurgencies. My entire family was devastated, broken-hearted. We never recovered from these losses. But those who were wise could foresee more deaths if retaliation took place. All the obstacles, the inconveniences, the delays, the losses that we suffered in our daily lives were nothing compared to these deaths. Eventually we moved to Syria, to another camp for Palestinians. That was Al Yarmouk camp. My family couldn't bear to stay where these sons had been killed. And in those days, before the civil war in Syria, life was actually better for us, more peaceful, and the schools were better. But as you know, tragedy has overtaken Syria. It is a broken country, devastated by war that seems to have no end. The civil war among so many factions is a deep well that has no bottom. And Palestinian refugees in Syria—'PRS,' we were called—used to be well treated in Syria. We are personae non gratae now in Syria and even in neighboring countries like Jordan and Lebanon. Conditions in Syria are now far worse than in Palestine."

Conrad spoke up. "This is a different subject, Ghadir, but do you know anything about the training camps for boys? I'm thinking about their location, how they operate, how many people are likely to be at the camps."

"After Yousef left with Jamil, I began reading and hearing about the DAESH program of recruiting young boys and girls," she replied. "It isn't just boys, and some are as young as five and six years old. They are trained to become soldiers, suicide bombers, or slaves to the fighters. DAESH has turned this immoral recruitment of children into a virtual industry. I also learned that many of these children are volunteered by their families but there is certainly an element of coercion as far as the children are concerned. There is actually a specific effort to encourage fathers who are becoming radicalized to bring their sons along. The sons get special training at what they call 'cubs camps.'

"There are at least three in Syria that I have heard about. One is in the area of Aleppo called Atareb, one in Al-Bukamal, in eastern Syria, and one in East Ghouta, which is on the outskirts of Damascus, not far from Yarmouk. That one is called the Zarqawi cubs camp. I am guessing that Zarqawi is where my husband will take Jamil. At least I am hoping so because it is not far from Damascus and should be within reaching distance for us. I have accumulated a lot of information about this camp and in general the way the training proceeds. This is all part of the 'DAESH cycle of radicalization,' as they call it, making sure that there are young boys to grow up to become fighters to keep the battle against infidels going. It's likely that there is another camp in Raqqa, the de facto capital of the Islamic State."

"I've read about the recruitment of boys," Levi said. "It's part of ISIS' brutal strategy of making sure there will be plenty of fighters in the future. It's indoctrination of the worst kind, brainwashing to get these boys to become brutal, to erase their consciences. They call the training places 'schools of Jihad.' Using children under fifteen has been declared a war crime under international humanitarian and human rights law. It's downright primitive. Civilized people do not do this. Of course, it's difficult to enforce because those who do it—like ISIS—evade detection and even when we know it's happening, they slip through our hands. I won't say what I really think," continued Levi before, characteristically, saying precisely what he really thought. "This is an Arab terrorist plot to undermine the fundamentals of human rights law and basic moral standards. It's an attack on our very civilization."

Ghadir looked shaken at the way Levi turned the conversation into an accusation. No one replied to Levi's implied attack on Islam until Conrad spoke. "Levi, decent people all over the world find this reprehensible. It's not an Arab thing or a Muslim thing. It's a lawless, criminal, immoral act that throughout history has been committed by people of all religions. We'll talk about that sometime but not now. This is not the time or place to attack anyone. We're united in seeking to liberate these boys from a fate they do not deserve in any way. These people—ISIS or DAESH—they are criminals, criminals of the worst kind."

"I don't disagree at all," Levi said, nodding affirmatively, but his body language suggested that he did in fact disagree, at least on the idea that Muslim barbarism was no different from the barbarism of others. He simply could not get past his disdain for the Muslim religion.

Frustrated, Conrad changed the subject. Looking squarely at Levi, he asked, "How about you next? I know you've held back your most painful experience. Will you talk about it?"

Levi shook his head, turning away for a moment. "This is very difficult, Conrad. It can only cause more hard feelings."

"Everyone should know what you suffered," Conrad said. "It had a direct impact on the way you feel about Palestinians and Arabs in general. Isn't that so?"

"Yes, of course it did. But it's private," Levi said.

"Holding it in only allows your pain to fester in bitterness and turn to hatred," Gaspar said. "You may be justified in feeling wronged but it can only tear away at your insides. Emotions like anger and hatred poison you."

"All right," Levi said. "But first I have to point out that Israel had a claim to its land going far back in history and it had international law on its side when it took possession. Okay?" He surveyed the room.

"Let's leave that subject alone for now," Gaspar urged.

Ghadir remained quiet and still. She made no move to interrupt.

※

"You all know I was a rabbi," Levi said. "It was my dream from childhood—to be a great teacher. I grew up in a Conservative family. There were also Orthodox and Reformed synagogues in Brooklyn. After college at Brandeis, where I studied religion and literature, I went to the Jewish Theological Seminary. I settled into a synagogue in Massachusetts and got married. That marriage didn't work out and we divorced. I won't go into detail but the divorce led to my resigning from my position. I began a career, of sorts, after that, in a university. This was not exactly what I envisioned as my teaching—I wanted to teach as a rabbi—but I have enjoyed it. And getting to know Conrad has been a great pleasure.

"Eventually, I married again. My wife was from an Orthodox family and was fully observant. This was a very happy marriage and we had two wonderful children." At this, Levi paused for a moment.

"My wife had a number of relatives who visited back and forth in Israel, a sister, two brothers, cousins, aunts, and uncles. Some of them decided to take up residence there, mostly in Jerusalem. They liked being on the frontier. They found it exciting and satisfying to be where the action was, so to speak. By that time we had our two children. We traveled back and forth to Israel quite often, three or four times a year. My wife was very close to her siblings and other relatives there. I usually arranged my teaching schedule so I could accompany her. Her family wasn't all that political. They were happy with life as it was there, although the tension with the Palestinians could be a plague on daily life. They disliked any restriction on their freedom of movement, but learned to live with it."

Levi glanced at Ghadir, sensing her reaction to that remark. He added, "I can almost hear Ghadir saying, 'Restrictions? Freedom of movement? *My* relatives dislike any restriction on their freedom, too, and they have a lot more to put up with.' Well, I can appreciate that. It works both ways, doesn't it?

"At the time of one of our fall trips," Levi continued, "there had been a lot of hostilities back and forth for several months.

There had been some of the 'lone wolf attacks,' as I call them, in Jerusalem. Our friends in the States warned that we should be extra careful if we insisted on going, which we did. Our family and friends in Israel warned us. They were limiting their trips into the city and being extra vigilant when they went. A few weeks before that, there had even been two suicide bombings downtown, one in a market and one in the business district. My wife was adamant that we shouldn't allow our freedom to be curtailed. It was unlikely that anything bad would happen, she said. I was afraid. I had a premonition. She was very courageous and said she needed to do some shopping for things to take home. We'd be leaving in a few days and there wasn't much time left to buy gifts. So, I gave in and said okay. The children begged to come along and she said yes. I argued that they should not run the risk but I lost the argument.

"We were in the market area where there was lots of outdoor shopping. We got separated. She had the kids with her. I had found an outdoor bookstore and got engrossed. I said I'd catch up with them in a minute. But I lost track of the time. Ordinarily it wouldn't have made a difference, but I will never, as long as I live, forgive myself for not staying with them."

Levi paused, trembling with emotion. "This part makes me shaky. I don't know if I can finish. It's been almost twenty years but it's like it happened this morning. There was an explosion and then another. I turned and bolted from the bookstore, eager to get a sense of where the noise had come from. When I emerged from the store, I saw people pointing in the direction my wife and children had gone. I dropped my bags of purchases, and ran, knocking people aside. I ran desperately, weeping, fearing that the worst had happened, knowing somehow that the worst had happened."

He paused to swallow and catch his breath, trembling. "I came upon a scene from hell. It was the worst I could imagine. It was a scene of destruction, just what you imagine the death scene after a suicide bomber would look like. Smoke was still rising, and burning pieces of paper, clothing, I don't know what, were rising in the air, blowing around, then settling. There were bodies everywhere. And body parts. I have no idea how many people had been killed. I screamed. I screamed my wife's name and my children's names. I saw nothing at first that I recognized. Then I did.

I saw bits of clothing and shoes that I was pretty sure I recognized. Then I knew the worst had really happened, the nightmare that we fear had turned into real life. I was too late. I stood transfixed among all the other people standing and screaming and wailing… and among the injured, bleeding, missing legs and arms, parts of heads and faces, hair. I can't go on, please. Forgive me." He paused again, bending over, putting his head down into his lap, sobbing.

Conrad reached over and put his arm around Levi's shoulder. "I'm sorry. I'm sorry."

"They were dead, all three of them," Levi said in the quietest of voices. "All three of them dead. And they had died in the most horrible way. Twenty-five people in all were killed. The market was very crowded and the explosives from two bombers were powerful. Another thirty were injured, including my brother's family. It was one of the worst suicide bombings. I lay down next to my wife, or what was left of her, touching her flesh. Someone eventually picked me up. Everything is a blur after that, and the next thing I remember is waking later at my wife's sister's house. I don't know how I got home or who came with me. But I have to say that for weeks, months, maybe even years after that, I lived life in a kind of stupor, going through the paces as if I were alive, but knowing that I was dead inside. Someone said I had PTSD, and I suppose I did.

"I once heard a Palestinian public health official say that all Palestinians have PTSD, all of them. That may be true but it works both ways. This horror changed my life. I was unable to forgive the people who inspired and caused this atrocity. I mean the Palestinians, all Palestinians. Some radical group claimed responsibility but I think responsibility is shared in a far broader sense. It's a society, full of venom and hatred and violence. I tried to forgive but I couldn't. My life was changed forever. Those three wonderful, beautiful people were killed and they were killed in the worst way. I might as well have died with them. At the time and for a long time after, I wished that I had. I cried out to God, asking him how this could happen. What could allow this? How could God allow this? Why, God, did you let those innocent people die?

"I was unable to resume teaching and kept postponing my return, week by week, month by month. I was then teaching at a different place, close to my former synagogue. After a year, I had not recovered my will to live, to go outside the house, to carry on life's routine. I had lost my faith, my faith in God. I know bad things happen to good people—but this? I drifted, dependent on the mercy and charity of friends here for a few years. Finally, I got an adjunct teaching position at the college where Conrad teaches. I managed to hold on and gradually recovered, if one can ever recover from something like this."

"Levi is a devoted teacher," Conrad said. "He has a large student following."

"I never married again," Levi said, "and I never resumed being a rabbi, and I did not go to Israel for two years. I finally conquered that fear and I do spend time there. I sustained myself with hatred, hatred for the Palestinian people who bred these murderers who kill blindly, out of passion for cold-blooded killing. I suppose it—the hatred—damaged me. I developed an ulcer. I still have it. I get the feeling of pent-up rage and hatred every time I meet Palestinians or when I read about events there. I try to avoid it and here I am now, agreeing to go to Syria with a Palestinian to intervene in an Arab-upon-Arab fight. How can this be?"

Levi slumped onto the bench where he was sitting, waiting for the flight delay to be over. You could sense the dissonance inside him. He was there with Conrad and the others, waiting to go to the place he saw as hell on earth. And who could blame him for feeling so?

The group was stunned into silence.

※

"Gaspar, how about your story?" Conrad asked. "Why did you decide to become a Catholic priest? What brought you to this point in your spiritual life?"

"Since I'm a bit player in this unfolding drama," Gaspar said, laughing, "I'm going to keep my answer very short. As you might have noticed, I have the freedom to come and go as I please. My motto is, 'Now you see me. Now you don't.' That's my role in this world, my God-given role, I believe.

"In the interest of time and relevance, I'll tell you about an incident that has haunted me all my life. Then I'll tell you about my religious order, which has something to do with our mission. The background is that I grew up in a poor neighborhood. It was dominated by gangs. I had no interest in joining a gang. It seemed to me they were always in a battle. But I had the same need as everyone else to be accepted by someone, I suppose. A couple of guys who lived near me belonged to one of the gangs. I hung around with them occasionally but did not join the gang.

"One time, when I was out late with a few guys from the gang, walking in a neighborhood near ours, someone got the idea of tormenting one of the vagrants sleeping in an alley. They woke him up and made him get to his feet. He was an old man. They started hitting him and kicking him. One of them stabbed him for no reason—just to do it, I guess. The man screamed in pain. He was so scared. He was shaking and begging them not to hurt him. But they kept on torturing him. They knew there would be no consequences. They kept it up until he was dead. There was so much blood, more than I could imagine. I felt sick. I stayed because I was afraid they would turn on me if I said anything. I never imagined it would go that far. It was like the feeling of power and the sight of blood excited them and they lost control."

"I once saw that happen," Levi said, "in Israel during one of those random stabbings that happen from time to time. I saw two innocent people stabbed to death brutally. Unbelievable. Sickening."

Gaspar nodded, then went on. "I had seen a few shootings in the neighborhood but I had never seen anyone killed in a murderous frenzy. I hung around in the background and finally started edging my way down the alley. One of the guys came over and threatened me. He knew I was not a 'made member' of the gang. He made me swear not to tell anyone. The others said they would kill me if I ever told anyone. I promised. I was really frightened for months afterward, afraid to go out, afraid they would come to my house. But I never heard or read anything about the death, the murder. Not a thing. I guess it happened fairly often to the homeless people and no one cared. No one ever reported it. I often wondered what happened to his body. This incident and my failure to prevent it has haunted me lifelong and, no doubt, motivated my decisions."

"That would be enough to change my life," Conrad said.

Gaspar continued. "I've drifted away from doctrine to some extent as a hospital chaplain but the nature of my religious order is still meaningful. I'm fascinated by religious symbolism and mysticism and how they relate to non-religious beliefs. I've been reading recently about how certain beliefs like the power and significance attributed to the periodic blood moons are a carryover from pagan times. We have a blood moon coming up, the last of the tetrad for a two-year period. The mysticism surrounding blood moons fascinates me. The symbolism of blood is interesting to me in itself especially because of my religious order. I know it is to you, Conrad, because of your disease. It's really remarkable that blood has played such a major role in religious history and belief. You are focused on trying to deal with your disease of the blood, just as Ayah is. I am spellbound by that little girl. I think there is something special about her, something unique. She has qualities that remind me of what was said about Jesus as a boy, his wisdom and his insight into the future...."

"Incidentally, there will be a total eclipse and a blood moon visible in the Middle East at the time of our mission," Gaspar related. "I can't wait to see it. There have been all kinds of predictions in the media about this blood moon signifying the coming of the Lord and the end of time. There are references to the blood moon in both the Old and New Testaments. There is a reference to the blood moon in the Qur'an, too, although it's not as well known. The Qur'an has a passage that seems to talk about Islam's fight on behalf of true believers. It even mentions killing and being killed. Then it says this curious thing: 'Their promise,' referring to true believers, I guess, 'is written in the blood of the moon.' I'm not sure what it means by 'the blood of the moon.' These passages are ambiguous, I have to concede."

"I'm not familiar with that," Ghadir interjected. "I can imagine that it is ambiguous."

"I'm interested to see if the blood moon phenomenon gets any special attention when we're in countries where Islam prevails," continued Gaspar. "Here in the States, it's viewed just as a total eclipse, without the religious symbolism and meaning. I've been looking closely at ISIS since I first met Ghadir and Ayah here at the hospital.

"Finally, I'd like to add a pitch," Gaspar said. "I'm very much opposed to the fringe, violent Islamist groups that aren't really Muslims at all. I can't understand why the peaceful world of Islam, which includes 99 percent of all Muslims, doesn't reject and control the tiny violent faction. I suppose it's because the violent ones turn to brutal violence and peaceful Muslims are not equipped to deal with that. I think all wars arise when one power tries to dominate others. I've learned that there is a whole spectrum of beliefs within Islam. There certainly are core beliefs, as with any religion, but Muslims, even those who aren't particularly observant, resist the idea of giving it up in favor of integrating in society. They don't want to see it become secular or pluralistic, or change the faith so much that it goes out of existence. Muslims should stand up against the violent jihadists, who do what they do for power, not faith and devotion to God. They shouldn't be asked to give up their religion and assimilate into society. No other religious group is asked to do that. But neither they nor any other religious group uses violence on society....That's my story."

⁂

"Okay," said Conrad, mustering the courage to speak of his condition, "now it's my turn to say something. We're getting close to departure time. Most of you have heard my whole story. I'm not expected to be around a year from now and that may be stretching it. I'm not giving up hope, though. I have bad days and good days. The good ones are when I am so absorbed in living that I push thoughts of early death into a far corner of my mind. This trip is the culmination of my life and all my interests. I've been warned by my doctors that it may be the last thing I do. I can't think of a better way to close out my life."

"I hope you don't discount all that has gone right for you," Virginia said. "The two of us finding each other after all these years is life-changing."

"Believe me, Virginia," Conrad said, taking her hand and bringing it to his lips, "I certainly do. It's the best thing that has happened to me in a long time—ever, I think. I do feel like I have a future."

Virginia smiled warmly. Conrad paused and shrugged his shoulders, as if to discount his self-pity, then he went on.

"I'm here today because this is the culmination of my life. I've put a lot of bad things behind me, toxic things, including people who have hurt me deeply. There are greater objectives and I want to be part of them. I can't afford dwelling on the past, the toxic past. The way I see it, the key to global peace lies in the Middle East. That's always been the case. This area was the incubator for some of the world's major religions, maybe all of them. It was the place that nurtured human life and civilization. Somehow, it developed into a cauldron for hatred and conflict as well.

"Almost all of the major world conflicts have some connection to Middle East conflict and bloodshed. It's where we need to concentrate our efforts to find a way for people of different beliefs to live in harmony. Most people have given up on the Middle East. They've given up on peace in Israel and Palestine, and peace in Syria, Lebanon, Yemen, Iraq, and Afghanistan. But it's the one place where we must *not* give up on peace. I don't think I've done any really bad things in my life, if you don't count failing in virtually everything." He smiled wanly, acknowledging the self-deprecation. "But I've certainly committed many sins and I've been a weak person, afraid to act, afraid to speak most of the time. I've done very little that is worthwhile. This is my chance, maybe my last chance. I dedicate myself to this trip and to fulfilling our mission."

The others were silent for a time after Conrad stopped speaking. Ghadir reached her hand over to touch his. "You are a very good person, Conrad. That is obvious. Ayah discovered your true nature the first time she met you."

"Ayah did?" Conrad asked. "How did she know what was in my mind?"

"I don't know if you observed this," Ghadir said, "but Ayah is a very special child. She seems to understand people's nature instantly. She recognizes good and evil in people. Her illness may have made her powers—I call them powers—more acute, but she had them even when she was a small child. She is, in many ways, a true daughter of Muhammed. I mean that seriously and it has implications for those who understand Islam.

"She understood what was happening to her father long before anyone else," Ghadir said. "Well before Yousef met the group of jihadists in Boston, she observed that he felt isolated from the people he worked with and that he was increasingly bitter about being singled out as different. She listened carefully and sympathized with his situation. I tended to tell him he was oversensitive and should learn to cope with it. She saw him become more isolated from his work colleagues and from her, too. She even told me he was having an 'identity crisis.'

"I was so busy with my own work," Ghadir added, "and with having full responsibility for the home and the children that I didn't pay enough attention. I also noticed that Yousef had more money than before. He spent more but not on us. I should have noticed that warning sign. DAESH is well known for handing out money to recruits as a way of inducing them, in addition to providing a sense of social belonging. As he became closer to them, he became increasingly distant from us. It worried Ayah because she had always counted on a close relationship with him as well as with me."

"You can't fault yourself," Conrad said. "How could you imagine this would happen? Both of you were so successful here in America. Why wouldn't he be satisfied?"

"It didn't seem like a real fear to me at the time. Ayah was concerned about her brother's welfare, too. She observed her father devoting all his attention to Jamil. She warned me that his life could be in jeopardy and that we should protect him, perhaps send him somewhere safe. I wasn't sure what to do. The worst happened. Ayah has urged me to see that Jamil is rescued without violence if possible, especially against her father. She still cares about her father despite what he has done. She anticipates, as I do, the potential of violence between her father and her uncle, my brother Hussein. There is long-standing animosity between them. I don't know whether it will be possible to save Jamil without violence, but I am committed to do all I can to avoid it. There will be hard choices to make, but I know that violence will never be a solution to the problem of violence."

"I am certain we will be met by violence on the part of DAE-SH," Levi said. "The nature of that organization is violence. It will not be defeated magically by some sleight of hand or by a prayer. I can't imagine that we can accomplish our goal without combating violence with violence."

"I know it appears so," Ghadir said. "I've talked briefly with my brother and I know that Ayah has talked to him once or twice from home. I won't know until we meet him, hopefully in Zaatari, whether he will have reinforcements along."

"I hope we can find your son in Jordan," Levi said. "I'm afraid, frankly, of going into Syria, afraid of everyone—Assad's forces, ISIS and the huge number of rebel groups, even the police. The Syrian border will be closely guarded. It is closed to most people, certainly to a motley crew as we are—a Jew, a Palestinian, a Catholic priest who promotes non-violence and Buddhist ideas, a leukemia patient, and a nurse. Some militia we are! No question that we are as unlikely a crew as Dorothy's as they journeyed to Oz. Bring on the ruby slippers!"

At Levi's description of the makeshift "militia" about to challenge a group of brutal DAESH warriors, the whole group burst into laughter, drawing curious attention from a passing stream of newly arrived passengers. But it was not so much humor Levi intended, as it was sarcasm.

"I would enjoy the laugh with you all if it weren't so serious," Levi added. "Here we are, about the least formidable group anyone could imagine. And yet we are about to take on the world's most brutal and violent military force. We expect to subdue them and rescue their prisoners, all without committing violence. We are about the silliest military force ever to go on a mission. I'm beginning to agree that our opponents will die laughing at the spectacle we present. Yes, indeed, we will take them by surprise."

"Wait," Conrad said, "can't we say that DAESH is every bit a group of misfits—people who don't fit into the world community—people who use religion as a pretext to prey on the weak, the innocent, and the defenseless? And for what? To establish a society of repression, of terror, of exploitation? I accuse them of being the world's worst cowards. We may be innocent, perhaps even naïve, to think we can succeed. But we don't lack courage.

We will not be rid of this gang for a while but they are doomed to utter failure and extinction. They are on the wrong side of history. But the enemies of ISIS must assess them correctly. They are not the type of organization that can be bombed out of existence, which is all some Western leaders seem to come up with."

Levi applauded Conrad's diatribe, which had attracted attention among the expanded crowd of waiting passengers nearby. Gaspar and Ghadir looked around, wondering if any terrorists were among the passengers within earshot.

❧

"You should tell us about yourself, Virginia," Gaspar said. "You are the only one of our Wizard of Oz bunch who has not said what you are in search of."

"While you all were speaking, I wondered what on earth I could say about myself that would be meaningful," Virginia replied, quietly. "My life has been traditional and ordinary. I don't think I experienced traumas at the level that all of you faced. I met my husband, Henry, and Conrad while I was in nursing school. They were roommates at college. Conrad and I dated before I started dating Henry. I had a happy marriage for many years until bladder cancer took over his body. He suffered quite a bit but managed to remain active with writing until a few months before the end. We did suffer a loss some years before, which was a great sadness to us. Our only child, a daughter, Nancy, died when she was twelve years old. Conrad doesn't know this, but she died of leukemia. That was long before leukemia got so much attention from medical researchers. When I went back to my nursing work, I chose to get additional training as a pediatric oncology nurse. I guess it was my way of contributing in a way that was related to my daughter's death. I worked in pediatric oncology for nearly ten years. As it turned out, the training and experience helped me take care of Henry through his severe illness. I don't mind mentioning that I developed an addiction to prescription medicine after Nancy's death. It took a while but I conquered that illness and it made me more sensitive and understanding of patients' problems of that nature.

"I'm satisfied with my life. It hasn't been problem-free, but overall, I'd say I've been very fortunate. As far as the trip is concerned, I'm one-hundred percent committed to this important goal and to helping Conrad stay safe and healthy on this trip. I'll make sure he takes his medication and I'll watch to see that he is not overdoing anything. Although Conrad and I have been friends for many years, we have rediscovered each other in a very happy way. I feel that the future looks bright."

❧

"We should talk about what we're going to do once we arrive," Ghadir said, adding some practicality to their conversation. "The last message from Hamza and Mona was that they would leave Yarmouk soon to head for Jordan and the Zaatari camp, which would be safer than Yarmouk. I expect that we will meet them there. At least, I think that's where we should get our driver to take us, once we hire a car and driver at the airport. Depending on what we find, we will have to develop our strategies on the spot, including how to get into Syria. I'll coordinate with Hussein as necessary."

"Agreed," said Levi. The others nodded. An announcement that boarding was to begin overrode the remainder of their conversation. Within a half-hour, the five were seated in adjacent seats across the aisle of the Royal Jordanian 747. Conrad suggested that they change seats periodically during the flight so each could talk with the others.

Levi looked resigned to the idea, but he was not enthusiastic. "I guess that's a good way to get to know everyone better," he said.

"It'll be good for you!" Conrad said, sounding like a camp counselor urging a bracing morning hike. "Don't forget, Ghadir probably feels the same hesitation about Israelis as you do about Arabs. The responsibility for the violence between your countries is not the fault of one alone. It's a shared responsibility. Both sides have valid points to make. You're both reasonable people."

Conrad, Virginia, and Ghadir began the flight together with Levi and Gaspar across the aisle. After the uneventful takeoff, they settled back quietly, each contemplating the uncertainties that lay ahead.

❧

After the plane reached its cruising altitude, Conrad turned to Ghadir. "Will you tell me what life was like at Dheisheh when you were growing up? You spent most of your first twenty years there, right?"

"Yes," Ghadir said. "I would divide the time into two parts—when active, continuous, violent conflict was going on between Israelis and Palestinians and when the violence was merely sporadic and localized. Violence was always a part of daily life in one way or another.

"During periods of active conflict, such as the second Palestinian intifada, the uprising around the turn of this last century, every day was a living hell. We worried about being destroyed every time an Israeli plane went overhead. The whole camp could have been wiped out with a few bombs. It didn't happen on that scale, but that was little consolation to those who were killed or whose homes were destroyed."

"I had no idea it was that bad," Conrad said.

"Life even during the quieter times was characterized by a certain numbness. Being numb was an effective way to cope with the delays, the crowds, the unpredictable flow of electricity and other utilities, and life without political and civil rights. As a child, one knows nothing different, and so I accepted this way of life and it acquired a certain normalcy. But to my parents and their parents, it was different. They remembered a different time, a better time, a time of freedom of movement and of homeownership. It was harder for them, but their past memories and the shared stories of the people faded away in time. We lived with the blackouts and the roadblocks when we were outside the camp. We lived with inconvenience and frustration. And we lived with the expectation of intrusions by Israeli soldiers, checking for this person or that one, but we never knew when they would occur."

"Was life worse at one time or another?" Conrad asked.

"That's difficult to say," Ghadir said. "In Palestine, we could come and go. But Syrians placed restrictions on Palestinians entering Syria. Syria is far more dangerous now to those of us who are labeled the PRS, than being in the West Bank or the areas near Jerusalem where Palestinians may live. Living in Dheisheh, which was by no means the worst camp, was like living in a prisoner of war camp although with more liberal conditions. You could also say it was like living in an occupied country. In some respects, it is both. Does that give you a clear picture? Of course, I have skipped the details of everyday life but I think you can imagine them. The presence of DAESH in Syria is unbearable."

About halfway through the trip, Gaspar took Conrad's seat next to Ghadir. In conversation with her, he focused on a different subject, Ghadir's husband. Conrad, seated directly across the aisle, listened intently.

"How do you think this educated, intelligent man, which I assume he was, suddenly decided to leave his wife and daughter and take his son to a country engaged in civil war to make him a soldier?" Gaspar began. "How could this happen? Did he become dissatisfied or did something happen that disillusioned him? Was it a religious thing?"

"I don't think it was sudden and I don't think it was religious," Ghadir said. "It happened over the course of at least a year, most likely. Of course, I can only piece it together in retrospect from what I observed and what my daughter pointed out. By the time I realized that he had separated himself from me and given his total loyalty to DAESH, it was too late. His brain had changed. As you know, this is far from an isolated case. Thousands of men are leaving their homes all over the world to go and fight for DAESH in Syria and Iraq and they are still recruiting. In fact, they have to keep recruiting to keep their strength. The survival of the group is everything, even more important than the political gains they claim are their goals. I believe the violence is more to attract recruits and maintain solidarity than to win any particular goals. An outsider can't be certain but many people study terrorist groups and how they survive—and how they die off."

"Could you focus on how it starts?" Gaspar pressed her.

"It starts on the personal level," Ghadir said, "with new friendships, giving the recruit a sense of belonging to a social group. Sometimes this is done through email and sometimes through personal contact as in Yousef's case. The recruit has to be susceptible to it—ripe for the picking, as someone said—and the people who proselytize recognize that they have—what do you call it in American slang—a mark."

"You mean it's what we call a con game, a scam, in a way," Conrad said from across the aisle.

"Yes," Ghadir said. "My husband was engaged in his graduate work for a while but then he ran into some frustration. He didn't like his advisor and nothing he was doing seemed to please her. He blamed that on who he was—a Muslim—rather than on the quality of his work. He felt picked on. He was afraid of failing to complete his thesis and get his PhD. He succeeded in that but when he started work at the university, he got paranoid again about being picked on, overlooked, for being different—for being Muslim. He became isolated, resentful, bitter, and eventually that turned to hatred.

"Yousef spoke about feeling isolated socially. He seemed to need to belong to a social group in order to give him identity as someone worthwhile. If he felt lonely, as many recruits do, it was his own fault. He had a family who loved him and wanted to spend more time with him. Somehow, that was not enough. He needed to define himself outside the home, I guess.

"We had money problems, too, even after he first started work in Boston. What we were both getting in grants and fellowships and pay for being teaching assistants wasn't enough to get by—at least not the way he thought we should. I was doing graduate study and taking care of the children. Ayah needed special care and a lot of my time for medical appointments. When we were working, it was the same story. There was never enough time or money. I suspect that the recruiters were giving Yousef money and he became flattered by that and dependent on it. I didn't have much time for Yousef and I wasn't very sympathetic to his complaints about his advisor or, later, his boss. I felt he should just deal with it, do his work, and share responsibility with me."

"There's a pattern to recruiting for marginal organizations like this, particularly with DAESH," Gaspar said.

"Around the same time of his disillusionment, of what Ayah calls his 'identity crisis,' Yousef met several men," Ghadir said. "I later learned them to be Islamic extremists. You'd be amazed if you knew how many DAESH sends to this country and all over the world, just to recruit and perhaps eventually do some damage. I think these men, whom he never brought to our house, of course, would play on his weaknesses and talk down the U.S. and made him feel as though it wasn't his fault. It was everybody else's fault. Of course, they painted a glowing picture of life where the Islamic State was in control.

"Eventually, he began to talk about fighting for a cause, an important cause. He would quote Abu Bakr al-Baghdadi, the Islamic State leader. He'd bring home reading material about al-Baghdadi. He'd follow all the terrorist attacks that DAESH claimed credit for. He admired the success of the attacks in Western countries. More and more, he would talk down America and he resented the American military invading, as he called it, Iraq, Afghanistan, and Syria.

"From what he told me, and he would not talk much about this as they began to influence him, they didn't talk about all the killing at this point. They would create a peaceful state, at least for Muslims. I didn't mention that these extremists have no respect for women. I was carrying the family on my back and had achieved the same level of success that he, Yousef, had but he became more and more disrespectful and abusive as time went on."

"What about religious aspects?" Gaspar asked. "Do you think these recruiters inspired religious beliefs in him? Was he religious before all this?"

"He was raised in a religious family, as I was, no more or less extremist. We observed most traditions but not all. We weren't as religious as many Muslims are but we didn't turn our backs on it, either. Even today, I'm not particularly religious. I observe the holidays and I fast at Ramadan but, for example, I don't perform prayer at home or at the mosque every day as some women do.

"I believe they reached him through religion as well as on the personal level. But religion was used as a political tool, not an end in itself. Religion was intertwined with power. It was one of many means to power. This is where the U.S. misjudges DAESH. The leaders—most of them, anyway—see it as an outgrowth of Al Qaida, at least now where they stop saying it's the 'junior varsity.' It took a long time to realize that DAESH has deep religious roots even though its goals are much more about power than about pure theocracy. They exploit religion for their own purposes and they keep or discard what they want of Islam, as it suits them. DAESH promotes the idea that its members believe in this extreme form of Islam which is militant in a way that is not accepted by the vast majority of Muslims. I believe their goals are power-oriented. They use religion just as they use violence to achieve their political and military goals. Although promoting Islam is held up as a goal, the leaders feel free to manipulate it and change it whenever it's expedient."

"I've read about how even in Raqqa, the headquarters of their political state, if we can call it that, they use Islamic law as they please," Gaspar said, "and they don't hesitate to enforce it brutally or simply change it when they please."

"It's complicated and inconsistent," Ghadir said. "They believe in the religious meaning in one sense. It gives them strength. That's why DAESH will not go away easily and why Americans need to understand the religious foundations. Until Americans and other Westerners appreciate the origin and internal functioning of this particular terrorist organization, they will not control or dominate it. It will self-destruct—implode—before it will be crushed by outright military force. That's the lesson.

"It seems to me that this is not entirely different from the way Christianity is often used. It is used as a justification for certain political goals and it's also called on as a rallying cry for political and military conquest. Historically, it has been used to promote violence, too."

"I can't disagree with that," Gaspar said. "It has been used by extremists in those ways. Right now, most of the world's people are appalled by the level of violence promoted by DAESH. The leaders seem to bend over backwards to challenge the morality that most people adhere to. Sometimes it seems to me like violence for the sake of violence, without being connected to political or military strategy or goals. It's an assertion of power and how the extremely violent use of power can cause great fear among many people."

"I agree," Ghadir said. "The violence seems to repel people more than attract them. It seems to thwart their own goals by so horrifying people that they want to destroy DAESH and everyone connected with it. The use of power is very short-sighted.

"As for my husband, I believe Yousef became convinced that he wanted to live in a country governed by DAESH. It gave him a sense of belonging, a false feeling of importance. My guess is that the militancy and negative aspects got to him, too, and he became excited to be a recruit in the holy war that they advocated. He began to see America and the West as evil and DAESH as good. Of course, DAESH promotes the idea that everyone who opposes it is the Devil—Muslims, especially Shia, Christians, Jews, not just Americans. In Yousef's case, he began to hate American society, for its practices and way of life that he once had aspired to enjoy. It was a gradual transition, playing on weakness and fear, offering friendship and belonging and then going in for the kill. He was ensnared and enabled to do unthinkable things. Now he is dangerous. That he can think of turning Jamil into a child soldier or even a suicide bomber is beyond my belief. But it is true."

PART SIX

THE TRIP

THE FLIGHT WAS UNEVENTFUL. After disembarking and heading for the customs area, they observed an extremely high level of security forces in the airport. This was not surprising in view of the recent terrorist shootings and bombings in Jordan, which had thought itself fairly safe from such activity. The Jordan security forces were known to operate effectively. The recent terrorist attacks had undermined the national pride in its security forces. Tightening of control was a natural outcome. The travelers had discussed the possibility that each of them would be subjected to close questioning by the customs officials. As individuals, each would be questioned carefully for different reasons. Had they appeared to anyone as a group, they would receive far more attention since they would stand out as a curious group traveling together.

As it turned out, Ghadir was the only member of the group who received extensive questioning about her purpose in visiting Jordan. She had anticipated that she would be thoroughly interrogated. She prepared for it with a story that did not involve Syria in any way. Ghadir was resigned to expect extensive questioning whenever she traveled because of her Palestinian background, despite her U.S. citizenship. She was passed through eventually by the single customs official and the group headed together for the ground transportation area. None of them had checked any luggage. Each of them had brought only hand luggage for ease in traveling during their expected short stay on this trip.

The next problem was finding a suitable driver with a vehicle large enough to accommodate the five of them plus, hopefully, the additional passengers including Mona, Hamza, and the two boys. As they expected, the lobby of the airport was overflowing with drivers and tour guides with signs, clamoring for the attention of tourists and other visitors. They waited until the height of the furor had diminished to select a few candidates who remained un-committed. Finding someone who could meet all their needs was a delicate matter. They agreed that they should say nothing about going to the border or crossing the border into Syria, much less going to Yarmouk. That would scare off legitimate drivers, which was a disadvantage. Finding a driver willing to cross the Syrian border illegally would be difficult and risky.

Ghadir, the only one of them who was fluent in Arabic, spot-ted a driver with a sign that said in Arabic, "Omran's Van ser-vice—fair prices."

"He looks like he has a legitimate driving service," Ghadir said. "I'll have a conversation with him."

She negotiated with Omran for twenty minutes and he agreed to take them to Zaatari refugee camp, the most likely destination in Jordan for the family. Zaatari was about 70 kilometers north of Amman near the town of Mafraq. Since Amman was 25 kilo-meters south of Amman, they should count on three hours, to be on the safe side.

Omran, a heavy-set Jordanian man in his mid-fifties, was friendly and chatty at first but kept glancing at the five passen-gers, probably trying to figure out what could bring such different individuals together and why they would want to go to a refugee camp. He asked a series of questions obviously designed to elicit information about their purposes. When his questions got no an-swers, he became more guarded as they drove on. He announced after they were underway that the fee would be sufficient to take them only to Zaatari, no further, and that he was licensed to drive only in Jordan. Gaspar, who wanted to brush up his modest Ara-bic, sat in the front seat with him. Omran asked why they were going to Zaatari.

"To meet someone," Gaspar said. "Why do you ask?"

"Just wondering," he replied. "Are you on a mission to work at the camp?"

"No," said Gaspar. "We're meeting someone there, someone who is on a trip. What does Zaatari look like these days? Is it overcrowded? Clean? Safe?"

"Most people say, 'Ah, I didn't realize it looks like a neighbor-hood in a city.' It's fairly clean, but I wouldn't want to live there. It is restricted and there's no free passage in and out."

"Is it safe?" Gaspar asked.

"Mostly. But there has been some violence. It depends on the population. And it depends on the police. They keep strict con-trol of the gates so new refugees don't enter the general popula-tion readily. Are any of you Palestinians? They usually don't let Palestinians in."

"Why is that?" Gaspar asked.

"They consider them troublemakers. They feel more com-fortable with Syrians. They feel that Palestinians should just stay home. They have a place to live. It's the Syrians who are home-less in this war that goes on and on. Palestinians are no longer welcome. Let them go back to Palestine. That is what I say, too."

"Does that seem fair to you?" Gaspar asked. "If some Pales-tinians were in Syria as legitimate refugees, why shouldn't they be able to go to a safer place, too? After all, aren't they refugees in the first place and the second place?"

Omran clearly disapproved of Gaspar's view and seemed wary of being drawn into an argument. He went silent, his face formed to a scowl. Ghadir was used to this prejudicial attitude against Palestinians. It was what she expected as the result of the long-term experience of her people. Conrad sensed that Omran would not be flexible about crossing into Syria and that he would be difficult to handle if pressure were put on him. Omran could be a problem if they did not find the family in Jordan.

❧

After they left the airport road system the van bumped along the rough road toward Zaatari.

"I have an email from Mona's sister. Shall I read it aloud?" asked Ghadir, glancing at Conrad for approval.

He nodded yes but whispered that she should read it very quietly to him so the driver wouldn't overhear. Ghadir added that she received the email today but it was written by Mona several days ago.

We reached Yarmouk two days ago. It was early evening and just starting to get dark. Although we were interrogated intensely by the guards, we were allowed to enter. They asked us where we were coming from, whether we were Syrian or Palestinian, and whether we understood this was a dangerous place with no security. They wanted to know if we were healthy and whether the children were our own. They said we might not have any shelter and that we could stay only three days. We told them we probably wouldn't stay more than two days.

They said to expect bombing every night. They wanted to know which area of the camp we wanted to stay in. They told us that various areas were controlled by ISIS, others by government forces, others by rebel groups like al-Nusra. Some areas appeared to be neutral at this point but there were no guarantees. We want the safest place, we said. We were assigned to a neutral area.

During the last few days before reaching Yarmouk, we encountered a lot of dangers on the road. We saw an increase in troop carriers of all kinds. Some appeared to be government forces, and others were troops wearing DAESH uniforms. We saw other rebel groups that were difficult to identify. I imagine al-Nusra forces were in the area too. This is a hotbed of fighting and bombing. Destruction is everywhere. Private and public buildings have suffered extreme damage. We experienced bombing very close by and a great deal more in the distance. We felt very much in jeopardy from the bombs. It was impossible to tell whose bombs were falling. We were told that the U.S. was bombing in Aleppo and that Russia had started in the Eastern portion. We heard that the U.S. was targeting DAESH but Russia appeared to be bombing only rebel groups that opposed the Assad regime, despite claiming to target DAESH. We heard that a Doctors Without Borders hospital encampment had been struck and that a training camp for child soldiers run by DAESH had also been struck.

It seems that much of the bombing is not well focused; civilians are bearing a heavy burden of injuries and death. This is the worst fighting and danger we've encountered since leaving Aleppo. But of course we are close to Damascus, the seat of the Assad government. The word on the streets is that Damascus may soon be taken over by either DAESH or al-Nusra. In either case, the government will lose and Assad will have to flee. Hamza doubts that Assad will give up that easily. Parts of the city may be held by DAESH and part by al-Nusra, an arm of Al Qaeda, which apparently is an enemy of DAESH now. Presumably they will fight it out for control of the city. It's difficult for me to keep straight on the various groups and their alliances.

We are going to leave tomorrow for safer territory. We are afraid of the bombing and other violence in this place. People here say this refugee center is the worst place on earth. With DAESH in the area, our fears about Yousef have increased. We fear he may be tracking us. We are too close to the boys' training camp to feel comfortable. For all we know, Yousef could be right here in Yarmouk. That is our greatest fear. We fear the rebel groups too. We expect to leave and head for Jordan. We have found two families who will travel with us. One has an old car. This will enable us to manage the trip more quickly. At least we can let the children ride along with people who are elderly or ill.

Many people are riding bicycles. In fact, we were able to purchase two for ourselves so we can nearly keep up with the car. We see bicycles everywhere, most of them old. We understand that the Netherlands donated thousands of bicycles. No one wants to stay at Yarmouk. I think this area is also a recruiting area for the thousands who are coming to join DAESH. They will receive training nearby along with child soldiers. We must escape from here and we hope to meet with Ghadir and her friends, whom you told us about, at Zaatari camp.

❧

"A second message has come in just now from Mona's sister," Ghadir said quietly. "I'll translate and summarize. They expect to leave Yarmouk before the end of the day, hopefully without being seen by any DAESH soldiers who might know Yousef. They will be on their way to the Jordan border. The car broke down and they are walking. They have only two bicycles so that doesn't help much. Maybe they will be lucky to find a taxi. They are only 38 km from the Jordan border. They will head for Zaatari but it is not likely that they will reach it for several days. Once they get across the border, which may not be so simple, they will be safe. Zaatari is a large camp and much safer than Yarmouk. There's more.

"Ayah has been in contact with Mona's sister. She has heard from my brother several times. As you know, he is affiliated with Ahrar al-Sham, a rebel group that opposes both Assad and DAE-SH. With the big push to take over Damascus, he is on his way to Damascus. They hope they can eventually defeat both Assad and DAESH. He will not be far from Yarmouk and if something goes wrong before they reach the Jordan border, he is close at hand. He will communicate a meeting place a safe distance from Yarmouk. Ayah has told him that there should not be bloodshed but that, of course, the main goal is to rescue Jamil and bring the whole family back safely."

"This is exciting news," Conrad said. "It would be a relief to resolve this without fighting. The five of us are hardly prepared for fighting. We have to rely on Hussein. And I doubt that persuasion will win if it comes to a confrontation with Yousef."

"I pray for Hussein's safety, too," Ghadir said. "He's in danger in the Yarmouk area. I hope he can avoid fighting until Jamil is safe."

"If Hamza and Mona are not here yet," Conrad said as they were nearing the camp, "do you think we should stop and wait or keep going to the border and try to intercept them? It could mean the difference of a day."

"I think we should wait overnight at least and then consider what to do," Ghadir said.

"We need to keep the driver from leaving," Conrad said. "We should try to negotiate a price for him to wait with us," Conrad said. "But we can't alert him that we may want him to take us to Syria. Can you persuade him to remain here?"

"I will do my best," Ghadir said. "Once we reach the camp, I'll tell him to stay because we will need him to drive us back and that it could take a couple of days while we find our relatives in this huge camp."

In a half-hour, they pulled into the huge camp parking area. Ghadir instructed Gaspar and Levi to remain in the car for fear that if they left Omran alone, he would disappear. She told Omran to wait and that he would be paid for his time. The excuse was that they had to ask permission to enter for the purpose of finding their relatives. Omran agreed grudgingly. Ghadir suspected that Omran was less than enthusiastic about having Levi as a passenger. She and Conrad approached the guarded entrance to the camp that now contained some 80,000 people.

An hour-long interrogation followed, with the Jordanian guards inquiring into their nationality, place of origin, purpose in being here, along with a wide-ranging inquiry. Conrad feared that they would be denied entrance and denied information. Eventually, the guards agreed to search their sparse records for Hamza and Mona's names. They found nothing. Another half-hour was required to persuade them to let the group stay overnight on the representation that the relatives they were to meet had not yet arrived. Ghadir handed over to the guards the expected bribes to guarantee the transaction.

Returning to the van, Ghadir informed Omran of the situation and that they needed to hire him for at least another day and perhaps another after that. He protested and said that was impossible. Ghadir pleaded with him not to leave them stranded without transportation. He said they could phone him in Amman when they were ready and he would come to get them. Ghadir rejected that suggestion, knowing that Omran was not likely to return. Hours of standoff passed and finally Omran agreed to remain until the next day. Ghadir insisted that she be allowed to hold the keys to the vehicle and, in exchange, Omran could hold a cash deposit on his additional fee. Reluctantly, he agreed. She knew there would be a problem getting Omran to stay longer.

Ghadir arranged for makeshift sleeping accommodations for the five travelers plus the driver. They divided into two groups of three and made their way to two vacant lean-to type shelters with nothing in them but filthy worn-out mattresses that had been abandoned by previous occupants. Conrad, Virginia and Ghadir occupied one shelter and the other three, including Omran, were a block away. Conrad spent a restless night, despite his extreme fatigue, wondering where the family was and whether they would arrive during the night. Morning came and, after inquiries of the camp guards, they were told that no family of four had arrived. Their own searches produced no information about the family. They were troubled to learn that new fighting had erupted in the vicinity of Yarmouk and in areas close to the Jordan border.

They decided to remain at the camp for another day and night in hopes that Mona and Hamza would arrive. Ghadir was concerned that perhaps they decided to go to Baqa'a instead, because of the large Palestinian population. An inquiry of Mona's sister indicated that there had been no mention of Baqa'a and she was sure Mona would tell her if they changed their plans. Omran protested loudly but the promise of additional money quieted his objections. Another night passed, with Omran becoming more and more agitated and declaring that he would refuse to stay any longer.

"I have a family, you know, and I have to get back to work," he protested red-faced and angry. "You are not paying me enough to stay. I will not let you force me to stay against my will. This is a dangerous place. This is criminal to try and force me to stay. I am leaving tomorrow morning and you will not stop me. I will go to the authorities."

⁂

Before sunrise the next morning, Ghadir informed Conrad and Virginia of a new message from Mona's sister, who was now aware of the location of the rescue crew and their plan. Ghadir, shaking and holding back tears, read the message aloud to them and to Levi, who joined them.

> *As we were approaching a point about ten miles from the border, amidst extensive bombing and shelling all night and all day, we were overtaken by a caravan of Humvees. We were walking, pushing the boys on the bicycles. No taxis or buses stopped for us so progress was very slow. The road was crowded with so many other people walking. By the time we spotted the caravan, it was too late to leave the road for cover. As*

the vehicles, which we recognized as ISIS carriers, were passing us, suddenly one stopped. Three men got out and waved us over. I was shocked to recognize Yousef. My heart sank. I knew we were lost. All three of them were heavily armed with automatic weapons.

"I've been looking for you," he said, with visible rage. "Why did you not keep in touch with me to let me know where my son was?"

Yousef didn't even greet Jamil. He directed all his fury at us. We tried to explain that we had to flee Aleppo for our lives. He began screaming at us, saying, "You kidnapped my son. You had no right." He said he could kill us. "I trusted you," he said to Hamza, "but you betrayed me." The caravan kept going slowly and I could see he was getting agitated. I pleaded that he should let us go to Zaatari where we would be safe and he could find us there. He was silent. I asked where he was going and he muttered something about an encampment. "I will go back to Yarmouk with the boys," he said.

I wept and pleaded, Hamza too, but it was to no avail. He ordered the boys into his vehicle. They were terrified. He said he was going to kill us. He talked with his two men and apparently changed his mind. He said nothing further but he spoke to the men in another vehicle. I heard the words, "I will take them to the training camp." He turned his vehicle around and headed back on the road to Yarmouk and, no doubt, to the children's training camp.

We were thankful for our lives but we are devastated that he has taken both Jamil and Karam. I watched them huddled in the back of the Humvee staring back at us, their eyes pleading. There was nothing to be done. We decided that we have no choice but to return to Yarmouk and try to secure help there to rescue the boys. We dare not leave them and continue on to Jordan. We will not go inside but will camp outside about three kilometers south of it in a tiny village that we passed. The name is Burraq, the Arabic name of the Temple Mount, a walled compound within the city of Jerusalem and the site of religious landmarks. We will wait for you there.

We can continue to communicate by text or email. This close to Damascus, there is both cellular and Internet service, although it is intermittent and not dependable. People who assist refugees have amplified the Internet service so we should be able to stay in touch. Please get help and come to meet us. We must locate the boys and rescue them. We will find out the exact location of the training camp.

🌱

Ghadir was pale and barely holding back tears as she finished reading the message. The group of five determined that they would let Hussein know the plan and ask him to meet in Burraq, the small village this side of Yarmouk. Ayah, who had been in touch daily with Ghadir, confirmed that she had communicated the message to Hussein. Now the problem was how to secure transportation across the Syrian border to their destination.

"There's no doubt in my mind," Conrad said. "We have to either persuade Omran to continue with us or we have to make use of his vehicle."

"He'll never agree," Gaspar said. "And we can't just steal his vehicle. That's a crime, besides being immoral."

"Right, he'll report it to the guards," Levi said, "and, being Jordanians, they'll back him up and we'll end up in jail. We just have to find someone else, even if it means calling the airport services or hiring someone here."

"No," Conrad said. "This is urgent. We have no time. The boys could be brought to another camp anywhere in Syria. I understand the main training camp is in Raqqa. It would be far too dangerous to go there and attempt a rescue. Raqqa is where DAESH headquarters in Syria is located. It is heavily armed. We can't risk that happening. We can't lose a moment. If he won't agree, we take it and we have to take him with us or he'll let the guards know and they'll follow us and arrest us."

"I have a plan," Ghadir said. "I'll tell the driver that we need to meet our family just this side of the border. They are waiting for us. It's just a little further and we'll pay him well. He will be in no jeopardy. Then after we're away from Zaatari, out of range, we'll do what we have to do."

"I don't think this will work," Levi said. "We'll all end up in jail. I don't want to be part of this."

"We have the lives of two young boys in our hands," Gaspar said thoughtfully. "Conrad is right that there is no time to spare. But we have to treat Omran humanely and we have to commit to return his vehicle or replace it if it is stolen or damaged. We can't just kidnap him. He can come with us or we will have to find a safe place for him on the Jordan side of the border. Maybe we can find a spot which is too far for him to walk to report it. By that time we'll be gone to Syria anyway. We can return the vehicle by dropping it somewhere once we return. It's best if we can get him to agree either to come with us or wait for us. But we have to find a secret border crossing. There must be many. We can't afford to have him tell the Jordanian guards at the border what is happening. This is a very sensitive matter."

With exasperation, Conrad directed his remarks to Levi and Gaspar. "If you don't want to go along with us, you can stay here, or you can wait for us with Omran near the border, or even by yourself if he chooses to drive his own vehicle and come with us. The moral decision is yours. Play it safe for your own good or help us save two innocent boys from a horrible fate and certain death."

Levi stalked off into the camp at this stinging criticism from Conrad. Conrad let him go, confident that Levi would come around to their point of view. Gaspar responded quickly, "I'll accompany you across the border but I prefer not to participate in the rescue itself. It could be violent and I'm not cut out for that."

Before ten minutes elapsed, Levi returned. "I'm going with you," he said. "I won't desert Conrad. He's okay so far but it's only been a few days. I have to be sure he returns home."

※

At the suggestion of driving to the border, Omran furiously shook his head in the negative. "I will not be party to this. I will report you to the authorities. You are committing a crime. You will all go to prison."

An ugly scene followed. After an hour of negotiating compensation, Ghadir persuaded him to drive them to the border, without mentioning any further plans. Ghadir had found out from camp residents about two unguarded, illegal border crossing locations that would enable them to avoid both the Syrian and Jordanian border guards. She directed the driver toward the closest spot. They had found out that the Syrian guards had sealed the border to prevent anti-Assad rebels from entering. And Jordan had sealed its border from any new immigrants, whether Syrian or Palestinian. The only alternative was one of the two known unguarded crossing points.

When the van stopped, Conrad, who was seated in the front passenger seat, snatched the car keys from the ignition. He and Gaspar got out and stood near the driver's door to prevent Omran from getting out. Omran slammed his body against the door but was unable to force it open. He shouted with rage and threats of arrest. Conrad had assured himself, by careful observation during the trip, that the driver had no weapon.

Omran threatened, then pleaded, then threatened again. "You are liars! You are thieves! You tricked me! I am an old man in poor health with a family. I must work. This car is all I own. I will have you arrested! You will not get away with this. I must return to Amman. I have commitments. You will pay for this!"

"We prefer that you continue with us," Ghadir said calmly. "You can protect your own car. You can drive it. We will pay you for your time—double the fee. If anything happens to your vehicle, we will reimburse you. We will put that in writing. No more than three or four days are involved. If you refuse, we will find a place for you to stay safely and await our return. We will pay for that, probably at one of the farmhouses that we see around here. Levi will stay to guard you. He would probably prefer that anyway."

"We don't have much time, Omran. Think it over but decide quickly."

"I will do that," Levi said, "but I am willing to go the whole way with this mission, as I said."

After twenty minutes of argument, Omran agreed to go with them and drive his vehicle. But not at the crossing that Ghadir had chosen. "I don't like crossing the border illegally," he said. "That's a criminal offense. I prefer to go to the official crossing."

"It's sealed now," Conrad said firmly. "And most of the illegal crossing points have been closed as well. It's grossly unfair to the Syrians who are struggling to get to safety. We've seen and heard of hundreds, maybe more, of sick and dying people, elderly, babies, everybody, on their last breaths some of them, lying on the ground, refused passage to Jordan. Returning to Jordan is going to be a challenge. The border control tightens every day, and the massive number of refugees living here in wait increases every day."

Conrad added to Omran, "We need to get to Syria and back safely before this crossing point gets sealed. We have no alternatives... and we have no time, either. You have to commit to us to cross where we determine, or it's out of your hands. Anyway, we don't trust you to keep still. We go here... or you stay on your own. If you become difficult, we may withdraw the help we're offering you. We will just take you with us, period. You'll get nothing. No pay, no nothing."

Although Omran finally agreed, reluctantly, to cross illegally, they could not trust him. They would have to watch his every move and keep the keys plus his passport the entire time. Conrad remained in the front seat beside him, having possession of his valuables, including his cell phone. He was never allowed out of their sight. Their chances of success hinged on not being discovered. Omran could be dangerous.

They crossed to the Syrian side and soon were on their way toward Yarmouk. Ghadir checked with Ayah and then attempted to contact her brother. Finally a return call came in. They arranged for the meeting place in Al-Buraq, a small village some 20 kilometers to the south of Yarmouk, which was in Damascus. She got an update from Mona directly to ascertain their location. All they needed was time and help from Hussein, who had promised to bring with him as many of his Ahrar al-Sham soldiers as could be spared. From there, after their rendezvous, they would find a location closer to the training camp, which was southeast of Yarmouk.

It took the group of five travelers, plus Omran, who was constantly in a bad mood, sulking and complaining, nearly an hour and a half to reach Al-Buraq. They pulled the van off the road into a field where it would not be easily seen by anyone passing on the road or by aircraft or drones. While they rested and awaited the arrival of Hussein and his small force as well as Mona and Hamza, they assessed what they had learned about the boys' camp and its surroundings. They had made use of their brief time in Zaatari by attempting to gather information about the size, layout, and security of the training camp, the number of boys likely to be there, and the number of Islamic State guards and trainers. They were gambling that Yousef would have made his destination—at least the first one—the Damascus area and this particular training camp. If that proved wrong, they would have to try the other camps but that involved a much more formidable effort in terms of traveling to the north through war zones.

After Hussein arrived, they would pool their knowledge. It was likely that he would have more current information about how best to attack the camp for the rescue operation. Although Hussein was in his thirties and university-educated in law and law enforcement, he had spent the past two years fighting for Ahrar al-Sham. Hussein, still single, had no personal obligations. Originally, he had aspired to travel to the U.S. for further education but that goal was put on hold by the Syrian civil war. His vision was that his rebel force would eventually take over the government once Assad was driven out.

Hussein and three members of his militia, one female and two males, arrived shortly before dark. The meeting between Ghadir and Hussein was emotional. Hussein spoke of numerous conversations with his niece, Ayah, and her insistence that no violence be used, and especially her plea to spare her father's life if they encountered him. Hussein had promised her to do his utmost to fulfill her request, despite knowing, based on their past relationship, that Yousef would not hesitate to kill him if the opportunity presented itself.

After a light meal of packaged food from the supply brought for the entire group by Hussein, the group of nine sat down to discuss their collective knowledge of the mission before them. Omran was required to remain in his van, although Levi estimated that, as a practical matter, he was now too far from the

Jordan border to escape and successfully return on foot to his homeland. Obtaining transportation was uncertain. As a Jordanian, he would be vulnerable to attack by ISIS forces or rebel forces. He was clearly intimidated by the presence of the four heavily armed soldiers.

Hussein had learned that the Zarqawi cubs camp was a few miles southeast of Yarmouk. It was located in an area with desert-like conditions, with a scattering of sparse ground foliage. The desert terrain stretched for tens of miles with slight rises and rock outcroppings at irregular intervals. The camp was accessible by means of a dirt road that branched off the main road and extended at least a mile. Approaches to the camp by way of any of the open areas would be risky because of the minimal natural coverage. There were no ideal approaches for their purpose, although one side of the camp appeared to offer a slightly better approach through a very lightly wooded area which bordered a dried-up stream bed.

Hussein's information revealed that there would likely be as many as twenty to forty boys in training and roughly a dozen DAESH personnel, consisting of equal numbers of trainers and guards. "The low ratio of guards to cubs," he said, "was by the pressure on ISIS forces throughout Syria and the heavy fighting in the Damascus area. Most ISIS troops were engaged in battling the rebel and government forces. Only a few could be spared to guard and train the boys as child soldiers and as suicide bombers."

Hussein had heard rumors that Zarqawi was being used now for fresh recruits and their fathers—or kidnappers—who had come from Europe or the U.S. After basic training, some of the boys were moved to more advanced training camps. The adults departed after the basic training for the front lines of fighting or whatever else they were deemed suitable for. In Hussein's view, Zarqawi in Eastern Ghouta was the logical starting place for the rescue group.

DAESH had captured more than 125 Kurdish schoolboys in the northern part of Syria in Kurdish-run areas. Ein-al-Arab and Manbej were mentioned. Some of the younger ones had been released because they would not be suitable for training but boys in the 14-to-16 age category had been held in the northern part of

Syria. The recruiting of children was a wholesale enterprise. Entire school buses were being stopped and boys and girls were forced to get off. The boys were taken to camps set up for the purpose of brainwashing them in radical Islamic theology. Some were forced to watch videos of beheadings and mutilations. They were threatened with death by beheading if they tried to escape. Similar incidents happened farther south but on a lesser and more sporadic scale. Kidnapped girls were subject to torture and enslavement.

The prediction that Zarqawi would be lightly guarded (because DAESH could not spare many troops at the camp) was encouraging news for a successful rescue—if, in fact, Jamil and Karam were there. Yarmouk had large numbers of troops which could be called upon in case of trouble. There were reports of several escapes by boys who took advantage of the light security of the camp.

Hussein warned the group that they should not assume that rescuing prisoners at the camp would be easy. "There is no telling what the circumstances will be on any day or night. We will not know in advance whether Jamil and Karam will be there. We will conduct surveillance for a substantial period to obtain as much information as possible to guide the assault."

One of Hussein's men had been close to the boys' camp on another occasion and was familiar with the surrounding countryside. He said it was remote and there was little traffic in and out. But it was exposed to surveillance from the camp itself on virtually all sides. There was very little cover for anyone approaching. The best strategy would be to approach the camp at night and take out the soldiers on the perimeter quietly and enter the camp unannounced. It was likely that the guards on the perimeter would have to be killed silently by individual attackers. They would be the only ones fully armed. It was possible that there were only four guards and the rest were military trainers. The latter might not have their arms ready because they would be engaged with other tasks at night. The hope was to kill only those who were the greatest threats to the mission's success, the guards.

He recommended surveillance for two days and nights to ascertain the population and how heavily the troops were armed. Hussein had not had time to attempt to establish contact with

U.S. military special force advisors in the country. His Islamist group, Ahrar al-Sham, was a consolidation of numerous rebel groups, which rejected radical Islamic causes. Since it was an enemy of DAESH as well as the Assad regime, he was hopeful about building a working relationship with U.S. military personnel. That remained uncertain in view of the changing alliances of the group with other Islamic groups such as al-Nusra. But he was not in a position at this point to request drone support to identify the occupants, including guards and prisoners or to assist with the rescue. That would have enabled him to determine the means of access and the likelihood of accomplishing a rescue with minimal violence. The mission would have to be undertaken with a goal of rescuing all boys if possible, hoping that Karam and Jamil were present.

"Hussein," Conrad asked, "will you tell us more about your rebel group? How does it relate to the large number of rebel groups?"

"Right now," Hussein asserted, "my group, Ahrar al-Sham, is one of the few Islamist coalitions that the U.S. recognizes as compatible with American goals. We reject anyone who stands against the true principles of Islam. We don't think ISIS has any claim to legitimacy at all. Right now, we have had a working relationship with the U.S. coalition from time to time and we want to keep it that way. So far, I can say that the U.S. has not put us on the list of designated foreign terrorist organizations. We see that as a step in the right direction. We foresee that we will be in a position to govern when the Assad regime is knocked out of Damascus and ISIS and al-Nusra go after each other in a death-struggle."

PART SEVEN

ATONEMENT

"The moon will be in full eclipse two nights from now," Gaspar remarked as the group gathered around Hussein to plan strategy for the rescue mission. Conrad glanced in Omran's direction to be sure he was in his vehicle and safely out of hearing range.

"When it does, we'll have about an hour when it will be completely dark over the entire landscape. The only illumination will come from the dull redness of the moon, the notorious 'blood moon.' This one is the fourth in a cycle of blood moons that have run over a period of two years and there have been all kinds of speculation as to their significance. Did any of you see the stories about this on television? The blood moon is referenced in the Bible—both Old and New Testaments—and when there are four of them—what they call a 'tetrad'—well, big things are supposed to happen.

"Most people don't give it a lot of credibility. In fact, some people think it's nothing more than mythology. But for those who do believe, it foretells the apocalypse, the end of the world. There's an oblique reference in the Qur'an, too. It appears to signify a time when Islam will be in apocalyptic conflict with Christianity. That reference is not as clear as the one in our Bible, but some Muslims may be spooked by the blood moon anyway."

"I don't know very much about this," Hussein said with a skeptical glance at Gaspar, "but I recall hearing about it when I was growing up. Do you think many Christians and Jews actually believe in this? I don't recall ever hearing Muslims speak about the blood moon, although I know that Islamic mythology does promote the idea of a clash of civilizations at the end of time. A redeemer called al-Mahdi will then appear. I have also heard that

Jesus will then descend from the sky and declare his allegiance to al-Mahdi, who is a descendent of Mohammed. This is all about justice on earth as predicted by the Prophet. But why are you bringing this up? I don't understand why it is relevant."

"I'm fascinated by the mythology that builds up around religious doctrines and practices," Gaspar said, "whether true or not. This is mythology. I'm not claiming that it's all true. But as to your question of its relevance..."

Hussein interrupted him. "Wait, now I remember," he said excitedly, "the story gets even more elaborate. Damascus has been alluded to as the site of the apocalypse, the great clash of civilizations. And when you combine that with what is happening now, well, think about how that prophecy might be realized by DAE-SH or al-Nusra. I mean, it's tantalizing to consider, but recent developments don't seem to support that. Assad's having success at retaking rebel territory in general, and a takeover of Damascus, is hard to fathom."

"Okay, sure," said Gaspar, eager to bring the conversation back to their mission. "But my main reason for mentioning the blood moon is that, on that night of the fourth eclipse, the one which is about to happen, there will be a period of extraordinary darkness. It will be an unnatural and eerie darkness with a reddish color in the sky and on the landscape. If the guards and trainers at the camp are superstitious and don't know about this in advance, they may be startled, even frightened, when the celestial event happens. If you've ever seen it, you know it can be very dramatic, eerie, I'd say. The combination of darkness and strange blood-red color spreading everywhere could give us a tremendous advantage in approaching the compound and overcoming the guards. I suggest that we time our approach—and the complete operation in fact—to coincide with the eclipse of the blood moon."

"Sounds like a good idea," Ghadir said. Hussein nodded in agreement.

Gaspar added, "I have a little more detail that I can tell you. But, first, do you have any questions?"

"Before we leave the subject," Hussein said, "is there more you can tell me about what the blood moon signifies for Christians and Jews?"

"I'd say the mythology is on the fringes of Christianity," Gaspar said. "There's an element of superstition that drives the belief. The New Testament reference to the blood moon is in the Acts of the Apostles, which is a major book. But the Old Testament reference is in the Book of Joel, which is not. I wouldn't call it a central idea in either Testament. The references are brief and ambiguous. The idea of the end of the world—the Day of Judgment or the apocalypse—seems to be central to all three Abrahamic religions. Christians would call it 'the Second Coming of Christ.' I suspect that it's mainly fundamentalist Christians who believe seriously in the apocalypse as a time of judgment. I can't speak about the other religions but I'm sure there are fundamentalists in all religions who believe in such things."

"What's the science behind the blood moon phenomenon itself?" Ghadir interjected. "I mean, how does it explain why certain colors appear during the eclipse?"

"The scientific phenomenon," Gaspar said, happy to prolong his explanation, "is that when the earth totally blocks the sunlight from illuminating the moon, just for an instant, there's a red halo around the earth that is reflected onto the moon, making it appear blood-red at total eclipse. Then the moon gradually becomes visible again. The whole event takes about an hour from start to finish, before the moon is bright and full again."

"Do you know more about the mythical meaning?" Ghadir asked.

"Yes. There's a little more to it," Gaspar said. "According to the myth, the moon is actually turned into blood. That's mythology. Understand? But I think there's truth in recognizing the spectacular coalescence of life forces in the universe. It also plays on the symbolic importance of blood which, after all, is the fluid of life on this planet. It represents a change in the natural order brought about by God or Allah as a sign that the end of the world is near. The forces of good and evil will battle in the End Time. Who is good and who is evil is very much a matter of opinion, of course. The prevailing view is that the good forces are led by al-Mahdi and Jesus and the evil forces are led by a tyrant called al-Sufyani and an Antichrist simply called the 'one-eyed deceiver.' The Middle East—Syria, in particular—is supposedly the battleground for this. I find the focus on blood to be particularly significant in view of Conrad's disease and Ayah's and, frankly, my own religious affiliation with the power of the blood of Christ. The supernatural aspects fascinate me.

"Setting all the mythology aside, they are all fascinating stories," Gaspar added. "For the sake of our mission, let's hope that the camp guards and trainers will be disturbed by the eclipse and the blood-red moon. That will give us the advantage we need to make the rescue while they're distracted."

"Sounds good to me," Hussein said. "Anything that will help."

Hussein started to walk away from the group. He turned abruptly to face Gaspar and the others. "I have no idea what some DAESH warriors might believe about this," Hussein said. "I am skeptical about the whole blood moon story but I can see there may be a practical effect. The entire DAESH doctrine is, in many ways, a throwback to ancient times. If any of these soldiers know about the mythology—or even if they don't—they may be uneasy. I would wager they probably do not know there will be a blood moon and probably do not know the mythology behind it. At least it may distract them. If we can cut off their electricity at the same time as the eclipse, they will literally be in the dark. This should enable us to take them by surprise. That's the way to prevent a lot of killing, which was my promise to Ayah and Ghadir. My biggest fear is that, once the guards are aware of our attack, they will deliberately set out to kill the children. They are their trainees but also their hostages in a sense. Some may have been turned over by their families, like Jamil, but some may have been kidnapped. I don't want to take any chances."

"You're right about that," Ghadir said. "That would be a horrible result. We must protect the children."

"The encampment has its own light sources," Hussein said. "We've observed light poles situated around the compound. But since there are no other sources of light in the vicinity of this remote encampment, we should have the advantage of being undercover until we choose to reveal ourselves. Surprise is everything.

We have an ample supply of flashlights and weapons of all kinds for everyone able to participate. Who will join us in the assault?"

Everyone but Gaspar volunteered.

"I'm not a fighter," he said. "I've taken a vow of non-violence. I'll guard the driver."

"I'm probably the least able-bodied or trained," Conrad said with a slight smile, "but I'm willing to risk everything for this. That includes my life. Tell me what I can do. Provide cover? I'm concerned this could turn out to be a fierce battle. I agree with Hussein that they will try to kill the lost boys, once they realize what's happening. That's standard procedure. I would expect that of these cowards. Their modus operandi is preying on defenseless people."

"I'm afraid so," Hussein said. "We'll have to move incredibly quickly. There are only four of us who are prepared to do the actual assault and three or four of you to follow up. We need to locate and protect every boy in the camp without delay. That's why we need to know exactly what to anticipate in terms of numbers."

"I'm worried about Hamza and Mona," Ghadir said. "We don't know whether they are aware of our meeting place or if they have new information about where the boys are. I'm concerned they might even attempt to enter the camp themselves and become targets. But we can't delay our assault without risk."

"What do you think Jamil's reaction will be?" Hussein asked Ghadir. "If Yousef is there, will Jamil feel divided loyalty? What if he refuses to leave with us? Is it possible he'll act to protect his father? I've seen that happen in these situations. Children get very confused. We need to be prepared for any or all of the boys to be conflicted, especially since the brainwashing will have already begun."

"In her message, Mona said that after the kidnapping both boys were very upset and frightened when they were driven away by Yousef," Ghadir said. "I don't think there's been time to brainwash either one of them. But that's why I need to be in the camp right away to reassure Jamil and Karam, in case Mona and Hamza don't arrive in time."

"We should assume the worst-case scenario and be prepared," Hussein said. "Those of us who attack and take out the guards—

my three fighters and myself—will have to use lethal force. After that, the rest of you should be prepared to use whatever force is necessary. We will still have the trainers to deal with even if we succeed in neutralizing the guards. Violence is unavoidable."

After a long pause, he added, "I keep wondering whether Yousef will be there."

"My guess," Ghadir said, "is that he will still be at the camp in order to ensure that Jamil and Karam don't try to leave and that they get indoctrinated."

"Bizarre, isn't it?" Conrad said as an aside to Levi. "Yousef will be concerned to protect them from being rescued so he can sentence them to their deaths."

"I may go tomorrow to Yarmouk to see if I can recruit more fighters to help us," Hussein said, "especially if we learn that there are more than a dozen DAESH fighters. I think that, with surprise, we can handle that many but not more. Even that is a close call. I can make some inquiries about Hamza and Mona."

Hussein's three militia companions headed out for the area of the camp, planning to spend the rest of the day and night with their binoculars trained on the facility. They would find cover during the day while they continued their surveillance. They would meet up with Hussein later that day and pool the information.

While Hussein was trying to gain information at Yarmouk about the camp and its occupants, and his troops were conducting surveillance of the camp, Ghadir attempted to contact Hamza and Mona. Late in the day, she received word from Mona's sister that they had gotten as far as the outskirts of Yarmouk and had been given shelter at a farm within a half-mile of the group's rendezvous point. Mona's sister informed them of Ghadir's location and within two hours, Mona and Hamza reunited with Ghadir. They had not seen each other in more than two years. Ghadir brought them up to date on the plan to conduct a raid on the camp during the blood moon eclipse the night after next. Any urgency, such as an apparent attempt to move out some of the boys, would move up the time of assault on the camp by one night and forego the cover of the blood moon. The militia members assigned to surveillance would attempt to compile descriptions of individual boys in an effort to ascertain whether Jamil and Karam were among them.

At noon on the next day, Hussein and his companions returned to the campsite to rejoin the group, which, with the addition of Mona and Hamza, was now seven in number.

Hussein reported, "I was unable to recruit other fighters from Ahrar al-Sham to assist in this mission. This is my personal mission and there are too many other battles going on. We'll have to go forward with the four of us plus you civilians."

"I can join the assault team if you need five," Levi insisted. "I'm an Israeli citizen. I've received military training. I'm familiar with the weapons you're carrying. I don't have any medical problems. I think I could take on a guard, maybe not silently with a knife, but with a pistol with a silencer, if you have that."

"That's good to know. We may need you," Hussein said, clapping Levi on the back.

"We've discovered that there are between twenty and thirty boys at the cubs camp," Hussein said. "The bulk of the trainees were moved to another site in the Atareb area of Aleppo. They apparently decided that the cub camp is too vulnerable for older boys. There have already been two escapes during the past three months. Only the youngest and weakest of the boys are kept here. We don't know for sure whether Jamil and Karam are among them but their ages would seem to place them in this category.

"According to my sources, confirmed by surveillance, there appear to be no more than ten to twelve adult males on site. They are likely well-armed and reasonably vigilant. They posted four guards last night and, from what we observed, they seem fairly casual about their duties, as if they were not expecting any trouble. They have made this whole area secure, so that makes sense. They wouldn't expect any interest from rebel groups or government forces in this small camp. Approaching the installation is going to be difficult. There is a broad expanse of desert with only a few scrub trees and some underbrush providing minimal cover. Our hope is that by knowing the logistics of the site perfectly and using the eclipse as cover, we can approach in the darkness and complete the mission before full moonlight is restored. We'll need the four of us who are trained fighters to approach quickly on our bellies and take out the guards with knives. We may need Levi if they post five guards. We can't afford to make a sound in the approach and entry, or in the course of taking out the guards.

"Then the rest of you, not counting Gaspar, who will stay and guard the driver, can enter immediately and follow up by locating the boys. Everyone will immediately assist in securing them as soon as his main assignment is done. Each of you will be armed because any of the trainers is a potential threat. Yousef will be a special threat. We have identified where the source of camp lighting is so one person, Levi, if we don't need him to neutralize a guard, will cut off the electrical supply and then the four of us will proceed into the camp, in darkness, to immobilize the remaining DAESH soldiers. We expect they number another six or seven, totaling ten or twelve in all, with trainers. That's just an estimate. We can't be sure based on our surveillance. It will be difficult to avoid killing because we're outnumbered—maybe even more than we expect. There is no room for mistakes. Time will be precious because one phone call could bring reinforcements very quickly."

"I can see some tragic choices coming up," Conrad said, glancing at Ghadir to get her reaction. "We want to avoid violence but every guard or trainer we avoid killing is a potential threat to one of us—or to all the boys together. We will try to spare Yousef, if he is there, but as for the others, they have to be immobilized quickly and completely. Remember, if we let Yousef live, he will be a continuing danger to you and the children."

"I understand," Ghadir said. "We have to think about saving the boys first. Protecting ourselves is next. We should not take lives unless absolutely necessary. That includes Yousef's."

"We can't lose time gathering all the boys," Hussein said, "and removing them to a safe place very quickly. My rough estimate is twenty to thirty boys. If Jamil and Karam are not at this camp, we are committed to this rescue anyway. If Yousef is among the guards or trainers, he will fight to the death unless we neutralize him. I know he would like to kill me. Seeing him would signal that his son is there and Karam, too, no doubt, since they are both in the same age group. I warn you that we are a very small force to take over a camp guarded by professional militia. They will not hesitate to kill the boys if they have sufficient warning or time.

258

They will kill anyone and everyone in sight."

Gaspar added, "There's also the chance that other DAESH troops will arrive between now and the time of the attack. The eclipse will begin at 8:30 and be full at 9:50. Then it will recede. You have that much time but, of that, it will be truly dark for only about 45 minutes. That's when you have to complete the mission. Oh, and I haven't mentioned the weather. If it's a clear sky, we have maximum advantage. If it's overcast, we lose the impact of the blood moon because the eclipse will not be visible. Pray for good weather so the effect of the eclipse will be the maximum possible."

"Yes," Hussein agreed. "Those of you who will be backups, including Levi, who will rejoin you, will have to follow our advance squad. Plan to move forward on your stomachs as we do. Get as close as you can to the perimeter fence while you wait for the darkness to descend. The perimeter is lightly protected by fencing. It does not appear to present a serious problem for us to breach it. We will cut an ample opening for all of you. The problem will be for us to approach and neutralize the guards without giving any warning to the trainers. We then move to neutralize the trainers. You will follow immediately behind, ready to secure the boys as soon as it is safe. I suggest that you divide into teams of two so that all of you will have assistance and backup. Does anyone have questions or doubts about your ability to participate?"

Conrad spoke up. "I'm sure we're all ready to go. I understand you have weapons for us, is that right? I doubt that any of us are skilled in using them but perhaps you can teach us the basics."

"I can help with training," Levi said.

The rest reported that they, like Conrad, needed basic instruction.

"We have time to get outfitted," Hussein said, as his three companions headed out for the DAESH compound. After training the support group of six, he would head out as well. Hussein made the decision to wait for the eclipse the night after, despite the urgency of striking before boys were moved out or reinforcements arrived. Taking the risk of waiting was unavoidable since success depended largely on the cover of darkness—the blood-red darkness that would distract the guards and trainers.

Despite his earlier protests, Omran had quieted down and remained in his vehicle, the doors secured and the horn immobilized. He understood that Gaspar would remain behind to prevent him from escaping.

❧

The day was spent training and observing the cub camp activities. A restless night followed. Finally, the day for the rescue effort arrived. The morning sky was overcast with a thick blanket of clouds, completely obliterating the sun and the sky. Disappointment at the weather conditions cast an aura of gloom over the crew. Hopeful that weather conditions would improve, the advance force spent the afternoon hours preparing for the evening's expedition. By late afternoon, the clouds had begun to disperse, allowing sun to shine through and patches of blue sky to be visible. The sky continued to clear. The blood moon would dominate the sky after all.

Hussein had obtained complete equipment for the support group of five plus Levi, including weapons, night vision goggles, camouflage clothing, and other essential gear. At 5 p.m., the support group headed for the launch site guided by one of Hussein's recruits who was familiar with the area. It appeared that the light and dark phases of the moon would be at their extremes. The group approached and lay down well out of sight of guards in the encampment. They were shielded by several higher points of ground between them and the encampment. But they could still observe regular movements within the compound.

Hussein and his three soldiers, the advance force, had found safe cover closer to the camp, protected by the uneven terrain. They were within five hundred meters of the camp perimeter. They planned a short sprint to bring the advance squad within striking distance of the guards. Since Levi was not needed to neutralize a guard, he was instructed on how to dismantle the electrical system. No vehicular traffic in or out of the camp had been observed. The presence of small figures visible within the camp assured the attack force that children were still on site. The soldiers observed demonstrations going on in which the boys were required to use rifles to strike adult figures kneeling on the ground in the center of a large dirt area. The victims appeared to be live people who fell forward after being struck. They were then required to resume a kneeling position repeatedly, until finally others took their place. Hussein speculated that adult prisoners might well be present as well, presenting another complicating factor to deal with.

The training camp had no elevated observation posts, limiting the range of vision of the guards to the ground level. It did not appear that the DAESH forces anticipated any enemy attacks, at least by ground.

ཉ

When the eclipse began at 8:30 p.m., the advance squad members, led by Hussein, began approaching the camp on their stomachs. By the time the eclipse had reached the halfway point, the celestial effect was becoming even more dramatic. A red hue began to color the eclipsed portion of the moon, casting a crimson light on the entire landscape. The barren, desert-like terrain with its occasional rock outcroppings and low-growing brush took on the unearthly blood color originating in the heavens. Conrad could see a figure he thought was Levi crawling toward the electric supply area at a corner of the property. Hussein had established signals for notifying the other participants when they should advance into the camp.

Through his binoculars, Conrad could see four guards patrolling slowly. Their frequent glances at the sky revealed they were indeed distracted by the eerie lightshow, and the palette of earth tones that covered the broad canvas of the once barren and colorless landscape.

Conrad could still make out in the semi-darkness the four militia members crawling forward. One by one, as they got within fifty feet of the compound, each would break into a sprint. He could see no immediate response or change of movement on the part of any guards. The attackers were out of sight now and Conrad believed he could hear faint sounds of struggle. He heard no warning alarm or shouting, leading him to assume that the silent strikes at the guards by Hussein and his three companions had been successful.

Flashlight signals flickered back toward the members of the support force, the signal that they should move rapidly toward the camp. They rose and began running in crouched positions. All the camp lights went out. Levi must have successfully sabotaged the lighting system. As he was straining to see where he was running, Conrad stumbled and lurched forward, losing his balance. He landed on his left side, striking his left leg, hip, shoulder, and head. He broke the fall partly with his hands and arms, although his left arm was crumpled underneath him. He was not strong enough to break his fall. He immediately thought of the likelihood of internal bleeding in addition to the certain external bleeding.

Conrad felt wetness on his left side, his face and scalp, and his hands and arms. In the red light, he could not make out the color of the fluid oozing from his body. He must have cut himself in multiple places on projecting rocks, hard-packed dirt, and harsh underbrush. He was bleeding profusely. He felt panic begin to take over. Was it only external bleeding or had he started bleeding internally? His platelet count was no doubt dangerously low, probably in single digits, more than one thousand times lower than normal. He felt weak from the exertion—or was it from fear of bleeding to death, or simply the uncertainty about what would happen? Where, he wondered, was his bravado about giving his life for this enterprise? Despite his fear and pain, he struggled to his feet and kept jogging toward the camp. His weapon and gear felt as though they weighed as much as his entire body.

Shouts of alarm resounded from inside the camp, all adult male voices, along with running footsteps. It was evident that the element of surprise had facilitated the assault on the camp. The support team members rushed forward the final 100 feet to the fencing, which had been neatly cut in several places. They entered without injuring themselves, heading toward the dormitory-like structures at the far end.

❧

Conrad could tell that the eclipse was nearly complete, gradually extending toward the point of maximum darkness. A strange silence hovered over the landscape, causing an atmosphere of unreality. The silence seemed to be threatened only by the presence of the blood-red moon hovering over the camp, promising destruction below. The blood moon cast an angry red over its domain, both celestial and terrestrial. Each member of the group attempted to find his or her assigned partner. Each pair was responsible for moving as many as ten to twelve boys to safety. Conrad and Virginia partnered. Conrad could see Levi and Ghadir together in what must have been the central area of the camp. Mona and Hamza were not in sight.

Since most of the noise was coming from the rear area of the camp, Conrad assumed that was where the boys had fled. Others might have gone to their dormitories. He could hear excited, high-pitched voices of children. The words were indistinguishable but the sounds alone conveyed terror. Still, other boys might be with trainers who had so far survived. Locating and securing a group of boys was far more difficult than any of them had imagined. They did not know how many boys were at large or how many trainers or guards remained free. Conrad and Virginia spoke in whispers as they approached the area where the boys were likely to be.

"We need to catch them unaware so we don't force the guards or trainers to act impulsively," Conrad said to Virginia, who nodded in understanding. "I'll be ready to fire," Conrad added.

"How is your bleeding, Conrad?" Virginia whispered.

"Not too bad," he replied. "But can you stop it with my shirt?"

After Virginia's treatment, Conrad felt safer.

At that moment, as they were at risk of losing contact with each other in the limited light, they heard gunshots from two areas of the camp. Obviously, the rebel soldiers were encountering other trainers who were still active threats. Screams ensued. They heard a cacophony of boys' voices, and the scurrying of many feet, with shouts of fear and danger.

Levi called quietly to Conrad, who was visible in the increasing light. "I suspect that, rather than going to a particular place, all the boys are scattering, running for cover, finding places to hide—running for their lives, for all they know."

"True," Conrad said. "They have no concept of what is happening, who is attacking the camp, or whether they're in jeopardy."

At that moment of indecision and confusion, an adult male voice shouted loudly in recognizable military tone, "All cubs report to the dining area and stand in order."

Conrad wondered if that was Yousef's voice and if the boys recognized his authority. He heard Ghadir say to Levi, "That's Yousef. I recognize his voice. We have to stop him."

Conrad knew that the dining area was in the rear of the compound. There was enough light now for him to see a large, pavilion-type structure. He could see rows of long tables and benches. Yousef's command was an unmistakable warning that the boys were now in jeopardy of being killed. Yousef's presence removed virtually all doubt that Jamil and Karam were there. From his place in the compound, Conrad could now make out the figures of individual boys—young boys of Jamil's and Karam's age—running toward the pavilion, following Yousef's orders. He could see three or four larger boys, probably teenagers, directing the smaller ones toward the pavilion. At least one other adult was visible, a trainer, no doubt. Conrad realized that those larger boys might well be trained to assist Yousef and other soldiers.

Conrad realized in a moment of panic that the mission teetered on the edge of glorious success or crushing failure. The boys could all be saved or they could all be killed. The rescuers had no idea who the boys were, their ages, how many there were, or whether they would accept or reject the authority of Yousef or any of the trainers or guards who were still alive. Conrad realized the rescue group could take advantage of the assembly of the children but they would have to subdue Yousef and probably at least one trainer before the boys would be safe. They would be trying to save the boys without the boys knowing if they represented help or harm.

Ghadir was huddling with Mona and Hamza, who had entered the compound. Conrad confirmed what he had heard—that the boys had been ordered to the dining room by someone, presumably Yousef. It was up to Conrad. He had no idea whether Hussein and his troops were still engaged fighting the enemy, or whether they were injured or dead. He couldn't afford to delay.

Conrad reported to the other five that they would have to approach the dining pavilion cautiously, silently, without alerting the enemy trainers. Then they would have to overcome at least the two men—and perhaps the older boys—in order to save the younger ones. "We have to be careful not to warn them. One of us needs to lead the way. I'll do that and will signal you. I'm prepared to use this weapon. We all have to be ready to fight."

"Conrad, you're bleeding even more," Virginia said with alarm, reaching to touch him. "Are you alright? We should stop the bleeding right away."

"No, later." Conrad said, "There's no time. We have to move forward to the pavilion. It's about 30 meters ahead of us. The two men, Yousef being one I assume, don't know we're here yet. We have to assume that they herded the boys there to kill them. They're in grave danger. We should split up and approach from three sides. Get your weapons ready. But we have to be very careful not to shoot any of our own in the line of fire. Get yourselves in a position in the gathering moonlight so that none of our own people are in your line of fire. Stay hidden behind the two men until I signal. We'll attempt to disable them without firing if we can. But if either has a weapon, we have to shoot."

࿆

Moonlight was beginning to brighten the sky again, now a luminescent white with only a reddish trace. Since the light enhanced their vision, they knew it would have the same benefit for the guards and trainers, including Yousef. Conrad moved toward the pavilion with Virginia following him. He could see outlines of various figures—two men and four teenage boys—sitting at tables in front of the room. A large group of smaller boys were lined up, sitting on rows of benches.

Conrad heard muffled voices and could see some movement on the benches. The support group headed toward the room without making a sound. They were approaching behind the men and larger boys and did not appear to have been spotted by anyone. As they approached, they could hear a male adult voice shouting at the boys and the sound of crying. Both men had pistols in their hands. Conrad approached with his pistol drawn.

Yousef was addressing the room full of small boys. "This is your time," he announced to them, almost as if he relished the encounter as a test of their mettle. "You know your duty. We have been at-tacked by enemies, those who mean to destroy us. You all have your destiny. You have been trained to serve as soldiers for ISIS for Allah. Your training is not yet finished, but a challenge is already upon us. You must call upon what you have learned to avoid the fate that these infidels would have for you. You must avoid capture, for they aim to dissuade you from your calling, to come between you and your god. Instead, you will be martyrs for the cause and when you do you will go to heaven. We will stay here and continue to fight the evil ones and do so in the knowledge that you have been pro-tected from the evil they would have done to you."

He raised his pistol. "Who will be the first volunteer? It will be my own son, Jamil. Bring him forward."

Two older boys took Jamil by the arms and brought him for-ward toward his father. But Jamil did not go willingly. He strug-gled and cried out in protest. It appeared that his trust in his father had reached its limit. He was aware that his father was willing to sacrifice him.

Yousef, now a trained warrior with a military mindset, had control of the situation. His expression showed no reluctance on his part to sacrifice his own son for a principle. Conrad real-ized that all the boys would follow Jamil to death if he failed to intervene. He had no choice but to kill Yousef before the rebel presence was discovered. Despite his natural aversion to violence, Conrad felt no compunction about killing Yousef. He hesitated one more moment, however, wishing that something would hap-pen to relieve him from his duty.

A moment of silence punctuated the violent sounds outside the pavilion, signaling more fighting between Hussein's squad and the trainers and guards. More and more light appeared with the receding eclipse. The atmosphere in the pavilion had a surreal appearance to it, with the reddish hue that remained from the receding blood moon. It appeared that the eclipse was slipping away, leaving a deep stain of blood on the floor of the room. Con-rad realized that his own blood was on the floor merging with the visual stain from the blood moon.

At this moment, with Jamil standing next to his father, a pis-tol in the older man's hand, Ghadir found herself unable to hold back. She stood upright and called to the boy. "No, Jamil, no! Run!"

As the words came tumbling forth from her, Ghadir herself ran, sprinting toward Yousef, causing him to turn partially toward the area where the group had been approaching him. Conrad followed quickly, aiming his pistol at Yousef. As Yousef dropped his pistol and raised his AK-47 to shoot Ghadir, Conrad released the safety on his pistol, aimed, and stepped forward so that he was facing Yousef head-on. Conrad pointed the pistol at Yousef's chest, an easier target than the head for an inexperienced shooter, although a less lethal one. The thought of issuing a warning flashed through his mind. But that would have jeopardized both mother and son. He knew he would lose control of the situation once Yousef knew he was there. Conrad fired and Yousef's chest exploded in blood which splattered in a wide circular pattern over the floor, reaching as far as the wall. He fell backward into a table. Yousef collapsed to the ground almost instantly, his weapon falling under him. Conrad followed instantly with a shot to the chest of the trainer standing beside Yousef. The man collapsed on top of Yousef.

Conrad moved forward, stepping on Yousef's legs in the process, grabbing his assault rifle and flinging it aside. Yousef did not lose consciousness but lay on the ground, struggling to get up but unable to overcome the shock to his body. He fell back motionless, blood staining his black military shirt in the receding moonlight… red on red, red on black.

Yousef was losing blood. It ran together with Conrad's and the trainer's on the floor, spreading out as the red haze from the moon eclipse was receding with blood still soaking the floor and the ground outside. The blood of the moon was mingling with the blood of three human beings, along with the group of some twenty boys, all of whom were apparently uninjured.

The trainer, who was lying close to Conrad, was severely injured. He managed to point his pistol toward Conrad but Levi emerged to deliver a fatal shot and the man's head exploded with blood and white matter.

Two of the older boys rushed Conrad and pushed him to the ground, bringing him excruciating pain. Pain layered on top of pain. Levi and Ghadir grabbed them and pulled them away. The other two ran for the rifles Yousef and the trainer had been holding, grabbed them and aimed at the group of smaller boys, who were huddled on the benches in shock. Conrad somehow got to his feet and joined Levi in tackling them, wrestling the guns away. Finally they were secured. The smaller boys sat silently, spellbound by the drama.

⋇

Ghadir, followed by Mona and Hamza, who had been gathering a group of boys together near the back of the dining room, rushed toward Karam, as soon as they spotted him. He looked confused and terrified at first, trying to avoid his parents who had appeared suddenly as though they were the enemy. Jamil had broken away from his captors as soon as Conrad intervened, and now he attempted to hide in the back of the room. When he saw his father lying on the floor bleeding, he seemed conflicted and ran around the perimeter of the room to his father. Yousef was struggling to get to his feet despite his wounds.

Virginia was bravely attempting to stop Yousef's bleeding and bandage his wounds, despite the fact that he was striking out at her with his free arm. Conrad could see that Jamil was in shock and did not fully appreciate the fact that his mother had come to rescue him. Ghadir was standing nearby, calling softly to Jamil to come to her. Karam had gathered his wits about him and had left the room with his mother. Hamza quickly bent down and restrained Yousef, then assisted Virginia in attempting to save Yousef's life. Despite the fact that Yousef was barely conscious, he was muttering threats and curses at Ghadir, Virginia, and Hamza.

"These cubs," Yousef said in a weak voice, "these cubs must die. It is my charge that they not be taken prisoner. They must die and then return to take the blood of the evil ones. I call for their blood. It is their fate. Jamil, listen to me. Jamil."

Jamil, still confused and conflicted, looked up and called out, "Father, I'm sorry. I'm sorry. Please don't die. Please don't die. What should I do? Someone help me. I don't know what to do."

It was plain to Conrad that the man he had shot and left for dead had become delirious. As Yousef became consumed by his wounds, he nonetheless continued to call to his son, alternating now between his wish to martyr the boy and his equally strong wish to flee with him.

"We must escape, Jamil. You have a duty to perform, a sacred duty. You will come with me. Step aside, woman, or I will kill you now. If you try to leave with him, I will kill you both. Jamil is a cub of the Islamic State! He has a destiny to fulfill! You will not stand in our way! The clash of civilizations is underway! The end of the world is at hand!"

At that moment, Ghadir knelt beside Jamil and wrapped her arms around him, attempting to shield him from his father. "Jamil," Ghadir said softly in his ear, repeating his name over and over. "I'm here to take you home. Your father will not die. We have done all we can to preserve his life. I'm here to take you back to our home to see Ayah. Ayah is waiting for you."

The mention of Ayah's name startled Jamil into understanding. "I want to see Ayah, Yamma. Where is Ayah?"

"Ayah is at our home, which is in America, where you were living before your father brought you here. We are going to return to our home very soon. You will see Ayah soon. She is waiting for you."

"Stay back, woman," Yousef called out harshly. "These boys have a destiny. Do not interfere, or you will die, too."

Jamil hesitated but then rose with Ghadir and walked out of the pavilion, gripping her tightly around the waist, sobbing quietly.

Yousef shouted, "Jamil, stay where you are. She is no longer your mother. You have a destiny to fulfill!"

No answer came from outside. Hamza and Virginia carried Yousef on a makeshift stretcher to the prison compound, which contained a small lean-to. They placed the stretcher on the ground, and brought supplies, including water and food, into the prison compound, placing them within his reach. Yousef had finally lapsed into unconsciousness. Hamza could not be sure how serious his bullet wounds were but the bleeding had stopped and his vital signs were in a safe range.

"We've done all we can for him," Hamza said to Virginia. "He doesn't deserve more. He doesn't even deserve this much, frankly.

I see two wounded guards here as well. They really should not be allowed to live. I know that's a terrible thing for a physician to say but I think leaving them alive will give them a chance for retaliation. I'm worried that if Yousef survives, he will be nothing but trouble for Ghadir and Jamil in the future. But we've carried out Ghadir's and Ayah's wishes."

Conrad had found a place to sit on a dining hall bench. He knew he continued to lose a large amount of blood from the injuries he sustained over an hour ago. He felt dizzy and faint. He lay down on a bench quickly, fearing that he was in danger of collapsing. He was too weak to get onto a table. Other people entered. Hussein announced that the compound was secure, at least for the moment. Two guards were killed. One was mortally wounded and another had a chance of surviving. Three of the trainers were killed. The less seriously injured soldiers had been rounded up and secured in the prison compound. One of Hussein's soldiers had been killed in his knife fight with a guard, who was also killed. One other was injured. Hussein warned that they must hurry and escape before reinforcements arrived. They were afraid that a trainer might have managed to call for help before being captured and secured.

⚹

Ghadir held Jamil in her arms for a few more moments before they had to leave. Jamil was frightened and in shock but had bonded with his mother, despite his distress at leaving his severely injured father. Hamza appeared in the doorway, uninjured, but exhausted from the ordeal and from doing all he could to safeguard the survivors until they could receive treatment from DAESH reinforcements. It occurred to Conrad that the guards and trainers, having failed in their mission to secure the cubs, or to prevent their escape, in the alternative, might face a fate worse than dying of battle wounds, perhaps punishment by torture or death.

"Karam," Hamza called out.

"Yes, Papa, here I am," called out a small voice, that of Karam, who was in his mother's arms. His parents embraced him and, with six other boys, began their exit. By this time, Hussein's soldiers had joined them in the search for other boys who might have run outside or into other buildings.

"The guards are dead or neutralized," one said. "Get all the boys out. Don't let any get away. They may be frightened. They don't know who we are."

"Is this Heaven or Hell?" Conrad wondered aloud as he moved forward toward Ghadir and Jamil. The other members of the group with their young charges held tightly to them began to move outside the compound. The landscape was fully illuminated by moonlight, although still bearing a slightly reddish tinge, as though the land itself had been soaked with red dye.

"I don't think Yousef will die," Conrad said to Ghadir, who was clutching Jamil, still sobbing with relief that his ordeal was over. Hussein and two of his warriors entered the pavilion, alarmed by hearing the gunshots moments earlier. They stood transfixed at the sight of mother and son, Conrad's condition, and the quantity of blood on the floor surrounding the two bodies.

Looking at Hussein, Conrad said, "Yousef deserved to die. He is a disloyal dog but at least we did not perpetuate the cycle of death. If we had not used restraint, we would have accomplished nothing at all. The blood of the moon and my own blood are flowing together with the blood of two DAESH warriors. The irony of it all is bewildering. We did our best not to disturb the natural order of peaceful resolution. Killing is not the natural order, although it seems to be the way of the world today. It is miraculous that the boys have been saved."

"We have secured everything," Hussein said. "We must leave immediately. We have no time. The gunshots will warn anyone within a mile. We can't be sure that DAESH warriors were not warned before we immobilized everyone in the camp. They will be upon us soon enough. We cannot fight off an army. Hurry. We will lock up all the DAESH soldiers and guards and the older boys who refuse our offer to bring them home to safety."

There were twenty boys in all, including Jamil and Karam. All four older boys, probably teenagers, refused to leave. It was evident that they had already been brainwashed by their captors.

Hussein and Ghadir argued with them, attempting to persuade them to leave. They refused.

Ghadir argued in favor of forcing them to leave with the group. "They should be returned to their families and rehabilitated," she said.

Hussein argued that they would escape at the earliest chance and that they would jeopardize the whole operation. Hussein prevailed. The decision was to leave them behind, locked with the guards and trainers who were still alive, including Yousef.

"What will become of my father?" Jamil asked. "Should I stay with him?"

"No, Jamil, you will come with us," Ghadir said firmly. "You will die if you stay with him. He will get well and perhaps he will leave this place and return to us someday. But we must save your life and not allow it to be used to take other innocent lives, as your father meant for you to do."

A short time later, the group of adults, Karam, Jamil, and fourteen boys were safely outside the camp and walking rapidly toward the meeting place, where Hussein's vehicles were ready to take them back to Burraq. Their plan was to use Omran's van plus the military vehicles to return to the unguarded Jordan border crossing. As they left the training camp, they heard Yousef shout in a desperate rage, "I will come after you! I will kill you all! You will not escape!"

Jamil trembled and sobbed at his father's frantic state. He had trusted the man for so long. How could he now leave him to die? Still, the boy did not try to turn back. Soon the camp settled into a painful silence.

Their plan was to take all the captive boys, except Jamil and Karam, to Jordan and leave them in a safe place; that is, if the authorities would allow them to. They could not leave them behind in Syria, so close to Damascus and the fortification at Yarmouk. They knew it would be a difficult task to elude the Jordanian and Syrian border guards, under the best of circumstances. They were now a large group of some twenty people, and Conrad realized it would be virtually impossible for them to return to Jordan without being discovered. They would be at the mercy of Jordanian officials.

❧

The group of rescuers, along with the fourteen rescued *lost boys*, ranging in age from seven to eleven, crowded into the waiting Humvees and sped toward their rendezvous base in the village of Burraq in the region of Yarmouk. As they approached the base, they saw Gaspar sitting on the rear bumper of Omran's van. The van was empty and Omran was nowhere in sight. Gaspar rose and walked hesitantly to meet them, his shoulders hunched forward. The expression on his face revealed discouragement mixed with amazement at the sight of the entourage pulling into the barren campsite situated among a few trees. He made a sweeping sign of the cross on his chest and raised his arms skyward, in what appeared to be a prayer of thanks or a plea for forgiveness.

"It's wonderful to see you all," Gaspar said earnestly, after they disembarked. "But I have bad news. I put Omran in the car and sat beside him with the pistol you left with me. I thought the driver's door was secured from the outside so he couldn't get out on that side. I sat in the passenger seat. I thought he was asleep. He probably faked it. I fell asleep myself. When I woke up an hour or so later, he was gone. Apparently, the driver's door was not secured after all or he released it when I let him have a stretch break. He probably headed for the Jordan border which is a long way from here. If he got a ride, he could have gotten there quickly and reported what happened to the Jordan border guards. I'm afraid we may have trouble getting back into Jordan. I hope Hussein knows of another border crossing so we can avoid going to the place we used last time."

He scanned the faces of his companions. At the looks ranging from frustration to anger flooding over their faces, Gaspar muttered, "I'm really sorry. Forgive me."

At this development, Conrad slumped down on the ground with his back against the van. For the first time that morning, everyone realized how desperately sick he was. Virginia fully appreciated his condition. She had cleaned the blood from his head, arms, and legs before they left the camp and given him all the medical care at her disposal. She was sitting next to him on the ground, cradling him in her arms.

"Oh my God, Conrad, are you okay?" Levi asked, kneeling beside him, with a look of deep concern suddenly crossing his face. "You're so pale. You really took a beating during our approach and attack on the camp. You did the heavy-duty fighting too. Are you as sick as you look, or are you just exhausted?"

"Both," Conrad said quietly, using all his strength to respond. "I'm totally out of strength. Nothing left. Have to sleep."

"Of course he's exhausted," Virginia said to the group. "None of us slept last night after the most strenuous activity most of us have ever been through. Here it is morning and we face a long trip to the border and a difficult crossing. His red cell counts must be way down and I'm worried about his platelets too. You're pale, Conrad, severely anemic. I can see it in your face. What can I do for you now? We should get you a blood transfusion once we get to Amman. There's a cancer hospital in Amman, the King Hussein Cancer Hospital. I checked it out before we left. It should be safe enough for a transfusion. They can check all your vital signs too. We may even be able to take a day to get you healthy before the trip."

"My core is totally out of energy," Conrad said, his voice faint and shaking with fear. "That's my heart and lungs and abdomen. I don't think I can get up. I'm sure my blood counts are all haywire. The whites are probably way up and the red cells, down. I'm sure tumor lysis syndrome is going to overwhelm my organs as soon as treatment starts. All those dead tumor cells! This was strenuous, Virginia, a lot more than I'm used to. I will have to sleep until we have to leave. I have to, I tell you. I have to! I'm about at my limit."

He looked at her and, despite his condition, felt an urge to deflect the conversation from himself. "Please know that I am so glad that I could take part in this. It makes everything worthwhile, including my life. I don't care what happens to me now."

Virginia stroked his face. "Of course you do. I certainly do. We all do."

"We have to leave immediately," Hussein said, with urgency. "We're lucky no one caught up with us yet. You can bet that a squad from DAESH will be after us as soon as they discover what happened. I have some regret that we left Yousef and the other ISIS soldiers alive. They know all about us—how many we are, how we are armed, everything. They will figure out where we're going. I'm afraid we made a huge mistake to leave them alive, especially Yousef."

Levi nodded in agreement. "We've put ourselves in jeopardy by leaving survivors. The Israeli military would never do that. Very poor strategy," he said, looking directly at Hussein. "I don't know why I went along with that."

He glanced at Conrad and then at Ghadir. Noticing her shocked reaction to the statements about survivors and Yousef, in particular, he quickly looked away, realizing that he had struck a blow at her cherished values with his remark.

"It was the only humane thing to do," Ghadir said. "We had to end the cycle of killing. I know Ayah's view of that was inspired by Allah. There was no other moral choice. We who oppose the violence of DAESH and the corrupt regime had to end the cycle of killing, even if it causes us greater risk. Besides, he was—is—the father of my children. How could I face them if I had gone along with killing him?"

Levi looked upset and dismayed that he had engaged in this argument. "As a practical matter, I agree with Hussein. Yes, as a practical matter, we should have killed anyone who could identify us. But I also respect your view on that, Ghadir. I understand. I spoke impulsively. I want to end the cycle of death, too. It is self-perpetuating."

Ghadir looked through tearful eyes directly at Levi and whispered, "Thank you, Levi. I know you understand. We have been injured over and over by this killing that has dominated both our countries. It has captured the souls of men and women and robbed them of their humanity. I know Yousef poses a threat to us as long as he lives, that is, unless he comes to his senses. I can only pray for that."

She looked earnestly at Levi, as if to reassure him that she had sought to spare Yousef out of humanity and conviction, not out of some tattered shred of love that remained alive. She extended her hand to Levi and he grasped it gently with both of his hands. They shared an intimate moment although they were in the company of two dozen people. Conrad, from his position on the ground, paid close attention to the exchange of affection in their words and gestures, even though he was drifting in and out of sleep. He recognized that a bond had been created during the trip between these two—the Palestinian and the Jew. He looked from one to the other, wide-eyed and amazed that such a chasm could be bridged in so short a time. That two lives so far distant in heritage and experience could be linked in some unfathomable way was remarkable. Mona and Hamza understood what had happened. Mona smiled almost imperceptibly; Ghadir did not miss her reaction.

❧

As the five travelers reflected on the events of the past hours, the magnitude of the killings overcame them. Levi, with his military background, was the least affected morally. Conrad, Ghadir, and Virginia, the most. Gaspar took the events in stride, having avoided direct participation. They had all hoped to avoid killing, but as Hussein starkly predicted, it was inevitable.

Hussein broke the spell lingering over the participants with a reminder that time was of the essence. "It's over," he said. "We are long past the time of moral decision making about killing or not. We have done what we had to do. Now we have to leave quickly. They'll figure out that we're heading for Jordan. They will come after us. They have probably started out already, with a force far too big for us to defend against. And we have to go along the Jordan-Syria border until we find a safe place to cross. The only one I know of is at least five miles northwest along the border from the place we entered. I haven't been there in months so I don't know if it's still open and unguarded. For all I know, they may have put up a fence or stationed guards. It's no secret that Jordan has cracked down on Syrians entering the country. We have no choice but to try. I have to keep in mind that Jordan has turned against rebel fighters. We are not welcome in the country. That policy will govern how they treat us or, should I say, dispose of us."

Hussein added a slightly encouraging note: "Fortunately, Omran didn't know the details of our plan so whatever story he told might sound incoherent. You can be sure he has reported us. He'll be mainly concerned about getting his vehicle back. We can't force our way back into Jordan or we'll have the whole Jordan military on our back. The Jordanians were good to allow so many Syrian refugees into the country but they are beyond their limit. They are overwhelmed with refugees. The period of hospitality is over. We can't expect a warm reception, especially if Omran has made criminal complaints against us. Remember that Jordan has renewed its toughness in security as a result of a few unexpected terrorist attacks. They took pride in their tight security but it's been breached. They have tightened up. And they are experiencing radicalization within their society. The wall that used to exist is no longer impregnable. It's true that Jordan is as hostile as ever toward DAESH but that does not mean it extends a warm welcome to other visitors."

They pulled their four vehicles onto the secondary road. As they negotiated the next leg of their journey, one that would take them from their base camp in Burraq to the Jordan border, Conrad, Virginia, Gaspar, Levi, and Ghadir looked forward to the chance for safe passage back to the States. They dreamed of new beginnings. Jamil, who was too young to comprehend all that had happened and how it would play out in the future, anticipated a new life reunited with his mother and Ayah in the only place in which he had ever lived. At the same time, he felt the pain of separation from his father whom he did not judge as an adult would. Good or evil, to him his father was his father.

For Hamza and Mona, there was the hope of finding a safe place to live in Jordan with their son, Karam, after his frightening experience of being forcibly taken to the training camp. For the other fourteen rescued *lost boys*, this was a time of fear and uncertainty. They had all been kidnapped and imprisoned in the training camp. They had been forced to view horrifying, brutal beheadings, been taught to use automatic weapons, and had been brainwashed for days or weeks to win over their allegiance to DAESH. They had no idea where their families were or how they would reconnect with them to restore their former lives—if it were possible to return to those lives at all. Many of them had lived through harrowing experiences of war for most or all of their young lives. Uncertainty about their fate was added to the problems they faced. For all they knew, their parents and siblings had been killed by DAESH warriors or government forces or by the devastating bombs that plummeted screaming from the skies every day. Memories of the cruel bombing of Aleppo and other cities in the north followed them and haunted their sleep.

For Hussein and his two surviving companions, the trip to the border meant lost time and exposure to being tracked down by the DAESH militia that, doubtless, was on their trail by this time. It also meant risking detention or other sanctions imposed by Jordanian authorities. Their interest was in getting their passengers to safety and then making a fast departure to rejoin their unit. It also meant continuing the fight to end the civil war and, for some, to bring about a peaceful resolution and a just government.

They would have to avoid main highways all the way to the crossing place. Conrad lay down in the back seat of Omran's vehicle, bleeding, and feeling weak, feverish, and nauseous. He had used up all his medication, by increasing doses according to the way he felt during the first few days. He now had no medication to suppress the malignant proliferation of white cells. There were no antibiotics, antivirals, or painkillers. He had no precise idea what was wrong because how he felt usually had no relationship to what was going on inside his body with the disorder. To him, it was just a series of chance and changing genetic mutations and resulting malfunctions within his marrow. He knew that the condition had progressed to an acute phase in which too many of the toxic white cells spewing into his bloodstream were blasts, grossly immature cells. That would mean that he had a severely reduced immune system. The acute form of leukemia was far more dangerous than the original CNL. He felt lucky that he had not been shot or otherwise severely injured during the attack. He should probably be dead by now. His fall during the approach to the camp was bad enough. In his weakened and vulnerable condition, he had suffered serious injuries.

"Oh what the hell," he said aloud, "I'll be home soon. If only I can hang on that long … with God's mercy."

⁊₹

After they had gone a few miles toward the border crossing that Hussein had in mind, they heard the rumble of large vehicles following them.

"Do you think it's a DAESH squad?" Levi asked Hussein.

"Could be, although they don't usually make so much noise," Hussein said, a look of alarm crossing his face. "We'd better get off the main road right away, just in case."

They turned down a rough, gravel road through a field but, before they were out of sight of the road, they spotted a small convoy of vehicles gaining on them.

"It isn't DAESH," Hussein said confidently. "They aren't wearing the usual black headgear, and flying their black flag. It's another rebel group. I think it's a splinter group of the Syrian Democratic Forces. They operate in this area. They are anti-Assad and anti-ISIS too. They are composed of Kurds, Christians, and Arabs. I think I recognize the flag on the back of the jeep. If I'm right, we're okay. I can't be sure yet. My group gets along okay with some of the other rebel forces, although we have different goals and different methods. Quite a few rebel militias oppose both Assad and ISIS. It's hard to keep track. We have no choice but to confront them in peace. There are too many for us to take on. I'll try to talk them out of delaying us—or worse. Sometimes these rebel groups are trigger-happy. I hope this isn't one of them."

As the three vehicles drew nearer, Hussein lay down his assault weapon conspicuously, hoping the approaching soldiers saw the gesture as one of peace. The men, six in all, exited their vehicles and approached cautiously. Hussein moved forward to meet them, sweeping his arm around to show that they were not a militia group, pointing out the two civilian women and the young boys. The soldiers approached, without lowering their weapons. Hussein spoke to them in a calm tone.

"I am a member of the military force called Ahrar al-Sham," Hussein said calmly. "We oppose both the Assad government and the military group called DAESH. Are you with the Syrian Democratic Forces? I recognize your flag."

"We are," said the man who was obviously the leader of the squad. "If you are with al-Sham, we have no quarrel with you. We share similar goals. What brings you here? Why are these civilians, adults, and children with you?"

"My soldiers and I came here to meet my sister," he said, pointing at Ghadir, who was standing five feet to the rear in order to translate for Levi and the rest of the group.

Hussein continued. "My sister's husband kidnapped his own son—their son—in order to turn him over to DAESH to be trained as a cub. Her husband, Yousef, was recruited by DAESH in the United States. We located the boy, Jamil, in a training camp east of Yarmouk, one of many kidnap victims. We rescued all of them, except for a few older ones who refused to leave. They were too far gone for us to deal with, already won over by DAESH. My sister insisted that our rescue mission be as non-violent as possible. Contrary to my own preference, we left injured fighters alive, including the boy's father. That has created a big risk for us and for my sister later on. We must get across the border quickly. We are certain that we are being pursued or soon will be. Can you accompany us to help in case an advance unit of DAESH catches up with us?"

"We cannot do that," the SDF spokesman said. "It is not our mission and we are on our way to support other members of our group in Damascus. But I can tell you that we did not encounter anyone in pursuit. We will not delay you. Where will you cross?"

"Coming into Syria," Hussein said, "our group crossed a few miles northwest of the main checkpoint but we dare not cross there again, because we fear the guards are waiting for us and they will detain us. We intend to go further northwest until we find a safe, secret passage across the border. We must get the boys to safety, along with my sister and her friends. They have to return soon to the United States. One of them, that fellow over there," pointing to Conrad, "is very sick, maybe close to death. He has cancer and needs medication and a blood infusion. We have to get him to a hospital soon."

The militia soldiers huddled and spoke in animated fashion. One appeared to disagree angrily with the leader. Conrad was barely conscious at this point, lying on the ground with Virginia comforting him. He felt there was a danger they would be held here while the rebel group leader contacted a superior officer. He wondered how long he could survive. He felt his strength and energy fading from moment to moment. His stomach was distended. He had hardly been able to eat for the last day or two, having no appetite and suffering from severe nausea. Eating was a distasteful chore. He was afraid his spleen and his liver were enlarged to a danger point. He had trouble urinating today as well. He was dehydrated since they had an inadequate fresh water supply. What if his kidneys shut down? That had nearly happened once before with this illness. He wondered how close to death he was. Could he hold out for another day if they didn't get him to a hospital across the border?

After what seemed to be an endless twenty minutes, the leader returned to talk with Hussein. The other soldiers began climbing into their vehicles. That was a good sign, Conrad thought. They mean to leave and they're not pointing their assault rifles in our direction any longer.

"You are free to leave," the leader said. "We will not detain you longer. I suggest that you go at least five miles northwest before trying to cross. Jordan has relocated its border guards over a longer stretch of territory than before. They are concerned about the refugee camp in the border area near the main area—where the sand berm is. They are trying to prevent any illegal crossings and limit severely any legal crossing. They're making a serious effort to reduce illegal entry into the country. We go back and forth for supplies often and it is getting more and more difficult. May Allah go with you."

With that, he joined his forces and they sped off.

"We were fortunate to be allowed to leave," Hussein said. "There was disagreement within the ranks. One of the soldiers wanted to take our vehicles and some of the boys too, not to be soldiers but to do menial tasks. He was the second in command today but usually he was in command of this unit. It just happened that the leader had joined the band today. We had a close call. Allah was with us. We have to be on our way and hope we don't run into anyone else."

After another hour of slow movement toward the border, the vehicles neared the vicinity of the illegal crossing point that the leader of the SLF had recommended. A lineup of emergency vehicles blocked access to the Jordanian side of the border crossing. Emergency lights were flashing wildly. Hussein recognized them all as Jordanian police vehicles, rather than military vehicles. Conrad, who was lapsing in and out of consciousness in Virginia's arms, realized they had no alternatives but to cross and surrender to the Jordanian authorities. Besides Conrad's urgent need for medical attention, the travelers had to be ready for their scheduled return flight to the U.S. in two days.

Mona, Hamza, and Karam sought to remain in Jordan so long as the endless civil war continued. Every attempt at a cease-fire and peace negotiations had failed so far. If anything, the level of military destruction had escalated. Even the rubble in Eastern Aleppo had been bombed again and again, destroying rebel encampments and trapping refugees without the means to leave for safety. At least, according to very recent rumors, the fighting in Aleppo had diminished now that government forces appeared to have the upper hand. Whether—or when—intense fighting would reappear in some other region, such as Idlib Province, remained to be seen. That there would be more bloodbaths before the civil war was over seemed likely.

Hussein and his two militia companions had hoped to make a quick crossing into Jordan, secure the travelers in safety, and then return to their encampment near Yarmouk. The entire group had discussed what to do with the fourteen *lost boys*. Hussein said he had no means for finding the families of these boys. The only safe alternative was to attempt to persuade the Jordanian authorities to allow them to stay in a refugee camp, while Mona and Hamza worked to identify the boys and their families and return them to their homes. It would not be easy to convince the Jordanian authorities to accept the boys. Some of them, whose families had been killed or displaced, could become permanent responsibilities of the already overwhelmed Syrian refugee operation in Jordan. If Jordan refused, Hussein had committed to taking the boys to a safe location in Syria.

"I don't see that we have any serious choice here," Hussein said to his companions. "We could leave without crossing the border but I can't bring myself to do that, not knowing what happens to the Americans and the children. I leave the two of you on your own to do as you wish but I will cross with them. I'm concerned that Jordan will refuse to release us once we're in their hands. We know what we stand for but to them we're just another rebel militia. We have the same enemies they do—the Assad government and DAESH. But they do not forget that our roots were once in Al Qaeda. I'm afraid we can expect a hostile reception from the Jordan authorities."

Conrad realized that being detained and interrogated was dangerous to Hussein's future plans and that securing safety for the rescued boys would not be easy. All of them could well be forced back into Syria, with the authorities washing their hands of the mess, or perhaps worse, imprisoned and charged with crimes against Jordan. They would be in for a long siege in either case, with no safe place or freedom. They had crossed the border illegally and had stolen Omran's van and coerced him to go with them into Syria. They had essentially kidnapped him. They could be arrested and imprisoned, as Conrad had been warned before departure. On top of it all, there was Conrad's condition. If they could not get aboard a plane for home immediately, he would need hospitalization. The situation threatened to become more critical at every moment. Time was of the essence.

Upon crossing the border, the entire assemblage was approached by a dozen armed Jordan border police officers and ordered to exit their vehicles. They were surrounded.

"Who is in charge of this expedition?" demanded one officer, obviously the highest-ranking official by the color of his uniform and insignias decorating his shirt. His suspicion was colored by a snide expression of humor, which he tried to suppress, as he contemplated the motley crew of soldiers and civilians and children in front of him.

Ghadir stepped forward with a nod to Hussein that she would take the lead. "I am Ghadir Younis," she said, "an American citizen. My brother-in-law and sister-in-law are also in charge of this expedition."

With that, Hamza took a cautious step toward the officer. "I'm a Syrian citizen," he said, showing his passport to the police officer. "I had a medical practice in Aleppo until a few weeks ago, when my wife"—he motioned toward Mona—"and I had to leave our home with our son and our nephew, my sister's son, Jamil. Our home was destroyed by bombs. These people"—Hamza motioned toward Levi, Gaspar, Virginia, and Conrad, who was outside the car now having risen, with difficulty, to an awkward standing position—"accompanied Ghadir from the U.S. in order to rescue her son. The boy was kidnapped by his father some months ago in the United States. He took the boy to join DAESH and become a cub of ISIS, a child soldier, or suicide bomber.

"These five people came to rescue Jamil and his cousin, Karam, from a camp near Yarmouk. As we were making our way from Aleppo, our son Karam was kidnapped by Jamil's father and taken to the training camp. With the help of Ghadir's brother," he pointed to Hussein, and his companions, "we rescued these two boys plus fourteen others who had been imprisoned at the camp. We want to re-enter Jordan to bring them to a safe place from which they can be reunited ultimately with their families. The five people from the United States need to take a flight back to the U.S. the day after tomorrow. One man," he pointed at Conrad, "is very ill. He is an American citizen. He needs emergency medical treatment. He must get home as quickly as possible. He could die if he does not get immediate treatment in a hospital."

The police officer looked overwhelmed and slightly confused at the complexity of the story and the number of young boys, although he had heard many bizarre and tragic stories arising from the Syrian civil war. Refugee problems knew no bounds and the problem was getting worse, not better, as the war raged on despite attempted cease-fires.

"We will take you to police headquarters, examine all your papers, and determine what to do," the officer said firmly. "I cannot let you go or make any decisions here. From what we have been told, you have violated many criminal laws. We had a complaint from a commercial van driver who claims you stole his vehicle and kidnapped him. You have these and other charges to answer to. It isn't likely that any of you will be permitted to remain in Jordan other than to answer criminal charges. We are not interested in giving entry to Palestinians and Syrians who commit crimes— or for that matter, Americans, either."

"What about Israelis?" Levi said, gently goading the officer. "I'm a citizen of Israel."

"You can expect the same treatment," the officer said, seemingly oblivious to Levi's sarcasm. "In fact, we have shut the border down to Palestinians and only let a few Syrians through now. Jordan is bursting at the seams from the number of Syrian refugees already admitted. And refugees continue to arrive at the camp on the Syrian side, hoping for entry. You must have had good fortune in entering Syria illegally but returning from Syria to Jordan poses an entirely different problem for you."

"Are you arresting us?" Ghadir asked the officer.

"We are taking no official action. I am merely taking you into custody for investigation. We are entitled to do that since you are alleged to have committed crimes against a citizen of Jordan and crossed a border illegally. There will be an interrogation and investigation at headquarters."

PART EIGHT

MESSAGES

288

THE OFFICER HAD CALLED FOR backup police transport vans. When they arrived, the entire group, all twenty-six of them, was loaded into the vans and began the short trip to Amman, where police headquarters and the central courts were located. After everyone had been taken from the vans into the central police headquarters, the boys, except for Jamil and Karam, were taken for questioning to a separate building for juveniles and children. The authorities made a point of noting that they did not recognize any relationship between any of the adults and the children except for Jamil and Karam. That, of course, was true except that the adults were their rescuers. But that was merely considered a claim, not a fact.

Hussein and his troops were separated from the others and taken to interrogation rooms in the basement of the police headquarters. They were detained in holding cells, since they were, by their own admission, members of an unofficial, unrecognized, and, therefore, illegal Syrian rebel militia. They were considered a danger to the nation of Jordan, per se. Rebel group members were not welcome in Jordan, even those who were opposing ISIS as well as the Assad government.

The remaining seven civilians who appeared harmless, but were, by their own admission, the initiators of this expedition, were brought to a waiting room where they would be called for individual interrogations. Conrad was having trouble sitting up, much less remaining conscious. He told Virginia that he felt desperately ill and that he needed medication and immediate blood transfusions. He had never experienced this level of weakness and overall body pain from his injuries and illness. The slightest movement produced agony in his legs, arms, core, and lower back.

Sitting still was acceptable but lying down was better. Virginia asked the officer in charge to get him medical treatment, but he did not seem to care.

"Only after we interrogate all of you," he said, glancing with indifference toward Conrad's undeniable suffering.

"But what if he dies?" Virginia asked. She became shrill. "He needs urgent medical help! He is in desperate trouble! I'm afraid for his life!"

"Have a seat, please," the officer said, as if he were scolding a child.

One by one, the group members were called into an interrogation room. All proceedings were recorded on video. Virginia was allowed to accompany Conrad because of his condition, and Mona was allowed with Hamza after convincing the authorities they were married. But Gaspar, Levi, and Ghadir were questioned separately. The authorities satisfied themselves that Jamil and Karam were, indeed, the sons of Ghadir and Hamza and Mona, respectively. But they, too, would be questioned individually. Each person was warned that the interrogation was under oath and any falsehoods could be the basis for further criminal prosecution. Conrad and Virginia were summoned first and Conrad was questioned first. He realized that he would have to gather his wits about him and answer honestly, but he had to be careful to not say anything that could cause further complications. It was a challenge.

"What is your name?"

"Conrad Frisch."

"Where do you live and what is your citizenship?"

"I am an American citizen. I live in a small suburban town in the southern part of the state of Connecticut. Do you want the name of the town?"

"No, we have that on your documents. When and by what means did you arrive in Jordan initially?

"We—the five of us—arrived by Royal Jordanian Airline— five days ago, I think. I'm not sure of the number of days at this point. I have my ticket in my jacket pocket. But I left my jacket outside. I am very ill. I need medical attention. Can you get me to a hospital, please? I think my blood counts are dangerously out of order. I badly need transfusions of blood and platelets."

"We'll take care of that when we finish here. Now, what is your purpose in being here?"

"We came to rescue Jamil, the son of Ghadir Younis. Ghadir is outside in the waiting room. She's an American citizen. Jamil was taken here without his mother's permission or knowledge. He was kidnapped, actually, by his own father, a Syrian, who had been studying in the U.S. and had been recruited by DAESH. His purpose was to have him trained as a child soldier, a Cub of ISIS, as the term goes."

"How do you know all this?"

"I work at a center for refugees in a small city in Connecticut. Ghadir came in one day to seek help. Then I met her and her daughter at the cancer hospital a week or so later. We talked and exchanged stories. I became convinced of the truth and urgency of her story. "

"But you have no personal knowledge of all this, right?"

"Correct. Still, I don't doubt it for a minute. I saw what had happened to him with my own eyes. The boy was virtually imprisoned in a DAESH training camp. His father was there with Islamic State soldiers. We had to fight to free Jamil and the other boys."

"This all took place in Syria, correct?"

"Yes, of course. We risked our lives to rescue this boy and the others, too, except for several older boys who resisted leaving. They were obviously brainwashed. They wanted to stay. So, we left them. We didn't harm anyone unless it was absolutely necessary."

"How did you enter Syria from Jordan?"

"We hired a car to drive us to the border and we crossed over."

"Was this at a legal checkpoint?"

"I don't know. I just followed along."

"What do you mean 'followed along?'"

"I guess we made joint decisions, the five of us, so I'm as responsible as anyone."

"Did you force the driver of the car to take you into Syria?"

"No. We persuaded him by offering him money to overcome his reluctance."

"Didn't he refuse?"

"No."

"But you coerced him to drive his car into Syria, isn't that correct?"

"No. Once we were there, we encouraged him to stay so he could drive us back. No one laid a hand on him. We promised him freedom and extra payment. We'll keep our promise."

"Did the owner give you permission to take his car into Syria?"

"Yes, I would say so, because he accepted our offer."

"Did you restrain him in his car while in Syria so he would not leave?"

"We did take precautions to ensure that he would not leave us stranded."

"In other words, you restrained him, right?"

"I guess you could say that we restricted his freedom of movement by securing his car and holding onto the keys."

"Are you aware that illegal border crossings constitute a criminal offense?"

"I don't know anything about Jordanian or Syrian law," said Conrad, his frustration with the interrogation building. "May I please be excused to go to a hospital?"

"I said, when we're finished. Now, where did you get your weapons?"

"Hussein, Ghadir's brother, let us use them for purposes of freeing the kidnapped boys who were being trained as cubs of the Islamic State."

"What military training did you have?"

"None. I've never been in the military service. But I was instructed on how to fire the weapon they let me use, in case it was necessary."

"Did you need it? Did you use it?"

"I did, twice. I shot one DAESH militia man who was about to kill Ghadir and her son, Jamil. This man was Jamil's father, the one who kidnapped him and brought him here."

"Did he die?"

"No. I purposely did not shoot to kill. I disabled him only and then declined to kill him, even though he will be a threat to

Ghadir's safety and that of her children so long as he lives. Virginia, here, who is a nurse, and Hamza, who is a doctor, stopped his bleeding and bandaged him up so he would survive. We left him alive in the makeshift prison compound they used to imprison the boys, along with a few other injured DAESH guards or trainers and four older boys who did not wish to leave. I'm not sure which ones will survive. Perhaps all of them will."

"Why did you do that—leave him alive, that is?"

"Because it was the wish of Ghadir, the man's wife, and his daughter, who is back in the United States."

"Who else did you shoot?"

"I shot one of the trainers who was about to use his rifle on Levi Weller after I wounded the boy's father, Yousef."

"Did he die?"

"He did, but not by means of my shot. Someone else killed him."

"Who was that?"

"Levi Weller, the friend of mine who was with us."

"How many Islamic State troops were killed in all?"

"I can't be sure. Four or five. The civilians were told to stay back and wait for Hussein and his troops to clear the way before we approached the camp to rescue the boys. As I said, several others were injured, but we—I should say, Virginia—bandaged their wounds. Our mission was not to kill unnecessarily but to free the boys peacefully."

"Admirable," said the interrogator, "but of course the ones whose lives you spared will go back to killing. Do you think that was wise? My country is no friend of DAESH. Why didn't you just kill them all?"

"Wise or not," Conrad said, "those were Ghadir's wishes and it was her son we were trying to save and her husband who was responsible. We did not think we should question her wishes. Besides, I have learned that we cannot kill all our enemies. That just continues the cycle of killing."

The interrogator snorted and laughed bitterly. "You don't look naïve," he said. "But that is absurd. We should kill ISIS warriors at every opportunity. None of them deserves to live. Do you intend to return to the United States?"

"Yes, as soon as I can. But I need to go to a hospital before that. I may not live through the return flight unless I get a blood transfusion and some medication."

"Are you also a doctor?"

"No, but I know when my red blood count and my platelets are dangerously low. I have a rare, acute form of leukemia and I take powerful cell-killing medication every day. I know I am in bad shape."

"We'll do what we can after we finish the questioning," the interrogator said firmly, without flinching. "And you, why are you here?" he said, turning his attention to Virginia. "Are you married to this man?"

"No, I'm not, but we're very good friends. I came along be-cause I'm a nurse and he needs medical care until he's home safely. I'm very worried about him right now."

"Your only function here is this man's nurse, is that right?"

"I am acting as his nurse, yes, but I am his close friend, too. I do not know the other people well. I met them just before the trip."

"What do you know about this man's condition?" the inter-rogator asked. "Is his condition an emergency?"

"I believe it is. I suspect his blood count is so low that his or-gans are in danger and, in fact, I think several organs, his kidneys for one, may be on the verge of failing. Will you please, please get him to a hospital?"

The guard showed no sign of sympathy and in fact continued the interrogation for another forty-five minutes. Conrad became exhausted and asked to lie down. They let him, but even as Con-rad showed such evident signs of strain, the questioning persisted until finally, an hour and a half after he had begun, the interroga-tor relented. The grilling was over.

"I will check on our progress with the separate interrogations of the rebel soldiers, the Israeli, the priest, and the Palestinian woman," he announced. "You may go back to the waiting area. The priest is already there. We are not concerned about any threat from him."

⛄

Conrad and Virginia returned to the plain, sparsely furnished lobby area, a drab place under any circumstances. The walls were painted in an institutional green, the kind of hue that has long been associated with old hospitals and government buildings. It was peeling in many places. It was no surprise to find that the room, designed for economy, not comfort, was lined with an array of well-worn, uncomfortable, upholstered chairs made of some inexpensive synthetic material. But there was one bench approximately five feet in length, just long enough for Conrad to recline on, if he curled up, cradling his head on his right arm, the uninjured one. He was in extreme discomfort now, a sharp pain in the left side of his abdomen, similar to the stitch-like pain he experienced preceding his diagnosis. He surmised that this was caused by his enlarged spleen, which signaled a dangerously high white cell count. The debilitating stomach cramps that plagued him periodically reasserted themselves. Conrad knew they were caused by his gastrointestinal system malfunction. His fatigue level signaled a drastically lowered red blood count, which indicated severe anemia. After a half-hour, Ghadir, Jamil, and Levi returned to the waiting area, their faces reflecting their concern for Conrad as well as their own exhaustion. Jamil lay down with his head in Ghadir's lap and was asleep in a few minutes.

"How was your interrogation?" Virginia asked Ghadir. "Were they hostile? Did they believe your story?"

"They seemed to believe me," Ghadir said quietly, with a puzzled look on her face. "It's hard to tell. They seemed suspicious of me and hostile, too. But they had no sympathy for Yousef, either, based on what I said and what Jamil said. Fortunately, we got Jamil away from Yousef before he was brainwashed. He isn't yet willing to talk much about the experience. I believe he was terrified by what was going on in the camp. But for the sake of his father, he was struggling to hold himself together. He did tell me they had him watch a beheading. They forced all the boys to gather around in a circle and, after a speaking program, they brought some poor infidel out and beheaded him right in front of all the boys. They were told that he was an enemy of Islam and the Caliphate and therefore needed to die. Half of the boys got so sick they vomited during the ceremony. Imagine that! They made it into an actual ceremony! They followed a set program as if it were part of a sacred ritual. Jamil didn't reveal many specifics but I think he actually passed out and had to be revived.

"When the interrogator here asked him to tell what had happened at the cub camp, Jamil started shaking and crying. I think it will be a long time before he will be able to talk about that experience and longer still before he can stop thinking about it. I'm afraid it may have a permanent effect on him." Ghadir's anger was building and her voice became agitated. "It's unthinkable that Yousef subjected him to that! Why did he? He is a far different person from the one I married, but perhaps I really never knew what kind of person he was. I don't know how I could ever look at him again, much less live with him. I can't help but wonder if he is driven by some innate evil. How else could he treat his own son this way?"

Conrad propped himself up slightly so he could look at Ghadir. "I've been thinking about Ayah," he said. "I don't want to alarm you, but I'm worried that she is in danger. If Yousef survives—and we have to consider that possibility—he will communicate with his colleagues in the U.S. about what happened to him, and when he does, it seems likely they will try to retaliate against you. They may try to kidnap Jamil again. Ayah is not safe either. None of us are safe, but it is you and the children that I worry about."

"That occurred to me, too," Ghadir said. "During the night, I woke up terrified about all that happened. It makes me doubt my decision to let Yousef live. He is evil! They all are evil! And they are cowards, the worst kind of cowards. Imagine that they prey on young children, not to mention killing innocent, unarmed people throughout the world, people who are going about their personal lives doing ordinary things, and not harming anyone. What kind of people can perform those acts of terror? What wouldn't they do? It seems that no evil act is beyond them. Yes, what if they come after Ayah? That could happen before we get home, if we ever get back home. I hope they will let us go so we can take our flight. Thank you, Conrad, for raising that. We should call my aunt and have her take Ayah to a safe place immediately. We must do that right away. Now I am worried."

"You should ask your interrogator now if you can make that telephone call," Conrad said.

"I'll go with you," Levi said. "Once we're home, I will do what I can to find protection for you and Ayah and Jamil. That much I can do. I have many friends who might be able to help. Yousef and his fellow ISIS criminals are my enemies as much as yours."

His face softened when he looked at her, melting away cultural and religious barriers that he had spent his life constructing. Their communication was human to human, soul to soul, no longer "Jew" to "Palestinian."

Miraculous, Conrad thought to himself.

୬

Ghadir returned soon to report that she was permitted to call home on her cell phone. She reached her aunt. "My aunt has a friend out of state. She'll go there tonight with Ayah and won't tell anyone else. I doubt that Yousef knows anything about her friend. We'll have to arrange for a hospital to give Ayah her chemo treatments. She is on an intense regimen of I.V. chemo. My aunt will tell the hospital to keep all the information confidential, especially from Yousef if he should make contact. We're vulnerable on that score but we have time to work out a safe plan."

"Wonderful," Conrad said, breathing a cautious sigh of relief. "You'll have to figure out what to do when you're back with Jamil. That will be more difficult. I'm afraid this will be on Yousef's mind as long as he lives—unless he should have a complete change of heart."

The security officer who interrogated Conrad came into the waiting area along with another official of the Public Security Force. They motioned Conrad to come with him. "We've arranged a ride to the hospital for you, sir. Come along. You, too," he said, beckoning to Virginia. They followed him.

"I'd like to go," Levi said, smiling broadly. "I'm his protector. This way I can keep in touch with the group to let them know what's happening with Conrad."

The officer responded without acknowledging the attempt at humor, but agreed to the request.

"What's the status of Hussein and his soldiers?" Levi added. "Are they being released to return to Syria? You don't really want them here in Jordan, do you? They're certainly on the right side of the civil war and they certainly don't belong here."

"We'll wait until tomorrow when a high-ranking member of the national police or perhaps the Public Security Directorate will be here," the Public Security official said. "I think this will be handled by the Public Security Directorate. These rebels—and all of you—have committed criminal offenses in Jordan, crossing the border illegally, stealing a car, kidnapping a Jordanian citizen."

"They didn't do that. We did," Levi said. "The five of us did that. Hussein and his men had nothing to do with it. They met up with us after we were in Syria. If anyone violated the law, we did. But we did it to rescue innocent children from DAESH."

"That is for the prosecutor and DARAQ to decide. We have no particular interest in prosecuting Americans or Israelis," the interrogator said. "But the rebel groups cause us terrible problems. They enter and leave illegally all the time. They use Jordan as a marketplace for the trade in lethal weapons, arms, and bombs. Many Jordanians, I'm sorry to say, have jumped at the opportunity to build up their arms-dealing businesses. Jordanians are buying weapons for themselves, too, but we know that many arms find their way across the border. Omran has his vehicle back, undamaged. We have persuaded him to withdraw criminal charges. You will simply have to pay compensation—a victim's fee— and the charges of kidnapping and theft will be dropped against you Americans."

"Compensation for a victim in a criminal matter? I never heard of that," Levi said. "We'll deal with that tomorrow. We need to get this man to the hospital now. We don't have much money with us, but don't worry. We'll arrange something.

"Ahar-al-Sham is fighting ISIS and Assad, your enemies. Why would you want to prosecute them?" Levi asked, in a tone of belligerence. "They are your allies and this is war. Yousef committed an act of war, as did all his fellow terrorists in the camp. They imprisoned children whom they had kidnapped from their parents. They were set to turn them into killers or suicide bombers. You should thank Hussein and his group, not punish them."

"I'm sure that will be taken into account," the interrogator said. "But that is not my decision to make. We need a prosecutor to do that."

Conrad spent the night at the hospital, accompanied by Virginia and Levi. Conrad had blood tests and then received two units of blood and a unit of platelets. Virginia and Levi slept soundly on cots in his hospital room. By morning, Conrad's continuous external bleeding had slowed to a mere oozing. He was relieved. They learned by phone that Ghadir and Jamil, along with Gaspar, were brought to a hotel near the police station. A police guard accompanied them and spent the night in the lobby. They were warned to remain in their room and that they would not be allowed to leave the country until they were cleared. They would be picked up in the morning and brought to Public Security Force headquarters. Conrad heard from Levi that Hussein and his soldiers remained locked in cells beneath the police headquarters, awaiting interrogation by the prosecutor later in the morning.

Conrad felt just strong enough to get out of bed in the morning and to be discharged for purposes of his return flight, with the notation AMA (Against Medical Advice) in order to protect the hospital and doctors, in view of the instability of his condition. All that remained was to obtain a release from the security police. The three rejoined the others at PSF headquarters, where they learned that Hussein and his troops would be taken to the border and allowed to return to Syria without charges. The officials assumed that the Syrian authorities would not block the move to return them to Syria, since they were Syrian citizens. They left behind anything that would identify them as members of a rebel militia. They were warned that, if they ever attempted an illegal entry into Jordan again, they would be arrested and imprisoned. Hussein intended to recover the body of his deceased warrior colleague, taken from Burraq, now in the hands of the Jordan authorities.

❧

Hamza and Mona had made it clear from the beginning that they would apply for asylum in Jordan with their son. They wanted to avoid returning to Syria so long as the brutal civil war was being waged. They related to Conrad that, even if fighting ceased in Aleppo, there would be more fighting in the northern part of Syria, wherever the defeated rebel forces reappeared. They also were convinced that Karam would be in jeopardy in Syria from Yousef and other DAESH warriors.

DAESH was stepping up its efforts to recruit young boys as well as adults. There was a constant need for new recruits since DAESH was under siege from so many different forces. So many of its soldiers had been killed trying to hold positions in Iraq, like Ramadi, as well as in Syria. All children in Syria were in permanent jeopardy from DAESH's recruitment efforts. Hamza and Mona had been told unofficially that they could remain in Jordan while their asylum applications were processed. They told Conrad they would remain in Amman and Hamza would begin looking for employment at a hospital or clinic while they waited, which could take many months.

The prosecutor had checked with government officials before issuing a clearance to Hussein and his troops to leave the country without having to answer criminal charges. Higher authorities in the government decided not to create an international incident since it had been verified that Hussein's rebel militia was actively opposing both the Assad government and DAESH. American journalists had gotten word of the incident and the full list of detainees and had run stories about the affair. The Jordanian government was eager to be rid of all of them to avoid unfavorable publicity. The government had been trying to extricate itself from involvement with the huge flow of Syrian refugees along with Palestinian refugees who had been situated in Syria. Because of the close ties between Jordanians and Syrians, it was difficult to stem the flow of Syrians. Refugees continued to pile up in the refugee camp on the Syrian side of the border, in hopes of entering Jordan.

Jordanian authorities had to also consider their country's delicate relationship with Israel. Since Levi was an Israeli citizen as well as an American citizen, and all the others in the original band of five were American citizens, this entire incident was more trouble than it was worth to the government of Jordan. The remaining problems were raising funds for the victim's fee to Omran, even though prosecution was being waived. The compensation, which was said to be a fixture of the civil law system, was adjusted to an amount that could be raised among the travelers in order to close the matter. The only other issue was how to allow Jamil to board the plane since he had no passport and was not registered on his mother's passport. In view of the boy's age, the official in charge decided to grant him a special exception in order to board and leave the matter of entry into the U.S. to the immigration officials in New York. Although deferring a decision on exit and entry at the departure airport was unusual, it was not unprecedented.

The six—the five adults plus Jamil—boarded their scheduled flight in the afternoon, destination: New York. The extra day had given them an opportunity to recover from the ordeal. Ghadir had already booked a seat for Jamil, in the expectation and hope that he would be with them for the return flight. They were exhausted and slept for the first half of the flight. Later they talked quietly about their adventure and tried to anticipate what each would face upon the return home. Levi joined Ghadir and Jamil in a three-seater, and Gaspar joined Conrad and Virginia.

The flight was marked by periods of extreme turbulence. But after the dangers they had all surmounted, no one paid it the slightest attention. Everyone but Conrad fell asleep. Although he dozed from time to time, it was a restless feeling and in the end he spent long hours awake, fretting over his illness, the successful expedition and rescue, and what the future held for him. Conrad already felt a longing to return to the Middle East. He felt sure that Virginia, who had done her best to comfort him, would be a vital part of his life. After a while, he found his thinking going around in circles and the repetition had a soporific effect on him, allowing him to finally drift off into the deep, restorative sleep he desperately needed.

※

The next obstacle facing the rescue squad would be the one presented by the United States immigration authorities. After landing at JFK, each of them joined the American citizen line. One by one, they were directed by an official to a small waiting area off the main floor. There, they were told, they would be interviewed by another INS official. The area was inhospitable. It offered no seating, meaning that as they waited their turn, the six—still exhausted from their ordeal—had to lean against the walls for support.

"I don't get it," Conrad said. "Why are we all being scrutinized? I knew you would be, Ghadir, and Jamil, since Jamil has no passport. But why the rest of us?"

Ghadir was prepared to show the Jordanian government document that authorized Jamil to board in Amman in the temporary custody of his mother.

"I'll bet the Jordan security officials notified INS about all of us," Levi said, "not just Ghadir and Jamil. That means a wide-ranging interrogation about traveling to Jordan and Syria, our destination, our purpose, and all that. They probably thought that U.S. officials would want information that citizens had traveled illegally to Syria, and violated criminal laws. I think we're in for a hard time. You know there are U.S. criminal statutes that come into play depending on how hard-nosed INS wants to be."

"Criminal statutes?" Conrad exclaimed. "What law did we break by going to Jordan? Jordan is a friend of the U.S."

"But we didn't limit our trip to Jordan. We went to Syria and that, my friend, is illegal. For God's sake, think for a second. Syria is an active conflict zone where the U.S. military is engaged in opposition to the government! You think they are going to just overlook that?"

"Okay, but how will the immigration people know that if we don't tell them?" Gaspar asked.

"Have you ever heard of perjury?" Levi asked, his voice dripping with sarcasm as he looked at Gaspar. "If we're asked questions under oath or penalty of perjury, we can't lie. We have to disclose every bit of what we did if we're asked. No doubt the INS people already know everything we told the Jordan officials. By the way, we will be questioned separately so each of us had better tell the same story, and it has to be the truth, no matter what the consequences. So, don't try to be clever or evasive. It won't work. It will make things much more difficult, and by that I mean, for all of us."

"Okay, so we disclose our mission and we convince them we did everything for a very good reason," Conrad said with authority. "Come on, now, are they really going to prosecute us for rescuing a bunch of boys? Or at least, rescuing the ones we cared most about, since we don't know the outcome for the fourteen other boys or, for that matter, for Mona and Hamza."

"There's a little statute that is very significant these days," Levi said. "It's called 'Providing material support to a foreign terrorist organization.' It's in the U.S. Code, according to my lawyer cousin. And, good reason or not, we got involved with what may be considered a foreign terrorist organization, Hussein's outfit. I'm not sure if the statute would apply to our conduct and it's too early for me to call my cousin. But we are on thin ice here. For instance, how do we prove we didn't go to Syria to join forces with ISIS? Proving a negative isn't easy."

"Do we need a lawyer?" Conrad asked. He looked worried.

"I don't think we're entitled…."

Before Levi could finish his answer, two hefty, middle-aged INS officials, their faces parked in a look that was both grim and menacing, arrived at the waiting area. Without even greeting the group, one of them simply told them to follow him to their office. The group moved forward silently, filed onto an elevator, and, arriving on the sixth floor, followed the officials down a long corridor to a large office complex with a multitude of small cubicles.

"You can all have seats and we will begin the process. We have some papers for you to fill out first; then we'll question each of you individually," the most senior-appearing official announced.

"Why are we singled out for this process?" Levi said, immediately confronting the officials. "We've just had a long flight with no sleep. We're beat. Why do we…?"

"Complete these papers and we'll talk later," the senior official said, cutting Levi off.

After they had filled out ten pages of papers explaining in detail the nature of their trip and every facet of it, the second official collected the documents and disappeared for an hour while the travelers waited.

When the official returned, Virginia explained Conrad's medical condition and asked if the two of them could be interviewed first. He and the others were still operating on Jordanian time, where it was now early morning, seven hours later than New York.

303

Although they had all dozed on the flight, they were weary. Conrad felt strange and dizzy, in fact, and wondered how he could answer questions in an official—perhaps hostile—interrogation. The official explained that they would be informed of the order of questioning and that they should not speak to each other about the questions or answers after their interviews.

"Are we in America? Is this our country? I can hardly believe we are being treated this way," Conrad said, looking at the others.

"Amazing," said Levi, stealing a look at their interrogators. "This is no different from the way we were treated in Jordan."

The senior official glared at Conrad and Levi.

Ignoring Virginia and Conrad's request, the officials chose Ghadir for the first interrogation. She asked if Jamil could remain with her, but her request was denied. In any event, he was sound asleep and didn't wake when she handed him to Levi. After an hour, she returned to her seat in the waiting room. In the moment, Ghadir, giving in to the officials' demands, said nothing. In fact, she even resisted eye contact with her fellow travelers. But later she would tell them that once she had disclosed to her questioners that she was a Palestinian-American, the tone of the interrogation changed. She was treated with suspicion, hostility, even though they had confirmed that she was in fact an American citizen. She felt abused by her own adopted country. The terrorist incidents in Paris, Brussels, and other European cities, plus new threats of terrorism on American soil, had resulted in tightened security, especially for foreign travelers and those American citizens who had Middle East connections. Conrad and Levi shared their concerns about a resurrection of the paranoia about outsiders that has occurred periodically in the U.S. since 9/11.

Later, Ghadir would recount that, true to their plan, she had told the whole story including the radicalization of Yousef, his kidnapping of Jamil, and their joint quest to rescue Jamil. The mention of Yousef's recruitment by ISIS and his hostile actions alarmed the officials. Supervisors were called. Phone calls were placed to DHS, the Department of Homeland Security, in Washington. Ghadir was informed that Syria was on a warning list for American citizens. Although travel there was not banned, it was discouraged. Ghadir admitted that the five of them had entered

Syria illegally and then had sought—before being stopped—to return to Jordan by means of an unauthorized border crossing. They knew that they were breaking the law, but they did not know how else to rescue Jamil.

Conrad was next. He was told to sit in the only free seat in the room, an uncomfortable, unstable wooden folding chair that cut into his back painfully. He asked for water and got only a small paper cup of it. He agreed to a video-taping of the interrogation and settled back, as best he could, to await the questions. He was feeling pain at a level of 7 of 10 and felt fed up with bureaucrats. This process, on top of the Jordan process, was virtual torture.

"Actually," Conrad asked, "am I entitled to the *Miranda* warnings?

"Did you commit a crime? Are you worried about being arrested?"

"No," Conrad answered. "I just wondered. As they say, 'I'm just asking.'" He smiled, nervously.

"No, *Miranda* does not apply here… This is not an arrest. It is an informational interview and you are free to leave. Do you wish to leave?"

"No, as long as this doesn't drag on too long. I'm very sick and I am tired. Very tired. We have all been through a lot."

The senior official began with routine questions leading up to the plan to fly to Jordan.

"What was your destination in Amman, after landing at the airport?"

"The refugee camp called Zaatari."

"Your purpose?"

"To attempt to connect with Ghadir's brother-in-law and sister-in-law."

"Did you connect with them?"

"No."

"What did you do next?"

"We asked our driver to take us to the Syrian border."

"Did he agree to do that voluntarily?"

"Yes, for more money."

"What was your intention when you reached the border?"

"To go to Syria to continue our search."

"Where did you cross?"

"I don't know exactly where it was but it was unguarded and wide open."

"So it was an illegal crossing into Syria?"

"I don't know the law but it did not appear to be an official crossing, no, so perhaps that was illegal."

"Did you force the driver to cross the border in an unofficial place?"

"No, he agreed to cross into Syria there for extra money."

"Did you enter Syria in order to make a connection with the Islamic State or a representative thereof?"

Virginia asserted an emphatic, "No."

She was met with a stern warning not to interrupt.

"No, certainly not," continued Conrad. "We went to rescue Ghadir's son from the Islamic State—that is, if we could find him."

"You are aware, are you not, that her husband was recruited by DAESH?"

"Yes, that is what I understand."

"Did you intend to meet with her husband?"

"Not if we could help it. We wanted to avoid him. We feared him. But we found out that he had recaptured his son and his nephew after the original kidnapping."

"Wasn't Yousef a lawful parent and custodian of Jamil?"

"I assume he would be, under lawful circumstances."

"What do you mean by 'lawful circumstances'?"

"I mean something other than a kidnapping," Conrad answered, anger boiling inside him.

"Didn't he have the right as a Syrian citizen to take his son to Syria with him?"

"I don't know. But I would think he would not have that right if the mother did not consent to taking him out of the country, and knew nothing about his plan, and not if he intended to make him a child soldier! Are you really telling me that in those circumstances we are to respect a parental right? That seems absurd."

"Did you intend to meet with and cooperate with a rebel militia leader in Syria?"

"We meant to meet Hussein, the uncle of Jamil, who would help us rescue him."

"What group does he belong to?"

"He claims to belong to something calledAAhrar al-Sham."

"Did you intend to assist Ahrar al-Sham in a military action?"

"Ghadir's brother, Hussein, was assisting us. But the aim was always very limited: to free Jamil and maybe others from the grip of DAESH."

"Is that rebel group a terrorist organization and did you intend to provide assistance to it?"

"I don't know its status right now but I believe it opposes Assad and DAESH. I think it cooperates with the U.S. military. My understanding is that it is not a terrorist organization."

"Did you accept support from the group, such as weapons, supplies, food, etc?"

"Yes."

"Without knowing whether it is a terrorist organization or considered so by the U.S. government?"

"I believed that it had a good purpose."

"Do you know that providing support or resources to a foreign terrorist organization, as designated by the U.S. government, is a felony under 18 U.S. Code Section 2339B?"

"I have never read that law or any part of the U.S. Code, in fact. I will take your word for it."

"Did you attempt to ascertain the law before you embarked on a trip to Jordan and Syria?"

"No."

"And yet you conspired with a foreign terrorist organization to commit crimes within Syria?"

"I did nothing of the kind," Conrad said, emphatically. He had reached a point where he did not know if he could suppress his anger anymore. "It never occurred to me that I or we were doing anything with a foreign organization, much less a terrorist organization. I don't believe I committed any crimes in Syria—I certainly never intended to. I merely knew that Ghadir's brother was going to help rescue his nephew. I felt that the rescue of this child from ISIS was a humanitarian mission. I viewed the uncle as helping with that effort as an individual. I did not for a minute think that I was providing support or resources to him or to his organization. I had never even heard of his organization until he showed up to meet us and mentioned his affiliation in passing."

"What inquiries did you make about Ahrar al-Sham?"

"None. He spoke on his own and he said that the group had a good working relationship with the U.S. military. In fact, I believe he said it was not on the list of foreign terrorist organizations."

"Did you communicate with or cooperate with other members of Ahrar al-Sham?"

"Hussein brought three colleagues along to help with the rescue. I assume they were members but I don't know."

"Did you consider that Syria could be on the list of countries prohibited for U.S. citizens to visit unless for official purposes or permitted humanitarian purposes?"

"No, I did not. Is travel there prohibited?"

"I ask the questions. You answer them," the officer said sharply. "Did you consider that it was a violation of the law of Jordan and Syria to make unlawful entry into Syria and that you committed other crimes such as unlawful restraint and/or kidnapping of the driver of the car you hired?"

"No, I don't believe I did any of those things."

"Was it your intention to re-enter Jordan without going through official security?"

"I can't speculate what our collective intention was. I think our actions were driven by concern for me and my condition. I was simply a very sick passenger in the convoy and we were looking for the quickest way to get me to some medical attention."

"I have no further questions at this time," the senior officer said. Then, surprisingly, he asked Conrad if there was anything he wanted to know.

Virginia responded to the question. "Yes. Is Ahrar al-Sham in fact on the U.S. list of foreign terrorist organizations?"

"We'll leave that for the two of you to ascertain. If you are allowed to continue your journey home, you will likely be instructed to report to the INS office in New York City upon demand. Furthermore, until this investigation is completed, you are ordered to turn over your passport to this office. I will give you a receipt. Upon conclusion, if no criminal charges are brought, it will be returned to you."

⸙

After complying with the interrogation, Conrad was ushered back to the waiting room, where he collapsed on the bench, head on Virginia's lap, and closed his eyes. Despite his weakness and pain, he felt outrage at the relentless bureaucratic questioning and what he felt was mindless strictures. He had no choice but to await the individual questioning of the entire crew of five. They were discharged, all on the same conditions. Levi was the only one to strongly protest withholding his passport, although he knew that he could travel on his Israeli passport. After some five hours of interrogation, the immigration officers reported that Ghadir had been cleared on the FBI watchlist. Jamil was allowed to enter the U.S. officially with his mother as temporary guardian. At this point, the travelers were beyond exhaustion. They hired a limousine to take them back to Connecticut.

"I have an idea," Levi said, whispering to the others in the passenger area. "Let's hijack this limo and kidnap the driver. But where could we demand that he take us?" Levi burst out laughing at his own proposal.

The group was weary to the point of giddiness, enough so to pause minutes before reacting to Levi's suggestion. At that point, they broke into hysterical laughter about the prospect of another kidnapping. The driver peered into the rearview mirror to see the cause of their strange behavior. But he had the window to the passenger area closed and so was unable to hear them. Despite himself, Conrad laughed at the idea until his stomach muscles ached in pain. He realized that laughs had been few and far between.

Conrad said aloud to no one in particular, "Laughter is one of the first casualties of despair. What a relief to laugh out loud!"

⸙

Arriving in Connecticut in mid-morning, they spent the night at Conrad's house rather than traveling on to their individual residences. That would help to alleviate immediate fears about DAE-SH threatening the safety of Jamil. Yousef, even if he recovered quickly and communicated with ISIS in the U.S., was not likely to know any details about Conrad or where he lived.

"We have to be vigilant," Levi said, "that is, if Yousef survived. How can we find this out?"

Turning to Ghadir, he asked, "Will you stay in regular contact with Hussein? It would be good to have someone on the ground who could warn you if he survived. We need to know what he's doing and what to expect."

"I made arrangements to stay in touch," Ghadir said. "But I'm thinking that I should move to a place where he won't be able to track us down."

"Sounds like you need to establish a new identity, at least publicly," Levi said. "It will be hard to disappear and not be traceable. DAESH has a professional-level digital network. Personally, I would like to stay in close touch with you. You need support. I hope you won't just disappear on me." He paused and added, "On us, that is."

"My first concern is the children," Ghadir said, offering Levi a warm smile. "I'll do whatever I need to for their protection. That's not to say that I would lose touch with any of you. You are my family now. To tell the truth, I'm frightened about the future."

"I don't want to be a contrarian," Levi said, "but I think it's impractical to think that you as an individual can disappear out of DAESH range. You need protection. What do you think about contacting Homeland Security to ask for some assistance?"

"I disagree strongly with that," Conrad said, his voice getting weaker with illness and fatigue. "If any one of us goes public, it would attract a lot of attention, especially going to Homeland Security. There's no guarantee that a government agency would keep it private. The department includes thousands of employees. Anyway, what would they possibly do to protect an individual from her own husband? Do you really think Ghadir would get their complete attention and support, given her background?"

"Good point. I'm not in favor of running and hiding or making futile moves," Levi said. "It occurs to me that Israel might be a safer place than the U.S. I know there are risks. I'm thinking about living in Israel part of the time. You would be welcome, Ghadir. The protection from DAESH is airtight. It's even possible to live in the Palestine territories, perhaps in an area where Israelis and Palestinians live peacefully together. I think the U.S. is far less safe. Security is really like a sieve, maybe not as bad as Europe, but not like Israel."

Ghadir was silent, looking as though she was taking Levi's words seriously and assessing their implications.

After a long pause, Conrad ventured to Ghadir, "This will be the last night for a long time when you won't have to worry about Jamil's safety in the U.S. Ayah's, too, I suppose, although Jamil will be Yousef's target. It's a fair assumption that Yousef and the other ISIS warriors were found in time to save all their lives. Yousef will be a permanent enemy, waiting for his chance to strike. Never let your guard down."

The group sat sprawled on Conrad's living room chairs and floor before turning in. Levi observed that Conrad was pale and seemed to have difficulty moving or getting comfortable.

"You look exhausted, Conrad," Levi said. "You're probably feeling terrible. Is that right? Will you be able to manage until tomorrow morning without medical help?"

"I think so," Conrad said, barely mustering the strength to answer. "After the transfusion, yesterday, I guess it was, I felt temporarily restored. I felt fine on the plane but, of course, I never sleep well. Whatever strength I had has dissipated. I suspect my blood counts are in bad shape. I could be in danger again. I'll be fine tonight, though. Virginia will be with me," Conrad said, looking fondly at her. "Tomorrow I'll go to the hospital for a checkup. I'm afraid they'll want to admit me in-patient. I hate that. It takes forever to get your strength back. And it's demoralizing... dehumanizing to become so dependent."

"I have to say, I continue to be amazed by all of you," Levi said, "every member of our expedition to Oz. I like that metaphor. It recreates a picture in my mind of how our unlikely group of soldiers took on a DAESH military training unit. Of course, we had a little help from our friends but we carried it off."

The reference to Oz brought laughter and tears to every eye.

"Conrad, your determination throughout this terrible but wonderful adventure has been remarkable," Levi said. "I know you consider yourself a healthy person with a serious disease. Through it all, you've managed it so calmly, so courageously. The fact that you went on this trip is incredible. You've been the driving force behind the whole quest. It wouldn't have happened without you."

Levi continued, "I know it does no good to be angry and depressed, but it's only human and I'm sure there are times when you feel that way about being saddled with your condition and facing, as you know, uncertainty in the future. I've never seen you sink into despair or fear, at least not for more than a few minutes."

"I've done more than my share of complaining and ranting about being saddled with this albatross around my neck," Conrad said, with a spontaneous laugh. "I guess that's a classic mixed metaphor," he said with a self-conscious grin.

"You are the one who helped me find my child and bring him to safety," Ghadir said, with evident tenderness. "I can't bear to think what would have happened if you hadn't organized our Oz rescue team. This was a pilgrimage, a sacred mission, to save a life—many lives, actually."

Conrad sat up for a moment and surveyed the room. "Thank you for all those inspiring words. I've had many moments of discouragement and frustration since I was diagnosed. But thankfully I've reached a point where they don't hold me in their grip for long. My condition is a condition of old age. It's just that my genes are wearing out, mutating, a few years earlier than I anticipated. Nothing I can do about it.

"My genes send spam messages down my neural pathways in my bone marrow. The cancer clone cells are so determined to proliferate and they don't care if they kill their host. How crazy is that? But we can learn from their suicidal determination. The genes keep changing to evade the medication we throw at them. They race to their deaths, like a bunch of buffalo driven over a cliff. 'Follow the leader' is the game. This is all very unscientific, you understand."

Conrad went on. "Now this is a metaphysical problem too, not just physical. I have a sense about how a person should live and how a person should face death squarely. I don't want to let anyone down, of course. I don't want to live too short a time but, then, I don't want to overstay my welcome, either, and wear everybody out. It's a tough situation. I want to face death without fear. I hope I can face the discomforts and the indignities that lie in wait for me. Lord knows, they come at me constantly—the bleeding, the catheters, the exhaustion, the fevers, the chills, the probing, and the midnight excursions to be examined and inspected. But I'll do my best and I certainly don't intend to give up until I'm dragged away, at which time I will raise the white flag to my old friend, death. No kicking and screaming," he stopped and gave forth a guttural laugh that appeared to come from deep in his chest. Everyone joined him in laughter.

"I'm not saying that I won't put up a little resistance, but nothing undignified. I'm no Dylan Thomas. He, who wrote, 'Do not go gentle into that good night.' I may not go gentle, but I will go relatively quietly once the final bell has tolled. I've already met death, several times, and I can accept the end with grace, I think. I hope. Actually, it gets easier each time we—death and I—greet each other. Gradually, in fact, fear lessens and you discover there's nothing left to fear.

"I'm almost finished," Conrad said, feeling as if he was boring his listeners. "Until that time comes, I want to live and be useful in every sense. I hope to feel strong. In fact, I have a formal announcement to make. No, I'm not announcing my candidacy for President or anything else. But I do want to return to the Middle East."

"We're with you," the group said, almost in unison.

"We're with you in spirit anyway, Conrad," Levi added.

Gaspar nodded. Ghadir did not flinch.

"I want to return to Syria and rescue other children who have been kidnapped by DAESH," Conrad said. "Training children to become killers and suicide bombers is abominable. Could anything be more immoral, more reprehensible? I've been thinking about our decision to let Yousef live. I'm at peace with that as a huge symbolic move on our part. There's been too much violence justified in the name of solving conflicts and if good people fall into that trap, what hope is there? I will be working on a plan."

"I agree that your goal is a fine one," Levi said. "I am thrilled at what we accomplished. The only thing I've been second-guessing is our decision to let our mortal enemies live. I accept what we did in principle, though. I think we should stick together...

see what we can take on six months from now. I don't think we should rule out planning another rescue, but maybe leaving it to professionals to carry out. What do you think?"

"I expect to have a happy six months with Virginia and be ready for a challenge," Conrad said. "I'm happier than I've been in a long time, maybe ever, despite my illness. I know I won't ever be free of this disease, but I've learned to live with uncertainty and, after waiting a long time, I'm learning to live with love."

Virginia laughed heartily as she leaned over to give Conrad a long hug and a kiss on both cheeks.

The next morning, as the radiant light streamed into his bedroom, Conrad awoke to find that Virginia was no longer beside him. He felt a momentary twinge of disappointment. He enjoyed the luxury of emerging from sleep slowly but was aware that his fatigue was so heavy it was truly an effort to move. He was content to lie still and give his body time to adjust to being awake. He was on his back, although he remembered going to sleep on his left side, the one that gave him the least pain. His body was protesting the physical stress and injuries suffered during the past week.

His mind reviewed the events of the past days and gradually reoriented itself. He remembered that he was safely in his own bed after five, or was it six, days on the road, on airplanes or riding in a Humvee. The events of those days flashed before him one by one and he felt a thrill knowing that their mission had been successful. Jamil and Karam had been rescued, although where exactly Karam and his parents were was unknown. Ghadir would get word, no doubt. He felt thankful for the success of the mission and he repeated his litany of thanks to God.

Just as he finished, the door opened slowly and Virginia peeked around the edge, her face brightening at seeing him awake.

"Hey," she said, putting her hands on her hips and swinging her body with sensuality. She came over to the bed and lay down beside him, tucking her head gently under his right arm and pressing close.

"We're home," Conrad said. "I can hardly believe it. What an experience. Are the others awake?"

"They are, all except Jamil," she said. "We have breakfast nearly ready. Do you want to come out or do you need more sleep?"

"I want to see everyone," he said. "Am I okay the way I am?"

He looked down at the unmatched, wrinkled sweatsuit that he had found in a pile of dirty clothes on his closet floor.

Virginia laughed heartily. "What else is new?" she added with a smile.

❧

One week later, as planned, the band of rescuers, the 'Oz Squad,' as they now called themselves, met at Conrad's house. Ghadir entered the living room with an anguished look on her face.

"What is it?" Conrad asked.

"Ayah had a relapse," Ghadir said. "Oh, that's not quite the right term but she's back in the hospital. Her condition is worse. The disease took an aggressive turn. My aunt said she was fine the whole time we were away. The doctors don't know what to make of it but they will put her on intensive chemo for a week. She's been hospitalized again. She's used to that. She accepts it. She doesn't seem like a strong person but she can tolerate doses of chemo and the side effects that adults couldn't stand. The worst symptoms are nausea and extreme fatigue. I know she is distressed at not getting her hair back but that won't happen until the intensive chemo stops. Children's survival rate, even for AML, which Ayah has, is much higher than adult rate. It's in the range of fifty to sixty percent. Adults are in the ten to fifteen percent range. My aunt thinks she used all her energy to follow our mission and it depleted her reserve for fighting her leukemia. She may be right."

Conrad and the others were devastated by the news. There was a pause in the room. Silence.

"I'd like to ask God to transfer my remaining time to her," Conrad said softly, looking off in the distance. This was not just some polite comment. He meant it as a genuine proposal. Over the past few months, Conrad had spent so much time thinking in the realm of the metaphysical, so much time contemplating his own death and looking for some magical, divine intervention, to reverse his condition. Who could be sure that facts alone governed outcomes?

"Does her God—Allah—bargain with humans?" Conrad continued. "I've been led to understand my God does not, but I am not so sure. I bet Levi would say his God does bargain. There's a history of that. It's called the Old Testament, right?"

Levi looked momentarily amused. "You got that just right," he said. But, in the grip of this news about Ayah, he was in no mood for a discussion of the world's religions.

"I've always believed there is just one God, no matter what we use for a name," Ghadir said, picking up on Conrad's lead. "That goes for religions that define God differently. God does not need to be recognized or defined by humans in order to exist. It does not matter what we do or what we say. God is God. Allah is Allah. The human story varies over time and cultures, but God is above and beyond all that."

Her response brought Levi back to the conversation. "I've always been a skeptic about defining who God is, although my God calls himself Yahweh, *I am*," he said, taking Ghadir's hand in his. "I, too, am becoming convinced that God is God regardless of the names humans give and regardless of the belief system."

He turned to Conrad. "How are you, my friend? Are you recovering?" Levi feared that bad news about Ayah might now be joined by bad news from Conrad.

"I'm still tired, but coming around. My blood counts were high, the whites, that is, the reds low, of course. The doctors said my disease had progressed to full-fledged acute myeloid leukemia, at least one of a variety of eleven acute myeloid leukemias, each one likely to mutate further just to keep us on our toes. The doctors wanted me to be admitted to the hospital so they could give me a transfusion and IV chemo. I refused and said they could treat me outpatient. They won't guarantee that it will work. In the meantime, they changed their minds based on the reduction of blasts in the bloodstream. I may not have AML after all. So, who knows? It keeps mutating. Now you see it, now you don't. Cancer is a grand illusionist—but an illusionist with sharp teeth. It can kill you while it has you reacting to the surprises it produces.

"I'm getting more comfortable with asserting myself with doctors, even when they threaten the magic letters 'AMA,' you know, 'against medical advice.' 'AMA' is music to my ears. It means I'm doing my job as a patient. They're starting me on a new drug used for the new genetic mutation that showed up in the latest genetic testing plus an injectable chemo. For that I have to go to the clinic seven days in a row every month. Not too onerous; it sure is better than being in-patient."

Conrad went on. "It took a long time and many, shall we say, frustrations, before I learned that the patient is in charge. I just had an experience that really convinced me. When I showed up at the hospital for a doctor's appointment one day with a fever and chills, I got shipped to the ER for testing. That was fine, but I got stuck there for the whole day. All the results were negative, but they wanted me to stay overnight for further observation. I almost gave in, but finally said no. I was fine the next day. I'm not saying that the protocol wasn't the safest plan. Infections can be deadly in immune-compromised patients. Most cancer patients die, not from the disease directly, but from one of the many secondary medical problems, like infection, that can emerge. I just felt that keeping me in the hospital was not a good decision. From now on, I'm the one who decides and they can 'AMA' me all the way out the exit door. A person is weakened from being in the hospital. There's loss of identity and autonomy. I'm better off outside, living in freedom. Of course, Virginia is taking good care of me, although I fear she will tire of it."

"I will not. No worry there," Virginia called from the kitchen. "I'll be here as long as Conrad wants me, maybe even longer. This is a privilege of love." She began laughing exuberantly. "I won't leave until he throws me out. We're enjoying the love affair of a lifetime, illness be damned."

Conrad smiled and said, "Yes, yes, for sure, the love affair of my life!"

"I'm sorry I didn't come around or call you," Levi said. "But I felt that Ghadir and the children should take priority in finding a new place to live and arranging for security. I'm afraid I wasn't a very good friend to you."

"I understand," Conrad said. "No question. Ghadir's needs are the first priority."

๚

One month later, the group of five, plus Ayah, gathered in Conrad's living room again. Jamil remained with his great-aunt for the day. Conrad got up to greet everyone as they entered. His face had good color and his gray-blue eyes sparkled with promise and enthusiasm. Virginia welcomed everyone and told them that Conrad had a short stretch in the hospital two weeks ago but a new treatment plan, layering three medications, was now underway and working at the moment.

"I thought we should wait a couple more weeks but he insisted on going forward," she said. "He wouldn't hear of postponing our first monthly gathering."

"You all are my lifeblood," Conrad said, grinning at the pun. "I want to hear how you're all doing. Have you had any problems, Ghadir? I've been thinking about you and the children. Are you in a safe place?"

"Conrad," Ghadir said. "Tell us what's happening with your disease first. Why were you in the hospital?"

"Don't worry about me," Conrad insisted. "I can tell what you're all thinking. This guy's on his last legs, one foot here and one foot in the great beyond."

He allowed a smile to break over his face. "I had a little setback, that's all. My blood counts were going in the wrong direction. They increased the chemo dose to reduce the white count and added a new medication. The bone marrow biopsy showed that the blast level—the immature cell level—was negligible. They actually think the disease has receded a bit from the acute phase. They've returned the diagnosis to a chronic state. Of course, I understand that once acute, always acute. Perhaps it's a temporary and partial remission. I'm not sure they know exactly what my diagnosis should be now, given the genetic mutations, but I'm going to concentrate on regaining strength. There are no guarantees for the future, of course, but I'll take good news over bad, any day. I just take it a day at a time. Time seems to lose its boundaries."

"That's wonderful, Conrad," Ayah said. "I know just what you mean. I've lived most of my life a day at a time and I don't know whether I'm six or sixteen or sixty years old. I've lived as long as anyone deserves to, it seems, and yet, the days keep rolling in one at a time."

Conrad smiled warmly at Ayah, reaching his arm out to her. "Ayah, my dear, you are wise. You know this at your age, and yet look at me! I'm just learning."

"We're determined to stay optimistic," Virginia said quietly. "He'll have another biopsy in two months to see if any new genetic mutations have appeared that might lead to a new treatment. The recent one showed no change in mutations. The hope is buying time while we search for new medications."

"Enough about me," Conrad said impatiently. "Tell me, Ghadir, are you safe? Did you go to the government for help—a protection program, perhaps?"

"We don't trust the government," Levi interjected. "I made some confidential inquiries to get a sense of what Homeland Security would do in a case like this. Nada, nada. Do you think our government would protect a Palestinian woman from her own husband, an ISIS recruit? No way."

"What Levi means," Ghadir said, "is that we've learned from cautious inquiries that the government has no program to offer protection in this situation. I'm afraid letting them know would just draw more attention to me, where I am, where the children are. It would just make it easier for Yousef to find me."

Seeing Conrad's surprise at Levi's intervention, she added, "Levi has been very helpful. He's actually helped to find me a place to live out of state where the children and I would have privacy but also warning if strangers came around asking questions."

"I'm still trying to persuade Ghadir to come with the children to Israel," Levi said. "Israel is more secure, I think."

"But wouldn't life in Israel for Ghadir be a restricted one?" Conrad asked. "Wouldn't she suffer prejudice and exclusion? How would that be better? Wouldn't Yousef have an easier time finding her there than if she stayed in the U.S.? It seems to me that Israel and Palestine are getting ready to explode in violence again, now that the two-state solution is fading as a meaningful option. Do you really feel this is a good time to attempt to integrate a Palestinian into Israeli life?"

"I don't think it would be unsafe if, let's say, she were under the protection of an Israeli citizen. She would have a much better life than other Palestinians, even the ones that are citizens of

Israel," Levi said. "DAESH warriors are not exactly welcome in Israel. Security is very tight."

"Oh, I see that you and Ghadir have, shall we say, a different relationship from last time. When did this happen? Where are you living now?" Conrad asked.

"We're living in an area where there is privacy but also enough people around so we can blend in," Levi said, getting a nod of approval from Ghadir. "But there would be enough warning if DAESH types suddenly appeared. They would stand out like the proverbial sore thumb."

"Nearby?" Gaspar asked, deciding to take the pressure off Conrad for being the interrogator.

"I can't give you our home address for security reasons, you understand," Levi said, sounding more than a bit formal, "but I will give you a phone number with a secure line so you can reach me, us. I use a mobile phone that can't be traced, obviously. And I still use my university address."

Conrad felt stung by Levi's seeming lack of trust. "Wait. Are you kidding me? After all we have been through?" Conrad asked, with a wounded expression clouding his face. "You don't trust us enough to even tell us where you are? Do you think I'll divulge that information to Yousef and his black shirts when they knock on my door? Please, Levi!"

"Of course we trust you," Ghadir said, concerned at Conrad's reaction. "But there's so much at stake, most importantly, the lives of Ayah and Jamil. It's not that we don't trust you. But mistakes can happen."

"I'm sorry to say this, Levi, but your refusal to share that information pisses me off," Conrad said.

Virginia moved closer and put her arm around Conrad, trying to calm him.

"I can't believe that you feel you have to keep that a secret from me. Where is your humanity?"

"I'm sorry," Levi said.

"Levi, we should tell him," Ghadir said. "Surely we can trust Conrad and Virginia. Gaspar, too."

"Leave me out of this," Gaspar said. "I don't need to know. I don't want to know. It's fine. I'm leaving here for a while anyway.

I'm thinking of returning for a short stay at the Buddhist monastery in New York State where I spent some retreat time before. If it works out, I might stay for a while, for a trial period. Who knows, I may convert to Buddhism. The peacefulness of it really appeals to me."

"Oh, great," Conrad said, his voice dripping with sarcasm. "So now you become a monk? Just stay in the monastery, away from the world?"

"I'll make that decision later," Gaspar said with hesitation that he, too, had offended Conrad. "Nothing definite. Of course, it's up to the order to decide what I'll be deemed suitable to do."

"I can't believe this," Conrad said, disheartened. "After this rescue mission, we're splitting up, falling apart. What happened to our trust, our bond, our future plans?"

"What future plans?" Levi asked. "Do you mean another rescue mission to the Middle East? Please!

"Yes, I do, Levi," Conrad retorted. "I plan to take on another mission as soon as my condition is stable enough. That's my calling, my destiny. It sounds presumptuous but what I mean is that my spiritual self tells me that doing this work would carry out God's will. We spend a lot of our lives figuring out how to live our lives. But most of the time, we consider only what would bring us pleasure or comfort and security. We don't think much about higher callings," Conrad added, "like fulfilling God's will, for example. It's that basic. I don't mean there's anything special about me. It's not that, at all. I'm *not* special. That makes it even more important to spend my life in a worthwhile way."

Conrad wasn't finished. "Listen, I want to get well, well enough, that is, so I can return to Syria. I'd like to make it my mission to rescue children who are being trained by DAESH to be suicide bombers and child soldiers. DAESH is the worst offender, although not the only one. They share practices of recruiting and indoctrinating children to be killers. There are no moral restraints on who they kidnap or recruit from their parents, or how they train and indoctrinate them."

"It doesn't seem realistic to me," Levi said gently, aware that Conrad was feeling abandoned. "But when you're ready, we'll be there to help if we can. For now, I'm committed to keeping this family safe—Ghadir, Ayah, and Jamil. Maybe this comes as a sur-prise to you," he said, looking at Conrad. "Me—an Orthodox Jew, the anti-Arab bigot that I am—or I should say, that I was—giving my life to protecting and caring for this Palestinian woman and her family. How did this happen?"

Levi paused, emotion welling up in his voice. "I'll tell you how this happened. You brought it about. You. You, Conrad, talked me into coming on this trip and it changed my life. I don't know what happened, except that I had some kind of revelation that this was right, and it was."

Conrad looked moved, but Levi wasn't finished. "Now, I should not forget to add, if it isn't obvious, that in addition to all of that, I have fallen in love. I have fallen in love with this won-derful woman. She, whom I would have looked upon as the en-emy just a short time ago. Let's just say that my eyes were opened on our journey. Ghadir went from being a caricature, something that I would look upon with disdain for no other reason than for her being a Palestinian, to being Ghadir, a person I not only saw as unique, but as an object of desire. I am in love, Conrad. I am in love with a beautiful Palestinian woman. Me, Levi! And I owe that to you!"

The mood in the room had changed.

"Frankly, Levi, I am not surprised. I saw it coming. We all did, right?" Conrad said, looking at Virginia and Gaspar.

They nodded in agreement.

"As a matter of fact, I've fallen in love, too, with this woman sitting next to me. Virginia and I are going to get married as soon as my divorce is final. It's underway at last."

Conrad's happy pronouncement was met with applause and cheers in the small, unpretentious living room.

"That's not all," Conrad said. "Levi. This notion of a new res-cue mission is not some pie-in-the-sky idea. I'm actually formu-lating a plan for one. With Aleppo falling to the government and refugees along with rebels expected to flee to Idlib Province, the chemistry is changing in Syria. DAESH will weaken as a land-holding force, splintering into what will probably become like the mythical Hydra with nine heads. There is talk of Raqqa eventually falling outside their control, too. That means the children in the cub camp in Raqqa could be in jeopardy. When DAESH leaves, the soldiers will kill the hostages, just as we feared before our mission. I plan to organize, with Hussein's help, a militia to attack the cub camp at Raqqa and rescue the children before they are killed or forced to commit suicide. This calls for entry through Turkey, probably flying into Hatay Airport, which isn't all that far from Raqqa. There is the ground transportation problem, of course, along with some grave danger to reach the camp and carry out a rescue. Turkey, itself, is awash in terrorism and other problems even apart from DAESH. I will need a ton of help—and God's blessing—but I realize that all of you have other agendas. I respect that but any help you can give I would appreciate."

"We'll talk more about this, my friend," Levi said, impressed by Conrad's pursuit of this dream. "We don't mean to leave you in the lurch."

Before Levi could go any further, Ayah stood and commanded the group's attention. She had gone to another room a few minutes after their arrival. The group had barely noticed that Ayah had slipped back into the living room and was standing quietly inside the doorway to the hall leading to the bedrooms.

"May I say something?" Ayah asked in a clear and confident voice. "I think it's important."

Everyone turned to her.

"Forgive me, please. There is some very important information not mentioned so far. First of all, my uncle Hussein informed us this morning that the cub camp where Jamil was held was destroyed two nights ago. The signs point to a U.S. or Russian bomb that may have been dropped accidentally. Uncle Hussein told us that cub camps don't seem to be on the target list usually. He said the casualties ran into the twenties, his exact words. The death toll included bodies of both adults and children. It seems that both adults and children were moved in after you rescued Jamil. He said that some of the children's wounds, and perhaps their deaths, were self-inflicted. The implication is that there were children's suicides prior to the bombing. This story hasn't even been reported in the media."

"Oh, that's horrible," Conrad said. "Unimaginable. Suicides? It's incredibly lucky we got Jamil and Karam out when we did."

"That's not all," Ayah said. "After the attack, my father got a few messages to Jamil through former colleagues of his. He was moved from the camp to a hospital for his injuries but now he is out again. Jamil is very upset by these messages. He says he loves his father and is worried about him. Apparently, my father is about to go to Raqqa and take on an administrative role since many warriors are moving out elsewhere. He wants Jamil to come there. Of course, we are worried that he will again try to turn Jamil into a soldier or suicide bomber. We don't know what to do. It breaks my heart that my father has not given that up. My uncle warns that he may try to slip back into the U.S. to do harm to us or he may enlist someone here to take Jamil to him. My uncle believes the only way we will ever be safe is if my father is dead."

Ghadir added, "We do not know how Yousef found out where we are, but we have moved since that happened."

Ayah continued, "My uncle doesn't know whether my father has commissioned others to try to kidnap Jamil or to retaliate against my mother. I know you made the right decision, partly at my request. We can't go on trying to kill all our enemies. I am hopeful that my father will change his heart and forsake this terrible path. But..."—Ayah looked directly at her mother—"...I think Conrad and Virginia should be trusted with information about us, Gaspar, too, if he wishes. If we can't trust them, who can we trust? We do our best to protect Jamil from harm. Jamil still feels a special bond with his father but he knows, I think, that he has to save his own life."

"Do you think we should talk to Jamil? What would convince him that he should never go with his father?" Conrad asked.

"My mother and I have to protect him," Ayah said. "We need to keep him strong. But we need to keep a watch on Jamil all the time. I would say that he is very disturbed by this conflict in his loyalties. You know that there is a high suicide rate among cubs, don't you, even higher than for Syrian refugee children?"

"Yes, I've read that," Conrad said. "That worries me and your mother, I'm sure. We need to help Jamil. And this points to the urgency of stopping this child brainwashing. It is inhuman."

"I watch out for Jamil around the clock," Ghadir said. "I bring him to school and pick him up. My aunt helps, of course, and

Levi, too. We guard him carefully and we have talked about his father and what his obligations are—and are not—to his father. I think he understands but, of course, he is still a child."

"This will be a continuing problem," Virginia said. "We'll all help, if you let us."

"I'm glad to know," Conrad said. "It makes me all that much more committed to eradicating this terrible inhumane practice of recruiting and brainwashing."

"Second," Ayah said, "this is on the lighter side. I want to ask all of you how it feels to have lived a part in a famous book? *The Wizard of Oz?*"

Ayah was holding a poster showing the five travelers marching down the yellow brick road, with bodies like the characters and faces of the five. "I remember when you talked about seeing yourselves as the characters of Oz."

"I love the ruby slippers," Virginia said. "They're exquisite!"

The poster was passed among the group, but the mood shifted back to Ayah's first bit of news.

"I was going to mention that about Yousef. I didn't get to it," said Levi. "There is a serious cause for vigilance. Perhaps there always will be. Conrad, you've managed to distract us all from your situation."

"I think we've brought you up to date," Virginia said. "We don't know what will happen but we are hopeful. Conrad may not have the orphan disease, CNL, any longer. The defining mutation is not detectable but that isn't the end of the story. Cancer is devious and persistent. It seems strange to say this but we can learn a lot from cancer, itself, about how to treat it. Cancer has a lot of tricks, such as how to survive and proliferate, how to bypass the immune system, how to create its own stem cells. There are lessons there if we pay close attention. We should see how cancer operates and, in some respects, imitate it, learn from it. Strange as it seems, cancer can be our teacher."

"But when cancer turns against its host and kills the source of its own survival," Conrad said, "that doesn't sound so clever, does it?"

"You're brave, Conrad," Ghadir said, sitting down beside him. "And you, too, Virginia."

"Conrad and I are thankful that we found each other and the love of a lifetime. I carry with me a deep sadness that he has to suffer from so much discomfort. And it grieves me that his life may be shorter than otherwise. I feel sometimes that my heart could break and tears could flow endlessly. My burden is to bear this deep sadness, but his is to bear whatever the disease inflicts and whatever the treatment inflicts—every day, every night. Conrad feels the frustration, and the fear of the known and the unknown. We will marry at the earliest opportunity, hopefully within two months. We'll let you know. In the meantime, we're living day by day and loving the time we have with each other."

"Every day I give thanks for Virginia and for this wonderful thing that has come to us," said Conrad, holding back tears. "We are blessed. There is no injustice here. We just ask for mercy and a little grace. I'm far from giving up, but I believe I've reconciled with death for about the fourth time. I'm sure it will not be the last. Each time is different and each time feels a little closer in time and space to the great unknown. I've been doing a lot of soul-searching about our mission—literally *soul-searching*.

"Each of us has uncertainties in our lives. We live with the potential of violence and loss and, of course, with disease. On a lesser scale, we live with uncertainty about whether the U.S. government will take action against us. Our passports are still being held. But I'm optimistic about that. My lawyer assures me that Ahrar al-Sham is not on the foreign terrorist lists. We should hear soon that we are cleared on that score, too, which opens up the possibility of future trips.

"We all live with the moral decisions we made. We used restraint to avoid violence even when that would have made our lives simpler—and safer. We left behind some injured people who might not have survived. We also left behind four boys who refused to come with us. And out there in Jordan there are fourteen boys whose fate remains to be decided, not to mention Hamza and Mona. There is much unfinished business. We live with the consequences of these decisions and actions.

"We're all better off in terms of happiness. Levi and Ghadir have discovered each other and Virginia and I have found each other. Gaspar is off to a new challenge. I'm looking forward to recovering enough to allow another rescue mission.

"But let me tell you something else I've realized. You all remember my telling you about how I *experienced* six words— 'HAVE COURAGE. DO NOT LOSE HOPE'—the ones I call *the first miracle*, the *Word*. This miracle led to the other two miracles, which I call the *Understanding* and the *Rescue during the blood moon*.

"One night late when I couldn't sleep, I begged God, 'Give me another message, please. Tell me what to do next. What do those words mean?' I lay in the dark, quietly, not moving, not making a sound. I lay there for a long time. Nothing happened. I felt very much alone, even abandoned.

"Then it came to me at once that there was no need to ask for another message. Those six words were complete. I realized that I had interpreted them to be what I *wanted* them to be about. The message was far beyond my illness and me. It does not belong to me in a sense. Why, I may have been just an eavesdropper for all I know. They are an eternal message. It encompasses the whole message of the Creator, and whatever other prophets, divine or otherwise, have said about God's message. It's the beginning of my understanding. It will guide me."

Turning to Gaspar, Conrad asked, "Do you think I've atoned for all the failures of my life?"

"Without a doubt," Gaspar said.

"What was it that brought atonement, then? Was it my suffering? My determination? Was it the rescue itself? In doing what we all did there, was I not only helping to rescue Jamil, but my soul as well? What was it?"

"Only God can answer those questions." Gaspar replied. He paused, and his voice receded to a whisper. "Perhaps God already has."

ACKNOWLEDGMENTS

The Honorable Barry R. Schaller asked me, his wife, Carol, to make these acknowledgments in his voice. I proceed to do so here:

Nearly five years have passed since I departed from your midst. Tempus fugit, as our Yale Class of 1960 classmates would say. The phrase, "Time Flies," has become a heartwarming family joke as well, since my first-born granddaughter, so many years ago, denied the concept at age three, proclaiming after a thoughtful pause, "NO IT DOESN'T…. IT'S JUST A CWOCK!"

Nevertheless, the world has continued forward on a path in these recent years that many of us would choose to redirect. By working together much can still be accomplished to benefit life on our incredible planet.

The financial divide. Politically-motivated misinformation. The wicked power struggles. The breakdown of gun control. Extraordinary levels of drug-trafficking and human trafficking. The rampant disrespect. The shortcomings in our educational and religious institutions. The failures to choose proper leaders. Ethical anomalies in our once-revered Supreme Court, let alone the Presidency and Congress itself.

Before the Covid pandemic befell the world, and before the Russian attack on the Ukraine, I was concerned about the way we, in the United States, ignored the critical issues in our country and neglected to choose leadership in a responsible way. We had progressed with true cooperation and great pride in our beloved America following WWII. Then suddenly, the downward spiral of values, and our country became an ugly, muddy whirlpool, threatening to plunge to irretrievable depths. It is imperative to reverse that trend now. Once lost, there will be no way to get our cherished freedoms back. And if burdened with poor egocentric dictatorship-style governance, the climate change will bring natural disasters that will destroy life-sustaining accommodations here on earth.

We must select the finest choices for leadership in the executive, legislative, and judicial branches. This will make or break our beloved democracy. The key issue rests with the exercise of our constitutional right to vote. It is truly vital, and we must guard it well. It is in your hands!

I acknowledge my gratitude to my colleagues and classmates, neighbors and friends, and members of my community, for caring about our future generations.

I wish to thank those who contributed to my efforts to make this book available to you.

I send a personal "Thank you!" to Dr. Amer Zeidan at Yale New Haven Hospital, Smilow Cancer Center, for the relentless pursuit of new research into forms of leukemia and other cancers, for the benefit of patients, including the extra time you gave me on this earth, which allowed me the precious time to complete this novel. I send gratitude as well, to the nurses and medical staff for their kindness, friendship and extraordinary care. This extra time enabled Carol and I to come to terms with the Gifts, as well as, the Meaning of Life. Together, you made the book possible.

I feel blessed to have had the opportunity to bring my father back to Switzerland, to explore the area of his birth, Porrentruy, and the beautiful mountains and nearby lakes, and to meet many inspiring cousins for the first time – on his 85th birthday. And then on his 90th birthday, to bring him to the Statue of Liberty and Ellis Island where we had inscribed his name on the Memorial Wall of Immigrants. He cried happy tears to see his name memorialized and we, the next three generations of his ever-growing family, were holding hands, singing Happy Birthday, and crying too. The American dream had been his reality, and on that special day, we were a group of four generations of his American family. It was wonderful singing the "National Anthem" and "America the Beautiful" on the boat trip back to shore.

It is important to me to thank the religious leaders who have impressed me over my lifetime, in ways that have impacted my soul with faith and spiritual guidance.

I give thanks to God, "Our Father, who art In Heaven", and those who taught me to understand, with true faith, the importance of the Ten Commandments and the Seven Deadly Sins. Those individuals who impacted my belief system the most deeply were:

The Rt. Reverend Jacques Bossiere, who served as Episcopal Chaplain at Yale, when I was a student there, also as Canon, American Cathedral in Paris, also as the Minister of the French Speaking Episcopal Church of New York City. His friendship and spiritual counsel throughout my lifetime provided eternal guidance and comfort. Thank you, dear Jacques.

I would also like to acknowledge the Rev. James F. Martin of Trinity Church, who married our two single parent families into our blended family of nine, at an outdoor, authorized Episcopalian, waterfront setting at a local Ecumenical center, Killam's Point, with about 100 invited guests. We arranged picnic tables, Japanese lanterns and chrysanthemums everywhere, and all nine of us took the marriage family loyalty oath, following the traditional marriage vows, upon which an extraordinary sunset took place and dozens of fish leapt out of the water capturing the awe of the entire wedding party for several minutes. Two fifers played a classical duet to capture the moment.

I would also like to acknowledge Rev. Henry Burdick, who arrived as pastor, also of Trinity Church, Branford. He earned my admiration and respect as a profoundly spiritual leader, always exhibiting modesty and God's selfless love for other. He was a great friend with much creative wisdom.

I would also like to acknowledge the Rt. Rev. Andrew Donnan Smith, Bishop of CT, emeritus. A man of high principals and great devotion. He cared about the underprivileged and unprotected, the homeless and the hungry. He fought tirelessly to improve immigration regulation.

I thank them for their unwavering gifts of love, respect and justice. They taught by example.

I hasten to include the names of friends from various walks of life to whom I owe acknowledgment for fun and laughter, interspersed with their illuminating insights which contributed over the years to my world perspective. With deep gratitude I mention some of those names here:

Dave & Ginger Toomey	Mavis & Tony Terry
Stanley & Laura Page	Felix & Heidy Thomann
Don & Nancy Rankin	Dwight Merriam, Esq.
Socrates & Joani Mihalakos	The Schaller Families, CH & USA
Don & Maggie Coolican	Jim & Tracy English
Prof. Peter Brooks	W. Peter Simon
Mike & Sue Klimas	Charles & Tazuko Schmitz
Dan and Anne Fisher	Leighton & Marie Lee
Jack & Dorothy Covert	Dennis & Meredith Carnelli
Todd Brewster	Bob & Margaret Brady

I take a special moment to address with deep appreciation Dan Pope. Dan, thank you for your uncanny grasp of my outlook, extrasensory perception, if you will, that has connected us from the outset. You have used your talent with understanding and expertise that have clarified my objectives, start to finish.

I would also like to thank layout designer, James Brisson of Vermont, who showed such sensitivity to the plot, and to my award-winning book cover artist, my dear stepdaughter, Donna H. Colburn, who has captured the heart of those who have seen early previews. I am sending my eternal gratitude.

Friends, neighbors, classmates, colleagues, teachers, law clerks, and most importantly, my beloved family. Thank you all.

I close by saying, I am deeply indebted to you, for whom this book was written.

—Carol V.C. Schaller
June 2022

ABOUT THE AUTHOR

BARRY R. SCHALLER was a justice of the Connecticut Supreme Court from 2007-2008. He served as a judge of the Connecticut Appellate Court from 1992 to 2007. Before that, he was a trial court judge in Connecticut for 18 years. A graduate of Yale University and Yale Law School, he was a visiting lecturer in public policy at Trinity College where he taught bioethics, public health law and ethics, health policy, and public policy and law. He was a clinical visiting lecturer at the Yale Law School, where he taught appellate practice and procedure. He also had appointments as visiting lecturer at Wesleyan University, where he taught bioethics and public health law, ethics and policy, and at the University of Connecticut School of Public Health. He also taught an appellate advocacy class at Yale Law School, focusing on Connecticut appellate procedure. Justice Schaller was a former chair of the Connecticut Board of Pardons, a charter life member of the Connecticut Bar Foundation, a member of the American Law Institute, and Chair of the Connecticut Judicial Ethics Advisory Committee. In May, 2008, he was awarded an honorary Doctor of Laws degree by Quinnipiac University School of Law. He is the author of *A Vision of American Law: Judging Law, Literature, and the Stories We Tell*; *Understanding Bioethics and Law: The Promises and Perils of the Brave New World of Biotechnology*; *Veterans on Trial: The Coming Court Battles Over PTSD*; and a prior novel, *The Ramadi Affair*. *Flight from Aleppo* is his second novel. After retiring from the Connecticut Supreme Court he continued his writing and his judicial work as a judge trial referee by hearing arguments at the Connecticut Appellate Court and mediating cases within the court system. After suffering from a rare form of leukemia, he died in September 2017.